PIGEON MOTHERS

a novel

PIGEON MOTHERS

a novel

Marty Correia

TRIPLE
DECKER
PRESS

Copyright © 2021 Marty Correia
www.martycorreia.com

To request permissions, and for educational or book group discounts, contact the publisher at info@tripledeckerpress.com.

ISBN: 978-1-953998-08-8 (paperback)
ISBN: 978-1-953998-00-2 (electronic book)

Library of Congress Control Number: 2021900277

First paperback edition: March 2021

Book jacket design by Kate Conroy
Cover photo by Andrew Bennett
Author photo by L.D. Salvatore

Printed in the U.S.A.

10 9 8 7 6 5 4 3 2 1

TRIPLE
DECKER
PRESS

New York, New York
www.tripledeckerpress.com

To my Kate for your unreserved love and our daily laughter.

Chapter 1

Red checked his wristwatch approximately every fifteen minutes. He rushed from building eight all the way to the break room in building one in order to clock out on time. As he stepped up to the time clock with less than a minute to spare, he pulled a black plastic comb from his back pocket and ran it through his thinning ginger hair. His fingers thick with work and age, held the manila timecard at arm's length so he could make out where to place the machine's arrow. It was Monday. The card, the same tone as his skin, recorded only three other punches. A.M. in, A.M. out for lunch, P.M. back in from lunch. His neck tensed as the large empty room filled with the machine's kerchunking gavel. P.M. out.

At exactly 5:30 p.m. when he punched that black plastic rectangle for the last time, the clock dutifully stamped Red's time out. Clocks shaped most of Red's days. Every morning he awoke to the bleep of his clock radio. His wife Helen had bought it after their daughter threw his manual alarm clock in the toilet back when she was a toddler. The week before his daughter's vengeance against time, Red applied for a Sears credit card to put two new tires on their car. Sears gave him three times the amount he requested, allowing Helen to buy some underwear for their little Cole, a bottle of Jean Naté body splash for herself and, when the need arose, or in this case descended, Red's clock radio.

It had been a few years since hundreds of Quality Electric employees rushed to punch their timecards under the "It's About Time" sign. Now as one of only twenty-three remaining employees, Red wanted to rip the sign down. He had started taking down signs the day after he climbed the stairs to where Hector ran a rotary switch line. The sign read "22E to 33E." That ten-inch square sheet of metal marked the area as Hector's floorboards before it became just another empty expanse peppered with rat traps. Gradually, the walls returned to their original barrenness. The vast open spaces once filled with men, their machines, parts and materials all started to look alike. Red found it easier over time to clear out things that reminded him of his former work buddies.

Red's last day on the job was all about time. When the blizzard started earlier than predicted he wanted to get home to Cole and Helen. He was still driving around on the tires they had bought back when they first got their Sears card. Even though his father gave him some cash for new tires, Red knew Vladimir would probably need it back soon. The money sat at the bottom of Red's sock drawer. It tempted Helen every time she put away the laundry but the old man was losing his mind. Every few months the Housing Authority manager called Red to report that his father had run out of money and needed groceries.

It felt to Red as though he worked at least two jobs but all at the same time. While he maintained the shuttered factory, he worried about his father, Cole and Helen. Whenever he boarded up the factory's broken windows, told Helen a joke or brought his father some of Cole's chewable vitamins, Red wondered why he bothered. What was the use of making things better if they just kept falling apart?

It was finally time to go home. In the parking lot, he cleared the snow from his car with a commercial-grade push broom and shoveled behind his tires to make it easier to get out. As he walked back to building five to return the broom, he noticed the third-floor lights on in building three. He could just go home and call Sal the night guy to tell him to shut them off. Then he remembered that they cut the phone lines to the boiler room where Sal smoked cigarettes and listened to his Radio Shack transistor radio. The wind seemed in a panic, not knowing which way to blow. An upward gust blew snowflakes into Red's nostrils as another burst pelted sleet into his left ear. He shook off the chill and jogged to the building.

Now that Red managed all the doors his keys didn't jingle any more. They let out flat metallic claps with Red's pace. The massive 13-building factory was one and half million feet of a continuous structure. Back when the factory was full of equipment and workers, the building made Red feel important. With his boiler operator's license and a knack for plumbing, he helped keep the master machine, The Monster, in operation. When his Monster was put to rest, Red was kept on as a janitor. Eventually, his black leather belt cracked and bent at the three spots where his key rings were clipped just like the dark red welted scars that steam and fire had burned into his hands and forearms.

Each building had a flashlight and a bucket of sand to the right of the entrance. For years Red picked up Sal's cigarette butts and placed them on the top of the sand, but Sal never took the hint and continued to throw his butts all over the factory's floors. The beam from the square red six-volt flashlight picked up the dust in the air that seemed to never settle. At the sunniest part of the day, Red watched the particles swirl in the vacant spaces as if people moved the air as they walked to the bathroom or grabbed Band-Aids from the first aid kit. At home relaxing in his chair on Sundays, he watched the specks in the sun. There they floated as if they were tiny astronauts until Cole or Helen walked in and unsettled them all.

When Red told his father he wanted nothing more to do with the family business of crime, Vladimir asked, "What else you got to do? It's in your blood. You won't be able to go any place without casing it." Red didn't argue but promised himself to think about how to clean a place whenever he thought about his father looting it. Eventually he found it relaxing to focus on dirt, dust, debris, messes of all kinds. It was in his father's nature to pry things open and lift things. Red felt safer with the world's decay and its respect for gravity.

On the third-floor landing in building three the flashlight's beam caught the dust behaving much like the squalls outside. Five banks of lights were on and the room was freezing. Two windows had been left open. Annoyed, Red kicked a fallen ceiling tile. Dried and hardened from no longer being part of something, it sounded like a scuttling shard of ceramic rather than a chunk of horsehair plaster. He placed the flashlight down where it shone a glowing polka dot onto the wall, waiting for his return.

In the hallway between the buildings, Red shut off the lights. Past the outskirts of the flashlight's glow, he slammed the first window shut but the other one wouldn't budge. On his way to find something to stand on, Red felt a blast of cold air from the stairwell that went to the roof. He patted his keys and headed up the steps.

Out on the roof the confident wind blew snow as if it knew where it was headed, not like the same storm frantically whipping around into a fracas five floors below. Two plastic milk crates sat a few feet outside the roof's door. Red wondered which two remaining employees had been sitting out there. He planned on taking the crates to his car for Cole. She always found a use for whatever work junk he brought her. He brushed off a few cigarette butts that the snow had stuck onto the makeshift seats. He turned in the direction the seats faced, toward the trees and pond behind QE.

When he first started at QE Helen visited with fresh sandwiches whenever he worked overtime. All the guys hooted and smooched out kissy noises as the couple left the building. Helen smiled and squeezed his bicep. The world fell away. It was simple back then. He loved. He was loved. As they walked over the bridge and onto the paths, he believed that he could cure Helen's loneliness. But now, he looked out onto the overgrown walkways and chained-off bridge, all covered in night and snow. He sighed.

Now that they had Cole and he loved Helen all he could, it was clear that there would be no end to Helen's achy clouds. He would have to just accompany her under them. It hurt him to watch Cole try to get her mother to feel better. Part of him wanted to explain how it wasn't possible to change Helen's mood. But the optimistic, desperate part of Red told him to keep quiet. He had some hope left that someday their quirky little daughter might just charm her way into Helen's heart and set off a change.

He tried to shake off those thoughts along with the cold seeping through his coat. Clapping his hands together he turned around. The blizzard's persistence made the parking lot's floodlights appear to struggle to stay on. The blanketing snow created a false sense of security by dampening all sounds except the wind.

A ruthless squall slammed the door shut. The veins in Red's neck pulsed hard. He dropped the crates and scurried over to the door as if rushing toward it would make it more likely to be unlocked. A wooden shim that the guys used to prop the door open sat next to his foot as he tried to turn the knob. It didn't turn but he tried to pull the door open anyway. The naked knob was locked. This was the only time he wished that a door had yet another keyhole. Regret slid down his throat with a gulp.

"Shit!" he whispered. He grabbed the cement block, lifted it above his head and slammed it down onto the doorknob. It bent and dented but it wouldn't turn. He hammered the knob with short firm strokes until the block crumbled in half. Other than Red, the crates, the cigarettes and that now-destroyed block, the roof was empty. Almost all the houses across the street had lights on; a few people could be seen through their windows. But there was no way they could hear him. No one was coming or going from QE until the next shift and he knew no one was going to do any rounds in the storm. He hoped someone across the street would come home. He stared at the bus stop as if to will one last bus to brave the slippery roads before the city shut them down. But no one came or went from the factory, a house, a bus or a car. For so many years that parking lot had bustled and was at least half-full at all times. After the layoffs, the few remaining workers' cars looked like pieces left on an abandoned checkers game board.

Red checked his watch. It was exactly one hour and eight minutes since he was first locked out. Thoughts of Helen and Cole came in flashes. Had they figured he was staying late because of the storm? Were they eating dinner without him? Maybe they would call the office and someone would look for him. He was mostly worried about Cole. Even though she had Helen there, Cole always treated his arrival home as a kind of rescue. Helen usually sat at the kitchen table staring at the floor as she hugged herself and chain smoked. No matter how much Cole tried to make her laugh or talk, Helen left her hovering like a seagull on an impervious, invisible wind.

That past Sunday night, Red helped Cole practice her oral book report. Really, all he did was turn on her tape recorder and then when she was done, cheered, clapped and shut off the machine. Cole's teacher assigned a book about a boy who lived on a farm and had to kill his pet pig because his family needed it to survive. Most of Cole's report was about how even though the family was poor, the young boy's mother loved him very much. The rest was about how people sometimes hurt animals even though they knew it's wrong. She went on to describe the trainers she saw whip the tigers at the circus. Although he had avoided ever reading a book from cover to cover, Red knew how people had a way of making things about themselves. Cole's report sounded like a description of the kind of mother she craved and an excuse to mention that she is P.T. Barnum's great-great-granddaughter. While they listened to the tape recorder play back Cole's report, Red heard Helen softly close the clothes dryer door. She folded the laundry on their bed even though there was space in the living room. Solitude comforted Helen, especially while people were close by.

Red rubbed his cheek to help him concentrate on finding a way down from the rooftop. There were other roofs. Twelve. Twelve other doors. Maybe one was open. Like an elderly Olympian, he carefully vaulted over the parapets between the buildings. The building had been built as if each giant unit could be separated from the rest. But in fact, the only way to extract one would be by explosion or to dismantle it brick by brick. By the fifth locked door, Red's feet were numb all the way to his ankles. Looking over the edge of the front of the building he pursed his lips. Maybe he could jump down to a cement balcony a story below. If there was no way to open that door, he could try to climb down each balcony until he reached the ground. But he'd have to safely lower himself down four times. He closed his eyes to think it through.

Then he remembered the open window. It was only one story down. The cold was exhausting. He trudged back five buildings, arthritically scaling the parapets again. He thought of the koala bears that Cole loved so much. She had shown him a picture of one resting on a branch on its belly. His body started to take longer breaks between motions but when he got to the right roof, he felt a slight energy surge.

He kept his eyes on his feet and planted them far enough away from the roof's edge. Leaning over, the view down seemed both daunting and not too bad. Maybe he could lower himself far enough down to angle his legs into the window.

Using a crate as a shovel, he pushed the snow off the edge as the wind whooshed more into its place. His ears were past stinging and burning and now felt like they would chip off if he touched them. The plan was to lower himself down until he couldn't hold onto the edge's six-inch lip any longer. Then, he'd take the fall and catch his toes on the window ledge or if he could manage, try to get his feet in the window. He counted aloud, "One, two, three, four...," as he clapped his hands fifty times to better feel his fingertips. Stomping gave him a fix on the boundaries of his shoes. A shiver ran from his gut up to his neck. For courage, he grunted a few times and then he growled out loud, "Don't make me angry. You wouldn't like me when I'm angry!" When he watched *The Hulk* with Cole, she taped the introduction and replayed that part often. Red said it whenever she gave him any trouble.

When he was a boy and afraid of burning his hands when he started fires, his father asked, "Just because you fear wolves, you won't go into woods?" The saying had been handed down from Red's grandfather, Boris, along with, "The eyes are afraid but the hands will do the job." To Red, his family's old Russian sayings were just shady ways to fool his mind into doing what his heart couldn't bear.

He got down on his belly at the roof's edge and looked only at his hands. He swung his legs over the ledge. As he plummeted, Red clawed at the air for a rope, a rung, a buoy, a railing, a hand. His own hands would have welcomed anything, anyone that would pull him up. His guttural bellow was thumped short by the metal A-frame vents that stood at the ground floor like a row of small houses. Red's spinal cord was severed upon impact. His loyal keys dangled securely from his hip but at the angle they hung during Red's naps at the boiler room janitor's desk.

The snow continued to dip in and out of the gully between the walls built to cover the vents. Amid snowy tempests, some flakes glided straight down.

Initially Red's body heat melted the snow. Later, more snow and ice coated his body in thin mottled layers. After a few hours, he looked dappled with sparkling white doilies.

Inside the building, the flashlight Red left on the floor was still lit; its beam was fixed on the wall where someone wrote "Out of Order" with an arrow pointing to the vacant spot where a vending machine had long ago been removed.

Chapter 2

In the middle of the night Vladimir slipper-shuffled from his bed out to the couch. For several days he spoke to no one other than himself. He scarcely slept for more than a couple of hours since Helen's widowed whimpers filled his living room. Her lament echoed in his mind and the room, which often felt like the same thing.

Vlad hadn't bothered to bathe or dare look in a mirror since he found out his only living child had died. When his grandfather died, his mother covered the mirrors so that her father's soul wouldn't see its reflection and refuse to move on to go wherever dead people go. Now that his son was dead, Vlad didn't want to look in the mirror. In fact, *he* wanted to move on, to be the dead person.

Red's death made Vlad think as much about his grandfather as his son. A Russian dictionary his Deda gave him sat on top of two thick scrapbooks on his coffee table. Stuck between its pages were pictures of his children, Oleg and Vera. It pained his stiff hands to pick up the heavy book, but Vlad's fingers suffered willingly in order to touch the evidence of his lost people, things and time.

Vlad last bought new eyeglasses in the winter of 1978, but lost them when they flew off his face into a tall snow drift during that year's epic blizzard. Every year his vision deteriorated but he liked not being able to make things out and living in a blur. But now he wanted to see clearly. See Vera. See Red.

A small toy magnifying glass Cole gave him is all he had. Passing it over a close-up of Red's face made the boy look like a Cyclops. But holding it over a snapshot of Red's tenth birthday, he could see the entire magic show they had performed for the neighborhood kids. Vera wore her star-covered black velvet cape as she held triumphantly overhead a playing card in one hand and a wand in the other. Red's face rested expressionless under a pilgrim's hat from his school's Thanksgiving play. Unlike Red, it thrilled Vera to try magic tricks, make people laugh and talk to neighbors as they pinched their sheets onto clotheslines. Vlad blurrily shuffled through the photographs. His thumb rubbed over the images as if it could feel what his eyes could not see. Instead of padding his sorrows with memories of their faces, the photos left Vlad aching for his children. Vlad grasped for a memory of Red, but not as little Oleg. It was about five years earlier, when Vlad, Red and Cole fished off the rocks at Seaside Park as the ferry chugged back and forth from Port Jefferson all day.

Vlad told Cole, "Your great grandmother was invited by P.T. Barnum to be on the very first ferry that left from Bridgeport to Port Jefferson. There was a band, dancing, and tables and tables of food." He snickered and went on, "She told me that the wooden ferry was built all catawampus. The water tossed it around so much that most of them vomited all over the place. She bragged that she and my father didn't get sick. He kept his balance as he danced his heart out, even after the band stopped playing. She always lit up whenever she talked about Clinton. I've said it before and I'll say it again, it's a damn shame they couldn't marry."

At that moment, Vladimir had noticed Red observing him closely. When Red realized his father had caught him staring, his crooked smile slanted down the opposite direction than his raised eyebrow; the classic Red smirk that Vlad found playfully stern. Ruddy from the sun, Red's sweaty face shone under his salt-and-pepper hair, some stuck to his forehead, some limping on the wind. A treasured moment frozen by no camera.

Vlad squeezed his eyelids as he rocked forward and back. It was his body's way of pushing off from the memory, as if it were a diving board or a pirate's plank. But he wasn't finished. His eyes fluttered as Vera's face appeared. He tried to simply envision her face. Recalling her actuality pained him. He avoided exhuming her jaunty walk and giggly voice. But similar to his failing body's disobedience, his aged mind continually failed to submit to his wishes.

Vlad's mind's eye traveled to 1951. Vera danced in front of the radio as he stood in the doorway of their living room. She watched the hem of her blue and white striped dress boogie along with her hips and Rosemary Clooney. Vera sang along, "Come on-a my house, my house, I'm gonna give you candy...." Her head bopped side to side.

As soon as she noticed Vlad watching, she pulled his arm, "Come on! Poppa! Dance!" He motioned for her to keep dancing without him. She flashed a wide grin with her tongue bulged pink up behind her new front teeth, four little white nubs.

This was the last time she would dance. The last time he would hear her feet thump on that rug and her free spirit fill their house. That floor, those walls, the curtains and Vera were gone by the time most of Bridgeport headed off to bed that night.

Old Vlad coughed in soft sobs. He didn't know his tears were soaking pocks into the onionskin-like pages of the dictionary left to him by his grandfather. According to his Deda, it was a gift from his boss, the Tsar Nikolai before sending him off to the United States with P.T. Barnum. Vlad had told Red that he should take the book after he died. He would have to tell Cole to take it now. This book is where Vlad had filed his life for more than seventy years. Birth certificates, leases, car titles, his marriage certificate, a lock of Red's hair, a lock of Vera's hair, a lock of Cole's hair. Cole always seemed more interested in the book itself than its legacy. "Why can't I read it? Can you do magic so that I can read in Russian?" she asked. "Please?" she whined.

"That's not how it works," he sighed. His patience had waned but especially with Cole's questions about magic. It had always irked him that no one wanted to hear the truth. There is no magic. When he started out as a young con man, Vlad posed as a party magician so that no one would suspect his actual job. The idea of magic captivated people and exposed that most of them want magic to be real. It comforts them to think that something is true about something that is fake. As a realist, he concerned himself finding the counterfeit in the genuine. It also made him a better scam artist. Still, living as a pessimist in a world of optimists eventually roofed him under a constant haze of grouch. Most recently, he thought he had mastered how to disregard everything, past and present, and wait to die. But Cole's curiosity about everything, including magic, made him feel as if living past eighty was simply surviving too long.

His mind rambled back to Cole and how occasionally he forgot her name. When he was a boy lighting small fires with his Deda he never understood how the old man could forget his only grandchild's name. But by then, time and despair had forced Deda to forget many places, names.

Some of his stories were fun but one continued to haunt Vlad. When Deda was only seventeen his first baby was born. Sometimes Deda said his daughter's name was Ludmila and other times he just called her dóchka. As he had kissed his newborn's forehead, the mother's father threatened to kill him if he didn't leave the village. He fled to Moscow that night. After he was gone for a week, he came across an old gypsy woman who said that his hometown of Teplovo was now known for insanity and horror. A young mother who was abandoned by her lover burned her baby's blood-drained corpse in the community baking oven.

Deda howled like a trapped animal. To console him, the gypsy pulled his head to her chest and sang a long lament. Deda sometimes sang it to Vlad. He once translated it, but only the last part. It ended with, "Neither in church nor in the bar, Nothing is held holy! No, my friends; everything's wrong. Everything's wrong, my friends!" He vowed never to return to his village and later, his home country.

Vladimir itched his head hard with his fingernails to scrape all the day's dead memories away. He hobbled to the kitchen. A thick slice of Spam on a buttered piece of toast always put him to sleep. He put a slice of bread in the toaster and took the Spam chunk out of the refrigerator.

Even though he barely left his apartment Vladimir never went hungry. His neighbor brought him Twinkies and Wonder bread from the bakery thrift store every Tuesday, when she got the 10% senior discount. He liked to dip the sweet yellow treats in his Sanka instant coffee lightened with powdered milk, both provided by a nearby church that delivered a bag of groceries every week. During the last delivery, Vlad had a coughing fit. The young man brought him a cup of water and rubbed a circle between Vlad's shoulder blades. He continued to comfort Vlad until he barked at the young man, "You may think I'm a shut-in, but really I'm a shut-*out* because I've *chosen* to say, 'The hell with you all,' until I die." The man rushed out. Vlad felt the uneasy satisfaction of having pushed away one more person who had made him feel as though life could be made better by not pushing people away.

When the toast popped up, Vladimir dropped it onto one of the Christmas-themed paper plates given to him around the Fourth of July. When he looked down at the toast, he thought maybe he hadn't put it on the plate and he was looking at a Santa Claus face. But after touching the bread and blinking a few times, a face still appeared in the bread. Holding the toast as if it were a bathroom tile, he carried it into the living room. Under the bright bulb of his side table lamp, he used the toy magnifying glass and now was almost sure the toast had an image of a face burned into it. He lowered his head toward it and squinted. "What the?" he whispered. It was the face of his Deda's friend and employer, P.T. Barnum. He turned the bread over and there were the initials P.T. in white, traced with brown edges.

He went back into the kitchen to knock on the toaster's side and unplug it. Shaking it upside down over the sink, Vlad heard the larger crumbs ping the metal sink like icy rain. He relocated the toaster onto the opposite counter and plugged it into another socket. While making another piece of toast, he stared at the now-cold toasted portrait. When the new slice came out like all other pieces before Barnum's face, Vladimir tossed the weird toast into the trashcan. The peculiar experience had caused him to forget to put the water on for tea. He poured a few ounces of brandy into a juice glass, plopped the Spam slice on his plate, turned off the kitchen light and sat on the couch and ate. He fell asleep with the empty glass in his hand as the paper plate and crumbs slid to the floor.

Chapter 3

Cole woke up to a distinctive stillness. Not a weekend tranquility, not a home-sick-from-school gray lull, not even a Christmas-morning silence. All other days there had been a plan, at least one of them, her father, herself, her mother, needing to do something, needing to be somewhere. Even a blizzard meant shoveling after watching the Action News 8 coverage of the I-95 crashes. But this was the day after her father was found dead and there was nothing to do other than to try to believe it.

The smell of scrambled eggs coaxed Cole from bed. When she passed her mother on her way to the bathroom, she wanted to give her a hug. It wasn't something they ever did in the morning. Hugs were for their "goodnight" ritual: a hug and a peck on the cheek. She stood beside her mother at the stove and huffed out a sigh, but her mother didn't look up from the pan. She shuffled on to the bathroom.

After Cole peed, she lifted her nightgown to look at her pubic hair. Every morning she checked to see how much closer she was to looking like the lady in the sex magazine she saw at a friend's sleepover party. She did this every day but this day it felt wrong. A wisp of dark hair growing near her left inner thigh caught her eye just before she dropped the hem of her nightgown. Was she supposed to care about things like this now? Do kids with a dead father have to always think of their dad's voice so that they will never forget how it sounded? Cole wondered if she could get out of this requirement since she had cassette tapes of her father's voice.

At the table, Helen seemed hypnotized by her thumb as it flicked her cigarette a few times, then several more past the point when any ashes were left to fall into the half-full ashtray. She didn't look up when Cole walked past her into the living room, picked up her tape recorder and brought it into the kitchen and sat across from her. A bowl of Kix awaited Cole. Cole stood up to go look in the pan still on the stove.

"I left the eggs on too long," Helen said.

Cole sat down.

The apartment was densely empty of Red but the kitchen was most bearable. It was the only place where they expected him to walk in at any moment versus thinking that he was already there in his green easy chair or in bed.

Milk dripped down Cole's chin as she ran a fingernail between the plastic grooves of the tape recorder's speaker. She twisted her neck and lifted her shoulder to her face to wipe the milk on her nightshirt. Cole tensed when her mother squinted at her.

Helen said through a flat haze, "What's that nightie? It's cute."

"It's a Christmas one," Cole said. She didn't say, "from Dad."

Cole pulled the pink cotton jersey cotton out, so she could look down at the cartoon candies on the front. Lollipops, candy canes, gumdrops, cupcakes, all seemed to be falling from above to be around the words "Sweet Stuff!" written close to her belly button area.

Cole didn't want to put on the same pajamas she wore the night her father died. Next to the plastic laundry basket in her room she piled everything she had worn while he was dead and she didn't know yet. She hadn't decided whether she would destroy them or just wash them by themselves.

The clock over the stove said it was a few minutes after eleven in the morning. Cole's class was in Social Studies right now, her favorite class. Yesterday, Mrs. Sutton rolled a television cart into the classroom, so the class could watch the space shuttle launch. Since her father had not come home from work the night before, Cole's attention was fuzzy. She didn't get much sleep. Icy snow pelted Cole's bedroom window all night while she listened to her mother make calls to phones no one answered.

In the morning, as Cole slotted two blueberry Pop-Tarts into the toaster, Helen said, "You better go. I don't want them to think I kept you home on count of the snow. You heard the news guy. They didn't cancel school."

Cole hadn't asked to stay home but had thought about it. She hovered her hand over the toaster as its squiggly radiant red bands bronzed her breakfast. Whenever Helen displayed any sort of motherly ESP, it was always to tell Cole she couldn't do something. In retaliation, Cole acted as though she didn't hear it but eventually did what she was told.

As she watched the television in the classroom, Cole worried about her father. To calm her nerves she gently bit down on the tip of her tongue. She looked around at the kids sitting close by. They had all stopped fidgeting and were watching the television intently as the voice said, "Liftoff of the twenty-fifth space shuttle mission and it has cleared the tower." The NASA men's voices sounded like they were coming from a small transistor radio as they talked about throttling and velocity.

The classroom was fuller than usual because the science class next door came in to share one of only a few televisions in the school, and Mrs. Sutton's classroom had a cable line. Some kids stood in the back while several sat on their textbooks on top of the counter that covered the hot radiator by the window. As the launch was at its most boring part, just a missile fading into the distance, the newscaster said, "This morning it looked as though they were not going to be able to get off."

One of the heater kids snickered, "Well, they're sure getting off now." The camera zoomed out to take in the sudden expansion of the shuttle's image.

Mrs. Sutton explained, "That must be the rocket booster releasing from the shuttle."

Half the room chattered about something going wrong while the rest silently observed the streaks of smoke scrape down the blue sky.

When the newscaster said, "It looks like the solid rocket boosters just blew away from the side of the shuttle in an explosion," everyone in the room took it to support his or her theory.

"Obviously a major malfunction," said one of the radioed voices. The science teacher took off his glasses, rubbed his beard and shook his head. Cole folded her arms on her desk and put her head down.

Someone close to the television cart said, "Cool, look at that. It's just like a two-headed snake." A voice from the back of the room said in a Porky the Pig voice, "Ble, bleh, ble, that's all folks."

Cole wished that putting her head down meant that the room was put on pause. That everyone would just look at her and see she wanted them all to stop, stop talking, stop everything.

"My class," said the science teacher, "go back to the classroom and open up your books to the solar system chapter we read last week."

"Yeah, and go find Uranus," someone behind Cole said.

"And please thank Mrs. Sutton for hosting us today," the teacher added.

"Thank you," a weak chorus rang out. Cole listened as a few others said their thanks directly to Mrs. Sutton, shoes scuffled and the door squeaked open and almost shut until all twenty or so students were gone.

Cole's face was hot and moist from her breath entrapped in the well created by her arms. When she sat up, the room's otherwise warm air felt cool on her face. Some of the students were still looking at the shut-off television when the principal knocked twice and then walked in.

Principal Connolly sat on the teacher's desk, making him the same height as Mrs. Sutton. Everyone watched the two adults as they faced the chalkboard with their backs to the class. Principal Connolly folded his arms and leaned in close to Mrs. Sutton. Cole wondered what the principal knew about the spaceship explosion that would make him come tell Mrs. Sutton. She thought that maybe since one of the astronauts was a teacher this time, all the principals had access to some sort of insider NASA information.

As Mrs. Sutton listened, right below where her hair was pulled up into a bun, the back of her neck blazed red. When they finished, Mrs. Sutton turned around and looked directly at Cole.

She wondered if the science teacher thought she was the one who made those wisecracks during the broadcast and told the principal. Cole straightened up and tucked her hair behind her ears. Suddenly she had to pee so she clamped her knees together. The lunch bell rang out but no one moved. They all watched Mrs. Sutton walk toward Cole's desk with the principal behind her. Mrs. Sutton put her hand on the back of Cole's head and said to the class, "Please all go to your lockers and then line up in the hall. Quick now."

Mrs. Sutton said to Cole, "Honey, you wait here. Principal Connolly needs you to follow him."

Cole tried to look into the principal's eyes but he avoided her gaze. Did this mean she was or wasn't in trouble? Maybe it meant her father was at the school to let her know he was okay and the principal was embarrassed that he didn't know which of the students Cole was.

As they walked the halls together, Cole felt like she should be holding the principal's hand. He walked quickly and she usually kept up with her parents walking fast but she was nervous and had to pee. When they got to the school's office, they walked straight through to the inner office with the door that had black capital letters PRINCIPAL stenciled on frosted glass. These rooms smelled like Murphy's Oil Soap, as if someone polished all the wood every day, not just during the summers like the rest of the school.

Never before had Cole been called into Principal Connolly's office. As they walked in, Helen and the school nurse sat with their backs to them. Cole peeked behind the door to look for her father.

That was just yesterday. That was when her lungs stung with tears that didn't make it out of her eyes because there wasn't enough room for how much she cried. That was when her mother held her in a way she had never before felt. That alien comfort brought the words Cole had just heard, "Your father died last night," from her head into her body. It was less of an embrace as it was a containment; Helen's hug squeezed Cole's arms into her sides in a desperate swaddle while her chin rested on her daughter's head. After she caught her breath, Cole became aware of Principal Connolly standing behind them like a businessman angel with his arms around Helen. They remained in this grieving Russian nesting doll formation until Helen started to rub Cole's back. Principal Connolly patted Helen's shoulder and then offered to drive them home.

Now, about 24 hours later, Cole sat at the kitchen table as her class was probably talking about the Challenger explosion and Cole's dead father. So many questions rushed over her, one after another. She didn't know who to ask and when. The school nurse told her that she could go to her any time but what did she mean? What if she never went back to school? What happens to kids when their fathers die? Do they have to go to military school or join the army? Would she have to go get a job now? Her mother hadn't stopped smoking since Principal Connolly drove them home. They were supposed to get picked up to go to a funeral home in the afternoon. Cole hoped there would be experts there that could tell her and her mother what would happen now.

Cole asked, "Can I go watch TV?"

"No, stay here," Helen said. "We got a lot to do today."

All they were doing was sitting, looking at things on the table and out the window. Cole thought that maybe that's what they had to do now. Sit and miss her father.

She pushed the empty cereal bowl away, sat cross-legged on the chair and pulled the nightgown over her knees. Sliding the tape recorder directly in front of her, Cole wanted to do something that also wouldn't be doing anything. She put her middle finger on the red "record" button. Unless the play button was pressed at the same time it wasn't supposed to go down. She pressed down hard. The button did exactly what it was supposed to do. It didn't budge.

Cole had hoped that crying again would mean some more time in her mother's arms. It did. But this time as the hug felt like someone saying hello, not even a decent goodbye moment. It made her want to ask for something different. If she could, she would have requested a hug just like ordering eggs at the diner, "Could I please get an extra hard hug with a side of a kiss on the head?"

Instead, she asked, "Can I go and watch something now?"

"Sure," Helen said as she gripped Cole's forearm. The touch felt like when her favorite gym teacher Miss Butler held her ankles during sit-ups, sturdily tender and fleeting.

After watching soap operas for two hours, Cole heard Red's car pulled up to their house. She ran to the window. It was her father's friend Hector from QE. Red knew him before Cole was born and they had survived a few barrages of layoffs together.

Helen exhaled her last drag, mashed the cigarette and swirled it in the gray ashy bottom layer. Her all-white cigarettes mixed with Red's brown Marlboros. A drop of water appeared on the table next to the ashtray. Touching her face, Helen realized she was crying again. No warnings, no lump in her throat, no quivering chin, no itchy nose, just tears.

The everyday Ping-Pong-ball sized tissue wad tucked into the cuff of her sweater was now a train of them stuffed up her sleeve to her elbow.

When Hector came to the door, Cole came around the corner. Helen told her, "Go back in and watch television."

Hector sat at the table and said, "They got QE people asking us lots of questions about Red. When he left, if he was a drinker, if he was depressed, that kind of crap. They took all of our timecards. Even looked through Red's locker. It's fishy, Helen. It doesn't look good."

After Hector left, Cole stayed watching the TV. "Tonight's news. A national tragedy. A country mourns," the newscaster paused with her sky-blue eye-shadowed lids closed just long enough to appear sad. She interviewed people who watched the Challenger explode from a viewing platform in *Cape* Canaveral. As if they couldn't endure the nippy morning air, some wore scarves; the more durable people simply wore sweatshirts. Cole felt a detached solidarity with them because they had to endure cold weather and such an awful disaster, but in a happy, sunny place like Florida.

The living room darkened from dusk to night while Cole imagined what it would be like if the news was about her father. "Tonight we have tragic news. A QE worker fell to a snowy death at the long-closed factory."

Chapter 4

Cole thought about how in the movies dead people always looked as though they were asleep. Her father looked dead.

That morning, the funeral director closed the doors to the parlor and left Cole alone with Red's body. Only a few days before she had made her father laugh by walking around with her shoes tethered together by their laces. Now, a thick gray line between his closed lips replaced his smile.

By the time the first person arrived, Cole had already decided to act like her father was ignoring them all. A friend from her father's job. She said to Cole's mother, "Oh, God, Helen, he looks like hell." Nothing absorbed her voice but the shiny furniture and Red's body. Her words carried out into the hallway where Cole was pulling a chain of Kleenex from a box. Cole's heart dropped to think that anyone didn't appreciate what the funeral home had done to make her father look as good as he did.

Some people brought pictures to the funeral to have something else to talk about other than the deadness of 48-year-old Oleg, the man they all knew as Red. The mourners formed congregations. Those with the photographs semi-circled around a potted ficus tree. Behind several rows of upholstered folding chairs three couples lined up elbow-to-elbow in paper-doll style. The smokers and shy ones stood outside under the funeral home's awning talking about getting time off from work or what buses they took to get there.

When no one was visiting her father, Cole stood motionless at the foot of the coffin, blending in with the floral sprays. Her nervous spasms, eyes squinting or biting her tongue, exposed her position, as did her occasional head nod as she acted like she understood something when the picture crowd occasionally erupted with laughter over a story about Red.

Helen sat in an antique wingback chair that the funeral home's janitor called "the snot seat." The chair's placement channeled traffic to her but Helen buried her face in her hands for most of the wake. As if passing a sleeping dog, each person kept their eyes on the widow until they safely passed. Cole stayed close enough to offer tissues from the baseball-sized wad she'd crafted or to answer questions. She thought that's what people would expect from a 12-year-old girl, almost a teenager.

After a lull in new visitors, a woman arrived who Cole thought looked a little like Marilyn McCoo from one of her favorite TV shows, *Solid Gold*. The woman took confident strides in her high heels and sat in a front-row chair. Bowing her head, she clasped her hands together in prayer. Cole stared at her until she popped up and took Cole in her arms, slowly soothing out the words, "Cole, Cole, Cole. His baby girl, Cole." She then gripped the girl's upper arms, pushing her away from the coffin and looked her up and down, saying, "I haven't seen you since you were as big as a bug."

As she took Cole's hand to approach the coffin, the woman whispered, "I'm going to need you." Cole had never seen such large teardrops. She watched each tear pause at the smooth shelf of her cheekbone before it rushed down her chin and neck, clinging to her skin down past the crucifix. The cross had stuck to some lace fringe, resting Jesus horizontally across the hollow between her breasts.

"My God. I'd braced myself but he looks good," she nodded. She turned to Red, "You remember me, Red? It's Gwen. Well, you look good, Red. You look real good."

Cole winced to stifle an anxious giggle. She snapped back to her duties by telling Gwen to look closely at Red's face. She said, "Remember all those little scars from his zits when he was a kid? You can't see them unless you get close, but they said they put some plastic over them and put makeup on it."

Gwen squeezed Cole's hand and said, "Oh, I can't imagine."

"It's okay. They said he didn't suffer hardly at all. The fall knocked him out and the rest … they said, the rest just did it and he died out there without feeling it," Cole said.

Gwen put her hand over her mouth, bowed her head and

walked away. Cole kept an eye on her as she visited each huddle. She wanted to hear more about when she was a baby, but Gwen left without saying goodbye.

Cole waited silently through a few visitors. Then she surveyed one man's clothing and his variety of "Vietnam Veteran" and "U.S. Army" pins. On his green military jacket, a patch was embroidered with "Gus Kenyon." His long, tangled beard and wafting sour booze smell made it impossible for Cole to imagine him as a clean-cut uniformed soldier.

"You know what about your father? That man called me every Valentine's Day," Gus said as he pointed at his dead friend. He blinked his teary eyes up at the ceiling and went on, "'Cuz he never forgot that's the day Ma died when we were kids." Cole wondered if she was related to the man, since he said "Ma" as if the man and her father shared this mother. She never met her grandmother and her grandfather rarely mentioned her.

"Me and your dad," the man smiled for a moment, closing his eyes, "Yup, we were like brothers. I even remember Vera. Little Vera. God bless her soul. Even after Red's mom left, Red's dad was like a father to me. I won't ever forget that."

Cole stiffened at the mention of Vera and her grandfather. She hoped the man wouldn't ask where the old man was. She wanted to ask about Vera but her mother had told her to never ask about Red's dead sister. And then Helen was furious that Vladimir didn't come to his only other child's funeral and Cole didn't want her mother to hear anyone say his name. That morning her mother said, "I bet nobody even remembers if that old man is dead or alive. He doesn't even know if he's Arthur or Martha."

Gus made a short salute in front of the coffin and then leaned over Cole's father and kissed his forehead, leaving a tear that pooled into a crater in the cake makeup under the dead man's right eye.

Cole said, "Sir, I think people are telling stories in the back there."

Gus interrupted her, "Well, I don't know none of those people, but I suppose I can stay until we all go to the reception … where did you say that reception was at?"

"It's at the Webster House. But not until we are done here."

"Well, I'll make myself busy for a while," he said, then turned and winked at Cole. "I'll see you there later, little lady." Watching Gus steady himself against a pillar, Cole wondered if he would be able to find the reception.

One of the funeral home people moved some flowers to the back door.

"It's time for the cemetery," the funeral director whispered to Cole.

Cole whispered back, "It's just going to be me and my mother. That's what she wants. That's all."

The funeral director nodded, "I've told people to go to the Webster House and wait for you there." He had mastered the art of positioning himself in a way that told people what to do. His square, tall frame was a room divider when necessary, especially at services with feuding attendees.

Red's wake was one of the smaller ones for someone so young. It required the funeral director to simply stand in the middle of the room between the coffin and the door, with his eyes fixed on the door to signal the end of the service. The chatting stopped, people shrugged at each other while they tried to figure out whether or not to say goodbye to Helen, who was still despondent. The funeral director shook his head as if to say, "No need. Just get going." Grateful for the prompt and relieved to be freed from their mourning obligations, they slipped hands into pockets and clutched purses, leaving the funeral home as if dismissed from Sunday school.

The funeral director stood in the back and motioned Helen and Cole toward the door. The three of them got into a black four-door car that Cole thought looked like an FBI car. He opened the back door, but Helen didn't like to sit in the back; she always sat in the passenger seat of every car they rode in. She never learned to drive and her claustrophobia kept her up front, where "I can see where we're going and can jump out, if I ever need to." Cole got in the back while he opened the front door for Helen.

The car's heater slowly cleared the foggy windshield. Cole sighed as she pushed her head into her side window to see the three men slide Red's coffin into the hearse and place four small flower arrangements behind it before closing the rear door.

At the cemetery Helen and Cole stayed in the warm car that faced the leafless trees that couldn't block the view of the QE buildings. Three new men maneuvered the coffin's gurney over the snow and ice-covered grass, struggling to keep it stable. Cole worried if her father would make it to his gravesite before toppling out again into the snow and ice. Once the casket was placed over the hole in the ground, the funeral director stood back with his head down.

Another man walked to the car and opened Helen's door. After he helped her over the ice he came back for Cole. A lump formed in Cole's throat; she chewed the inside of her cheek.

Relieved that she was no longer facing QE, Helen looked up at the tall trees in the middle of the cemetery. The path to the gravesite was shoveled but slippery. After Cole slid over the icy ground to her, Helen put her arm around her shoulder. Cole wore a pair of Helen's shoes, since she had outgrown her own good shoes. They were at least one size too large. Her mother insisted she stuff newspaper in the toes so that people wouldn't notice. At the wake, Cole distracted herself from crying by scrunching her toes into the crumpled edges of the paper, until one of the mourners asked, "What's that sound?"

The red, cold hands of the two twenty-something men on each side of the grave lowered the casket. They executed the slow descent perfectly despite looking tired and cold. The funeral director watched the men work the cranks until he looked away and noticed that the digger had knocked over a headstone with the backhoe again. Cole saw him shaking his head and she thought the man was thinking about her father. So many people had shaken their heads in the past few days with "What a shame" or "I am so sorry."

The squeaking belt gears lowering the coffin and a frigid low wind gave Cole something to listen to other than the blood rushing in her head.

This burial reminded the funeral director of two others. Most burials have a priest or minister or family member speaking, but sometimes, the person goes down with no fanfare. As he thought about the day they buried Ozzie Palm, a down-and-out drunk they found floating in Beardsley Park Reservoir, Cole's red eyes surged with tears and she let out a yelp, then sobs. Helen closed her eyes for a few seconds. When she opened them, they again fixed on the cemetery trees. Her head tilted to the left as though she had just asked a question. And as if there was an answer, she jutted her chin and nodded. She rubbed Cole's shoulder in fast keeping-you-warm strokes. Cole didn't take her eyes off of what would be the last place she saw her father. She wiped her snot on her red mittens.

When the squeaking stopped, the funeral director's shoes crunched into iced-over snow as he pulled some flowers from an arrangement. He handed a few flowers to Helen and she stepped over to the hole and tossed them in. Her face was exhausted of emotion, sketched over with despair.

Cole continued crying, looking at the ground in front of her feet until the funeral director's boots appeared on the other side of the flow of tears. He handed Cole three white carnations and she choked out, "Thank you," spitting a little onto her chin then wiping it away with the soggy mitten. She stood with her head down while he walked back to his spot. She pinched the flower stems in her yarn lobster claw grip and then pulled them close to her face. Everyone waited. The moment Helen opened her mouth to tell Cole to throw the flowers, the funeral director's crunchy footsteps interrupted her. Helen followed him to the car and then Cole followed her.

Helen opened the back door to let Cole in but she wasn't there. Still clutching the flowers, Cole was hugging the funeral director, who awkwardly leaned over the girl patting her back.

"Come on, Cole," Helen said as she strained a smile.

"Thank you," Cole said just above a whisper as she turned with her head down and walked away. Helen caught his eye, so he shrugged, as if to say, "What're you gonna do?" and turned away.

After he dropped Helen and Cole off at the Webster House, the funeral director stopped at Madison Cleaners. Cole's snot on his black wool coat took it over the edge to call for a dry cleaning. When the counter clerk asked how he was doing, he told her all about Cole. He changed Cole to being a young boy, an attempt at privacy, but he had also thought Cole looked like a little boy dressed in his mother's clothes. Right down to her shoes that were too big.

"That's just heartbreaking," the clerk said.

"We see it every day. Some days are just harder than others," he said.

As he jogged coatless through the chill to his car, the clerk brought the coat to the back bench to tag it. She looked over her shoulder, saw her boss on the phone and then stamped PAID on the dry-cleaning ticket.

Chapter 5

In McDonald's, Janet slid her tray onto a table where someone had left a *New Haven Register*. Hunching over the paper, she tucked her straggling hair behind her ears and flipped through to only section she ever wanted, the comics. She slid the Egg McMuffin wrapper around the page as she nipped tiny bites off the sandwich, sipped a black coffee and read.

By the time she finished *Garfield*, who she always kept for last, Janet's feet had warmed up from the sidewalk's slushy snow. Ready to leave, she poured two unused creamers onto the tray and trickled her leftover coffee into the egg-shaped splotch. Janet liked leaving messes. It was as if knowing that someone would have to clean up after her made her feel like someone had helped her, or at least had thought about her.

As she arranged the newspaper to hide her creation, a photo caught her eye. It was a picture of a man wearing a white shirt, a black bowtie and a top hat. The headline read: "QE Worker Dies in Blizzard." She knew this face but didn't recognize the name, "Oleg "Red" Sevic, 48, Quality Electric employee and Bridgeport native, leaves wife Helen and daughter Nikolaevna." The photograph and these names appeared to belong to an old-fashioned time and place. Janet was sure she knew this man. She picked up the paper and rolled it into a tube, held it out in front of her at an angle at which only his eyes were visible.

"Holy shit!" Janet shouted. She usually swore to force people into a respectful repulsion for her presence. The polite New Englanders often made space for her that they promptly rescinded with Pilgrim-like sighs. But this time Janet's exclamation was internal, primal. The outburst won everyone's attention as she rushed up to the counter. Holding the newspaper up like a lit torch, she slammed her Styrofoam cup on the counter with her other hand. "Can you fill 'er back up, please? I'm having a big day here, lady," she said. The thin gray-haired white woman left the cash register mid-order to refill the cup and place two creamers, a stirrer and two packets of sugar on the counter. Slapping the newspaper against the counter, Janet asked for two more stirrers.

"Here, dear," the cashier said in a soothing voice as she handed her a fistful of stirrers.

"Thanks! I love the shit out of that tiny little spoon at the end. Don't you love that?" Janet tucked the newspaper under her arm as she held the spoons up to the faces of customers on line. No one dared reply; they played possum with cold downcast smiles until the wild-haired woman left.

Chapter 6

Helen had stopped answering the phone after an unnerving call from the woman who claimed to be Cole's real mother. Helen had already stopped communicating with just about everyone, from Red's father to the telephone company. She half-hoped her service would be cut but she needed to make calls about getting money. After three months of no rent checks, their landlord posted an eviction notice on their door. Helen had called about a few cheap apartments from the newspaper, so now she needed to answer the phone, no matter who might be on the other end.

The phone rang. Helen put the receiver up to her ear and let out a soft, "Hello?"

"Hello? Am I speaking with Helen?" She didn't recognize the woman's voice. Her tone was officially confident, like a bill collector. Helen held her breath and thought of hanging up. "How has it been? How is Cole?" She thought of hanging up. When Helen didn't respond, the woman asked, "You still there, hon?"

Helen finally took a breath and then sighed. "Oh! It's you! Yes, Gwen," Helen finally answered. "It's just hard. I'm not getting anywhere with the company."

"Which company? The insurance company? His company?" Gwen asked.

Helen squinted and reached for her cigarettes. Her husband was dead and Gwen still called Quality Electric Company "his," making Helen unsure if she should answer honestly or defend "his" company with her silence. She said, "All of them. I'm getting nowhere. We haven't gotten a dime yet. Except for Social Security. They were pretty good to us."

Helen's phone had been off the hook when Gwen called for the past two weeks, so it was not surprising things weren't moving forward. Gwen once helped her uncle with his Medicare and swore never to get involved in these kinds of problems again. Flustered, she made something up, "I'm sorry I don't have a lot of time, I have a doctor's appointment."

"Oh God, I just went on and on. It's just that…."

Gwen interrupted, "I called to let you know about a good deal on an apartment. It's small and it's in the East End. Only two hundred."

Even though they were about to be evicted and this was one hundred dollars less than their rent in the Hollow, Helen thought she should answer shrewdly. "What about the electric, heat and telephone?" The sting of her foolishness hit her at the word "telephone," both because landlords never paid for that and everyone called it a "phone" now.

"Everything's included, but not phone service." Gwen's cheerily annoyed edge reminded Helen that she worked for the phone company.

"Of course, it's not. I'm sorry," she said.

Gwen gave Helen the phone number and rushed off the phone.

After the call clicked off, Helen rested the phone on her thigh. She watched Cole repeatedly flick the light on and off while staring at the light fixture. She would have to finally break down and call Vladimir to give Cole something to do. The phone moaned out a dial tone.

Their apartment's odor had changed since Red had died. Helen didn't cook meals from scratch anymore and all the Renuzit air freshener gels had dried up. There was no money to waste on replacements, so the two of them left the empty decorative plastic cones throughout the apartment: on an end table, the bathroom sink, the kitchen windowsill and Red's bureau next to an untouched stack of coins and a used Band Aid folded neatly like a trifold wallet. Their entire home now smelled like Cole's bedroom always had, far from the waft of cooking food and self-sufficient in the fight against stink.

The pulsing off-the-hook tone blared from the receiver. Cole scrambled to pull down the phone's receiver and then took the phone out of Helen's hand. After hanging it up, she went into the living room to watch television. She sat on the floor in front of Red's chair so that she wouldn't have to look at it.

At the supermarket Helen tucked the Hydrox cookies next to a package of toilet paper. Cole knew that they were for her grandfather. Lagging behind to hide her joy, she picked up a box of soup/dip mix. Adding cans of soup and baked beans to their shopping cart, Helen said, "We got to stretch these food stamps, kid. Two for a dollar. Nobody's giving away steaks like this." The perishables (a plastic net bag of oranges, a pound each of American cheese and bologna, a gallon of milk, a dozen eggs, two loaves of Sunbeam bread and a pound of margarine) were teamed up with mustard, four cans of baked beans, six cans of soup, Spam and Saltines. Helen justified a budgetary dispensation for a box of Oyster crackers by saying, "When you are eating soup like it's going out of style, we got to fancy it up a little, right?"

That night they ate baked beans on toast. Red used to call it "shit on a shingle" to make Cole giggle. Helen said, "You're going to your grandfather's tomorrow for a few hours. I told him he didn't need to feed you, so bring what you want. It'll be lunch and supper time."

Cole buried a smile under exaggerated chews. As her knee bounced under the table in time with her racing heartbeat, she said "Okay," as flatly as she could muster.

Chapter 7

Always a little different than all the other little girls, Janet was the outspoken and sarcastic one. This didn't change after she found her older brother David hanging in their garage on her fifteenth birthday. In fact, her parents were relieved when a year later, Janet was more of a spitfire than ever at her sweet-sixteenth birthday party. Along with her friends she sang along to records and made sure that everyone was having a fun time.

But the next morning, when her mother looked in on all girls who had slept over, Janet wasn't there. When she noticed the door from the kitchen to the garage was slightly open Janet's mother started moaning, "No, no, no, no, no, no." When her courage elbowed aside her fear, she looked behind the door. A living, breathing Janet sat cross-legged in the center of a large circle of small candles they had bought that summer at Cape Cod Colonial Candle. Patchouli and bayberry merged with the marijuana's sticky skunk. Janet blew a smoky plume up to where she had found David. Her mother's tears dropped onto her floral housecoat as she backed away, closed the door and went on to cook dozens of pancakes for the sleepover crowd.

Since that moment, every time Janet was brought home by the police or stumbled to her bedroom drunk, her mother flashed to that image of her in the garage. Guilt rose in her like nausea when she felt relieved that this memory helped blur the ones of David's suicide.

As an adult, Janet's plans and schemes always lacked a couple of steps and included several unnecessary ones. It was as if her brother's death had forced her to complicate every problem into a laboring distraction.

Now, the morning after seeing the article about the dead man,

Janet hit her boyfriend up for weed and spent the afternoon getting high in his apartment. As she ate one little tin can of butterscotch pudding after another, she obsessed over the man's face. He had to be the man who took her baby to the adoption agency. She recalled how nervous he was, and the weight of her baby in her arms, as if it had happened that morning. Under the fog of pot and sugar, Janet convinced herself that she needed to break into the Catholic Charities building to find her file. It was the only way to find out where that man brought her baby.

The agency's yellow pages listing said they closed at 5:30 p.m. She sat at the bus stop across the street from the building from 5:00 until 7:00, watching everyone leave. When she took off her gloves to blow heat onto her hands, there was a bluish tint under her fingernails. After the last person shut off the front office lights and drove off, Janet crossed the street and walked into the parking lot. She strolled to the back of the building where there was an alleyway between the administrative offices and the orphanage. There were no windows on that side of the orphanage. But there was a row of high windows on the other building.

The metal door was locked. Even on her tiptoes on top of a snow pile, Janet could only reach the bottom of the windows. She tried pushing on the pane of the first one. Nothing. The second one had duct tape over a crack in the window but didn't budge. Before approaching the third window, she heard sounds come from the tall bushes that shielded her actions from the street. She froze. After Janet took two slow steps toward the bushes, a beagle wagged out. It sniffed and wiggled its nose at her. "You fucking ass beagle!" she hissed quietly at it. The dog didn't detect the disdain and kept up its joyful tail waving, snuffling at her shoes. "Get outta here, you piece of shit. Jesus Christ. Why are you back here anyway?" She kicked at it. It scuttled back and growled playfully.

Janet looked around for something to help her prop open the window but snow had covered almost everything and it was dark so far from the streetlights. In a sing-songy voice she coaxed the dog, "Hey, it's okay. I love the puppy-wuppy. Just find me a stick, or get the hell outta here, lovey-dovey."

The beagle sat down and watched her as she tried the third window with a broken yard stick she found back near the locked door. She pushed it against the pane and it gave. "Yes!" The window opened on an angle into the room.

"Here doggie. Come here. That's right. I have a little job for you. Come here. You little fucker," the dog rolled onto its side, thinking Janet wanted to pet him. "I gotcha!" she told the tranquil animal as she scooped him up in her arms. Humming the bouncy tune of Kool and the Gang's *Get Down on It,* Janet cradled the dog's butt in one hand and steadied the rest of his rubbery body with the other. With a hard stomp, she planted her foot in a snow heap below the window. With one smooth push, she raised him to the window above her head, hesitating only when he turned his head as it hit the window.

Grunting the tune now, she gave one last shove and the dog fell through. Her humming stopped suddenly as she listened for the drop. There were two thunks, one on something that sounded like a file cabinet and one that sounded like the floor. The dog was silent the entire journey but coughed out a loud wheeze after its mission was complete. Clicking toenails trailed off as he walked out of the room. Janet gave herself thumbs up for such a brilliant scheme and threw the promise, "I'll be back soon," up to the now-open window.

While at the bus stop, she had spotted a ladder propped against a nearby house. The bottom rungs were stuck in the snow so she had to knock it over flat in order to try to lift it. It clattered against the aluminum siding, but no one was home. Janet dragged it several feet before dropping it in the middle of their front yard. She didn't have the strength to move it any farther and passing cars had slowed down to watch her.

"Fuck this," she said.

She abandoned the break-in and headed back to Tim's apartment. As she passed the agency, the beagle scratched at the office's front door. "Fucking ass beagle. Tough shit," she said as she stuck her middle finger up toward his whimpers.

Chapter 8

As soon as school ended for summer, Cole half-heartedly brushed her hair and teeth. But this was the day she was going to see her grandfather. She woke up early to wash up and comb out her two-week-old rat's nest.

Since her dad died, Cole trimmed her hair in the shape of her last haircut from Red's barber, Eddie. He swung the cape in front of Cole and snapped it around her neck, smirking, "Here's our Russian girl getting the Dutch boy." After the commas of her dark straight wet hair fell onto the cape's white tent, Eddie brushed them onto the floor. While Eddie trimmed her dad's ginger locks, Cole watched the other barber sweep up her tumbleweed of hair. She tracked it until it became part of the large stubbly caterpillar edged along by the broom. After Red died, Helen continued to go alone to get her hair done. The first time she left to take the bus downtown to her hairdresser, she called out, "I'm going to Nancy. I'll be back. Don't go out." Cole picked up the phone and dialed zero. She asked the operator, "Do you know if it's the mom or dad that's supposed to get their kid a haircut?" The lady laughed as she disconnected the call.

Now, Cole shuffled around the kitchen as she munched on a piece of toast topped with a slice of yellow American cheese. She piled everything she wanted to share with Vladimir on the kitchen table. There, she packed up six Hydrox cookies in a piece of foil. Tearing the aluminum foil reminded Cole of when her father wrapped cold cans of soda for summer days at Seaside Park. She kept a mental list of all the foods her grandfather never bought because he swore he would eat an entire package in one sitting, including these tougher-than-Oreos cookies, coffee ice cream, and to Cole's mortification, chicken livers.

Helen and Cole got off at the stop closest to Vlad's apartment. They spent the two-leg bus ride from the Hollow arguing over whether Cole could walk alone to Vladimir's. The winning argument ended with an exasperated, "Dad would have let me!"

They parted on Boston Avenue where the widow watched the half-orphan cross one of Bridgeport's busiest streets. After taking a few steps away from one other, each felt relieved to be alone but also noticed that it was warmer out than either of them had thought. Helen's breath shallowed and she blew her nose into the same tissue she then used to blot sweat from her forehead and neck. Cole rolled up the sleeves of her favorite shirt that had epaulets and buttoned breast pockets that she never undid.

Turning onto Sheridan Street, Helen's eyes tried to spot differences in the houses. She noticed that some roofs were pointed and some flat, hoping that theirs was going to be pointed since that made it seem more like a home, not just a building. To most people the houses appeared unique and identical all at once. Like a room full of first graders, most were the same height and came in a limited range of shapes. There were different colors, some looked like no one took care of them and only one or two looked like someone spent a lot of time on their appearance. It looked as if someone moved the Hollow to a new location but took out all the cute little green Monopoly houses and plunked down big red hotels. But only after they bought lakes full of pale Easter egg colors and dipped every third house in light yellow and the rest of them in baby blue.

The apartment Gwen suggested was in a faintly distinctive yellowish tan house with something better than a pitched roof: its third floor had four peaks, one on each side. Helen met the landlord, Allan, at the apartment. He started the tour where he had run a rope across the wide doorway to the front room. "This area is off limits. I come up about three times a year to get my stuff."

The door was missing, so a sheet draped over the rope cordoned off where he kept his Civil War memorabilia collection. When Helen asked about it, Allan explained, "My sister Lisa calls it 'the dork squad' and makes me rent out the rest of the apartment." He told Helen that he planned local re-enactments of battles fought by Connecticut Volunteer Infantry regiments. The civilian area of the place seemed halfway packed up and a radio played rock and roll in one of the rooms off the kitchen. "Bertha's in here. She's moving back to…," Allan whispered, "*Mexico*," as if his tenant were defecting to the Confederacy.

When Allan knocked on the open bedroom door, Bertha acted as though she hadn't already heard them in the apartment. She said, "Oh! You are here already. Hello, I am Bertha," as she shook Helen's hand. They then exchanged the delicate glance that confirmed they had just performed the greeting because that's what women do when men are around.

The three small-talked and Helen volunteered Cole as a helper for Bertha's packing over the next few days. In return, Bertha complained that the apartment was very hot in the summer. Fanning her face with a large birthday card, she said, "You can feel it already. You are hot now, no?"

As Bertha had expected, Allan immediately gave in. "All right, I'll put two A/Cs in here and I'll throw you a couple of fans, but maybe you can pay an extra ten bucks a month electric in the summer?"

Before answering, Helen looked to Bertha who nodded once. "I agree to that," she said stiffly.

After signing the lease and giving Allan four hundred dollars cash, Helen left to pick up a job application at Caldor. She decided to walk and stop at the cemetery on the way. The lease transaction and thoughts about the apartment, about Cole, and distant screams from the neighborhood kids, worried Helen's head as she walked.

She didn't feel ready to make this move but she was at a dead end. Their car sold for only three hundred and fifty dollars, even though she thought it would get twice that. According to the shop it wouldn't keep a charge, something about the alternator. Still angry with Vladimir for not going to the funeral, she couldn't ask him for help. She had the food stamps and was on a list for Section 8, but she wanted to see if she could work. Just before Cole came along, she had a part-time job in a CVS. Now, she was unsure if she could handle being somewhere all day and learning new things.

If she were away at work, it would help Cole to be close to Vlad. Gwen would now be their neighbor too. Maybe Cole could spend time with her; Gwen was smart and professional, a good role model. Cole played with her tape recorder and watched television and talked softly, when she even spoke. Never knowing what her daughter was thinking, Helen wondered sometimes if the girl somehow sensed that she wasn't Helen's real daughter. Helen was afraid of doing the wrong thing. She would always follow Red's lead on how to be Cole's parent. Now she felt like an actor without a script with all the cameras focused on her.

The only way to the cemetery took her past QE. The closer she walked toward where Red fell, her legs swung out faster. She folded her arms and locked her gaze on the cars zooming past to avoid looking at the buildings. There was a time she was grateful that QE kept Red working even after the factory had shut down. Now, she wished someone would just tear it all down.

Once the buildings seemed a merciful distance away, Helen stopped outside the QE fence to look at the only good thing about the plant: the huge pond and walkways QE had built around it. It was on that path that led to the small bridge that Red told her that Vladimir was going to help them get a baby.

"You don't believe me, but my father will help us. Trust me." Trust him? How was she supposed to trust a fake magician who was a thief and burned things down for a living? On their first date in 1966, Red took her to a Jerry Lewis comedy that was set in 1989, a future where a married couple is sent to live on the moon. After the film Helen said she'd love to know what it was going to be like in the future. Red promised to someday either build her a time machine or make magic. Helen pushed him playfully, saying, "You're a joker, buddy!"

Red pulled a deck of cards from his jacket pocket, which was in itself amply charming. He then shuffled the cards as they walked and used a double lift and some bottom dealing to impress Helen with his card tricks. Helen snidely replied, "If that's all you got, you still owe me a time machine."

Twenty years later, she lingered at QE's black wrought iron fence trying to remember the pond's name. Candy wrappers, beer cans, and huge industrial drums dotted the parking lot. In the marshy spots, discarded car tires looked as if they grew there from sprinkled seeds. They were rooted into the dirt as snugly as the long grass and brush that sprouted up through their empty centers.

Helen's life was full of ghosts. Even her city had vanished yet could still be seen. Everything that had lost its vitality was crumbling or taken over by nature. Even Red's grave was already blanketed with grass.

That morning, Helen and Cole waited for the bus downtown. Pointing across the street at a lineup of soot-smudged extinct store windows, Cole asked, "What if all of these buildings were people? They wouldn't leave their bodies in the streets, would they?" It shook Helen up that Cole was seeing everything as dead or alive, here or gone, her father or no one. For Helen, Red's death left her at a crossroads of dead ends that she needed to fly away from in order to survive. But for Cole, her father's absence was an exposed cavity that hurt more when the world pressed into it.

Still young, Cole had not felt the discomforts of abandonment that Helen had by her age. Until meeting Red, Helen had never belonged to anyone. She had a better life with Red than she would have on her own, but now without him, she didn't know how to be Cole's mother. This seemed like another one of life's blind games. One moment you're with your boyfriend watching Jerry Lewis kiss Connie Stevens on the moon, and the next you are alone in that formerly hard-to-imagine future with a daughter who fell into your life, as if from outer space.

A breeze unhitched the hair tucked behind her ears and a few strands stuck to her tear-streaked cheek. A long-legged white bird aired its wings in the march. Perched on the fence a few feet away, a bright green monk parakeet squealed its response to the loud motorcycle that had just snarled past. It was the only bird, other than typical ones like seagulls and pigeons, whose name she remembered. Red often pointed them out, telling her the story of a shipment of the birds that busted open at Kennedy Airport in the '60s. Just like many of his stories, like the ones about being related to P.T. Barnum, she didn't believe that's how these birds ended up in Connecticut.

She asked herself if this parakeet was his way of being with her. The bird's head tilted from one side to the other as she spoke to it. "I think I'm doing the right things, but I don't know. I'm scared. That woman called asking about the day you took Cole. What should I do?"

The bird's chest puffed in and out quickly. In nervous flits, it hopped away from her before it flew out over the pond and disappeared into the trees lining the cemetery. She pulled the damp tissues from her purse to blot her eyes and blow her nose again.

The cemetery's entrance was only a few hundred feet away. Drawing in a few short huffs, she turned around to face the street. At the first break in traffic, she ran across the wide avenue. The crossing helped pad the distance between her heart and Red's grave. As Boston Avenue stretched toward Caldor, it became two streets with strips of grass and trees that would be called parks if anyone ever spent time there. She walked on the sidewalk that curved like a river that eventually opened out to the sea of parking lot tarmac.

At the store, the automatic doors opened, and a billow of air conditioning kissed her face. She went directly to the service desk, and despite feeling like a boxer's sweaty rag, asked for a job application.

On her way to Vladimir's, Cole stopped to watch a man on one knee on his walkway, crouched over to gut a fish. Lingering long enough to be recruited to help, she was asked by the man to go to the side of the house to turn on the spigot and drag the garden hose to him.

"What kind of fish are they?" she asked, approaching with the hose.

"Hey! Watch what you're doing!" He told her as the spouting water splashed him. "Brown trout," he said, pointing the curved knife at two fish in an Igloo cooler. "Bluefish," he motioned his head toward about five fish in a white plastic bucket labeled with a black marker, "Pickles."

"They look mean," Cole said as she bent over to look into the mouth of the sharp-toothed fish.

He didn't not want Cole there, but he didn't want her to stay either. He asked, "You one of Rob's kids?"

Cole didn't want to talk about her father. She froze, silent.

"No?" he asked. "Well, you from here or what?" He was annoyed.

"My Grampa lives over there," she pointed down the street, adding, "and he's a senior citizen." The man wiped sweat from his upper lip with the back of his arm as a hot breeze wafted his hands' fishy scent to Cole's nostrils. She pinched her nose, saying nasally, "His name is Vladimir Sevic." The man looked at her for signs that she was Russian or something like that. He never really thought about what Russian girls might look like. He thought about movies he'd seen with Russian spies and none of them were children. He wondered why kids were never used like this in movies. People trust kids and they could be getting information and stealing things with their little hands.

The man positioned the hose to spray away the scales and guts as he kept moving, refusing to be slowed down by his uninvited visitor. He asked, "You ever go fishing?"

"A couple of times. With my…." She stopped.

He shook his head at the girl who couldn't seem to finish a sentence. He offered, "Father? Brother? Uncle?"

To avoid talking about her father, she blurted, "Know what? I'm P.T Barnum's great-great-great-great-great…." Cole lost count but kept going, "great-great-grandkid."

He stopped the knife again and rested his elbow on his bent knee. He looked up into her eyes for the first time, putting her on the spot, "Naw. Really?"

Looking down at her hands, she said, "My grandfather's father was P.T. Barnum's grandson?" as if it were a question.

He shrugged and went back to jerking his knife just fast enough to keep it from catching on the skin. "You just said the old man's name and it wasn't no Barnum name. You sure you're really related to the King of Bridgeport?" he said.

"Maybe he had to change his name because he was wanted by a bounty hunter," Cole instantly regretted embellishing what could have been the truth with something she saw on *The Fall Guy*. He didn't answer. She added, "My great-grandfather knew ladies that were half fish, half girls. They were called mermaids."

"I know what mermaids are," he said as he rolled his eyes. Pointing to the bucket, he said, "You want to bring some to your grandpa or something? You can take a couple of those."

"No. No thanks. I wasn't trying to get fish from you. I just was telling you something," she said.

"That's fine. I just ain't good with kids," he answered. Intentionally, he splashed her shoes with the hose and then turned away.

Stepping back, she said, "I better go."

He pretended not to hear but when she got far enough way not to come back, he called out, "See ya!"

Cole pretended not to hear and kept walking.

At Vladimir's apartment, she put the cookies on his coffee table and went into the kitchen to get him a glass of milk. "Grampa, where's your milk?"

"I ran out. Just give me some of that coffee on the stove," he said as he opened the foil dumpling filled with Hydrox. The foil crackled delicately as his shaky fingers unwrapped it.

Cole cupped her palm closer and closer to the saucepan until she felt it was cold. "You mean heat it up?"

"Yes, please. I don't think I can wait for it though," he looked into the kitchen but he only saw a blur of Cole.

"Come on! It'll be better if you wait." So many things had changed and everything seemed to be happening around her and to her, but not because of her. She tested if she could make something not happen by pleading in a way someone half her age would, "*Please* wait."

He pinched the top shut and put the packet on the couch next to him and sensed Cole's unease ease. Although he hadn't spent much time around her lately, his intuition for her feelings was still sharp.

The height and the awkward hesitation of the figure walking toward him revealed to Vladimir all at once just how much Cole had grown up yet how young she still was. Unable to remember her age, he asked, "So, now. What grade is it you go into?"

"I am going into sixth," Cole said. Before Red died she had never been asked so often about her age and her grade. Used as distractions, these questions worked to comfort only the inquirer. In fact, these questions now seemed to represent the fact that she was fatherless.

She brought Vladimir his large, misshapen Styrofoam Dunkin'

Donuts coffee cup that stood alone in the dish drain. Cole had filled it to the line in the foam that she had fingernailed into the foam during a past visit. Vlad usually sloshed onto himself any drink that was filled any more than that.

Both their attention focused on the first cookie's dunk. The treat and half of his hand disappeared into the cup. Cole was relieved when the cookie survived its wobbly navigation to his gaping mouth. After he savored and swallowed the bite, he let out a guttural signal for her to keep talking.

Cole sat on the floor with her legs splayed out under the coffee table. She smoothed her hand over the top of two overstuffed scrapbooks stacked on the table's corner. "Do you think I could take these to our house?" she asked

"Why the hell not? Hell, I can't see much more anymore anyway," Vlad sulked as he waved a cookie in her direction.

Cole answered a question that Vlad didn't ask, "Because Mom told me not to ask you or her about the old days anymore."

He wiped his mouth with his sleeve and licked his lips, not wanting to be that old man who always has crumbs and dribbles. "Aw, just take them. But you ask me what you want. Don't worry about her."

Cole flipped through the older scrapbook that cracked with each page turned. The glued-down pictures and newspaper clippings seemed more important than the scraps of paper and photographs that were left loose.

Cole ran her forefinger over a postcard that merited its own page. It was one of her favorites. She asked, "So, your mom used to spend time with the animals?" Cole read the sign at the top of one of the long buildings, "At the Winter Quarters? Isn't that where she used to meet up with your father?"

"You could say that. My grandfather, Boris, and his wife weren't together after a while so my mother spent many summer days with her father. He spent a lot of time P.T. Barnum. That's how my mother met Barnum's grandson Clinton." Vlad closed his eyes and pointed at Cole, "*Your* great-grandfather, Clinton Seeley."

Cole had a hard time keeping track of all the people in Vlad's memory. He told stories about his mother, his grandfather and P.T. Barnum all the time. Every time the stories seemed to shift.

When she repeated Vlad's stories, Cole tried to tell the truth but sometimes she couldn't remember which details she had decided were real. She wondered if telling the man with the fish that there was a bounty hunter after Vlad made her a liar and, if so, whether the man could tell she was a liar.

Helen had warned Cole that Vlad closed his eyes whenever he told lies, so she asked, "Then why isn't your name like his?"

"Back in those days, a baby born before the mother was married wasn't supposed to get the name of the father. She wasn't even supposed to keep me to start with. But Clinton made a deal with Barnum," Vlad said. Cole couldn't keep track of what he said while his eyes were open versus closed.

"Did you ever meet him?"

"No, he died before I was born," Vlad said.

Cole remembered different details from each time Vlad told her these stories. In this case, she knew he had spent time with his father. She asked, "Not your grandfather. What about Clinton?"

"Yep. Many times. He lived in New York City. But when I was a little kid he came back to Bridgeport with his wife during the summers," Vlad explained.

Cole asked, "Why don't we know any other people you're related to?"

Vlad rubbed his palms against his thighs. "I'm cold. Is there more coffee?" The apartment was warm but Cole got the blanket off the back of the couch and put it on Vlad's lap. As she walked to the kitchen, she asked, "Do you ever talk to dad's mom?"

Vlad went on as if Cole had asked him another question, "Yep. Before I was born my mother used to meet up with Clinton every Christmas and New Year's and they used to get fresh in one of the winter barns. My mother said that's why I was born early. I had to be a Leo because I was made next to the lion's cages."

Cole was a little embarrassed about hearing about sex from Vlad so she focused on his long unbending fingers waving in the air as he spoke. He seemed to grow slighter each year, almost flimsy. It was as if someone could have let off a flashcube behind him, to show her his skeleton through his ash-gray translucent skin. He went on, "So, that's how we are related to the great P.T. Barnum."

The story sounded pretty much the same to Cole as the other

times he had told it. She still didn't understand why she didn't have aunts and uncles like other kids did. She knew Helen was an orphan so she understood why she didn't know any of that family but she wanted to feel what it's like to have more relatives, especially Wilda, Red's mother. In the pictures of her from a long time ago, Wilda looked more like her son than Vlad did. Wilda and Red both had thin lips and thick eyebrows. Cole wondered if she moved like Red, talked like Red, maybe she would instinctively squeeze the back of her neck like he did every night when he came home from work.

Cole asked, "Do you ever see Wilda now?" The name felt foreign in her mouth.

When Vlad raised his arm to wave off the question his sleeve brushed the foil, calling his attention to the remaining cookies. "I need another one of these to help think about that," he smiled reaching for the cookies again.

A box fan propped in the window hummed against the wood sill as it drew in the smells of someone cooking, prompting Cole to unwrap a now-limp bologna and mustard sandwich she had packed. She sniffed it. It sagged in the middle like a sad cheap mattress.

"You got a hot dog over there?" He squinted, trying to reconcile her food with the aroma.

Giggling, she said, "No. It's a sandwich."

"You put hot dogs in a sandwich? That sounds good."

"No. It's bologna," she said.

"Yuh-uck! Bologna?" He opened his mouth as if for a doctor's examination. Cookie residue embedded a neat brown stripe down the middle of his tongue as his top dentures levered down slow enough to seem as if they were sneaking away from his gums.

The sensation of his false teeth reaching his tongue triggered a gasp that flung a spray of spit to the back of his throat. A violent coughing fit erupted with wheezes, phlegm, tears, snot and a few drops of urine. Cole ran to the kitchen for water.

He couldn't see the dripping glass she held over his knee. Thinking that his peeing had progressed down his pants, he clapped shut his thighs and grabbed his penis. His instinct made him lie down on his side to keep what he thought was the contents of his bladder from soaking the couch.

Scared her grandfather was passed out, or, worse yet, was dying; Cole threw the glass of water in his face as she pushed him onto his back. She was ready to attempt CPR like she saw Punky and Margaux do on Cherie on the Punky Brewster Show episode she recorded the week before her father's accident. The two girls saved their younger friend Cherie after she was locked in a refrigerator while playing hide and seek. To start CPR they did something they called "Look. Listen. Feel."

Vladimir looked like he was choking. He sure sounded like it. Cole didn't want to waste time feeling for a pulse since it was obvious he was alive. She pinched his nose and lowered her face to his.

He rasped, "No!"

Cole stepped back. He called out, "Stop."

Cole sat on the coffee table in front of the couch and stared at him.

After his coughing died down, Vladimir closed his eyes. In about fifteen minutes he went from breathing heavily to falling asleep. Cole picked up the blanket from the floor and pulled it over him.

As he snored and let out a weak squeaky fart Cole went into the kitchen with the empty glass and the Styrofoam cup. Standing with the refrigerator door opened she thought about the Punky Brewster episode again. She remembered that they said that CPR was for when someone wasn't breathing, not when they were choking.

The refrigerator light flickered and then went out. She shut the door and opened the freezer door and wondered why there were no lights in their freezer at home or Vlad's. Maybe the bulbs that would not freeze and bust were so expensive that poor people can only get the kind without any freezer lights. She wanted to ask Vlad if rich people have well-lit freezers and to apologize for doing the wrong thing when he choked. But when she peeked out into the living room, his large quiet banana-like shape rose and fell with his snores.

She opened one of the lower cabinets to use a shelf to help her hop onto the counter. Reaching over, she grabbed the saucepan and sipped the rest of the cold coffee from it. It made her feel like the cowboys she saw in old Westerns. She wondered if the president ever drank his coffee like that when he was in those movies. Some of the old Ronald Reagan movies played all day a few weeks prior but they weren't the kind where cowboys slept outside and spent time by a campfire. Maybe he always knew he'd be president someday and didn't want to look dirty or sleep on the ground like most cowboys had to do.

She wanted to watch television to pass the time but Vlad was the only person she ever knew without a television. Normally when she was bored at his apartment, she played her cassette tapes of television shows and songs from the radio that she'd taped at her house on the old toy tape recorder she kept under his couch. To avoid waking him, she slid down off the counter and slipped out the front door.

A tall rosy-cheeked security guard poked his head around the building to check the back of Vlad's row of apartments. After he gave Cole a silly salute, his shoes churned the asphalt bits as he walked away out of her view. Sitting cross-legged on the cement patio, Cole looked beyond the cyclone fence to the hills and trees, and made up arguments between the nagging crows. She imagined they were fighting over how one of them was so loud it woke the baby crow. When one flew closer to her and cawed, she thought it said, "Blah, blah, blah. That's what you sound like. See? You can hear me from all the way over here!" She tracked the annoying birds while she untied and tied her sneakers.

Being alone with her grandfather was more boring but less lonely than when she was at home with her mother. Vlad fell asleep or stopped talking because he needed to rest. Her mother's frequent naps and bouts of silence gave the impression of covert escapes from Cole. Red once told Cole, "It's like that math test. You tried the best you could and thought you did good. But you just got a 54. That's how Mom loves us."

Cole worried about what her mother was doing at that very moment. What if the new landlord asked her something and she just sighed and lit a cigarette? The crows continued squabbling as they flew away. At first it looked like they were together but then there was one that pulled out ahead. She thought that maybe there are people, and crows, that would glide away by themselves and never return, if there wasn't someone that needed them.

Chapter 9

During their riskiest heist ever, Vladimir and Red wore matching long-sleeve blue oxford shirts, blue Dickie workpants and their best shoes. The disguises were the perfect hybrid uniform for the men to pass as both electrical outlet inspectors and the adoption caseworkers from Catholic Charities. Equipped with makeshift confidence and bogus credentials, the men slunk into Bridgeport Hospital's maternity ward.

Red knelt next to an electrical outlet just a few feet from where Vladimir bent over a metal trashcan. As his father lit the edges of a full Fritos bag, Red steadied a trembling hand near the clipboard on the floor next to his knee. His eyes darted all over the document. How did it have a doctor's signature? Helen's middle name was Edith not Eleanor. Should he correct it? There was no time. His father instructed him to put it in the maternity desk's big yellow folder. As soon as he saw a blur of his father pass behind him Red strode with purpose toward the front desk.

"Smells like someone exploded something in that goddamn microwave again. I hate that thing," a heavyset nurse said to an even heavier man spraying solvent on a coin of gum on the floor. "Go check the break room. Make sure the idiot cleans up after themself." His spraying continued, so she added, "Please?"

As if they understood the concept of job security, the cleaning man's shoes left black scuff marks. Red thought about how difficult it must be to keep hospital floors clean. The man waddled in a circle and yelled, "We need the fire thing! The fire thing!"

When the nurse leaned forward to look down the hall Red spotted the yellow birth records folder behind her but didn't catch sight of a nearby outlet right away. He fought an urge to shake out his nerves from head to toe like a wet dog. Instead he wiggled his right shoulder and stopped breathing as he held up the Radio Shack battery tester for the nurse to see. She waved him through, saying, "Knock yourself out." That morning, he had deliberated for about fifteen minutes about which gizmo looked most believable for gaining access but now it seemed like he could have made it behind the desk if he held up a Flash Gordon superhero doll.

"What now?" she called out as she walked down the hall with her hands on her hips.

Vladimir had set another fire in a trashcan on the other end of the hall but he had run a fuse on that one. He had practiced these strikes at home several times since he usually lit to burn, not to smolder and die out.

No one was within sight when Red opened the LIVE BIRTHS folder and slipped their document under the first two. He glimpsed his soon-to-be-daughter's name and shook his head. His father had a way of giving him indelibly marked gifts. Like the car he had given Red and Helen when they married. One of the Gamboni brothers had been shot in the back of a 1969 Dodge Polara and the father called Vladimir for the burn. Vladimir saw that the backseat's upholstery had miraculously soaked up every drop of blood from the single bullet in the guy's forehead. He convinced Vinny Gamboni to let him torch only the seat and keep the rest of the car. Then Vlad bolted in a backseat from another car and had something he could give to Red.

Helen believed Red's story that the vehicle was put together from a few stolen cars. He registered it in New Haven with Vlad, where they did all the business that they didn't want sniffed out in Bridgeport. Waiting on line Vlad joked, "When we get up there, let's tell them that we want to register a hearse."

Red couldn't complain because no matter what, Vladimir always followed through on a promise. Even when Helen miscarried two years into their marriage. Vlad said, "Don't worry Red. You two will have a baby. I swear you will."

Red told his father he wanted his daughter's name to be Nicole. Nicole Marie. Instead Vlad did what his grandfather had done to him, and what he had done to his son; he imposed on the baby a traditional Russian name. It was as if these men had a compulsion to leave evidence of their actions. They knew everyone would be stuck with it because any change would bring attention to the crime that pulled everything (and in the baby's case every*one*) into the Sevic realm.

When Red entered the small private room at the end of the hall, the baby was already in Vladimir's arms. The mother talked quietly at first. "So you say that I sign this and she goes to a good home? I don't care if anyone's Catholic or anything. They should just be decent people," she said to Vladimir. She locked eyes with Red for a few seconds in silence. "I said, decent people," she repeated, but this time she moved her mouth as if someone were reading her lips.

Red's pulse throbbed in his thumbs and neck. Vlad said to Janet, "He's got the form for you to sign right there on that clipboard. But you take your time." Purposely condescending to her, Vladimir hoped that she would rebel and act swiftly. She did.

"Give me the form," she motioned for Red to come to her. He placed the battery tester on top of the clipboard. "What's that? Are you recording this? You better not be doing some Candid Camera bullshit to me." Janet swiped her arm out to snatch the gizmo but Red backed up.

Vladimir stepped toward Janet but didn't want to get so close she could grab the baby. He said, "That's just to take the baby's barometric pressure and make sure she's healthy. Hold it up, Re…Roger."

Janet looked at its numbers and wires and told him, "Then put it away and check her later. She's healthy. They told me she's fine. They said you people would be happy. Lots of people wanting healthy little babies like her." She looked over to Vladimir as Red put the gizmo in the duffle bag next to a bottle of baby formula and diapers. "And that bitch nurse already gave me the whole speech about me being some kind of shitty bird mother. I get it."

Red nodded his head, even though he didn't know any of the procedures or conversations that happen for a mother to give up her child. It sounded as though they had promised that this baby was going to a good family. He had already felt bad about stealing the baby, but now he wasn't so sure he was saving her from a less fortunate life.

"Can I see her one last time? Please, mister?"

"Of course," Vlad said as he held the baby up.

"Bye for now, baby Kimmy!" Janet's voice cracked. Her eyes blinked, releasing two chubby tears in tandem down her cheeks. Shallow breaths made her mouth the shape of what could have been a laugh or just her mouth making room for more air.

Red didn't want to force the girl to sign the paper. He didn't see any sense in having her go through genuine feelings for a counterfeited adoption form they were going to destroy anyhow.

"You give me that before I change my mind." Janet bent forward and pulled the clipboard toward her, against Red who held it haunted-house tight. She asked, "I don't want to disrespect your job or nothing, but are you new at this?" Turning to Vladimir, she added, "He's sure a nervous guy."

"This is hard work for men," Vladimir said.

Janet looked down at the form. Barely legibly, she scribbled the name "Janet Nobody."

From the hallway, a woman's voice floated in, "Another one? You got to be kidding me!" The fire at the other end of the hallway had been spotted.

Vladimir left the room with the baby as Red patted Janet's shoulder and said, "You did the right thing. Thank you and God bless you."

Janet turned her head away.

Red walked out the door and bumped into Vlad who was bent over their tool bag. He was gingerly placing the baby in it before he covered her with a small blue towel. As they escaped the hospital with his new daughter, Red's heart churned like an ocean wave that tugs a swimmer farther out only to plant him, rattled, exactly where he started.

Chapter 10

Helen answered the telephone expecting the lawyer. It was both a greeting and a question. "Yes?" Did they say yes?"

"Is this Mrs. Sevic?" Janet's voice cracked.

"Yes," Helen said. This "yes" was not a question.

"Look, I'm sorry about your husband's accident. I wish he was alive. I really do. But I need some answers. Because then he might know where my daughter is. You see, I met him back when he worked for Catholic Charities."

"I don't think you have the right number. My husband never worked there," Helen said.

"No. I'm sure he's the one. Very jumpy guy. He took my baby girl," Janet insisted.

"You don't know anything?" Helen asked.

Helen's tone miffed Janet. "Yeah. I don't. I didn't get any names of these men. They took my girl. They didn't give me any papers. I don't got a thing about it."

Helen's brain went hot white blank. Red often said that in order to force the higher-ups at QE to get to the point, he had to ask specific questions. "What do you want?" she asked

"Well if you want to know I'll tell you," Janet spit back at Helen. Janet paused long enough that Helen enjoyed a moment of relief. Maybe the woman didn't know what she wanted. Janet sighed into the mouthpiece or maybe she exhaled from smoking. "I want to get my daughter back, duh," she said.

Even though Cole was at school, Helen cupped her hand around the phone's mouthpiece so no one could hear her. She hissed, "You can't have her. She doesn't even know you."

Janet drew in a deep breath through her nostrils and choked. Through a cough, Janet said, "How the hell do you know?"

"She's ours now. I mean, she's mine now. You just leave her alone. Leave me alone." Helen put her finger over the receiver.

"So *you* have baby Kim?" was the last thing Helen heard before she slowly pushed the button down and ended the call.

Helen put down the receiver gently even though she was angry. Back when she lived in foster homes, Helen learned that when her rage met fear, she didn't get angry. Ever since Red and Vlad came home with Cole, she feared getting such a phone call.

She needed to get the full story out of Vladimir. Just like Janet called and took her by surprise, Helen needed to corner the slick talker.

His number was on the back of an envelope taped to the wall next to the phone. A list of numbers was compiled in all their handwritings; Red's scrawls were large and crude yet seemed overly formal, Helen printed in all capital letters and Cole had neatly printed in tiny letters, "Jenny-867-5309" with a happy face next to it.

Red wrote, "Vladimir, Father." There were many numbers for QE. As the factory closed section by section, Red wrote out "Quality Electric" every time after scratching out its previous obsolete number. The last QE number standing was the one Helen called repeatedly the night he died. There was the number for Cole's grade school, which Cole wrote in neat square printed capital letters and drew a roof over them. Helen called that number the day after Red died. Gwen's and the lawyer's numbers were the list's only post-Red additions. Helen considered rewriting the list, so she could put this one away with other things that reminded her of Red. But she wanted to call Vladimir straightaway. What if the woman who just called her called him and Helen lost her chance to catch him off guard?

Helen dialed, clenched her fist around the phone receiver and closed her eyes. When Vladimir answered, she tried to sound cheery, "Hi Vlad, it's Helen." She waited until the count of three for that to sink in, "How are you?"

"I'm waiting for my neighbor to bring me back some milk for my morning joe, so I'm not sure yet," Vlad answered.

These types of answers were how Vladimir communicated. When she was younger, she often asked herself why he wasn't capable of a simple, "Fine, Helen. How are you?" His father often annoyed Red but he always came up with a reason why they should just tolerate his demeanor. It annoyed Helen how men had to wear emotional armor to protect themselves from each other but it just clanked around like empty booze bottles on garbage day when they dealt with women.

Even though he hadn't asked, Helen continued, "Cole is fine. I really don't know how school goes for her until her report card."

"Well, she seems smart enough," Vlad said just before he whispered, "Shit." Helen heard something hard fall on the floor. She took the audible tour of Vlad's phone receiver as it was placed on the couch cushion and then dropped to the floor. "Hold on," Vlad called out from a distance. Helen heard shuffling and Vlad's voice coming in and out like a hard-to-get radio station, "Dropped…think…goddamned…case…damn you."

Winded, he got back on the phone and bellowed, "Hello? Who is this?"

Helen wanted to hang up but said something she had not prepared and had no idea where she came up with the idea, "Vlad, the school said something is wrong with Cole's birth certificate and I told them what you told me to tell them about the copy of it not being that great."

"Yeah, so?" Vlad said.

"Red never told me anything. But now I want to know more about what happened. Can you tell me?" Helen left the question open.

"I told him not to tell you. I hope you never got angry at him over that. Did you?" Vlad asked a question to a question.

"I don't know what to say. Can you tell me more?" she said.

"It was a long time ago," he stalled.

"Twelve years ago," she pushed.

"You got a baby girl. Just like he wanted. There was no other way to get her that easy," his voice sounded younger, and as if he were trying to sell Helen a stolen car.

"Yes, I thank you for that, Vlad," Helen heard an edge in her voice that she needed to smooth out fast. She softened the moment with a little laugh, "It's not like I'm the FBI. You can't just tell me what happened?"

"I knew somebody who knew about a girl in trouble," Vlad paused. Helen waited. "She was a nurse who knew the girl real good. Someone from the adoption place was heading there to pick up the baby. So, she just told me when the hell to go in. Easy as that."

"A nurse? Did Wilda have anything to do with this?" Helen asked.

"She knew what we did. But oh, no, she wouldn't help. She can be a son of a bitch about stuff like that. But that nurse was good friends with her though. Wilda was like a mother to her."

"Uh huh." Helen stalled to think of more questions. "Do you think I could ask this nurse some questions about Cole's mother?"

Vlad's explanations became shorter the truer they became. Vlad started to sound like a telegram. "No. You can't. Ginny died. Cancer. Left behind two grown kids. They went to live with Wilda."

Helen switched her focus and asked, "So, you and Red just went in took a baby? What adoption agency were you two supposed to be from?"

"I don't remember that," Vlad answered. "But you got to know, no one saw us but that girl. And believe me, this girl wasn't ready for a kid. You know, the kind that's always in trouble. She had problems. The baby was better off with you and Red," Vlad assured Helen. He added, "Honest." Helen thought Red must have learned how to say that word from Vladimir. They both used it the same way. "Honest" was their code word for, "Don't ask any more about this because 'honest' will be the last truthful word you'll hear from me."

"How did no one ever figure out there was a baby missing?" Helen asked.

"The woman from the adoption place just figured that the girl had handed off the baby to a friend to hide until she got out. It was her last week at that agency. She just didn't care," Vlad explained.

"How do you know that?" Helen asked.

"What do you mean? I'm telling you. Ginny told me."

The story made less sense to Helen the further he explained. "And why did the nurse do this for you?" Helen probed.

"She owed me a favor. A big one." Vlad filled the silence with a long, "Uh … " while he acted as though he couldn't remember the favor.

"Did you ever stop to think about how the girl might try to find her baby?" Helen asked.

"Naw. Not a way. There was no way in hell," Vlad said. "You're fine. Don't worry!"

Helen wanted to tell Vlad about the phone call but didn't want to make the situation worse by involving him. She smiled in order to sound convincingly compliant and said, "Alright. I won't worry then. Thank you, Vlad."

"Finally! I almost gave up on you!" he bellowed.

Helen was taken back by his enthusiasm. She said, "I hope that … "

Vlad interrupted, "She's here with my milk. I gotta go. Goodbye!"

Helen hung up the phone. She placed her forefinger at the top of the phone number list and whispered, "No," as she ran it over each name. When she got to the final one. She ran her fingertip over "Gwen" as if it were braille. Then she pushed her finger back up the list to the words, "Landlord/Jerry."

He agreed to forgive the unpaid rent as long as she moved out by the first of the next month.

She sat at the kitchen table and lit a cigarette. As she blew the smoke out of the window, she thought about Cole and how she didn't have her raincoat. That morning Helen noticed Cole's hair needed a trim but didn't think of the weather. Now it was pouring and the tiny spits that made it through the screen felt like the pins and needles she got after her arm had fallen asleep when she slept on the couch.

Helen was never the one to know the weather forecast. She hoped the school janitor made the kids ponchos out of garbage bags again because she didn't want to go out in the rain. As she lit another cigarette, she wondered if Cole's real mother had a raincoat and boots. Would she have put them on and trudged through the storm to give her baby Kim her raincoat? Would they have stopped at a diner on their way home to sip hot chocolates and eat English muffins dripping with butter and grape jelly, just the way Cole liked them?

Sometimes Helen felt like motherhood was simply a string of moments that proved to a woman whether or not she was really meant to have a child. She watched other mothers at the parent-teacher conference nights. They smiled to themselves as they flipped through the folders on their children's desks. Helen never felt like smiling at the graded papers and other things Cole had carefully placed there for her review. She felt as though she were a spy, seeing into Cole's life in ways she didn't want to understand. The teachers usually said something positive about Cole and that she was a very serious student. Helen didn't care either way. She never understood why some parents asked to take the folder home with them. She didn't want a souvenir from this foreign parental township.

Who would Cole be if someone paid more attention to her and treated her like she belonged to her? It made her heart thump like she was looking over the edge of a cliff, but Helen let herself consider a world where Cole could be Kim, and with her real mother. A cold guilt overcame her when she felt relieved by the thought. She rested her forehead in her palms. A wild strand of her hair singed at the tip of her cigarette, giving the air a tinge of that distinctive scent that always seemed like it was never going to dissipate but when it did, it was hard to remember it.

Chapter 11

Before seeing the dead man's picture in the newspaper Janet could never remember the faces of the men who took Baby Kimberly. Her parents begged her for information. "They don't tell you shit. You just sign the papers and these guys take your baby," she insisted. Her father blamed drugs for her lack of recollection but her memory was just fine. She knew that she did sign papers and two men did walk out of Bridgeport Hospital with her newborn.

Janet was determined to find her daughter. She wrote "Operation Kimberly" at the top of a pad of paper that had a cartoon of a water pipe around its edge with a drop of water coming out of a faucet. Written in the bulbous drip were the words "Got a leak? Call Deke!" In the middle of a blizzard Janet dropped off some weed for her boyfriend Tim to a plumbing truck in the Stop & Shop Supermarket parking lot. She asked the plumber to give her something, "Whatever you got. I fucking fishtailed it here the whole way, man. Give me like a pen, a key ring or something. You know. I love that kind of shit."

She filled the first few pages of Deke's pad with all the information she had. Just by dialing information she got the Sevic's phone number and she believed she also found Oleg's brother, a man named Vladimir. If anyone answered she was going to hang up, but no one did. If his wife answered, she planned to ask, "Did your husband ever tell you about how he picked up a baby for Catholic Charities twelve years ago? Where'd he bring her?"

She was going to need a lot of money to take back her baby girl. On the pad's second page she wrote "Coney Island, NY" with an arrow pointing down to "Animal."

Janet was up all night with Tim in his dark, musty apartment across the street from The Mart. Just that morning Janet shopped for supplies for the trip to Coney Island. The Mart was jam-packed with cheap food and clothing, sometimes even shelved together for maximum use of sales space. While she tried on a pair of pants that day, Janet noticed a security guy who sat in a room above the dressing rooms watching people while they tried on the $3.99 pants and one-dollar t-shirts. After changing in and out of a few shirts, she gave him the finger and yelled out, "You fuckin' perv!"

Just a week before at Caldor, Janet stole two pairs of jeans, sunglasses and some metal bangles—a plunder worth more than thirty dollars. Two old ladies talked about how stupid their manager was because he insisted they wear nametags. They went on about how most of the customers knew them by name anyway, and the ones who didn't know them were just there from the housing projects to steal anyway. As they chattered, they didn't notice Janet walk out with a full shopping bag that she had brought in with her, empty.

At The Mart, she filled the shopping basket with crackers, peanut butter, baked beans in tomato sauce, Little Debbie cakes, plastic forks, knives, spoons and enough cola to keep her going for days. After she paid $10.81 for the supplies, she pushed the cart out of the store and up the hill. She threw it all in the trunk of a tan Thunderbird. After she pushed the shopping basket onto the sidewalk, she tipped it over on its side, so it wouldn't roll down the hill. Tim used the Thunderbird only every couple of weeks to go see his mother in New Britain. When Janet went with him they slept in his mother's basement. His mother was remarried to the brother of the guy who played Willie the Whistler, a cut-rate Bozo the Clown on Boston television. There were photos of them with the clown brother all over the living room. Tim's mother liked to think they were famous, or that Charlie's brother was as well-known as Ronald McDonald.

His mother worked as a waitress at the Hayes Diner and her husband was a security guard at the VA hospital. He hated Tim. He fancied himself to be more of a cop than just a guard and always threatened Tim with exposing his drug dealing, telling Tim that he had connections with the Bridgeport PD. Tim knew he didn't and that his mother would always protect her only son.

Janet borrowed $200 from Tim a week before her planned exodus but that had to last her for at least a month. She saved almost another hundred from money they split from pawning some tools they stole from a New England Bell truck and from the money she made selling the acid that Tim thought he had lost.

That day, Janet went to the car and made sure there was enough of everything to start her off in Coney Island. She even splurged on a carton of cigarettes. She took a box of butterscotch Krimpets, a pack of cigarettes, a bottle of Jack Daniels and a six-pack of ginger ale up to his apartment and waited.

She didn't expect that he'd take this as a gesture of a "romantic evening," but he turned on the radio and sat close to her on the couch. In the past year, they had fucked a few times but usually so that Janet could just keep staying at his place. He never threatened to kick her out but she knew it was part of the deal. He danced on his way to piss and they made out on the couch but he was so stoned that he just ended up with his head on her tits.

Maybe it was because he was drinking beers instead of the Jack but he didn't pass out as usual. After he finished each bottle of beer, he smashed it against the wall over a five-gallon bucket. After they busted, he yelled, "Poontang." The ritual usually made Janet laugh the first few times but it grew tired. That night was no different. After the seventh bottle smashed, Janet went to the bathroom to check if she had everything. The money was in her pocket, the car keys taped to her calf. She knew he would flip out if he found out she had them. He was looking for them all week. She kept telling him, "They'll show up soon, baby. They are probably just under the couch or something," as she squeezed one of his ass cheeks. She thought of making copies of the keys but she didn't want to have him take the car before she left or find her stash in the trunk.

It was almost three in the morning when he came out from the bathroom with his jeans around his hips, zipper opened and his cock out.

"You know what, Jackoff Janet? You need to stop being such a tease and suck on this."

"I do, do I? I thought you were too drunk to fuck." She didn't think that he'd be awake this long.

"No, no. Look at him. He's alive!" he laughed. He started stroking himself as he walked up to the couch where she sat.

Normally, Janet would be drunk by now too, but she only drank ginger ale with some Jack and wasn't well-oiled enough to suck Tim off and not think about it. What was worse, he was awake enough to be horny but drunk enough to take a long time to come.

He straddled Janet's lap, facing her, and put her hand on his cock. She stroked him a few times and then took off her shirt.

"You got great tits, man," he started to move his hips.

Whenever they got it on, Tim talked to her as if they were just hanging out. One time, while coming, he said, "Janet, your pussy's tighter than a vice grip."

Her t-shirt trick worked. He got off her lap and stood in front of her. She took off her bra and took his cock between her breasts. She incrementally tried to get him to come without much work on her part. He told her to wet it down with her tongue, and then put him back in her tits. All she could smell was Patchouli and his old sweat. She never understood why guys think that putting some cologne on their nuts covered up their scent. It's not like it covered up anything, it just added another layer. Once he was in her mouth, he held her head and pushed her on him. Janet thought about other things, like the tape on her leg and how it pulled on her leg hair. She thought about the baby she heard crying in the apartment next door, she thought about Madonna as she heard *Lucky Star* drift up from a car in front of the building.

Ready to come, Tim grabbed his balls and told her to, "Suck me dry." Janet just kept the same rhythm and wished he would come already. She looked up and saw him in a state of bliss. His wince stretched from his eyes to the rest of his face and his entire body was taut. She wondered if she could just tell him her plans. While he was vulnerable like this, it was easy to believe that he would tell her to go ahead and take the car and maybe even give her some more cash. Since he hadn't taken off his jeans, he backed up and tucked himself into them and zipped up. He flopped down on the couch, draped his arm around her and asked, "Now, what can I do for you?"

"Nothing. It's a freebie."

"Cummon. I could have a boxed lunch at the Y," he half-heartedly pulled at her belt.

"Really, Tim. I'm tired." To reassure him, she pulled his face into her chest.

He stayed with his head there for a few minutes and then got up, "Man can't live by pussy alone. You wanna beer?" He held two bottles in the air.

Janet said, "Nah," as she yawned. He put her beer on the counter. When he came back, he twisted off his bottle cap and toasted with the bottle mouth onto one of Janet's nipples, "Here's to those hot titties."

It was three thirty in the morning by the time he fell asleep. Luckily, he was on the couch. She waited a while in the kitchen, standing in the middle of pizza boxes, wrappers, and bits of broken bottles. Would she miss Tim? There was something charming about his two chipped front teeth that marred his otherwise good looks, his easy laugh and how he talked bullshit all the time. At some point he seemed to be fated to make some girl a great husband, but that possibility waned as each year passed.

Janet thought about leaving a note. If she didn't, he might not notice the car had been gone for a while. She guessed that he wouldn't report it missing since he stole it from a chaotic druggie commune out in the woods of East Lyme. She tucked the beer bottle Tim left on the counter into her hammocky leather pocketbook.

Janet shut the door quietly behind her and tiptoed down the wooden stairs. The streets were empty, except for two cop cars in The Mart's parking lot, facing opposite directions, with their driver's doors kissing, so the cops could talk from the comfort of their driver's seats.

For her new audience, she acted scared and clasped her bag closer to her. She wanted the cops to think she was just as leery of the area as the cops. In the stairwell on the way out, she peeled the keys off her calf so out at the car, she unlocked it and slipped into the driver's seat as if it was hers to get into.

The clock on the dash read quarter past five. She expected to have left by two or three in the morning. She pulled out, swerved around the shopping cart someone had dragged into the street and headed up over the hill to avoid driving past the cops.

She'd taken the first leg of the trip many times, so she didn't yet need a map. Her eyes jumped more to the rear-view mirror and the side mirrors than out the windshield. She remembered when her mother would tell her father not to look at the mirrors, nagging that it made her nervous. Her mother, a conservative Southern lady who married an upper middle-class Yankee, never understood why her husband put on his high beams either, saying, "If you can't see, you should simply slow down. I swear."

The hills and trees on Merritt Parkway brought back memories of when she took that route from New Haven with her father. He was born and raised on City Island, so they visited there for a week every summer until she was a teenager. It was a long ride but her father would always let her choose what to listen to on the AM radio.

On every trip, Janet's father repeated the histories of the Wilbur Cross and Merritt Parkways. "When I was a boy, people still had picnics on the sides of the Merritt," he'd reminisce, "but my father, your Grampy, said the men making Wilbur Cross were far less inspired by the time they got to that project." He once ventured to the New Haven Public Library to find out the weight of the stones used to build the West Rock Tunnel. He read that it cost almost three million dollars just for the tunnel, so Janet's father wanted to know how much it cost per pound. A man of numbers, he once figured that his $1,500 car cost less than 53 cents per pound. Janet's mother half joked to Janet, "Don't worry, he's keeping track of how much he spends on you and will calculate exactly how much you're worth per pound by the time you get married." Janet never minded his calculations. He sat at the kitchen table every morning with a pencil and pad, and the *New Haven Register*. When the newspaper reported how much pipe the city used per mile for a drainage project, Walter scribbled out how many millions of feet that would be.

That's all she could manage to do to keep from freaking out on this trip. Take herself far away from the stolen car and this desperate trip to the memories that hummed into her mind like radio waves. She didn't know if somehow cops could be looking for her, so she plotted her first stop in New Rochelle. She would stop there, get some food from the trunk and use the bathroom.

She gripped the steering wheel hard, pushed her shoulders into the seat and with a twist of her neck, a loud crunch filled her head. Reaching into her pocketbook for a cigarette, she said, "Hell yeah," as she pulled out the forgotten sweaty beer bottle.

Chapter 12

Cole walked downtown to take the bus to their soon-to-be new apartment. Helen told Cole to bring a can of ginger ale and some peanut butter crackers. There were other ways to get there, but Cole liked walking downtown, cutting through the arcade and spitting into the Pequonnock River near the railroad tracks.

As the buses stopped under the transit building's awnings, Cole thought about third grade, when her class learned square dancing. The girls lined up opposite the boys to create a tunnel of arms for people to pass through. When the person emerged and then became part of the tunnel it moved the group that much closer to the end of the room. Somehow, no matter how much she maneuvered in the line, Cole never walked through the canopy before they reached the wall. She had longed to look up and see what it was like to shuffle through the smiling faces and feel the group jostle her from all sides.

Fewer buses ran Saturdays and Cole had just missed one. She had to pee but didn't want to go inside. From where she stood outside, she watched the waiting room through the glass door. Every time the door swung open she heard chaotic snippets: the squealing children spitting water at each other while running to and from the bubbler. The old white man wearing three coats and two baseball caps, yelled, "I told her the tuna was bad, it stunk like cat food," as he checked the coin return slots on the pay phones and vending machines. Someone had burned the acrylic sheet that covered the bus schedule attached to the wall outside. Cole ran her fingers over the melted brown plastic bubbles that covered the section she needed. Her bus finally pulled up, letting out a whipping noise, making her wonder if they purposely planned for the buses to make this sound. Her grandfather said that he often missed the days when people got around by horse. He loved the sounds, he told her, but not the smells. She would have to ask him if buses made that sound to mimic horsewhips.

One of only a few people on the bus, she sat in one of the front seats reserved for old people. As the bus pulled away, she saw the payphone man throw something at one of the children. Wires splayed out from where he had just detached the payphone's mouthpiece. Coming from the back of the bus, Cole heard music she mostly heard when she took the bus, or during the summer months.

A chubby twenty-something black man sat in the back. Wearing sunglasses and a baggy yellow t-shirt, he clicked buttons on a small boom box, searching for a song on his cassette tape. Cole looked out the window. She hoped this bus driver didn't make the rider shut it off. During one of her last rides the driver yelled, "Turn that down. You ain't sharin', you blarin'." Cole put the guys blasting their music in two categories. There was the guy who had fun, smiling, saying hello to people, a mayor of the beats. His raps were usually fun. Sometimes he would even play Michael Jackson and sing along. The others were usually younger, and Cole felt like she shouldn't look at them and smile like she did with the music ambassadors. These serious guys usually turned up the volume just in time for the swears, much like when she took *Are You There God? It's Me Margaret* out at the library, returning it within two hours after skimming it for "breast" and "period."

The next song the man played was sad. He appeared to be looking out the window but Cole saw behind his sunglasses that his eyes were closed. The singing of "It's a shame," seemed familiar to Cole, but the rest was different. "Hey, preacher! What? Talk to me! About what? Hope! There is no hope!" His music was just loud enough for her to hear. He was different from the other men and so was his music. At the song's end, he said, "Uh huh. That's right," into the face of the boom box, as though he wanted only the speakers to hear him, and let them know that their music reached him.

To stop staring at him, Cole looked out the window again just as the bus was passing Lakeview Cemetery. She locked her eyes on the entrance. It was not visible from the street but she knew her father's grave was still without a headstone.

Cole snooped through her mother's mail and read the letter from QE. They promised to pay for his coffin, funeral and burial, adding, "…this contribution towards said expenses shall not create a precedent and/or admit responsibility."

Helen and Cole had sat across from Karl, the funeral director, as he made a phone call to Mr. Ken Price. This was the letter writer and general counsel for QE who had instructed that he be contacted for details. Karl focused his eyes on the point of his pencil pressing into the blank note pad, poised to write down the amounts or terms Mr. Price was about to offer. The pencil waited. Helen placed a cough drop in her mouth and handed the wrapper to Cole, who liked to smooth them out on her knee and then fold them into tiny triangles. She kept a handful of them in her pocket to flick when she was bored.

Mr. Price's gruff burbles spilling from the receiver were answered by Karl's calm, "I sees," "Uh huhs" and "Is that rights?" Karl rested the pencil on top of the still empty pad, putting a palm across his forehead. Cole thought this made him look like he was in a Tylenol commercial. Mr. Price had told Karl that they had to do everything very cheaply and that QE would not pay for the headstone because that was not necessary to the burial of the deceased.

Helen didn't cry until Karl said, "He said some big wig at QE argued with him over the funeral and he got *that* paid for you. So, he's kind of stuck in the middle here." Karl didn't tell Helen and Cole that Mr. Ken Price had in fact said, "I know you hear this shit all the time, so I'm going to level with you. No headstone. We are not doing all of it. If we do, they want more. They see this as a gravy train. I mean, this place is closed, and between you and me, this guy wasn't even on the clock, so you know what that means, don't you? We don't have to do shit. They're lucky we're giving him a box and a hole. Just keep our part under two grand." When Karl offered to check with the cemetery if they would put her on a payment plan for the headstone, Helen said she wanted to wait for insurance money or some sort of settlement from QE to get Red one of the fancier ones.

Now, the bus waited at the stoplight to turn onto Bond Street and Cole pulled the cord for her stop. She got off the bus through the front door as the music man used the rear door. As he walked away, his music faded into the Boston Avenue traffic. As the bus pulled away, the building where Red died appeared behind it. All at once, Cole wanted to look at the fateful roof and pretend she wasn't there at all or that the building wasn't there, or hadn't ever been there. At first, she compromised by looking at the QE logo that matched the ones on the many letters her mother had received and the ones on her father's jacket and shirts. It looked like a compass with an arrow on the top of a circle. And the letters Q and E. The E was indented and curved in on the left side, making it look like the Q had eaten too much and pushed into the E.

Each of the interconnected thirteen buildings looked the same and was capped with the QE logo. Cole's disquieted hands wrung the top of her paper lunch bag. The windows were all closed, but even if one were open, who would be there to close it? Would they remember Red every time they closed one of the QE windows?

She had snooped in the pile of mail in her mother's bedroom to read the QE letters. One told Helen that Red had punched out on QE's time clock before he re-entered the building, so they had no liability. Cole wondered if someday she would find a letter from Mr. Price that said her father fell from a part of the building that didn't have a QE logo on it, so they wouldn't pay for the coffin or anything at all. With the lack of shade or a cool breeze, Cole's racing thoughts and the muggy air insisted she get on her way.

Just across Boston Avenue, at the apartment on Sheridan Street, Gwen checked her watch every few minutes. Bertha had handed over her keys to Gwen so that she could finish clearing it out with Cole. Cole was due to arrive sometime after eleven but it was going on two o'clock. She didn't want to call Helen. What if the girl didn't want to help?

WEBE 107.9 was giving away tickets for Stevie Wonder's Madison Square Garden show. There were going to be twenty lucky winners over the weekend and Gwen thought that they already had given away almost half of them. That morning, she got through three times, "Sixty-four," "Ninety-three" and the closest call, "One-hundred and one." She wondered what she would say if she won. She thought about how most lucky callers asked, "Did I really win?" Her favorite was a shocked man who said, "You gotta be shittin' me! Hey, honey, I won!"

When Cole showed up, she wiped her sneakers as if there were a doormat there and then stood at the door until Gwen told her to come in. Gwen didn't realize the girl lingered in the doorway until she turned around to hand her a box and she wasn't there.

Gwen called out, "Please, come in," and Cole walked quickly through the kitchen to the bedroom. "You can relax," she said. "Put your things on the counter out there," pointing back to the kitchen. She rolled her eyes when Cole rushed to do what she said. She turned the volume up on the radio to let Cole know that this was going to be more fun than work. "You like music?" she shouted to Cole, now standing in the middle of what was soon to be her bedroom.

"I like *this* kind of music," Cole said, pointing at the radio.

"I do too," Gwen said as she stepped closer to Cole. "That's why your big job today is to listen for the music of Stevie Wonder," she pointed at Cole. "When you hear Stevie Wonder, you call the radio station over and over until they announce who wins, okay?" When Cole laughed a little nervously, Gwen said, "I am *very* serious about this. I want to win these tickets for Kevin and me."

Kevin? Did Gwen mean her godfather Kevin? Helen told Cole to be nice to Gwen and do whatever she asked. "She used to work with Dad," Helen often explained things to Cole like she was still in elementary school.

Only one of the bedrooms had a radiator. The room with no heat seemed cool and dark, and was completely empty. That's the one Helen said she would take. Cole couldn't imagine how her mother and she would inhabit this half-space. The kitchen seemed normal, but the pantry was empty of food and looked as though it always had been. The only things left were a wall-mounted telephone, a small stack of newspaper clippings and a few photographs on the counter next to WEBE's number. In one of the photos was an older woman wearing glasses holding a birthday cake covered in dark pink frosting. Her pupils were red like someone possessed. Cole wondered if the frosting had actually been white, but turned reddish like her eyes.

Cole didn't know what to say. She didn't want to ask about Gwen's family. In the past few months since Red's accident, she dreaded people asking her those kinds of questions. She decided she would never again ask people about their mothers and father because they might be dead or just hard to put into words, like her mother.

Gwen said, "I'm like you," Cole tensed thinking she was going to talk about a dead father anyway, but she went on, "I grew up here in Bridgeport."

"*Like A Virgin*," caught Cole's attention. She hadn't been listening for Stevie Wonder, but was somewhat sure that he hadn't played.

"You stay near the phone and put those things in with these," Gwen pointed at the clippings and photo, and handed her a box half-filled with pens, pencils and rubber bands.

Cole put the photograph in upside down. The newspaper clippings all took the shapes of their stories. Some were just words on a long thin strip, others were wide and folded around their captioned photographs. They were all about the same thing: an earthquake, or a terremoto, depending on the news source. A *Time* magazine cover called it, "Mexico's Killer Quake." Cole wondered if that's why the lady Bertha moved out. Maybe she needed to go back to Mexico to help someone put a house back together. The pictures mesmerized Cole. On all the clippings in Spanish, someone had printed "BERTHA" in all capital letters at the top with a blue pen. The newspaper photos were in black and white, accentuating gaps in the rubble of crumbled buildings.

"Oh, yes. That's all the stuff she left behind," Gwen said when she saw Cole going through the stack. "That's where she's from."

Worried that Gwen thought she was nosy, Cole put down the clippings fast, "Sorry."

"No. It's okay," she said, patting Cole's back. "Her mother lived through it and still has her home. But lots of people died. One of her best friends from school was found two months after, crushed in between two walls," Gwen crossed herself. Cole didn't know if she should make the motions too. It happened so fast, she just tapped her heart once and let her arm drop. "She said that they still find people who were trapped when the buildings came down." Some pictures made Cole imagine that a giant spatula slid under all of those buildings and flipped them like pancakes.

"You can keep those if you want," she offered.

"No, I can't," Cole shook her head and quickly placed some more into the box.

"No, no. Just put the ones you want in that drawer and then when you move in, you can look at them."

Cole met Gwen's morbid suggestion with an earnest, "Thanks!"

"Maybe you can write her a letter after you move in. I think she'd like to know how you like it here," Gwen said.

"Yeah, that would be good," but Cole worried if she would have to write it in Spanish. She always wanted to learn to speak Russian but wondered if she would be able to do it. It seemed like it would be very hard.

Cole heard the first few tinny drum machine beats from "I Just Called to Say I Love You," waved her arms and then picked up the phone. It was slow to give a dial tone and then she had to be careful to let the rotary dial spin all the way back before twirling it for the next number. Every time she hung up, she reported to Gwen, "It's busy." Someone answered and said, "Eighty-nine!" and hung up. Cole shouted out, "Eighty-nine." Another busy signal, and another. Then it rang, "It's ringing," she yelled out. Gwen heard the song's end with the three beats, cha cha cha. She listened.

"You're the hundred and seventh caller. What's your name?" She heard Cole say, "Cole." Gwen screamed, "We won!" and heard herself with a slight delay on the radio. "Sounds like you got someone excited over there. Where are you calling from Cole?"

Cole said, "A lady named Bertha's house. But we're moving in soon."

Cole heard Gwen's voice, "Give *me* the phone now," close up and from the radio speaker about fifteen feet away.

"Hello! I am Gwen! Did we win?" She knew they had won, but she didn't know what else to say.

"You sure did. You are going to see Stevie Wonder at Madison Square Garden September twenty-seventh. Now, stay on the line. Next, here's some Prince," the deejay put on "Raspberry Beret."

Cole's heart raced as Gwen gave her information to the radio station, so that she could pick up the tickets. After she hung up the phone, Gwen hugged Cole and laughed, "You are good luck, kiddo."

Cole started to cry and didn't know what to say when Gwen asked, "Aw! What's wrong?" She hugged Cole, and then sat her down on a short stool. In the kitchen she soaked a clean dishcloth with cold water. Handing it to Cole, she said, "Here. Put this on your forehead and sit here and relax." She closed the pantry door and turned up the radio. Gwen remembered the first time she, too, had fun and had forgotten her father died.

Chapter 13

A few feet from Vladimir's living room window the sloppy security guard, with his shirttails out, lit a cigarette. Vladimir stopped moving his eyes and little by little lowered the paper cup into his lap. An illusionist once told him that most tricks rely on what humans are wired to notice. In some situations the slightest flick of a man's eyeball can have the same effect as his arms waving. There was a time when Vladimir would have tried to get the young Italian guy's attention to say hello but he simply didn't want to bother with anyone anymore. He had napped in and out of consciousness all day. An interaction would ruffle this lull.

When Tony turned to stamp out his cigarette he startled a little at the sight of the old man in his rocking chair. Vladimir closed his eyes and pretended to have fallen asleep. A loud knocking rattled the thin pane, accompanied by Tony's voice, "Are you alright? Vlad?" Tony repeated the phrase until Vladimir lifted his hand and gave a thumbs-up while keeping his eyes closed. "Oh good! Thank God! Good!" Then silence. Vladimir raised his head just enough so that peeping through one eye would let him know if Tony was really gone. He was.

Having relocated to the couch, Vladimir dozed off just in time to be awakened by a knock on the door. "Fuck off," he thought. More knocking. "Fuck off!" he yelled.

"Hello? Hey, Vlad. I'm checking in on ya," Tony shouted.

"Okay. Hold your horses," Vladimir sat up, used his cane to stand up and hobbled over to the door.

"I'm sorry about before. I didn't know you were there. They told me people complain about the smoke. I was sneaking a ciggie and you scared the hell out of me," Tony laughed.

"I figured," Vladimir said. He was relieved that Tony didn't go on about how he thought Vlad had died in his chair. This spared them both. "So, you've checked on me. Not dead yet!" Vladimir looked down so he could more easily close the door in Tony's face.

Tony quickly spat out, "Wait, wait, wait, wait," using his palm to keep the door open.

"What is it?" The visit and his paining knees annoyed Vladimir equally.

"Over the weekend. We got some calls about you. They say in the middle of the night you were shouting," Tony shrugged and shook his head as if he thought the complaints were ridiculous.

Vladimir didn't know what to say. He retorted, "Yeah, so what?"

"I'm supposed to make sure you're okay. You know how Anderson's douchebag son comes down and hits him up for money all the time." Tony punched his fist into his cupped hand, "I got to make sure no one's making trouble for ya. You'd tell me, right?"

Tony's added gesture of protectiveness softened Vladimir to a smirk. "I think I'll be fine." Vladimir thought he'd just be honest, "Just old and confused."

"I hear ya, Vlad. We'll all be like that someday. That's what I say to my girlfriend …." Vladimir gave in and opened the door and motioned for Tony to sit down while he hobbled to the kitchen. Once in the apartment, the tall, ruddy-faced thirty-something in his dark blue polyester uniform stood out like a shiny football trophy on a dusty shelf.

None of the things Vladimir accumulated over the years retained their original luster. Most of his furniture was from the giant green dumpster next to his building. The chairs and tables were his profit from previous owners heading to the graveyard. The stuff's dullness matched Vladimir in body and spirit.

Tony talked about getting old and how people have to really love each other to get married because it's for life and then he said something about changing diapers. "I see," Vladimir called from the kitchen as he poured a can of orange soda evenly into two paper cups. He remembered that Cole had pointed out the yellow urine stains on his white tube socks. Dipping a forefinger into the soda, he flicked a few orange drops at his socks for a camouflage effect. He gave the toaster threatening looks. No one had been in his apartment since Barnum's ghost had started his shenanigans.

"Thanks, Vlad," Tony drank the soda in four gulps and slammed the cup on the coffee table as if it were a shot of whiskey. Vladimir furrowed his brow when he thought that Tony may have drank fast in order to leave. Now that Tony cut through the old man's fog, he wanted him to stay.

Tony screwed up his face pointing at a jar of twigs and leaves on a shelf near the wall phone, "You smoke marijuana, old Vlad?"

"That's not what you think it is." Vladimir squinted at Tony, "But I've smoked my share of things. What about you?"

"Off the record?" Tony stalled.

"Your boss is my boss," Vladimir sipped his soda and pointed to heaven.

"I smoke. My little brother deals," Tony added, "but just weed." Vladimir appreciated that Tony wanted to protect his brother's reputation. Tony leaned forward and conspiratorially asked, "You interested in some of the ganja?"

"Do you have to ask?" Vladimir laughed.

"Old Vlad! You're a mad man!" Tony pulled a joint out of his sock, smoothed it out and tightened its ends. Tony sighed, "It's the end of my shift anyhow."

After shuffling to the kitchen and back to the living room Vladimir slid an olive-green glass ashtray onto the coffee table next to Tony's empty cup. Dust floated off the window blinds as Vladimir pulled the cord to lower them. He blew out, coughed and ran his hand over his face.

Hearing Tony's voice in his apartment made Vladimir remember the first evening the two had spent together. A few years prior, Tony had cried on that very couch on his fifth day of working security for the Housing Authority. The shaken rookie had just spent over an hour trying to resuscitate Evelyn Joseph on her bathroom floor. Death always made Vladimir hungry so he fixed them peanut butter and jelly sandwiches and filled two juice glasses with Wild Turkey. They never talked about that again but ever since that night Tony often checked on Vladimir.

As he made his way back to the couch, Vlad winced as he imagined Tony finding his lifeless body on the floor someday.

"What you thinking?" Tony asked as he lit the joint.

"What I'm always thinking about, life and death," Vladimir

said. He looked down at his yellow and orange-dotted socks but couldn't see well enough to know if his soda-sprinkle-camouflage trick had worked.

"Deep. You're deep, aren't ya Vlad?" Tony sucked and held. Vladimir took the joint as Tony looked at him with eyes that asked him to take it easy.

"I can handle it," Vladimir was relieved it stayed lit, took a drag. He clicked the back of his throat to keep from coughing.

Time and stress unfurled into the smoke. Silence settled. The refrigerator cycled loudly and Vladimir hoped Barnum's voice wouldn't emerge from its hum again.

"You know, life and death are a lot easier to deal with than we think," Tony's tone seemed different than before. Vladimir wondered if the difference was real or if smoking had changed his ears. "I think we are here, just here and now. And then we're gone."

"That sounds pretty simple," Vladimir said. "I'm sorry, but that doesn't make it any less terrifying. To die, I mean."

"Why do you have to think about it? It's going to happen anyway," Tony talked to Vladimir like he was explaining how to register a car or get out of a traffic ticket.

Vladimir's thoughts floated, "But what if you don't know how to die?"

Tony chuckled, "You are now officially high, Vlad."

Vladimir felt panicky but it was on a delay and hadn't reached him fully. "I really am scared to die. I don't know if that's true but it's what I can say."

"You know what? Why don't you have an accent? I just maybe heard a little bit of one, but you got that crazy Russian name. Where the hell are you from?" Tony looked at Vladimir as if for the first time.

"I was born here, but my grandfather was from Russia. When I'm drunk, or, I suppose, high, it comes out," Vladimir was a little surprised at how easily he answered. He usually skirted personal questions.

Tony closed his eyes and kept talking, "Maybe you got to do everything you want to do before you die, you know. In order to not be afraid. Maybe you got to finish something? See somebody. Somewhere you got to go?"

From the kitchen, Barnum's voice called out, "Coney Island."
"You hear that?" Vlad asked.
"You're getting paranoid already?" Tony joked.
"Coney Island. He said, 'Coney Island,'" Vlad said as he pointed to the kitchen.
"Feeling real good, aren't you?" Tony teased.
"Maybe that's where I'm going," Vlad muttered.
"Coney Island," Tony said it as if it were a sexy ex-lover. "I haven't been there since … fuck," he stopped to inhale again.

Vladimir bit on the knuckle of his middle finger. Hurting it somehow relieved the joint's arthritic tension. He also used this method to stay awake when Cole stayed past when he would normally take a nap. But at this moment he gnawed on his knuckle because Barnum was back, and talking. He was probably using the refrigerator. It was the only kitchen thing Vladimir couldn't leave unplugged. He thought about what it would take to do without it.

"You got someone out there? Yeah! That's right. You used to live there, right? There's a ton of Russians out that way," Tony filled in where Vladimir left space. Other people often talked to Vladimir about Brighton Beach as if it were his second home, or that he must have relatives there. Vladimir had never lived there, but he had helped his ex-wife Wilda buy a house there.

Vladimir hadn't been to Coney Island since his grandfather took him during the summers. Deda had pointed out to his grandson where there used to be a farm before it got so built up. He also showed young Vlad where he and P.T. Barnum had visited Charles Feltman at his restaurant. The three sat at a corner table where they were served as much lobster and oysters as they could eat. Deda said that almost immediately, Barnum was struck with a bout of gout and walked with a cane for days after.

Vladimir missed his grandfather even though he had been gone for more than seventy years. If it had not been for him, Vladimir might have lived without ever knowing how deeply the love of a friendship could embed in one's soul. His grandfather talked about Barnum as if he were a beloved brother.

He wondered if maybe he should talk about his grandfather with Tony so maybe Barnum would listen and stop talking. "You know, my Grampa knew the guy who invented the hot dog out there," Vladimir told Tony, "a funny Kraut named Charles."

"What? The hot dog! That's something you never even think about being invented. Like what the hell was going on before there was a hot dog?" Tony stopped. Sat up straight and looked at Vladimir. "You're pulling my leg!"

"Nope. Go look it up for yourself. No one was putting a sausage in a bun like that and then this Kraut knew that people didn't like spitting out all the gristle that used to get caught in your teeth. Back then, people put whatever shit in sausages that they could get away with. Real garbage." Vladimir made a face, remembering his grandfather talking about the bits of rancid meat and cartilage that they used as filler with good meat.

"Jesus. Nothing like a Nathan's, huh? Aw, what I wouldn't do for a Nathan's right now," Tony looked at his watch.

"You know, you're not going to believe this, but that Nathan used to work for Charles. That's how Nathan got the idea. He made his own stand and sold them for half, five cents." Vladimir had read this in Nathan Handwerker's obituary. "Yup. He died about ten years ago. They said the heart attack was caused by eating so many damn hot dogs."

"Let's go to Coney Island," the voice called again to Vladimir from the kitchen.

Tony got up to stretch back his arms. "I gotta use the can." Through the door Vladimir heard a strong steady stream, something he hadn't experienced in quite a while.

Tony came back out into the living room zipping up his pants and his shirt was still untucked. "Okay, my friend. We are going to Coney Island. It looks like you got to go remember the old times. You know, like before there were hot dogs. You are as old as dirt, man."

"You want a peanut butter and jelly sandwich before you go?" Vladimir immediately regretted offering the sandwich that might remind him of Evelyn Joseph. But Tony didn't seem at all phased.

"No thanks. You got my gut set on a hot dog now. I'm going to The Greeks for a chili dog," Tony said patting his belly, "then home. We got way stoned, Vlad."

"We did. We did. Thanks for the trip, as they say. It's bedtime," Vladimir said as he walked him to the door. Tony shook Vlad's hand and awkwardly hunched over him for a hug. Tony's heavy hand slapped his back then gave a comforting rub on his bony shoulder.

Waving at Tony as he walked into the light of the parking lot Vladimir smiled at the idea of Tony going to Tomlinson's on the way home. It was the type of bachelor food that he missed after he married.

Tony shouted, "Don't forget! Coney Island," pointing at Vladimir as he turned the corner.

In bed, Vladimir's stoned thoughts flowed to Bridgeport's Seaside Park of the 1930s. He was single then, spending Sundays at the park to take a stroll with one of Tomlinson's hot dogs. It was just a tiny stand out there. He sat next to Barnum's statue and imagined his great-grandfather taking in the Long Island Sound. Sometimes, when not many people were around, Vladimir climbed up to sit in Barnum's larger-than-life lap. He talked to his silent great-grandfather about what was happening in Bridgeport politics. Vladimir told him about Jasper McLevy and how Barnum would have likely endorsed him for mayor. The despair of the times and the hope that McLevy symbolized made Vladimir wonder if his great-grandfather could have run for president if he had lived in in a different time. Maybe the skeletons in Barnum's closet wouldn't matter as much in the 1930s as they would have in the 1800s. People seemed to long for a strong leader with business expertise to get the country back on its feet. Looking up at the statue Vlad tried to imagine the charisma that mesmerized his mother and many other people. Her face always glowed when she told Vlad stories about Barnum.

He wrapped his arms around himself and pushed his head deeper into his pillow. Something was shifting. Vladimir hadn't longed to be held by his mother since he was a boy. Maybe Barnum speaking to him through the kitchen appliances had brought it on. It was as if his mother should be there but wasn't. Falling asleep, he heard her say something but maybe it was Barnum again or maybe just a jilted memory. Vladimir hoped he would die in his sleep, warm and stoned.

Chapter 14

Helen sent Cole to clean the apartment with Gwen so that she could make more phone calls about Red's case. The last time Helen made calls about the case, Cole sat on her bed and listened to everything. When Helen told her to go into the living room to watch television, she cranked the volume so loudly that Helen gave up making calls. It wasn't until Red was gone that Helen realized that there was only ever the three of them or the two of them, Cole and Red. There was never a Helen and Cole. And there was only a Helen and Red when she worked hard to believe that she could have a person and in turn, be that someone's person. Cole and Helen's hours and days without Red were like the pages of a book stripped of its glue, strings and cover. They sat static together, dreading a wind or anything else that could disrupt the illusion of affinity.

Alone and finally motivated to go through the mail, Helen checked for new QE letters before calling her newest lawyer, Gary Sargent. A Fingerhut catalog was folded over an envelope with the Hallmark imprint, addressed to Cole with no return address. She thought it could be a lost sympathy card from someone at Cole's school. Helen opened the envelope and barely looked at the card's front that had three cartoon rabbits holding hands under the words "Some bunny misses you!" A tattered clipping of Red's obituary fell to the floor as Helen read, "Dear Baby Girl, I think that this newspaper article was about your father, Oleg Sevic? If it is about him I send my thoughts to you. And, if it is about him then there is something I have to tell you. It's kind of scary. You are not this man's daughter, but you are my dear darling girl. Your father came and got you from the hospital where I had you and he took you away before I knew what I was doing because I was so young." Helen started to cry as she slumped down onto the kitchen floor, her back against the refrigerator. She turned the card over for the rest, "I wanted to call you 'Kimberly.' Maybe I still can call you that when I come to get you someday. I am getting together some parts of my life that would make it work for you to be with me again. I am your mother and I should be able to take care of you finally. You are not a mystery to me anymore. I think after the summer I might be able to have you live wherever I end up." Helen turned the card sideways, "I am running out of room to write here. I didn't want to call you or come get you because I can't do that yet. I am not ready. I love you. Until we meet again, Your Real Mother xo"

Helen cried as she inspected every inch of the card and envelope. After putting the card back in the envelope, she used packing tape to seal where she had opened it. She placed it back in the middle of the Fingerhut catalog and then put the catalog on the bottom of the mail stacked on her bedroom dresser.

After digging a pack of Trues from her purse she smoked out the kitchen window while she racked her memory about anything Red told her about the teenager who gave birth to Cole. She fought the urge to call Vladimir. She took comfort in the fact that the woman didn't seem equipped to do anything. Yet.

Back when Red and Vlad first brought baby Cole home, Helen wondered about where her mother might be and whether maybe neither that woman nor herself were fit to be mothers. Being Cole's parent seemed more like being a copilot than being her mother. The shared burden was always very much in the present. If she were Cole's parent at the teacher's conference, at the library downtown or at the doctor's office, everyone knew that right in that moment she was Cole's adult. Motherhood is to be a mundane deity. It means so much more, and less, than being a parent. Sometimes Helen wished people knew that her body did not birth Cole. Maybe they would expect less from her, grade her mothering skills on a curve.

Sometimes Helen wished Red would walk in the door and do what he always did, take care of every little detail of their lives as she stood by watching like a child at the carnival's cotton candy stand. But unlike a kid, she was aware of the worker's sticky pink arm and that someone else had to pay. But Red was gone. And the one paying for Helen's despondency was Cole.

The corners of her mouth turned down as she smashed her cigarette's tip into a cramped pond of other butts and ashes. Helen's connection with Cole transcended beyond Red for the first time. She shook her head side to side as she accepted that neither of them had at least one decent mother among the few they were dealt.

Chapter 15

Navigating through Westchester, Janet was confident of her landmarks until signs appeared for towns she didn't recognize. She started to take all exits ending with the word *south*. As the uppers wore off, she popped another, and another, so that the *Manhattan* sign beckoned her as if they were kindred restless spirits, rather than a warning that she was off course.

While the city's pulsing lights nudged her out of her daze, Janet flicked down the electric lock switch. The clunks of all four doors securing themselves comforted her. She did it again. At a stoplight two men rushed toward the car. Honking the horn, she screamed, "Get the fuck out of here!" as they squeegeed the windshield. She pushed down the turn signal thinking it was the wipers. The men looked like brothers. Janet tried to figure out which flag was tied around the taller one's neck. The star on the flag hanging over his shoulders made it look as though he wore a miniature superhero cape. Janet said, "Puerto Rico!" when she recalled the pattern from the Puerto Rican parade that she had happened upon during one of Tim's Hartford drug pick-ups last year from a big Russian-looking guy named Butchy.

The shorter windshield cleaner couldn't hear her, but he grinned, yelling, "Calm down, lady. We ain't hurting nothing!" She flicked a few things around the car looking for change but the honking chorus behind her insisted she hit the gas pedal. "Whoa, whoa, whoa!" The taller man hollered as he stepped back so that Janet wouldn't run over his foot.

The city's pulse and her high were nearly a perfect match, but Janet had to wind down a little. At a Times Square gas station, she stopped the car in front of a tire air pump machine and turned off the ignition. She sighed and closed her eyes, but then panicked that she was still driving. Her eyes flashed wide open as she and grabbed the wheel. She pulled herself out of the car and reached under her seat to grab the Mountain Dew that had knocked against the seat frame throughout the morning's journey. Gulping the very soda that helped frazzle her nerves, she washed down a pill from the "downer" pocket of her handbag.

Back in the driver's seat with the door open, she thought about making a stop in nearby Newark, New Jersey to visit her grandmother. Although she had never driven there herself, her father brought her to visit his mother several times.

Ribbon candy and jellybeans. That's what Nana fed Janet when she was a girl sitting on the couch to watch television while the adults caught up. Her father explained why Janet's mother couldn't make it, usually lies. Even though no one ever said that Janet's mother was a depressive who never left the house, Nana always sent Janet off with, "You send my love to your poor mother. When she hugged Janet goodbye, she whispered, "I pray for her." Her Nana wasn't the only person who let Janet know her mother wasn't quite right in the head. Teachers, her pediatrician, friends, relatives … they all took pity on the little girl with the crazy mother and bookworm father. At first Janet liked the attention. She used it to get what she wanted. But eventually she couldn't tell anymore why she constantly calculated how to manipulate people. Was it because her mother was bananas or had Janet broken out into her own case of the cuckoos? Either way, getting high outshined a consoling third-grade teacher's hug and the thousand callous pities Nana breathed into her ear.

Janet hoped the old bag would offer her an uncomplicated place to spend the night. She didn't know her grandmother's address, but Janet believed she would be able to find the apartment building after she took the exit.

Driving west from Times Square, Janet was both scared of and intrigued by everyone out on the sidewalks, especially the hookers and the dodgy men looking them up and down. She imagined herself living in New York someday. Living with a drug dealer, someone like Tim, but more successful, more professional. They wouldn't have to worry about money because rich and famous people in New York must pay a lot more to have their drugs delivered discreetly to their posh apartments. Maybe after she made the Coney Island money, she would move to New York with her daughter and not have to deal drugs anymore.

Janet made it to the Holland Tunnel, but didn't remember driving there from the gas station. She did remember making sure the street numbers were going down. As she passed the streets, she called them out, "Thirty-fourth…thirty-third…thirty-second….." But once she was sure she was headed downtown, she started dreaming about what she was going to do with all the money. If she stopped at any red lights, she couldn't remember.

Once through the tunnel, signs for Newark bolstered her confidence that she would be able to find Nana's place, but then several miles into New Jersey, Janet doubted she should go see Nana at all. They hadn't seen each other since just after she had her baby. Her father wanted to see if Janet could live there, telling Nana, "To get her away from the element that's making her like this."

Nana shook her head at Janet's father, "I love you all dear, but I think your Janet here *is* the element." Wincing at Janet, she went on "I'm sorry, but you know what's happening. You've never been a stupid kid." Janet knew Nana was right.

As these fresher memories overtook the candy and ice cream moments, Janet again followed signs that ended in "south" to get off the Newark course. After driving for a while, Janet worried she was headed toward Newark despite the detour. Despite her altered state, she kept a slippery sense of direction. Her father instilled this awareness by quizzing her. Taking a drive was the best way to escape his wife's distress. Yet he somehow replaced her deranged uncertainty with his obsession of the physical orientation of his own marbles. Although both he and Janet knew that he was about to ask, he burst out, "Okay, Janet. Point west!" Or east, or north, or whatever direction made him feel anchored. She pointed as fast as she could, but after she reached her teens, her father's game faded into a meager comfort.

The final time he popped a direction question, she refused to answer. He lectured, "Janet, if you don't know where you are, then how do you expect to get where you are going?"

She snapped back, "All I know is that I'm going nowhere faster than you!" This proved that once someone has nowhere to go, no safe place, no future, a compass is as useful as a spoon to a corpse.

When all of the exits started to look familiar , Janet grew paranoid that the car was trying to make her go to Newark now, no matter how much she intended not to go. She rolled down her window and lit a cigarette. Now, she was dead against seeing Nana. Looking ahead on the highway, she thought she recognized a Newark bridge and swerved to take the exit that she had almost passed. The car tires skidded as they kicked up gravel and bits of debris.

Hoping to turn around and go the opposite direction of Newark, Janet drove under and over overpasses, along docks and freight yards. After an hour of trying to leave what turned out to be Bayonne, New Jersey, she stopped at a convenience store.

In the parking lot, she made a meal from the vodka flask stashed in the glove compartment, tortilla chips and a cold cut-up hotdog smothered in orange machine-pumped liquid cheese. Her Coney Island plan was still in motion but delayed by this detour. Success was dependent on her keeping a low overhead until the money started flowing when she got in with Animal. That called for drinking this liquor straight, eating whatever she could steal and sleeping in her car.

Janet woke up the next morning to the beat of uneven rain on the convertible's vinyl roof. At first, the drops sounded as if they wished not to wake her, gradually working themselves up to a tap-dancing pour. For more than ten years the weather had frozen and baked the car's roof over and over. Like a pie or loaf of bread put through the same trials, the material was split open in random areas; some were just above her head. The leaks' positions seemed cruel, even calculated, to Janet, who grumbled, "My own personal fucking Niagara Falls," as she accordioned her legs and waist up to position her head out of the water's way.

Neither the uppers nor the downers had fully worn off. Though exhausted, her mind raced. Nothing made sense. How long had she driven? How far was Coney Island? Staying on her side, she tried to relax, even though her heart raced. She said aloud, "Okay, Jan, breathe in the nose," and she pursed her lips as her nose whistled air in. Her mouth opened as she exhaled. Nausea hit seconds after a cold sweat burst from her palms and forehead. She screwed her face up as she chewed a bitter downer fished out of her purse. A queasy slumber took over. The soggy remnants of cheese sauce and chili sauce were just one layer of the car's many sickening scents.

An hour into her nap, she turned the ignition just enough to power the window, out of which she tossed all the garbage within arm's reach. Leaving the window open a crack, the cool air made the leaked rain seem less intrusive. At first, the slight breeze gave her hope of righting her gut, but the Thunderbird insisted on its own fragrance, something fusing sweaty gym socks and mushrooms that smell like cum or the other way around. Popping in the car's lighter, she took a cigarette from the pack she had stuck in her sock. Her eyes crossed as she focused on the cigarette tip clenched in her front teeth. She sucked, then balanced it in the ashtray, burning it as an incense while she slept for another hour.

The midday sun and the car's dankness awakened Janet to a stomach-turning sauna. Coughing and kicking her legs, Janet floundered until her hands found the door handle. After scrambling to get outside the car, she stood on her garbage and coughed up some phlegm, followed by watery regurgitation. She exhaled the word, "Fuck," several times after breathing in deeply, letting her saliva's string yo-yo up and down until she snapped her neck to one side with one determined, final spit.

In the store she steadied herself by placing both palms on the checkout counter.

"Tell me something," Janet nodded to the woman's nametag, "Amy. Am I still in Bayonne?" Janet pronounced Bayonne with a playful southern accent.

"You sure are," the clerk held her forefinger up to ask Janet to wait as she answered the payphone behind the counter. "Hello? Yeah, we got that. What do you mean, say it? Say what?" The girl hung up and rolled her eyes. "Some creep. So, where did you say you were from?"

"I didn't. It doesn't matter. How the hell do I get *out* of Bayonne?"

"Where are you going?"

"What are you, a cop or something?" Janet asked. "Doesn't matter. This place is fucking Hotel California, but it's not a lovely place, not a lovely face," Janet closed her eyes to sing the last few words to the song's tune. "Not bad, right?" she asked Amy, whose hands rested on her wide hips, elbows out, as she shook her head, smirking at the latest lunatic to spend a morning at Get Going Convenience.

"Not bad," Amy agreed.

"I thought you'd like it," Janet said as she bee-lined to the back of the store, past "Keep Out," "Do Not Enter " and "No Rest Rooms," each with the tagline, "Per Management," as if to absolve the cashier of the inhospitality. On the bathroom door Janet opened, the "Employees Only" sign was the last gasp of attempted authority over anyone who carried on in the face of all the other signs.

While on the toilet, Janet imagined living in this bathroom; where she would put a single bed, a night table, a hotplate and toaster, a shelf for some magazines and a mini-TV. She could survive on the store's food and drinks. She chewed a nail while trying to figure out how she could make the room work when she got her daughter back. "Bunk beds!" she thought. The problem and its solution made the once-feasible space seem small, dismal. She noted the piss smell and the non-bloodied, but dingy maxi pads stuck on the wall spelling out "HELLO" in capital letters. She flushed and tried washing her hands with the coarse gray powdered soap from the wall dispenser, but only the faucet's cold water worked and the sandy paste stuck to her skin. "Goddamn dump," she said as she carried a can of Lysol and two rolls of toilet paper back out into the store.

"Your hot water's for shit in there," Janet told Amy as she tossed everything in her arms on the counter. "Got a bag for these? Now, don't go calling it stealing. I say, 'I'm taking it for free.' You hear the difference?"

A clerk at another convenience store once told her that as long as the taken-for-free food was in a container that wasn't counted by the managers, the food was up for grabs. Every morning, a manager took a count of the cups, cardboard hot dog sleeves and plastic nacho trays and checked it against the register's count of those items. If the store were a school, its principals would be obsessed with the attendance of cigarettes, milk and the convenience foods, and far less concerned for delinquent newspapers and gum. Knowing that, Janet grabbed a newspaper for her meal and picked a cup out of the garbage to rinse it in the store's little sink. After running a tooth-brushing finger over her teeth and gums, she also rinsed out her mouth.

Customers came and went, none of them needing more than cigarettes or to pay for gas. There were six pumps outside that Amy controlled by taking people's cash or credit cards and pinching them in clothesline pins Sharpied with each pump's number. Only one person seemed to notice Janet. He shrugged to Amy and then twirled his finger next to his temple, sign language for, "What's up? That chick looks crazy."

Amy nodded and gave him a thumb's up, waved him off and mouthed, "She's okay."

Janet walked to the back of the store again and swung open the walk-in refrigerator door. "You never told me how to get the hell out of here, so I'm taking a break in here to chill out," Janet snickered. One low-wattage bulb illuminated the giant square metal room. In the corner farthest from the door were expired items the store couldn't sell any more, but employees stockpiled. Janet saw treasure in the eight plastic milk crates full of stale food, cigarettes, magazines and several other odds and ends. Humming, she placed in an empty milk crate about twenty candy bars, a few packages of English muffins, a jar of peanut butter, three dented cans of tuna fish, a half-empty box of birthday candles, three cartons of generic menthol cigarettes, a rubber-banded stack of greeting cards, and a handful of dirty magazines. These items were of little or no use to Amy or other store employees, but Janet computed their value in making future contributions to Animal for sleeping on his couch. Before lifting the crate, she slung a cold and discarded red-and-white striped hula-hoop around the back of her neck. Walking up the middle of the store, Janet yelled out, "Hey Amy! Have you called the cops on me yet?"

"I should. My manager's going to be here soon," Amy had picked up the phone during Janet's refrigerator spree but hung up before dialing. Whenever she called the cops it wasn't worth the trouble. Amy noticed that they never stopped by any other times, but right after any incident, they came by to check in, milling around the store until she offered them a coffee and a packaged sweet bun. After they left she had to log the items as "police hospitality." Sometimes they would take things she hadn't offered, like a Snickers bar or a cigarette lighter. Next to those items she wrote, "police rudality."

Tracking Janet's movements throughout the store started to irritate Amy. "Okay, now. I think you've got plenty to get to wherever you're going."

"Alright, alright. What about some idea on how the hell to get out of Bayonne?" Janet said the city's name with a British accent this time.

"It would help if you told me where the hell you were going, right? Jesus!" Amy was over Janet.

Certain words triggered Janet's love of using accents and her latest destination was one that called for a voice like an announcer at a boxing match, lingering on each syllable, "Con-ey Is-land, is where I'm headed."

"Okay. Wow. I got an uncle near there. Let me think," blinking her eyes as if she were a medium conjuring a connection with the dead, Amy deftly split open an empty cigarette carton and threw it on the counter. Leaning over it with a pen, she drew what looked like many rivers using squiggly lines and straight ones that symbolized roads.

When Janet approached the door with the crate in her arms, Amy called out, "Hey, don't you want to know…."

"Keep your panties on. I'm coming back," Janet went to the car and put the crate in the back seat. She pulled out the Lysol and sprayed it in the back of the car and on the floors and then opened the driver's side door to spray the front seat. The car's cigarette lighter was burned into the front seat hump's carpet. She must have dropped it there after lighting the cigarette that morning. Yanking the lighter created the same effect as grabbing a stray piece of yarn from a homemade sweater. The carpet came up in ramen noodle strings attached to the lighter, which she then threw onto the passenger's seat, saying, "Fuck that." She finished spraying the front seat and slammed the door.

Amy watched Janet through the window and thought maybe she should have called the police. She wondered if people who know psychologists or doctors called them when things like that were happening. Having worked at the store since she graduated high school, Amy was often told, mostly by her parents, that she wasted her abilities as a compassionate person at Get Going, that she should work at the hospital or with children in a school. Sometimes she thought about starting at Hudson County

Community College to become a nurse or a social worker. Right now, she asked herself what she would have to become to help someone like Janet. Would that be a psychologist or a parole officer?

Janet came back into the store and leaned her elbows on the counter to look over the directions. "What we got here?"

Amy was surprised by Janet's apparent normalcy and even Janet felt as though she were floating somewhere between racing and crashing. Pointing outside and then at the paper, Amy talked Janet through all the buildings and businesses she would pass on the way to the exit onto I-78.

Janet snapped back into the jitters a little, sort of dancing in place as though she had to pee. "How long is this going to take me?" she asked as if the answer were determined by something other than distance and speed.

"Only about an hour, at the most. We go there all the time to see my uncle," Amy assured her.

"Who's your uncle?" Janet asked.

Amy couldn't come up with a lie fast enough and answered, "He owns an ice cream shop and a couple of Laundromats there."

"I just got really lost last night and I have to get to Coney Island, soon," Janet said. "Like right away. I got money to make," she clapped her hands then rubbed them together, "real bucks." Amy let out a relieved breath.

Amy felt that somehow now she was keeping Janet from what she needed to get to, saying, "I better let you go then." It was awkward to say goodbye to someone she barely knew.

"I'm on my way. I'm going to get my little girl back, by the way," Janet felt like Amy deserved more information since she had helped her. "After Coney Island, I'll get her back," Janet repeated.

"That's sweet. I bet she misses you," Amy answered.

Janet looked at the floor. Amy felt like she had gone too far because maybe they didn't get along. She was afraid Janet was going to cry.

A deep breath and closed eyes got Janet through the moment without tears. "It's not like that, but when I do get her back, I'm thinking we'll move to New York City and...," Janet went on about getting an apartment where her daughter would have her own room with a television. Amy thought that the entire story was possibly a lie. The plan sounded flimsy and Janet didn't mention her daughter's name.

Janet detected that she had lost Amy's attention and wrapped up. "You've been great and I'll never forget how much you've helped me."

"Just drive safe," Amy said as she gently joined her hands together as if in prayer, pointing them toward Janet to wish her well.

Amy's heart jumped when Janet gripped both her wrists and pulled the cashier toward her. Regret flashed in the pit of Amy's stomach.

Janet's teary eyes pleaded for a kind of dignity neither woman was given or ever knew how to give, the unconditional kind. "Really. You don't know. You helped me a lot. A shit load. People don't…" Janet's mind drifted.

Amy relaxed her arms, but it made her feel more awkward. Janet shook Amy's wrists as if they were shaking hands at the passing of the peace during a church service. The motion must have triggered such feelings in Janet, who said, "God bless," as she let go. Janet walked toward the door, filling the uncomfortable goodbye air with her voice. "God bless. Really, God bless," leaving Amy no opportunity to respond with anything other than a wave.

Chapter 16

Helen's job at Caldor started two weeks after she unpacked the last box, all of the flour, sugar and other baking supplies she never used, but felt like she was supposed to stock in the pantry. Before leaving for work, Helen cautioned Cole, "I don't want you going out. I hear there are some tough kids around here. It's not like before."

"I *know*," Cole answered, annoyed. She was relieved that her mother didn't go on further about how they didn't have health insurance anymore so she needed to be extra careful.

Cole knew what she meant about the area. Not only was the neighborhood less friendly, but nothing in their life was like it was before. Her mother was now just that, a mother, no longer a wife. And Cole had a mother but not a father. They were two, not three. Cole saw it as there not really being a "they" now. When her father was alive, Cole saw them as three people on one team. Since Red's death, she felt like two people not on any team, not playing, just alive.

She thought her father would not have liked this new apartment. He often sat at their dining room table and looked out at a maple tree that attracted lots of squirrels and chipmunks. In Sheridan Street's kitchen, their table barely fit near the window with a folded towel that soaked up rainwater that had leaked in. Her mother's bedroom was in what the landlord called the "sewing room," with just enough room for her parents' bed and dresser. The apartment didn't have a living room and that's where her father liked to sit in his dark green wingback chair to watch television or just fall asleep, exhausted from work. Before they moved, she begged her mother to take it to the new place, but Helen explained, "The more we try to hold onto Dad's things, the harder it will be."

After it was moved onto the sidewalk in front of their old apartment, Cole sat in it smoothing her hands over the arms where her father wore down the fabric. In hopes her mother would change her mind after seeing her saying goodbye to the chair, Cole stayed in it for two hours. After getting no attention, she went back in the house, where she stuffed some of her father's old t-shirts into a shoebox. She taped it shut and wrote "Cole sneaks" on it with a magic marker. This was her way of reminding herself not to open it in front of her mother.

When they moved in, the landlord told Cole not to touch his Civil War memorabilia that was stored in what was once a living room. The summer night was humid, so Cole ventured past the black drape across that doorway and through the large room that her mother called "No Man's Land." Next to a clothes rack full of capes and jackets, there was a door to the third-floor screened-in porch.

Cole untied the cushions from their wooden kitchen chairs, ventured out to the porch and laid them on the green painted floorboards. Stretched out on them, she flipped through *Tiger Beat* magazines she stole from the public library. The librarians taped long metallic security strips into the magazines but she easily sacrificed that one page to take the whole magazine home. Sometimes she wondered if libraries were supposed to be quiet so that the librarians could hear pages being torn out, not because people need silence to read. She carried the magazines upstairs where their clanking photocopier masked the ripping sounds.

Cole never thought about celebrities until she spent a night watching television with Gwen. During *Friday Night Videos* Gwen seemed to know every singer and the names of the bands. Cole's parents had only watched the news and some sitcoms, like *Night Court* and *Who's the Boss?* Now that Helen was going to be gone most nights and forbade her to go outside, Cole wanted to watch the shows and think about who these people were in real life.

Even knowing Gwen seemed something like knowing a celebrity. She was simply one of the people at Red's funeral to Cole. Almost everyone Cole saw that day and the few weeks after it, were absent from their lives. It was as if she watched a show for that time and the actors all went home. Cole had a hard time picturing what shape her new life would take. It was summer, there was no school and her mother's mandate of solitude prevented Cole from meeting other kids. This all pushed Cole into getting lost in the unusual details celebrity magazines offered: David Lee Roth was dating Brooke Shields, but Cole didn't know that until it was announced that they broke up, Michael J. Fox loved frosted strawberry Pop-Tarts, and George Michael from WHAM! slept with a Strawberry Shortcake doll, a gift from a fan in Ohio.

She went inside and retied all the cushions onto the kitchen chairs. Out of magazines and tired of watching television alone in the kitchen, Cole turned on the radio. Upon hearing the rolling guitar and the quick drum snaps of *We Got the Beat*, she jumped around and waved her hands above her head. Her socks glided on the linoleum floor as she chanted along, "We got the beat ... round and round and round," twirling in circles until the song ended. Breathless, she sipped from a can of Coke and looked outside. Three kids stood under the streetlamp right outside her house. Cole decided on black Converse sneakers; her red ones weren't serious enough to meet people who were supposed to be tough kids. She grabbed her tape recorder in order to look like she had something to do.

Taking the back stairs down from the triple-decker, she strolled out from behind the house on the side with no walkway. She didn't want it to look like she came out to see them; she wanted to appear to just be taking a walk and they happened to be there. She nodded to the kids, saying, "Hey," as she passed by them.

She put her head down after the tallest boy answered, "Yeah, hey," and continued using the toe of his shoe to pick away the crumbling curb. Cole continued on her fake journey toward Boston Avenue.

Cole had walked almost two houses away from the kids when the boy yelled to her, "Hey! You live here?"

She turned around. The jitters from the dancing and her new freedom seemed to swallow her voice. A couple of notches above a whisper, she told him, "Yeah. We just moved in."

"What?" he asked.

"We moved in," she said, but realized that was not what she wanted to say. It didn't make sense.

"Yeah. I heard ya," he said. A girl a little taller than Cole laughed along with the boy and leaned against the streetlamp pole, looking down.

Her mother was right. From upstairs they looked like kids she had played with before. They stood in a circle, focused on the space in the middle as they talked. In her old neighborhood the kids talked about school, other kids, stuff their parents said they shouldn't have heard. But close up, these kids seemed different. Cole tried not to let them bother her. After all, *she* was the new kid. Instead, she said, "Are you as bored as shit as I am?" She bargained that swearing would win some points.

"Yeah. My fucking father stole my smokes," the girl said. She seemed much tougher than the boy.

"That's shitty," Cole said.

"Your parents smoke?" the boy asked. The darker the sky became, the more the three kids looked like their eyeballs were hollowed from their faces. The smallest kid hadn't said anything yet. The clothes and hair conveyed a young kid in maybe first or second grade, but not clearly a boy or girl.

When Cole walked back toward them, she nodded her head at the youngest one, "You smoke?"

The kid giggled. Cole walked up to them and said to the little one, "My name is Cole." She held the recorder's handle with both hands in front of her thighs. She shifted her weight left to right a few times until the little one answered, "I'm Paul," he motioned to the other two, "but they call me Puke."

The older boy said, "Coal? Like you're what I get in my stocking when I've been naughty?" The girl snorted another laugh.

"Yeah, sure," Cole said.

"Coal? That's not your stupid name." The girl and Cole finally made eye contact. "Don't let people fucking disrespect your name."

Cole could hear her heart beating in her ears, "I'm not. He's kind of right. It's the same way to say it. C-O-A-L is what he said. My name is C-O-L-E."

"Well, fucking say that. Don't let people shit on you like that. Jesus Christ," the girl sighed. "So, do they smoke?" she repeated her brother's question as she pointed up to Cole's apartment, as if her parents were in the apartment at that moment.

"They're not home," Cole said and immediately regretted revealing too much.

"That's not what I asked you," the girl started blowing a bubble with gum that must have been in her mouth, but she hadn't been chewing.

"No, she doesn't smoke," Cole lied. "You got more gum?"

After fishing around in her jean jacket pocket, the girl handed Cole a piece of grape Hubba Bubba. Cole held it up next to her face and in a low voice said, "Big bubbles, no troubles."

The older boy snickered, "Wise ass."

Cole grinned and asked him, "Where do you live?"

"Over there," he waved toward the next street over, "on Shit-view."

"What about you?" Cole asked the girl.

"We're related. It sucks, but someone's got to be their sister." The girl tussled Puke's hair.

Cole nodded her head and laughed a little. Having to work at moistening the stale piece of gum gave her an excuse for keeping her mouth busy without talking. The older boy said, "Like it's a privilege to hear you snore and fart all night, Princessa Vanessa."

She pushed him hard in the middle of his chest. "Shut up, Toad!"

Vanessa seemed embarrassed. Cole wondered if his nickname was Toad, like Paul's was Puke. She said, "My parents didn't have any other kids. Just me."

"Lucky," Vanessa said. "You got your own room?"

Cole stretched the gum from her mouth down the length of her arm and nodded her head. After pushing the gum back in her mouth, she said, "But we don't have a living room. The TV's in the kitchen."

"Can we go up?" Puke asked. "I have to pee."

"Shut up," Vanessa snapped. "God. Don't be rude," she rolled her eyes.

Cole looked up at the apartment, thinking about how she left it unlocked.

"Can he go up?" Toad asked Cole. He looked apologetically to his sister, saying quietly to her, "I don't think we should go back yet."

"Sure, you can all come up, but my mom's coming home later,

so …" Cole led them to the back of the house the same way she came out. Puke said something about how dark it was at the side of the house but once Cole put her finger up to her lips to signal them to be quiet, they walked silently.

In the apartment the four stood looking at each other under the kitchen ceiling's bare round fluorescent tube. Cole noticed that Toad and Vanessa looked alike. Puke rushed into the bathroom as soon as Cole pointed to it. Cole hadn't heard the toilet seat flip up and hit the tank since Red's death. She told herself to remember to make sure everything was back to normal in the bathroom before her mom got home.

"This isn't bad," Vanessa said of the apartment.

Cole nodded and looked around, seeing it through eyes not her own. The stove looked newer but she noticed large gouges in the floor where someone must have dropped sharp knives.

"Your TV is small," Toad said.

"Toad, I thought I told you to shut the fuck up?" Vanessa hit him hard in the chest with her fist. The boy gasped for air as Puke came out from the bathroom.

"Is his name really Puke?" Cole asked.

Vanessa said, "*I* call him Puke. It's short for Pucas. And that came from Lucas."

Cole kept an eye on Toad, who went into Helen's bedroom for a moment and then into Cole's. From in there, he asked, "What grade are you in?"

"I'm going into sixth," Cole said.

"So are we," Vanessa said.

"I am not. I'm starting second grade," Puke called out from the bedroom.

Vanessa said, "I was talking about Toad and me. I stayed back a couple of times."

Cole shrugged to show that she didn't care that Vanessa was kept back.

"Get out here, you retard," Vanessa called out to Puke.

"No, you come in here," Puke insisted.

The four of them stood together in Cole's bedroom facing a poster board covered with newspaper clippings and photographs. At the top in all capital letters it read, "P.T. Barnum $ His Animals," in black marker.

"That's my old science project. I won honorable mention. I think I could have won better but I wrote a dollar sign instead of an and," Cole said as she pointed at the dollar sign. "My grandfather told me to leave it. He thought it was funny."

"I wouldn't have noticed it if you didn't say nothing," Toad said as he touched some of the display's pictures.

"So, what the hell do you know about P.T. Barnum's animals?" Vanessa asked.

Vanessa's question came across to Cole as hostile, so she jumped to a subject that usually got people excited, "I'm related to P.T. Barnum. My grandfather is his great grandson."

"Wow! Did you ever meet him?" Puke asked.

"Shut up, stupid. The guy's been dead for almost five hundred years. Right?" Vanessa said with the confidence of someone who needs to be right.

"Yeah. He's dead. But there's a statue of him at Seaside Park," Cole said enthusiastically.

"Well, Encyclopedia Brown, why don't you tell us about this thing?" Vanessa pointed at Cole's project.

They sat on her bed and waited for Cole to speak. Her face flushed as she tried to remember the speech she had made to the judges almost two years ago. She started, "I am a direct descendent of P.T. Barnum and I am here today to tell you about the animals in his museum and circus."

Puke clapped. He looked up at Vanessa glaring at him and said, "I know. I should shut up, right?" Vanessa nodded.

Cole couldn't remember all the dates, "A really long time ago my great-great-grandfather was good friends with Bridgeport's very own P.T. Barnum. I stand here today to tell you about the animals that P.T. Barnum had in his museum and circus."

"You already told us that part," Vanessa snapped.

"Okay, okay. I'm trying to remember. Well, he brought whales, monkeys and tigers into his museum before it burned down." Pointing at some newspaper clippings glued to the board, Cole said, "Here are some articles about one of the biggest fires ever in New York City. A lot of animals died in that fire. And then he bought his most famous animal. Jumbo. He was the biggest elephant in captivity at the time." Cole stretched out her arms like Red had coached her to animate what she was saying.

In their old house, she had practiced the speech over and over as her father nodded his head. There was less little physical distance between Cole and her audience but the kids seemed much farther away than her father had been. Cole wished she were back in her old living room. It was much larger than any of their rooms in Sheridan Street. These kids would enjoy listening to her more there. Her voice could meander and not get eaten by the tiny room's walls and low ceiling. Cole's left eye twitched as she bowed her head. As she tried to shake off her nerves, she imagined her father watching her from heaven and reminding her what to say next. She felt like she could cry so she cracked her knuckles by pulling the ends of her fingers out one by one.

Vanessa snapped her fingers. "Hello? Is that it?"

"Yeah. I have more," Cole said before she took a deep breath. Her voice shook a little, but she didn't cry as she said, "P.T. Barnum brought Jumbo here from somewhere and had him in his circus." Cole couldn't remember what she used to know but the three bored yet expectant faces kept her talking. She said, "And then a few years later a train hit him and he died. The elephant. Jumbo. Not P.T. Barnum."

She wasn't done but she stopped talking and took a hurried bow. Puke clapped again.

"Wow, that was depressing. No wonder you didn't win," Vanessa said.

Toad got up and walked back into the kitchen, "Do you have anything to eat?"

Vanessa followed him, as did Cole as she said, "I got some bologna and bread."

"Nah. Thanks," he said.

Vanessa crossed her legs and arms, making her body seem to fold in half.

"Did you have to go?" Cole asked Vanessa.

"Yeah, we should go back. I think it will...," Vanessa was interrupted by Cole.

"No, I meant do you have to go to the bathroom?" Cole motioned toward the bathroom.

Vanessa mumbled a self-conscious, "Nah." She stretched her arms out and let out a fake yawn. "Let's head home. All right, douchebags?" she pushed Toad toward the door. "Hey Puke! Get out here. We're going! Thank her so we can get the fuck out of here."

Puke came out of Cole's bedroom and said, "Thanks Cole."

"Smell you later," Toad mumbled.

Vanessa waved over her shoulder and gave Cole a devilish grin as she kicked Toad's ass. His "Hey!" was quashed by Cole's loud whisper of "Shush it," as she closed and locked the door.

After she checked the bathroom, Cole flushed the toilet for good measure. She got ready for bed and took one last look out the window. The kids either went home or were standing under a streetlamp on another street.

Taking off her gold cross necklace, Cole noticed that a few pictures and newspaper clippings had been ripped off her science project board. As she thought about the evening she wondered if she should ask Puke to give them back when she saw him alone. Vanessa could beat him up over it.

Just as she nodded off to sleep, Cole was jolted awake by knocking on their back door. Her heart raced, thinking the kids were back and her mom would be angry if she caught them there. Helen's voice called out quietly between the knocks, "Cole, Cole. It's me. Come unlock the door."

Dazed, Cole unlocked the door. Helen asked, "What the hell happened?"

Panicked, Cole stood silently staring at her.

"How did you get gum on the lock? I stuck the damned key in it," Helen looked at Cole as if she had done it.

"What gum?" Cole was confused.

"Never mind," Helen said. "Go back to bed."

Chapter 17

Janet made it to Animal's house in Coney Island. The house wasn't much to look at. Three stories with two mailboxes and one doorbell. Janet rang it. Someone had assembled dozens of water pipes and fittings to make railings up the steps and around the porch. They painted them a brick color but after they started peeling, dark green paint was brushed over the flakes. The shiny paint seemed melted over the peeled bits and cracks. The paint detailed the bumps and grooves as chronological markings of a blizzard wind, a car key's scraping, a heat wave, an errant ice skate blade and other objects drunkenly dropped or thrown in anger.

She rang the doorbell again. No answer. Janet knocked on the one of the windows and looked in. No lights were on except one at the top of the stairs. She walked back to her car parked in the street, looked up at the house and thought about honking her horn. Shadows moved behind sheets slung over the third-floor windows.

Back when Animal moved to Coney Island, he made it sound like a breezy ocean town but Janet found it to be about the same as New Haven or Bridgeport. The drive jangled her nerves so she needed something. She took a few maintenance drags from a dried-out cigarette from the glove compartment. The inside of her elbows sweated as she propped herself up over the car's hood. The car engine's heat rose up, making the smoke burning her lungs seem less biting. Janet watched the very top windows to try to tell whether the voices she heard were coming from Animal's house or the one next door.

Animal told her to come visit any time and that he lived in this nice big house. She wondered if "Victorian" only meant when a house was built and not that it was special or beautiful. She had imagined stained glass windows, not the same white window frames she saw on the kinds of houses that no one bothered to name.

The engine pinged now and then as its temperature dropped. Sweat under Janet's breasts soaked through her gauzy blouse and left moisture on the hood. This moisture, flanked by two lines where her arms were, formed a large sweaty "W" on the hood. Janet took it as a sign that she should cool out with some weed.

From the trunk Janet grabbed a crumpled brown paper bag and a golf club Tim kept for protection. Stomping back onto the porch, she pressed the doorbell again. Each push yielded only one ding and one dong. After a few more tries, she banged the golf club's head on the dark green aluminum siding as high as she could reach, hoping the people upstairs would hear her. Just when her right arm had tired and she was switching hands, an old woman with Albert Einstein hair swung open the front door, yelling, "Don't you dare! What the hell you think you're doing? You dented the goddamn house." The woman pointed up to the spot where Janet had hit it. "Look at that, you dirty bum."

Janet froze mid-way into a whack she was about to deliver and lowered the club as the woman rushed toward her. "Are you trying to act like you're going to the ninth hole with that thing now?" She wrenched the club out of Janet's fist and threw it onto the sidewalk behind Janet. The woman left the door open as she went back in the house and yelled "Animal! Animal!" up the stairs. Janet waited. She wasn't going to cross that threshold without Animal.

The woman grumbled angrily as she slipped into a door under the stairs. She came out smiling, saying toward the ceiling, "Put that in your pipe and smoke it." She walked back into a part of the house Janet couldn't see and a door slammed.

"What the fuck?" came a holler from upstairs. Heavy footsteps thudded down the stairs, making Janet hopeful it was Animal.

"Don't worry, they're on down here," Animal's voice called upstairs. Only in his mid-thirties, Animal seemed in his fifties. He told Janet and Tim that he started smoking in third grade and started going gray a few years later. Janet didn't believe the part about the hair but his smoker's voice sounded like a coffee can of pennies and a broken kazoo were stuck in his throat. Nearing the bottom of the stairs, he yelled, "Fuckin' ay, Wilda! Why the hell this time?"

"Hey?" Janet called from the doorway, "Hey. Animal?"

"Who the hell is that? Maddie?" Animal clomped down the stairs faster.

"It's Janet," she said smiling at the bearded giant moving toward her.

"What the fuck? Are you shittin' me?" Animal said.

Squinting to see him clearer through the screen door, Janet said, "Yeah. I finally made it out here to Coney Island, man."

When Animal hugged Janet his sour body odor made her less concerned with her own far weaker stink. His breathing was heavy from the trip downstairs. Also known as "The Bear," Animal had a torso like a wine barrel covered in flesh and black hair. He played off his panting as short sighs, saying, "Wow," breathing out, "Janet," breathing in, "Bridgeport Bomber Janet." After catching two more deep breaths, "Well, get in. I mean, come on in."

He led her to a kitchen in the back of the house, gripped her shoulder and guided her to sit at the table. After he took two beer cans out of the refrigerator, Janet tossed the paper bag into the middle of the table. "Here's my dish for the potluck."

Animal grinned, leaning against the kitchen sink, "You know I'm always stocked. You keep it." Janet reached for the bag, put it on her lap and took out a joint. He motioned toward the three closed doors off the kitchen, "By the way, she's not happy when we light up anywhere but way upstairs."

Janet looked at the bag like a child who was just told she couldn't eat her chocolate Easter bunny until after church. Animal opened the freezer and tossed Janet a Saran-wrapped brownie. "That ought to hold you over." In magic marker, "NO WILDA!" was written on a strip of masking tape wrapped around it.

"Now, let me get this thing in here," he said while going through the door under the stairs.

The doors off the kitchen were closed but only one had that old woman behind it. A television laugh track was coming from the middle one. Small bells hanging from the doorknob reminded Janet that she did hear some tinkling bells along with the door slam.

Animal shouted out from under the stairwell, "Yeah, Wilda unscrews that friggin' fuse whenever she feels like it."

Janet said, "Well, I knocked on the door for a while so…." Janet knew how to say nothing about something in a way that could exonerate her if the person didn't pursue more answers.

When Animal screwed in the new fuse, cheers and hoots rang out from the top floor. "We're in the middle of it up there. You want to come see?"

Janet shrugged, "Why not?" She tucked the brownie in her paper bag and followed Animal upstairs.

"I call it the Watchtower. You know? Hendrix?" Animal explained.

"Dylan actually wrote Watchtower. Did ya know that?" Janet didn't wait for Animal to answer, "But man, good ol' Bob sounds like a retard when he sings it, so he's lucky Jimi took his shit and rocked it into a real jam, right?" She played air guitar as her hair fell into her face and she stomped her foot. Janet bellowed out, "No need to get excited!"

Animal wheezed out a chuckle. "Janet, you're one wild chick, ya know that?" They climbed a few more steps, Animal apologized, "Well, anyway, sorry it's kind of way up here." Animal's insecurity had endeared him to Janet during his runs to Bridgeport. Tim would posture and tell stories about fistfights he'd won while Animal stopped the conversation to not miss a guitar solo or to get them to watch Tim's cat play with Animal's ponytail.

Several steps from the very top, Animal stopped to let her by. Once in the room, he wheezed, able to only whisper, "This is…."

Three men sat at card tables. "Janet," she finished the introduction. Each man had his own table and two other folded tables leaned against a refrigerator. Janet stared at the fridge, wondering if that's what it really was. It had been spray painted black and was in front of a window.

"We got some mac and cheese I made last night. You hungry?" Animal asked.

"Oh! I got some food in the car that's got to go in the fridge. Should I bring it in?" Janet raised an eyebrow and grinned a little, her way of asking if she would be allowed to stay.

"What do you guys think?" Animal asked the room.

No one answered. Animal said, "Keith?" to a skinny black man with hair that puffed from under a blue Citgo baseball cap, like half of an inner tube. Not taking his eyes away from his hands rolling joints he said, "What she got?"

His voice was deeper than Janet had expected. Now his disposition seemed that of a man twice the age she had guessed. Focused on his thin, veiny hands, Janet realized he could be a lot older than Animal.

"I got some cold cuts, candy bars, sodas, you know, the regular stuff." What had seemed like a treasure trove at the convenience store sounded far less impressive now. Even the drugs she brought were nothing compared with the piles of powders, pills and weed piled on the tables in plastic bags and Saran-wrapped bricks.

"Maddie brings us lasagna," Keith clicked his tongue.

"I don't care," a short elderly man smiled at Janet. "I like a hot meal, but if that's what you got, I'll take a sandwich or something." Although his table had small bags of pills piled on one side, he worked at a scale holding rings, chains and other bits of jewelry. When he looked up, he had just placed a thin gold ring on top.

"Okay. Go get the stuff," Animal said as he clapped Janet's shoulder chummy hard, not sexy hard. "Put it in the Black Sabbath," he motioned toward the refrigerator, "or Wilda will get at it. I am beat as hell. Going to crash. Get me up if any of you need anything. There's a run tomorrow and the Big Dog's in Sheepshead Bay tomorrow night."

The three men waved, nodded, grunted acknowledgment. Janet and Keith's eyes met. He smirked. She didn't think Animal had plans to get into something with her, but now it seemed clear he did. Janet needed something soon. Hours had passed without a pill or a toke. She followed Animal down the stairs and into his second-floor bedroom. "You know what? I mean, I got to get a little high."

"Okay," Animal picked up a beer can from his dresser and shook it. It sloshed at half-full; he sniffed it, shrugged and swilled it down in three gulps.

"What about this?" Janet asked holding up the brownie.

"Sure. That'll get you high all right," Animal smiled and nodded.

Working around his round beer belly, he used gravity and momentum to pull off his black motorcycle boots. He peeled his gray tube socks onto the floor and fell onto the bed, telling her, "Ah! I need some zees, man."

Janet stood stone still. Would he fall asleep and forget she was there? He kept his eyes closed and asked, "So, what you looking for, Janet?"

"I need a hit." She started to pull at the tape around the brownie.

"Yeah. I got that. But, why are you here? That's Tim's car, right?" he asked.

In order to stall, Janet used the distraction of getting the brownie unwrapped. "You could have dropped this from an airplane. It's fucking impossible." Animal waited. "And I'm so tired too. I've been driving for fucking ever. You know, I got lost and ended up in the damn city and then Jersey. Fucking hell driving there. Those people are nutso."

Animal said, "You can stay here but if Tim shows up, that's it. The guys all know the rule. No chicks. But I know you and I got a special thing coming up that I can't let the guys know about. Don't tell them shit. Any time about anything. I'm serious as shit."

"I got it, man. I'm good at secrets and covert shit. The car's running fine if you want me to run," she offered.

"Naw. I got a runner guy. Hold still for a few days." Rolling from his side to his back, he opened his eyes to take two twenty-dollar bills out of his pocket and held it out to Janet. He undid his belt, unbuttoned his jeans and pulled his zipper down.

Janet motioned one hand to tell him to wait. "I got to get high first." She chewed a large bite of the cold, crumbly dry brownie with her mouth open.

"Take it," Animal shook the money.

"Hold on," she sat on the bed. "I can't fuck straight, man."

"Oh Christ," he said. "No, this is just…. It's not for that. I'm tired. Got to leave early tomorrow morning. I can't even dream of pussy right now."

Janet laughed, "What? You're turning down this?" She squeezed her breasts together and leaned over him, as some brownie crumbs fell out of her mouth.

He ran his fingertips across her cleavage and up her neck to her chin, then patted her cheek. "There's a room upstairs. The one with a mattress. It's yours. I got to sleep. Big drive tomorrow." He rolled back over.

"Thanks man," Janet said. She wanted to add, "I'll give you a rain check," about the blowjob or whatever she thought he wanted. But she already regretted misreading Animal's intentions. She closed the door as if she had just put a child to bed.

In the bathroom across from his room, she sat on the toilet peeing while she finished the brownie and threw the wrapping in the toilet. During the two flushes it took to go down she tried fixing her hair wreck and picked at her face. The brownie started to kick in; she stuck her tongue out and it didn't look half as dry as it felt. Saliva collected at the tip. She waited until there was enough for it to drip into the sink, but it didn't. Turning on the faucet, she bent over to gulp water from her cupped hand. The car keys seemed to fall from out of nowhere, but reminded her about her original mission to get the food from the car.

After getting all the perishables and some other snacks all in one box and in the front door, Janet managed to lock the front door and grab three beer cans from the downstairs refrigerator without rousing Wilda.

Back up in the Watchtower Janet filled the Black Sabbath with her Bayonne food. The seats were empty and the stereo was silent. She didn't know she had been in the bathroom for over an hour.

The guys had figured she and Animal were doing what Janet had thought Animal wanted. They usually left a little after eleven, when the cops changed shifts. Animal had figured out the Coney Island police shift changes were every eight hours just like at the hospital. Knowing where and when the cops lurked protected Animal and his guys from being noticed for eight years.

"Take me -- Free magic" was printed on a piece of masking tape stuck diagonally on a Ziploc bag. A second, smaller piece of tape had a heart drawn with a face in it and the signature, "Animal." Janet examined the bag. It was about a half cup of tiny bits of mushrooms and their dust. Janet shook almost half of it into her palm, tilted her head back and tossed it in her mouth. She felt a cough come on but gulped down a flat open beer from a can on a table.

She hooked a finger into the plastic ring of a half six-pack from the Black Sabbath and grabbed a bag of Doritos to take down the hall, calling out, "Hey, anyone here?" She opened the first door. As she walked into the dark something tickled against her face. Dropping everything, she batted it away. The ceiling light turned on when the string cord that had swept against her face wrapped around her flailing arm. The piss scent made sense once she saw she was in the bathroom. One of the cans rolled behind the toilet but Janet didn't try to get it. She left with the beer that had landed near her foot.

The bathroom light lit the hallway and the two other doors. Janet was relieved to find the mattress room first. This room had a light switch on the wall and a large mattress in middle of the room with sheets and a pillow.

Janet fell to her knees on the mattress and opened the beer she needed before getting too high. A breeze strong enough to make it through the tree branches and the window screen hit her face. She rubbed the cold sweaty beer can on her forehead and arms before she chugged it down. After she ultimately gave in to the mushrooms, the empty can ended up under her shoulder. Unfazed by the discomforts of the can or the humid room, she held up the top sheet and looked at the green and blue dots encompassed by squiggly lines. They reminded her of the sidewalks of Rio de Janeiro she learned about in fifth grade. She said aloud that teacher's name, the way he used to pronounce it -- "Mee-ster Coe-stahs" -- and then she said it the way she always did: "Miss-ter Coss-tuss." She said it over and over until she thought again about the sidewalks he taught them were built by the Portuguese, his ancestors.

She sang out, "Her name is Rio and she dances on the sand, just like the river twisting through a dusty land." Janet liked hearing her voice and felt that the sound somehow made the breeze stronger. When she heard cars go by the house now and again, she wondered who could hear her and got quieter. Hushed, she sang, "When she smiles she really shows up all she can. Oh Rio, Rio dance 'cross the Rio Grande. Oh Rio, Rio, Oh Rio Rio. Rio…." She changed her pace and held her arms up like an orchestra conductor as she segued into, "Oh arh eeh oh. Ice cold milk and an Oreo cookie. They forever go together…." She stopped.

Janet's leg had rubbed against something in the bed. Pulling the covers up her leg, she saw a glossy magazine opened to a full-page photograph of a man holding his erection at the ass of a woman on all fours looking back into the camera lens. In her haze, the picture didn't make sense.

She said to the woman in the picture, "What? Why are you looking at me?" She put her forefinger on the man's face. "He's the one with the prick."

Pulling the sheets close to her face, she squinted as if that gave her special vision to see cum stains. The sheets' green and blue dots alternately looked like many eyes, and then eyes and noses and mouths together. After watching the sheets change faces and colors, Janet's attention floated back to the magazine. She flipped to its cover and said, "A hundred pages. Gourmet edition of The Queens of Anal Sex." It listed some of the queens, whose names Janet pronounced as if they were being introduced on a stage: "Suzie Silk, Tiffany Clark, Rose Torres." Looking at the cover, she said, "Ow. That's got to hurt like hell, girly."

Janet wanted to turn on music but there wasn't a radio or stereo in the room. She thought about looking for one, but she didn't feel like moving and, besides, an old hippy that bought from Tim once told her that she should never go roaming around on mushrooms. She pointed to an imaginary person in front of her. "You, Janet. You are staying here. Don't go out that door." Her heart raced when she heard her name and it was her own voice. For that moment she felt like two people at once.

She wiped the sheet on her face and down her arms like a towel to absorb her sweat. The room was getting hot again since the breeze stopped. Janet thought she had to sing again but didn't know what to sing. She opened up the magazine again. "Shake for me girl, I wanna be your backdoor man." Laughing, she turned onto her side and looked at the pictures again. She rocked in time to the music in her head and softly sang, "Keep a coolin' baby, Keep a coolin' baby, Keep a coolin' baby," then added, "Whole lotta love…" before making the descending guitar sounds.

Janet looked closer at the pictures of two women with one guy. Their names were Misty Dawn and Crystal Dawn, but they didn't look like sisters. Janet thought about how these names were probably all fake. Especially Suzie Silk's. She stared at the women's faces, thinking about how her baby's name had been changed from Kimberly. Janet wanted to call her Kimberly when she finally went to get her. She wondered if her daughter would like that. It would be something that would pull them closer, since

Janet would be the only person in the world who would call her by her real name. The bare breasts, makeup, high heels, anuses, erections all remained in front of Janet's open eyes, but her mind was focused on her daughter.

How old would she be now? Janet thought about how she had to keep writing letters so that when they met it would be less awkward. Thinking about the whole situation made Janet's heart race again and she felt that the trip could take a bad turn. Tears cooled her face although she hadn't felt as though she'd been crying.

"You're freaking out. Stop," she said as she got up from the mattress and paced around the room a few times. "Okay, okay, okay, okay," she said as she nodded her head and tried thinking of something else. Each time she circled close to the door, she put her hand up as if to tell the door to stop trying to get her to leave.

Janet pushed her forehead into the front window's screen at the very moment a cop stopped in front of Animal's house. "Shit, shit, shit," is all Janet could think. Her car trunk was left wide open, so he sauntered from his car to shine his flashlight into the messy trunk full of junk food. He grabbed a box of Little Debbie Swiss cake rolls, slapped the trunk shut and got back in his squad car. Janet watched him unwrap and stuff an entire roll into his mouth before driving away. This scare got her blood racing, causing her high to burn off faster.

She was afraid to shut off the light because even when she wasn't tripping she could get spooked in the dark. Back down on the mattress she flipped through the magazine again. She found a picture on the amateur page that didn't look staged and flooded with light like the rest of the pictures. And the couple's faces were blurred. The names seemed more believable. Under the picture of a man giving a thumbs-up to the camera while he appeared to be fully in the woman from behind was the caption "Joe H. takes Jackie A. for a ride in Fort Lauderdale, Florida." Janet imagined being Jackie A. while Joe H. was in the right hole, the one Janet was touching at that moment.

She'd never been to Florida but she imagined being in a man's fancy house that seemed to be near the water, not at all like the one she was in now. A house where Joe H. had a bar in a big living room where he made drinks and then served them to her next to his pool. She looked at Joe H.'s wristwatch. It looked like a nice gold one; he would probably have a ceiling fan in the bedroom and lots of pillows on his bed.

She felt a light twist of air blow over her. As she sighed, she got up to shut off the light to be with Joe H. On the way back she took off her jeans and underwear. The streetlamp lit the room enough for her not to be afraid to open her eyes now and again. She visualized Joe H.'s body with another face, but it kept reappearing as the magazine blur. The many cocks in the magazine were sliding in and out of her one after the other, mostly cut and with high and tight balls. When she came, Janet opened her eyes and the shadows of the tree's leaves shook on the ceiling above her bed. After a few minutes she went for another orgasm, but this time she just rocked her body from head to foot, taking deeper breaths.

During a sluggish try for another, she heard seagulls in the distance and liked the idea that anything could be true at that moment. Little by little she fell asleep while getting her mind to believe she was still in Bridgeport and she was going to wake up to her daughter Kimberly making her breakfast, then that she had made it to Coney Island and she was in a fancy Victorian mansion by the ocean, and then that she was going to wake up next to Joe H. in Florida and they were going to do it again in the morning.

Chapter 18

Splashes sounded out past the open bathroom door as Helen rinsed away work grime from her hands, arms and face. At the stove Cole supervised two pots: four bobbling hot dogs in boiling water and baked beans puffing out tiny hot sighs. Helen's work schedule changed every week. She explained to Cole, "Sometimes people screw up and the managers take it out on them. Make them work nights all week or days if they don't want to workdays." Cole worried her mother had done something wrong because she had just worked five nights in a row, but if her mother worked days that would keep her from being able to hang out with Vanessa, Toad and Puke.

Her mother talked as if Cole were listening. "Larry said that I may get to be a head cashier soon. My till comes out almost perfect every day." Something Toad said was still bothering Cole. At the corner store earlier that day Toad whispered, "Watch it with Vee. She's a freakin' maniac." Maybe he was just jealous because the girls were becoming friends.

A small piece of wet paper plate was on Cole's forkful of beans. She put it in her mouth and her tongue searched past the lukewarm beans to the mushy plate ball, nailing it behind her front teeth.

"You're quiet," Helen said in the way that she often asked a question, with a statement. Sometimes Cole answered her mother's not-questions, other times she let the impotent inquiries bounce off of her like Nerf darts.

Cole shrugged. Without her father there, her mother didn't seem like a mother anymore. Her mother didn't act any differently than she did while her father was alive. But without her father saying, "Bring your mother some ginger ale, her stomach's acting up again," or "Don't think your mother doesn't love you, she just never had a real family," Cole wasn't reminded that the woman that barely ever hugged her and looked worried to be alone with her was that person, "mother."

Cole had tried a few things in their new place to make things nicer, but Helen didn't say anything about the Garfield cartoon she had taped on the refrigerator or the clock she put on the windowsill. She wondered how her mother couldn't have said anything about their old owl clock whose eyes moved back and forth with each second.

This night, she wondered if her mother could see the golf ball-sized toy koala bear she clipped on the window shade tassel. The lazy night air swung it near Helen's shoulder. Cole got the toy from the drawer with the Mexican earthquake newspaper clippings. In fourth grade she learned that koala bears and kangaroos were from Australia but now she wondered if there were some in Mexico too. They had learned about Egypt, Australia, France but never Mexico. Her new school might teach them about Mexico. Maybe she could impress her new teachers with what she already knew about Mexico City and the earthquake.

Her mother continued to go on about her job and about a woman named Penny who smokes at the loading dock when she is supposed to be looking for abandoned shopping carts. "She doesn't come back not reeking. We all can tell."

Where Cole had cut her hot dogs was now a crescent shape in the plate. She used a fork tine to carve out two circles above it to complete a drawing of a face.

"Funny," Helen said. "Tonight was probably boring for you."

"I watched shows," she said as she swirled a nose through the plate.

"That's it? You didn't go no place, did you?" Helen asked directly this time.

Cole shook her head. She stretched across the table to turn on the small square portable television that was on the table where Red would have sat. It blinked on as if it were waking up from a nap. A newscaster announced that the Statue of Liberty was opening on the Fourth of July after being closed for repairs. When Cole heard they were going to have the concert and fireworks on TV, she pointed at the screen and said, "I'm going to tape it. I'm going to tape it." She repeated herself when she got excited.

Tired from work, Helen half-smiled and let out something between a "yeah" and "good," "Yah-guh." Whenever either of them spoke, the room seemed to cover the sound with a hollowing shroud. This is how voices not part of a genuine conversation vibrate against being needless or unheard.

Disappointed that Helen didn't notice the koala bear, Cole focused on everything the newscasters said. She slowly repeated the name of the lady tennis player who they said just won a big match, "Mar-teen-ah Nav-ruh-till-o-vah."

Cole remarked on everything that came on. During the commercials she sang along with the animated raisins that danced to "I Heard it Through the Grapevine."

A QE commercial came on. Cole crossed her arms and leaned back in her chair.

Helen closed her eyes but kept facing the television. They froze in those positions as a montage showed people using computers, opening up refrigerators, getting on trains, listening to boom boxes. It ended with a beaming woman getting a sonogram on her pregnant belly.

Helen opened her eyes again once the news came back on. A special report explained how the government was going to spend millions of dollars for research about drugs for AIDS. When they showed images of Rock Hudson, she pouted a little and said, "So sad." They had switched roles. Cole sat silently while Helen continued to make comments. When the screen filled with people standing silently in the street with pictures of the dead AIDS victims and holding candles, Helen said, "Lots of young people. Just awful. "

The report ended with a clip of Elizabeth Taylor making a speech about fighting against AIDS. Helen pointed at the screen and said, "How many cans of hairspray do you think…." She stopped. Cole's chin was tucked into her chest and she was crying.

Helen looked back at the television with an accusatory glare. She then searched Cole's face as if somehow she couldn't tell what brought on the tears.

When Cole cried as a baby, Red was the one that would go to her. She rubbed her eyes and took a deep sigh.

Cole said, "It's okay." She tried to smile but it made it look like she was in physical pain.

Helen stood up, turned and bent over Cole to give her a hug. Cole's shoulders tensed. She spoke into Helen's collarbone, "It's really fine. I just got sad about all those people dying. And then I thought that at least Dad didn't die of AIDS. And then I...." Cole wriggled out of Helen's hug. She got up, shut off the television and threw the paper plates into the garbage.

Through a yawn, Helen said, "We'll go to the mall tomorrow morning. We'll get some of your cassette tapes at Sears. I need shoes too. My dogs are barking." Helen kicked her foot out in synch with a few "woofs." Her attempts at humor usually fell flat since they were all at once not expected yet predictable.

Cole mustered a reassuring facade by raising her eyebrows and nodding. She asked, "Can we go to Womrath's to get a birthday card for Grampa?"

"Really? It's his birthday? When is it?"

"No. It's not. But I want to cheer him up," Cole said.

Helen went into her bedroom and changed into her nightgown. Sitting at the kitchen window, Cole looked out over their neighbors' rooftops at clouds tinged with pinks and reds. Her father used to tell her that this happened when God was making cotton candy.

After the light drained out of the sky Cole checked in on her mother. Helen's sleeping feet were stacked on their sides. The koala bear drunkenly thudded against the window frame in time with the breeze. Cole shut the window, went into her room and closed the door.

As she listened to her radio at a low volume, Cole flipped through the clippings and pictures that Vlad let her take home. She lay on her side and propped her head up with her hand. Mixed in with articles about P.T. Barnum, his houses, his museum, his political life, were clippings about fires. When her hand started to tingle from the weight of her head she turned onto her stomach but the pictures were so close she couldn't focus. With her head turned to the side on her pillow, she propped up pictures one by one.

Ever since she could remember, Cole loved listening to the radio. Some songs didn't make sense but those were some of her favorites. Deep down, she knew those were about love and things she didn't know about yet. Peter Gabriel's *Sledgehammer* came on the radio making it hard to concentrate. She leaned over and twisted the tuner knob until she landed on a station playing *Never as Good as the First Time*. Images from music videos often played in her head while the radio played. This video made no sense. Sade rode a galloping horse but it didn't match the mellow beat. When Sade's first videos came out, Cole found it odd how she seemed glued in place like a ballerina in a jewelry box. But then what came out of her red lipsticked mouth was as hypnotizing as the waves at Seaside Park.

Cole continued to study each photograph and tried to imagine what the people's voices sounded like when they were alive. On a photograph of Barnum with Tom Thumb someone had drawn on the mini-man a moustache, beard and a pointy hat. Photographs from many time periods were all together like different decks of cards shuffled together. She barely recognized her grampa in his wedding picture. He had dark hair and was dressed in a tuxedo. Cole had only met his wife, her grandmother, a few times. Whenever she saw her in pictures she was like a stranger in a magazine rather than someone in her family. The black-and-white photos seemed washed out with a bright light. It had been touched up with some sort of red ink for their lips and cheeks, making their white skin look ghostly.

Dozing in and out, Cole focused on a picture of her father and his sister Vera, who they said died in a fire when she was only eight years old. In it, Red hugged Vera from the side with both his arms. She smiled up at him as he looked at the camera.

Some people at her father's funeral said that he was up in heaven with his sister now. It made Cole feel a tiny bit better thinking that he was with this little girl in the picture, who had to wait so long to see him again.

Chapter 19

The Watchtower was empty when Janet woke up in the afternoon. Fully rested, she was taking the day moment by moment. Most of the time she felt like time was a linebacker slamming into her even though she wasn't anywhere near a football field. Always late or early, or too high to know where to be, she needed the structure Animal's operation offered.

After taking a shower, she set up her folding table close to the Black Sabbath. This became her table the way things often became Janet's. She started by wanting something, then needing it, and then she possessed it. Instinctually, she ruined things so no one else wanted it. Sometimes these were things no one wanted or would become hers anyhow. The table was taken into such custody while she painted "JANET" in all capital letters with neon yellow nail polish she had in her purse. The color, "Keep Back," clashed with the "Cinnamon Lollipop" she used to outline each letter.

When Keith showed up Janet had just pressed the power button on the stereo and Journey played on the radio.

He asked, "You playing more of that skinny white boy music?" He walked over to her table and asked, "You making food on that table, girl? Those colors make a man lose his appetite."

"You don't know shit. It's art. It's an original."

"That's unsanitary art, then. Look," Keith pointed. "Some of your hair is stuck in that gunk."

"Hell then. Don't eat. I don't care," she said.

"Cheese and rice," Keith sighed.

"What the hell is up with your cheese and rice shit?" she asked.

He explained to Janet that not using the Lord's name in vain was an example of his decent West Indian upbringing. Janet squinted at him to see if he was kidding. He wasn't.

After he sat back at his table, she shoved a bowl of potato salad into his chest. "But you got to try this. It's good shit. Me and the hag made it." She had just brought it up from what everyone called "Wilda's lab" due to some odd meals that made their way upstairs. Animal loved the food Wilda cooked but Keith said that even the names of the dishes sounded inedible: Tuna Succotash Salad, Hawaiian Fish Loaf, Lima Bean and Ham Casserole.

Janet straddled a folding chair backwards across from Keith. "Why don't any chicks come around here?"

"No one knows we're here," Keith said as he pointed a fork toward the bowl and nodded his approval. "I walk here, the other guys park over a bunch of blocks and we don't tell anyone a thing. The only girl he lets around is my little cousin Mia. She's into all this rock and roll thing. So when we chill out, she comes over sometimes. She's just fifteen, so I tell my cousin we just go to the park."

"Hold on. How many cousins you got?"

Keith laughed, "We got hundreds of cousins white people don't got. Everybody's cousins. Get with the program, girl."

Self-conscious about not knowing much about Black world things, she changed the subject. "Animal told me I could park out front," Janet bragged, stretching her chin out, smiling.

"You're a chick. You're a *white* chick. Plus, you don't know anyone, so it's not like the pigs would think they know something when they see you."

"More?" Janet asked with her hand out to take his now-empty bowl.

"Yeah, thanks," he bowed his head. "You know what? A little sweet pickle relish would make that perfect."

"Okay, Julia Child," Janet smirked.

"Try it," he said. "Maddie ended up liking it that way. She used to sneak it in after Wilda left it in the fridge."

"Yeah. I think the hag hates my guts enough already. All I need is to fuck with her potato salad shit with your genius relish thing." Janet shook her hair into her eyes and her voice got higher, "Wow. I haven't seen Maddie in forever."

Keith shook his head, making a sour lemon face, "Oh, you know that stuck up girl?"

"Yeah, we all kind of grew up together. Animal and me go way back," Janet bragged. "His mom helped me a lot when I had my baby. I wish Ginny were around now to see me get her back."

Keith nodded, "Yeah. Animal says she was a great lady. How she raised two people like that? One night and one day?"

"That wasn't her fault. Maddie was always a bitch to get what she wanted. What happened with her? I thought she lived here too," Janet said.

"Well Maddie, now. She moved out after she went off dating a cop. Dan. She met him when she got locked out of her car outside the post office. The last time she came by with food, she told Animal that Dan proposed to her. They hugged and cried. Then she stop visiting, bringing food, getting high with the guys." He added, "The old lady asks me every other day when Maddie coming back. I think Maddie and Animal the only people that lady likes."

Keith shook his head and said, "I miss Maddie's food though."

"She doesn't come see Animal anymore?"

Keith lightly pinched Janet's chin and moved her head from side to side, and said "Open them eyes, girl. Look."

Janet pushed his hand away, "Okay. I get it. But isn't blood thicker than water? All that happy horse shit?"

"You know what I say? Jerk sauce is thicker than blood. Aha! Right? So that person who feed you, who there with you every day? Ah ha! They your family now." Keith pointed at Janet and winked as he got up and put the empty bowl in a plastic yellow bucket by the stairs. This was their system for dirty dishes waiting to be taken down to the kitchen sink.

Janet's throat tightened. She chewed her thumbnail as she stomped to her room and slammed the door. Animal did treat her more like a sister than a possible fuck. Now she knew why. She had walked right into Maddie's empty shoes. He wouldn't be back for another day or two. Until then, she needed to make a plan. Either she would seduce him or get something else from him. To serve as Animal's stand-in sister wasn't her thing. Whether he knew he did or not, according to Janet's logic, he fucked her over.

The rest of the day she smoked weed nonstop and wrote Kimberly a letter that ended up being a decree about trust. She ended it, "When we finally reunite I promise to never fuck you over. I know you can't swear around kids but for you to know how serious this is I need to say fuck. You won't ever be anything but my sweet baby. Don't let anyone tell you anything else. We're blood. We are fucking blood. I love you. Making enough money to take you back and we are going to have a nice life. I am going to put some money in this for you too. I just came up with some extra today and want you to have it. Love from your only real MOTHER."

Before writing the letter to Kimberly she stole four twenties from Animal's room. When they got high on his bed, she saw cash sticking out of a bulging record jacket. She was about to tease the die-hard rock-and-roller for having Marvin Gaye's *What's Going On* album but stopped herself. Only two years ago Marvin was shot dead by his own father and deserved some respect, and she also didn't want Animal to know that she saw the money.

When she pulled the bills out from the album it was as if Marvin watched her hand take the cash. She quickly turned it over in order to stop feeling guilty from his look of disappointment. But he faced the same direction on the album's back and had a depressing disheartened expression, despite wearing a gold colored shirt and tie under a shiny black coat. For a moment, it felt like she was taking the money from Marvin Gaye, a man who couldn't bear to lose anything more. Then her anger toward Animal resurfaced. The sisterly bullshit he laid on her inspired her to take even more than she planned. Undoubtedly, he would have no idea that she took it. It seemed that he never took the time to count or organize the tens and twenties he indiscriminately shoved in there over time.

After writing "MOTHER" in all capital letters and underlining it twice, Janet tore her three-page trust manifesto from the notebook she bought for only fifty cents from the CVS clearance table. After several letters to Kimberly there were only a few pages left. She folded the two twenties in the middle of the spiral-frayed pages and tucked it all into the notebook. On its cover, the brown and white cartoon beagle wore headphones under the words, "Sound hound!" His droopy brown eyes looked bored as he listened to a Walkman. The longer she took in his disinterested expression the more she thought that the beagle wanted her to know something. "What the hell do *you* want? A goddamn medal for being cute or something?" she sneered at the dog. She flipped the notebook over to break their eye contact.

Chapter 20

When Animal came back, he backed up his white panel van as close to the house as he could. Inside the van, Animal and Janet pulled on ropes tied around a washing machine-sized hunk of something covered in a blue tarp. Wilda rushed onto the porch waving a Charleston Chew like a cop's baton. She screamed, "What the hell is it this time?"

"It's just part of an engine I'm gonna work on," Animal winked at Janet.

"It's just another goddamn piece of junk you're bringing in the house," Wilda yelled over her shoulder and slammed the front door.

"You going to let her talk about you that way?" Animal teased Janet.

Janet wasn't as strong as Animal but she knew how to use leverage to move things. "Sure. Because I'm not the fat fucker that's going to have a heart attack and die lugging this thing down to this cellar," she said as she repositioned the rope.

"They said it's 500 pounds, but it feels like a fucking whale," Animal grunted.

"That's why you're staying at the top as a counterweight," Janet jibed.

They dropped the colossal contraption on a moving dolly to haul the machine to the back of the house through the narrow alleyway between Wilda's and the nosy neighbor's houses. Animal pulled the massive machine as Janet pushed it. Once they heaved it into the back door, they had to get it down the cellar stairs. Animal leaned back as he slowly lowered the machine by the ropes one by one as Janet guided it down the stairs. Scared that it could tumble and smash, the pair worked quietly, outside of pants and groans.

At the bottom Janet placed it on old sections of carpet. They then pulled it by the carpets into a spot a couple of feet from the stairs.

Back up in the Watchtower, Animal told the guys to take the next few days off. They had just worked nonstop breaking down a giant load of jewelry, "separating the stones from the bones," as Animal called it. They were paid extra for those days since it was a weekend. Pushing through Saturday and Sunday always meant he didn't have to worry about nosy neighbors or cops. Everyone was too focused on getting laid, drunk or high to care about the pickups and drop-offs coming and going from the house every few hours.

Annoyed that Animal insisted that she hid during the pickups, she asked, "What the fuck? Why do they have to be here every five minutes? Does he think you're going to skip town with all his loot or something?"

"Naw. They just know that if they drop it all off at once some dick could just come in and clean us out," Animal said. "He keeps it moving. Just keep low. You know," he winked.

Janet told Animal that the few days of quiet would give her the mental break she needed to figure out how to use the press. It came with two cases of ready-to-print blank sheets. A stack of sheets of fifty-dollar bills caught Janet's eye but Animal made her promise not to use them. They were rejects and could uncover the whole operation. Janet convinced Animal that she'd use them only as a guide for practice. On top of the stack were instructions on how to prepare the paper. Written on the last few pages left on a yellow legal pad, the previous press owner wrote out what cotton paper to buy, how to treat it with RIT dye and iron it between pieces of parchment paper.

A few days later, Janet hadn't mastered the printing. She grabbed about fifty blank sheets and stuck them in the middle of the stack of the fifties they weren't supposed to use. She cut them with an X-Acto knife and stashed the stack of money at the bottom of a box of Kotex in her bedroom closet.

No one knew about the printing press but Janet, Animal and the guys that sold it to him. Animal said that his boss would probably want a cut or find some way to get something out of it. So, for now they had to keep it under lock and key in the basement. Brainstorming about how to explain Janet's new project to the guys, they decided to say she was working on some new drugs and she had to concentrate and use the huge sink in the basement.

Janet filled some glasses with blue and green food coloring and water and put them on a table by the bottom of the stairs. When the guys snooped down to the cellar, she lit a few matches to make it smell like she had just cooked something up. The press stayed concealed behind two hanging sheets, next to a folding beach lounge chair where she popped pills to stay up all hours to write out directions for the press. As Janet wrote letters to her daughter and scribbled directions for the printing press, the act of writing didn't seem to help her realize *how* she could be Kimberly's mother or finally print the money, but *if*. The shame and frustration made her stay in the basement.

Instead of going to an upstairs bathroom Janet peed in the sink. After a few weeks everyone's curiosity waned, and the basement's scent was a mixture of piss and ink. She thought running dish washing liquid down the drain would mask the piss smell but it didn't.

Janet used black ink for test runs. The stains on her hands and forearms brought back memories of when her parents moved the family from New Haven to Bridgeport. She had carefully undressed Barbie and packed her doll-sized pink and white-checkered dress and a red bathing suit in a miniature suitcase. Janet then wrapped her choice Barbie in newspaper and put her in the box her father had labeled "Janet's Planet." A few weeks later Janet unwrapped Barbie to find the newspaper print had rubbed off onto her body as if she were made of Silly Putty.

Now, sitting on the beach chair, she licked her thumb and used her spit to try to rub the ink off of an arm. Janet remembered how she didn't want her mother to scrub the Barbie. She liked the way the bits of advertisements and articles were backwards on Barbie's skin and didn't want to put any clothes on her again. It disturbed her mother but Janet insisted that Barbie wanted to show off "her new tattoos."

When she heard Animal lumber down the steps, Janet jumped out of the chair to grab her machine notes.

Animal walked through the hanging sheets holding a beer can. As he inspected the press now covered in ink smears, Janet asked, "Remember Barbie?"

"Who?"

"Barbie!"

"I don't know any Barbies."

"Sure you do! Everyone used to have one. Even my cousin Robbie had one. He loved her! Now that I think about it he was either a fruitcake or he jerked off on her. I swear."

"Barbie dolls? Of course I know what a Barbie is. I thought you meant a real broad named Barbie. What about them?"

"Just thinking."

Animal finished the beer and tossed the can onto a pile in the corner that Janet had amassed. He asked, "Ever notice you're always 'just thinking?'"

"Ever notice you're never thinking?" Janet retorted.

"Don't forget. I'm the one that got us that press."

"Well, I'll wait to call you Boy Genius until we get some cash money flowing out of it."

"It stinks like piss down here, Janet," Animal said as he sniffed his way to the sink.

She turned the faucet on and squirted dishwashing soap all over her arms. She made a big show of trying to scrub the ink off her arms and hands.

Animal went back to the press. "Nothing yet? I thought you said you're good with machines?"

"I am. But this thing is old. Why don't we just cut up the sheets they gave you?" She pulled at Animal's t-shirt to dry off her arms and hands.

He pushed her away and shook his head, "They told me they'd cut my nuts off if I did. That's why."

"Well, they'd have to find them first."

"Funny."

"You could say someone stole them." Janet hoped that flapping her arms around to dry them would distract Animal enough to change the subject.

"No way."

"You could even tell them it was me. I'll be long gone…."

"No. Janet. Chill out. You got that crap on your face. Are you rubbing that shit on you like lotion?"

Janet laughed, "Yeah. Instead of that dildo president I'll smash *my* face onto the money."

"Don't trash talk Ulysses S. Grant," he chided.

"You're such a dork," Janet said as she kicked at her pile of beer cans and threw one at Animal.

Wilda yelled down the cellar steps, "What the hell is going on down there? Cut it out! I'm not trying to watch Cagney and Lacey or anything, you idiots!"

"See? Even that old bitch thinks you're a dumbass."

"You know what? What we're missing is tunes. She doesn't hear shit if I got the radio on."

Janet turned on a Radio Shack radio that she had chained and locked to a water pipe.

"Why you never trust anyone?" Animal asked.

"Do you?"

"Yeah. Sometimes. You have to."

"Well, I don't," she said.

"You don't *have* to or you just don't?"

"You go to community college or something?"

Animal laughed. "See? You can't talk to you."

"I don't trust anyone. You know why not?"

"Why?"

"I said 'why *not*'!"

"Hey, now who sounds like a college asshole?"

"Fuck you, Animal." Janet turned away and started to cry.

Animal tried to comfort her, "Hey, Jan. I'm just fucking around. I don't think you're an asshole."

Janet's head shook forward a couple of times.

"Really. Seriously. Jan. Don't…." His chubby palm rubbed a circle in the middle of her back.

She sniffled and softly said, "You know, I just didn't think you…."

She turned, whipped her hair around and plunged her face toward Animal's. With red eyes and a wild smile, she shouted, "You *would* fall for that! Sucker!"

Animal pushed her shoulder and said, "You're a fucking freak!"

She laughed as she headed up the stairs and said over her shoulder, "But I'm going to make us rich! You know you love me!" Animal followed her up the stairs and then locked the basement door.

Janet rushed up the other two flights of stairs to get to her room before Animal hefted up. She grabbed four fifties out of the Kotex box to get an oil change and fill up the gas tank. Tim never took care of his cars and the engine seemed to shake a little. She didn't want the car to be useless when the time came for her to get her little girl back. The car needed tires too, but she didn't want to use too many of the bills in one place.

The day before, Keith had told her to ask for Angelo at Buy-Rite, a car repair place on Cropsey Avenue near Neptune. It hadn't taken long for Janet to feel at home in Coney Island. She fit in with the guys in the Watchtower but then wandered around Astroland, getting lost in the shadowy crowds. She felt invisible as she watched shirtless boys shouting over the barkers to get the attention of girls sipping sodas through straws and pulling at their cotton candy fluffs.

Just as Janet headed back out of the Watchtower, Animal got to the top of the stairs. Janet gave him a peck on his bearded ruddy cheek as she slinked past him and teased, "I was hot and ready for you, but your fat ass took too long getting up here."

A few steps down, Janet stopped and turned, "Hey! If you dropped some of your blubber and shaved, you'd be like a cute Meatloaf."

"Well, if you didn't piss in sinks and pull so many all-nighters, you'd look like Valerie Bertinelli, not smell like her cunt!"

Animal's raspy chuckle disappeared as he walked into the Watchtower. Janet cackled loudly as she ran down the steps. As she got into the car, she thought if her brother David hadn't killed himself, they would have joked around like she did with Animal. She once heard her mother tell their neighbor, "I think a part of Janet died along with him."

But David's suicide wasn't just a fatality to Janet, it was a declaration. He gave the world what it always wanted from him, a dowsed gay flame. After the funeral, she promised herself that she would live for both of them. Sometimes she made herself bigger to fill the void and other times she'd disappear into getting high enough to feel close to him, just short of dying.

Chapter 21

Cole and Puke walked along the fence that surrounded a massive pile of bricks that used to be a factory.

"They look like tombstones," Cole said as she pointed at the few surviving walls in the rambling heap's center. "You just need some flowers there and it's just like when they buried my dad."

"Why did they put bricks all over him?" Puke asked.

"No. He had dirt. It's a big bump in the ground like that though. It takes a long time for it to settle down and for grass to grow over it. The bump is almost flat now."

"Oh," Puke sighed. After scratching his leg again, he stretched his fingers out to drag them across the diamond-shaped wire fence. His fingers vibrated so fast they seemed almost to disappear.

She wanted to do the same with her fingers but he was in her way. "Go!" Cole barked at him when he slowed down.

Walking behind Puke, Cole looked down at his calves. "Mosquitoes sure love you."

"Yeah, we slept out in the backyard. I got all bit up."

"Outside?"

"My mom told us to go camping. We used some jump ropes and some sheets for a couple of tents."

"Your mom sure doesn't like you being in the house. Mine never wants me to leave."

"Vanessa says it's better to just be away from my mom anyway. We hate being there with her getting high with that big fat pig, Jack."

"That guy in that blue car that day? That's Jack, right?"

"Yeah."

"He's not fat."

"Vanessa calls him a big fat pig 'cause she says he feels like one when he's all over her."

"Well, I guess he's tall, too." Cole didn't want to know any more.

"Look! Don't they look real?" Puke pointed at three charred mannequins that someone had burned inside the fence in the middle of a circle of bricks. Parts of the factory were just piles of bricks while others still looked like buildings.

"Wow. They do," Cole was afraid for a moment that the stiff legs pointing out of the charred rubble were real dead bodies.

"Vanessa threw a pile of shit at me through the fence once," Puke giggled.

"Why you laughing?"

"That she did that. It was gross but kind of funny too," he said.

Cole thought that maybe he had brain problems. She didn't know what a real retarded person was like but Puke seemed like what she thought they'd be like. This was something she would have asked her father.

"Hey. There are a couple of good ones," she pointed at two empty beer cans that had not yet been flattened or dented.

Puke put the middle of his sneaker down across the can and then did the same with his other foot. Squished into them just right, he walked as they hugged his shoes.

"My feet are too big for that," Cole said.

"Well you're almost a grownup now," Puke said.

"I guess so, right?" she said and by saying it she felt like part of her just oddly matured. Cole felt a warm pressure in her chest. With brand-new confidence she picked up an empty glass vodka flask from the curb and hurled it over the fence. It smashed on the other side. When she tried to see where the broken pieces ended up, she couldn't distinguish her bottle from the other scattered shards and other jagged bottlenecks with their caps.

"Why you alone today?" Cole asked as they checked out the glass and a shopping cart full of bricks and dirt with weeds growing out in a few directions.

"Vanessa and Ritchie had to go see their dad," he clacked the can-shoes louder.

"Where does he live?" Cole shouted.

"In jail," he said.

She felt him look at her for a response. Cole looked down.

Bloody smears made tiny garlands around his bite-covered calves. She said, "You should put some stuff on those."

"Vanessa told me to spit on them. It made them feel a little better." He used the toes of his sneakers to pry the cans off his shoes and kicked them into the street.

Cole was ready to go home. She was still tired from listening to the radio late into the night. And her mother was probably worried. No kids ever came over to their apartment while Helen was home and then Puke showed up to ask for her to come out and play. Helen told him to come back in about an hour so that they could eat lunch first, but part of the reason was so that she could grill Cole why the boy knew her name.

As soon as he left, Cole started to make bologna and cheese sandwiches with just mustard. She liked them more with mayonnaise and tomato but that would take longer and the tomatoes they bought that week tasted like someone stole the taste from them but somehow left them in the package. . They looked like tomatoes but they felt more like sponges in her mouth.

After convincing Helen that she had talked to Puke only a couple of times on her way to Vladimir's, Cole was set free but had to come back before dark. When Helen asked why his name was Puke, Cole answered, "I don't know. I think he said his parents are German or something." Helen let out a light chuckle. Cole smiled and nodded her head as if she knew something but was sure she didn't know what her mother was thinking.

"My mom said to be home sometime around now." It wasn't even close to sundown yet but Cole wanted to go home.

"What time did she say?" he asked.

"We don't have watches anyway," she answered.

"Well if you don't know what time it is then how do you know it's time to go home?"

Maybe he asked Vanessa questions like this all day, making her want to whack him and throw crap at him. Cole thought it would feel good to say, "What woke you up? Did dawn finally rise over marble head?" That was a joke her father used a few times with her but not in the way she would like to say it to Puke.

He tilted his head and licked his flakey chapped lips, throwing his hands in the air and saying, "I can't go back in. They locked it."

"Locked your house?"

"Yeah. They might not get back tonight either."

"Why did they do that?"

"They never let me go to the jail with them. Vanessa says their dad don't know about me."

"But why don't they let you go in your house?"

"They say I can't be trusted. And when they called Gramma up she hung up on Mom, so I can't stay with her either. She says she's a bitch."

Cole wondered if his mother said his grandmother was a bitch or the other way around. She was afraid to bring him to her apartment because he would probably talk too much and reveal everything.

Puke kept walking even though she stopped. The extra distance helped her see him as someone else might. His thick brown hair stuck up in several directions, and his t-shirt was jaggedly cut along the bottom and didn't reach his pants in the back where she could see that his legs weren't the only place the mosquitoes had feasted. When he wasn't doing something with his hands he held them in fists close to his thighs. He stopped at the base of a telephone pole and bent over. Without moving his head, he waved his arm back at Cole. "Come here! Come here!" Despite his arm beckoning faster she walked over at her normal pace.

It was a dead bird with its wings out as if in flight but its neck was twisted back as if it were about to talk to them. He asked, "What kind of bird is it?"

She knew this bird looked smaller than a robin but bigger than a chickadee but she lied, "It's a chickadee."

"A chickadee, huh?"

"Yeah."

"What do you think happened?"

"It probably just flew into this pole and fell here."

"Do we have to bury it?"

"No. We only bury pets. But my grandfather told me how his grandfather used to bury circus animals around here. He says that we walk on top of hundreds of dead things every day. Especially at Went Field"

"Really? What happens when we pee on them? I peed there. So did Ritchie."

"I don't think they care. They're dead."

"Do you think your father cares what you do to his grave? He's dead too."

Cole ignored his question and looked closer at the bird. From its smooth head down past its wings, it was all dark gray. But his bottom half was pure white. It looked as if he had sat in a bowl of milk.

Puke looked up at Cole and clasped his hands together. "Let's have a funeral for him."

"Let's not and say we did." Vanessa said this whenever she didn't like an idea so Cole tried it.

"Please? I've never seen a funeral before and you know what to do. You can be the priest person and we can record it on your tape machine." He pulled her arm in sync with his voice, "Please, please, please?"

"You'll have to get some flowers or something," she said.

Puke's sneakers slipped over the dirt as he made a quick pivot and ran toward a patch of weeds near the fence. He pulled up anything that looked more interesting than a blade of grass but none of them were flowers. He held up a plastic green ring decorated with a tiny frog head as he called out, "A ring! It must be out of those toy machines at Pathmark. It probably came in one of those plastic bubbles. I choked on one of those once." He picked up a small branch that still had leaves attached and shoved it in his back pocket.

Cole knelt in front of the bird. She was afraid to touch it, even with the stick she picked up to tuck in its wings. It looked asleep. She never thought about birds having eyelids but this one did. That must mean they blinked. Maybe this one blinked at the wrong time and ran into the pole.

She looked back at Puke who was picking things up as if he were on one of those game shows where people have to choose items but not go over a certain price. His arms full, he balanced the load to pick up a six-pack plastic ring. He let it drop when he saw something better. Cole turned back to her task.

When she pushed the bird's wing, its entire stiff body shifted in the dirt. Then she pushed at one leg and it didn't bend. Had her father been this stiff? Maybe nothing was left inside to make him bend, move or even blink.

Puke dropped all his funeral treasures behind Cole and then carried things over to the bird a little at a time. "What do we say? Don't we cry?"

"Yeah. Some people cry."

"Did a lot of people cry when your dad died?"

"I don't know. I guess. My mother did."

"Did you?"

Cole arranged some weeds over the bird. She tried not to tear up. After she bit her lip hard, she said, "Of course I cried. Everyone cries when their parents die."

"I don't know if my mom will cry when her mom dies." He put the ring on the bird's head.

"Maybe not. But if someone's parents are nice to them then," Cole stopped. "Let's just do this."

"Put the machine on!" Puke pointed at the recorder that was on the ground next to Cole.

"Okay. But you have to stay quiet for it to work. We can't talk at the same time." Cole liked knowing details about what made a tape sound best. "Come here! Hold this part up to my face. That's where the microphone is."

"That's a microphone? It's just some holes!"

"Shush! I'm going to turn it on."

Cole pushed the record and play buttons together. "We welcome everyone to this dead bird funeral. We are here at the telephone pole where he died in a blink of an eye. But God's eye never blinks. Or closes. It's always watching us."

Puke took one hand off the recorder to scratch his leg. He held up the weight with his one rubbery arm balancing it near Cole's face as she continued.

"We don't know where this bird's family is but we are sure they are crying. We don't know about birds but they aren't mean like people and they aren't rich or poor. They don't litter." Cole thought about it. Maybe they do litter. "If they litter, it's only because they don't know how to throw away garbage."

She tried to remember what was said at her father's funeral but the only thing that came to mind was something about God being a shepherd. "Just like there are sheep in the pasture there are birds in the sky over the pasture. And then God is higher above that so that no one can see above him. This bird is with God now. May he rest in peace."

During her father's funeral, the priest talked about the Space Shuttle explosion. He named each astronaut and then said, "May he rest in peace." Except for Christa McAuliffe, when he said, "May she rest in eternal peace." He said people all over the world were sad and that their deaths, along with the loss of Red, showed people that they shouldn't take life for granted or be in conflict with God.

Tired of standing and holding the recorder Puke sat on the ground cross-legged and held the machine up with one hand above his head. Cole remembered something about borrowing. "Like a library book, we only borrow life from God for a while and we have to give it back when it expires." This isn't what the priest said, but she thought it sounded even better.

"Ashes to ashes, dust to dust," she continued. Puke twisted around to look at the bird again and started to cry. He wiped his runny nose on his shirt.

Cole tried to think of all the things people say when people die because she wanted to make Puke really break down. She figured the more things she could say the more likely he would react. "The bird is dead and gone. He's in a better place now. He would want us to be strong and not stop living. He's in God's hands now. " She was right. Puke put the recorder on the ground and put his face in his hands to sob.

At first, she thought it was cruel to make Puke cry harder. But the tiny guilty pang didn't outweigh the warped gratification his grief gave her. "Look at those wings. They will never, ever fly again. Those eyes will never, ever, ever see again," Cole wanted to mention the beak but couldn't think of something fast enough. Puke cried louder.

Cole went on, "Just like when you die. You won't ever be able to walk again or eat pizza." Puke's favorite food was pizza and he rarely got to eat it, so Cole added it to her speech. It worked. He grunted and bared his teeth at her. She went in for the final swoop. "And your eyes will never see your mother again. Forever and ever."

Still sitting cross-legged, Puke threw himself to one side into the dirt, and put his head on his arm. Cole stopped talking and pulled the recorder close to the bird. She pulled the branch Puke had gathered out of his back pocket. Holding it over the bird, she shook the leaves.

Puke sat up and then crawled over to the bird. Tears ran down his face as he whispered, "Don't feel bad for me. I just never been to a funeral or anything before. Sorry you died, bird."

Cole moved her arm to stop him from getting closer to the bird but then she stopped. He delicately plucked the ring from the bird's head and replaced it with his puckered lips. His mouth stayed in the same place while his head shook as he cried. When he finished the kiss he laid his head sideways on the ground to gaze at the bird.

His arms and hands were dirty from the street's grime and collecting the funeral items. Tears squiggled clean streaks that made his skin look as if there were maps of rivers on them. Covered in a thin layer of soilish dust his mosquito bites appeared to be dulled into healing. When Cole held the branch again and shook it over the bird, the recorder made a soft squealing sound and shut off.

Puke didn't move but asked, "Why did the machine stop?"

"Because that's the end of the tape," Cole said.

"Do you think we should cover him with the other stuff now?"

"The funeral's over. We should just leave him alone now."

Puke's voice got higher as he whined, "But we got to bury him somehow. We don't just leave him here now. Right?"

"There aren't any rules," Cole said.

Puke pushed himself up and got to his feet. He stood above Cole with his hands on his hips. "Yes there are. We gave him a funeral so now he gets to be buried."

"If you're going to have a nervous breakdown about it, put some rocks on him." Cole pointed at the bird.

Puke's small hands could only carry two or three rocks at a time. Cole realized again how young he was. His face usually seemed far older with his constantly furrowed brow, and he didn't laugh very often.

Cole said, "Maybe you'll be an undertaker when you grow up."

"What's that?"

"Someone who does all the stuff after someone dies. Like take the body and make it look nice. And they talk to…."

"Fuck you," Puke said.

"What?" Cole asked.

"That means that I'll be sad my whole entire life."

"We're all going to be sad our whole lives anyway," Cole said.

As the bird slowly disappeared under the rocks and bricks he stacked on it, Puke said, "Well, *I'm* not."

Chapter 22

Animal held up a gold bracelet that arrived that morning to be sorted. He shouted across the Watchtower, "Hey Janet, you want this for your daughter?"

"You think I want to send her some stolen piece of shit?" She pumped her middle finger at Animal. "What's wrong with you?"

Animal didn't want to argue since he thought it was a pretty piece of jewelry and that it was generous of him to offer her something.

She'd been in a rotten mood for a few days. Whenever they had a moment alone, she talked about the press, "What the fuck would the thing need a vacuum for, you think? Does it clean itself? It does make a massive mess of itself whenever I try to make it go."

Animal interrupted her, "You know, I'll get someone to come over and show...."

"You're not getting anyone. I can figure this fucker out," she insisted.

Animal paid one thousand dollars for the press but told Janet that he got it for free. She had lived with him for a short while but he already noted that she couldn't handle much pressure. She had a tendency both to take things too seriously and appear not to care at all, or worse yet, to sabotage herself. Any attempts he made to help her seemed to make her angry.

It was impossible for Animal to gauge if or when Janet was going to move out and finally go get her daughter. She said she wasn't going to leave until she made a stack of money with the press but he was aware that could never happen.

He joked, "Do you think you're going to move your daughter in here? She can have a job! How old is she again? Fourteen?"

"What kind of question is that? No! You are crazy if you think

I'll let her be involved with shit like this!"

"I was just kidding. Can't ya take a joke?"

"No I can't. It's not funny. Cut the shit. That's my kid, my daughter."

"Well, excuse me. You can joke about me dying of a damn heart attack, but I can't stir shit? You're rich, you know that?"

"You can say all you want about me and her when I'm long gone with her. I've been thinking maybe we'll move up to a country house in New Hampshire. You can carry a gun on your hip around there, you know. Live free or die."

"Since when do laws stop you from doing anything?"

"Well, Retardo Montalban, if you were listening, you'd know that I don't want my kid to grow up with this bullshit." She waved her arm, then swigged from a Jack Daniels bottle that was next to the bracelet Animal offered her. The dark circles under her eyes highlighted her pallid tone.

"You got to get out in the sun more, girly. That basement is doing shit for your tan." Animal tapped a finger on her face.

"What gives?" She pushed his arm away. "You haven't stopped riding me all morning! Who the hell do you think you are, my goddamn father? Go to hell," she stormed back into her room with the bottle.

Animal sighed. He shook his head and picked up the bracelet again. It was in primo condition. He tested himself. If he had a daughter, would he feel okay giving it to her? With an outstretched arm he pretended to hand it to a young girl with long dark hair like his, but without a beer belly, moustache or beard. She would take it from him and run her fingers over the tiny rubies in the middle of the heart shapes pressed into the gold. Then she would ask him to put it on her wrist.

Animal held the bracelet against his belly with his head down. He was less concerned about the morality of the jewelry now. Now he questioned if he would ever be a father, let alone the kind that gives his kid hot stuff.

In a car-key-rattling fury, Janet stomped out of her room and tossed the empty whiskey bottle into the garbage can. She pulled back her shoulders to thrust her breasts at Animal while she jabbed her forefinger into his chest. "When a grizzly bear fat fuck like you tells you that you look like dog shit you better do something pronto! *This* mole woman is getting some sun today. I'm getting the fuck out of here." Although Animal felt the urges to both slap and hug Janet, he froze throughout her drunken tirade.

Janet's sharp whiskey breath and her sweaty sour pong whirled into his nostrils. He locked eyes with her to find any good in the person he had let into his life. Animal believed in a good Janet as much as the bad Janet struggled to push him into faithlessness. Behind her vibrating eyeballs and spitting furor, she suffered from a compassion that he guessed came from being a self-detained hostage.

Chapter 23

The break room was full of the stock team during Helen's break. The only female was dressed like the men in heavy boots, work gloves and a leather box-cutter holster. She didn't sit in the metal folding chairs with the rest of them. Instead, she leaned against the wall near the door. The oldest and best-looking stocker just finished telling an animated story about his mailman getting attacked by his neighbor's pit bull when their manager came out from his closet-sized office. Upon seeing their strapping bald boss who everyone called "Mr. Clean," the men jumped a little.

He pointed at the woman. "See that, guys? Harriette's on her toes. What's going on here? Get the hell up now and back on that load," he said as he clapped to rouse the men. Helen acted transfixed by the receipt for the Dr. Pepper and peanut M&Ms she just bought.

The men's groans clattered around the cement block room. Their dangling key rings clanked on the chairs whose legs dragged out dull laments of their own. The short dirge was followed by shuffling feet and cutter blades clicking in and out. The last to leave, the storyteller, tapped the table next to Helen's soda, said, "See you later," and winked.

Helen's lips and cheeks defied her brain that told her not to smile. He strode out like a much younger man even though he had a slight limp. The clock above the door was five minutes fast but Georgene, one of the other cashiers, told her just to set her watch to it so the managers never fooled her into a shorter break. This thirty-minute break was more than half over. Five minutes were wasted by waiting in line for her snacks and then a customer insisted that she escort him to their lampshade section. Georgene had warned Helen to take off her apron during breaks so customers wouldn't stop her. But now that Helen finally had a job, she wanted to get raises and wanted to be a head cashier someday. At least that's what Gwen told her she should want. Helen twisted shut the half empty M&M bag and put it in the pocket of the apron she now wore from the time she left the house until getting back home, even on the bus.

Back at the front of the store Helen stood at her register waiting for a manager to use his key to turn it back on. Georgene rang up a man who looked comfortable in a suit and dress shoes buying spray-on deodorant, a package of Fruit of the Loom underwear and hemorrhoid suppositories. Helen thought about how she threw out all of Red's underwear while she packed for the move to Sheridan. They seemed like the only things no one else should have been able to wear or use.

As a foster child, underwear was one of the only things that the families insisted she take with her when she was sent to another home. They could always pass down dresses and socks, and once she arrived at a new family where they gave her someone else's toothbrush. The rules of underwear were even stricter than those of marriage. Underwear must be disposed of after its wearer dies, but people seem to expect a surviving spouse to find another person.

"Have a good night, ladies," the customer raised his eyebrows at Helen.

After the automatic door shut behind him, Georgene said, "Now, Helen, you know that man was interested. Why did you just stand there...like a ghost?"

Helen liked to hear Georgene talk; she made up words and she stopped and started at odd times as if she were waiting for someone to transcribe what she said.

"I did not," Helen said.

"He looked like he was an out-of-towner. No one in this city, wears a suit. And in...the summer," Georgene started to straighten up the candy shelves at Helen's register. She slipped one Snickers bar in her apron pocket and another in Helen's.

"Georgene!"

Georgene whispered, "Oh, shut up. You have the receipt, from your break to cover it, and besides, they are all, in the back with the police. They finally caught that girl, with...the giant-gantic coat. She had, ten bottles of cough mixture! Aren't you glad, you're…on the night shift?"

Helen thought about it. There were only a few customers in the store most nights but they usually were people that didn't want to be seen: nurses still in their blood-freckled uniforms just after their shifts, or bored teenagers. The girl with the big coat came in a night or two a week. She looked at the earrings until a manager came over and asked her if she needed help. She became known as, "Just-Looking Laura."

Something about the shoplifter made her think about the woman writing the letters to Cole. "Laura" seemed the same age as the girl would have been when she had Cole. It was hard not to think about it. The letters and the woman. She never revealed her name in the letters.

"Do you think he's ever going to turn on my register?" Helen asked.

"Nah! Go front some shelves."

Helen pretended to work while she shopped for shoes. The predictability of the store's music and the humming fluorescent lights comforted her. Since they put her on full-time hours Helen liked being at work more than home. She figured this was why Red worked long hours all those years. Even though Helen wanted to work when Cole started school, Red insisted that he would take on more shifts instead.

The clothing section was deserted, so she tried on a pair of brown shoes. They felt much better than her worn out Skippies but they were a style she would never wear. While she considered the shoes on her feet, an emotional tug pulled her deeper into herself.

The bright multi-colored beads sewn onto an otherwise simply styled shoe somehow made her think about how she never felt she ever really knew anyone. Even Red.

When Red proposed to her, she balked and said they hardly knew each other. He told her, "That's why people get married. We'll get to know each other because we'll have to." It didn't sound romantic at all but she didn't understand anything about love anyhow. No one she knew ever wanted more than to work, eat, live, maybe take a vacation on Cape Cod once in a while. She asked herself why songs and the movies made it seem like everyone had amazing feelings and interesting lives when really everyone is just tired and bored.

She put the shoes back on the wire rack and tied her Skippies back on. They felt flat and too loose as she walked to the bathroom. Sitting on the toilet with her pants on, she ate the Snickers bar, and then tore the wrapper into small enough pieces to flush.

Back at the register, Georgene said, "You missed them take out that girl. She smiled at me. And said...goodnight, like she does every time she leaves. Now that I looked at her, she looked high...on something. Never really gave it much thought before ... but she was probably high as a kite, every time she...came in here." Georgene looked around and threw a yellow bag of peanut M&Ms to Helen. "For the bus ride home."

Chapter 24

Janet liked the idea of shooting a gun again. Waiting for Animal, she thought about the New Haven hockey game she had gone to that past winter. During the first half she snorted coke with some guys she met after she slinked into the VIP section. One of them said, "So it looks like you like to party. What about you and the three of us party tonight?" She knew what "party" meant but she was into the heaviest part of her period. Flirting until he gave her money to go get some smokes, she then went to the bathroom, changed her tampon, took three extra ones from a basket full of them in the fancy VIP lady's room and left.

After watching a Phil Donahue episode about PMS, she carried a gun whenever she was menstruating. An expert on the show said that a woman's hormonal chemistry goes haywire during her period and Janet thought that she needed something to back up her period-induced attitude. Every twenty-something days she felt her brain turn into a knot of bare hot wires.

She had left the Coliseum by walking down the parking lot's spiral driveway. A car driving down swerved around her, almost hitting the curved cement wall. A woman yelled from the passenger's side window, "Read the sign! Pedestrians not allowed!"

Janet pulled Tim's gun out from her coat pocket, cocked the trigger and aimed at a back tire. With one eye shut and the other squinted over the gun and yelled, "I'm not a pedestrian, I'm a goddamn Mac truck, baby!" The bullet pierced the trunk.

She rushed through the cars on the next floor to get back into the Coliseum and shuffled out the front door with the boring people who left early to beat the traffic. The horny guy's cigarette money paid for the train back to Bridgeport. As she fell asleep cuddled next to Tim on his couch, the gun smoke lingered in her nostrils.

Now, at Animal's house, she recalled that scent when she sniffed an unfamiliar dark blue and white bandana. It was on one of the sorting tables but something made her suspicious. None of the guys ever wore bandanas and this one was just crumpled into a ball, smelling of gun smoke and whiskey. In the ashtray one cigarette butt was a different brand than all of the others too. She unpeeled the cigarette's filter and pulled apart the stained cotton plug, and sniffed it like she smelled everything.

A whiff told her a lot about things: the last time someone wore a pair of shoes, how many times someone had re-worn the same pair of jeans, the height of the man that made a pizza pie (she swore that short men made the best pizzas) and in this case, when a cigarette had been put out. It had been smoked there the night before, most likely when she went out to get Chinese takeout. She stuffed the bandana into an empty Pringles can and pushed it under the top layer of garbage in the trashcan.

She worried about who was there while she was gone but would have to keep it to herself. Animal left her in charge of the operation while he went to Trenton to get a new hot load of jewelry. He told her that he hoped to get a gun. Having loads of cash in the house, even if it was poorly made fake bills, made him nervous. It would make him feel safer about the money but having the weapon would give him a different kind of stress. She warned him, "You got to grow a set and get some guns. You're a sitting duck here. We all are."

The missing stereo was back in its usual spot. Keith returned with it a few days following its disappearance. It had stopped turning, so he brought it to his cousin's repair shop. When Janet asked him why he didn't tell anyone he took it, he asked her, "Why didn't *you* say that you spilled a bowl of cereal all up on it? Did you not see that half your Honeycombs went under the turntable, girl?"

She laughed and kissed Keith's cheek. "You know you love the fuck out of me though, right?"

"Sometimes. But you got problems."

Janet glared at him and shot back, "And you don't? We're both doing the same thing here, Mister I-don't-say-the-Lord's-name-in-vain."

"Yeah. We both in deep shit here. But when I leave here I do okay. My people. We get high. We get high better than you white people," Keith said.

Janet rolled her eyes and pretended to yawn, "Are you done?"

"Hey, I think you a great woman. You funny and nice. But when you get messed up, girl, you messed…*up*. You ever hear of A.A.?"

"Sure have. I probably made those bastards go for broke. I kept getting to one month, got the golden coin and then back to square one. Then again. I think I got a bunch of those fuckers. Too bad I couldn't trade them all in for a year medallion for time served."

"You want your daughter back right? You think she want a Mommy Dearest when you got to buy food and not the drugs?"

"Aw, Keith. You don't get me do you? I'm at my best on drugs," she said while she reached into the Black Sabbath for a beer can. The metal tab pushed down to open the can. "I kind of miss those old pull tabs on these cans. Like, right now. I would be able to throw it at you before doing this," Janet said as she guzzled the beer down in one take. She forced a burp and tossed the can at Keith's feet.

He shook his head and opened his mouth to say something but Janet stomped to her room and slammed the door. On his way out he picked up the can and threw it at her door.

Out the window, she watched him leave the house and walk up the street. Now, alone in the Watchtower, she went out to get another beer. She swished the beer around her mouth and then hummed while picking a record. Van Morrison was on the turntable but Janet thought he sounded like someone's creepy Irish uncle trying to be cool. Jimi Hendrix never got old.

A large flat mirror they used to cut drugs was next to the records. Janet held the mirror up like a book. "God damn," she whispered. She hadn't really taken in her appearance since getting to Coney Island. Propping the mirror on a shelf freed her hands to touch her face.

Her crow's feet looked deeper than they felt under her fingertips. When she had turned thirty on Easter she'd wanted to tell Tim about possibly finding her baby and her plan to get her back. She had planned on being the mother she couldn't be when she was eighteen. But she didn't tell him a thing. They split a large pizza and got so high that Janet didn't eat again until Tuesday when she woke up in Tim's empty bathtub wearing nothing but a red plaid wool blanket. In her twenties she would have bounced back in a day or two, but she didn't recuperate until the following weekend.

Waiting for Animal, she started her first letter directly to Helen Sevic. By now Helen probably read all the letters to Kimberly but Janet wanted to let her know that while her husband shouldn't have taken Kimberly, Janet appreciated that they had raised her. As she wrote, she resented that she had to work so hard to take back something that was hers in the first place.

She ended the letter, "You won't understand but I don't want people thinking I never did anything with my life. When I take Kimberly back people will think I did something. Having a teenager makes it so you earned all your wrinkles. But it's not like I want her back because I want to feel younger or get the credit for raising her. I want her back because…." Janet stopped. She would have to think about what to say because this woman deserved an explanation. She was going to have to give up someone she loved, after all.

Animal walked in and said, "You look like you're trying to solve the world's problems!"

Janet was so deep in thought she hadn't heard him on the stairs. "You know me. I could be president of the United States!" She stood up next to the table and saluted Animal. "I am Commander in Chief! Show me your arms."

Animal put down his bags and held out his arms. Janet said, "You know what I mean."

He unzipped a black duffel bag and pulled out a revolver.

Janet punched Animal's arm and gave him a side hug. "You fuckin' did it! I thought you were going to be a pussy but you proved me wrong. Fuckin' A. You *are* an Animal! Hand it over!" Janet said.

"No way! It's all mine," Animal said. "You won't want it anyhow. It doesn't have any bullets."

"What the hell is it with you? You get a counterfeit machine without directions and a gun with no bullets. Are you sure you're not retarded?"

"Is that any kind of question for the guy that got us a goddamn money-making machine? You're priceless!" Animal bent over and took a box out of the bag. "Say you're sorry and I'll give you your present."

"What if I'm not sorry?" Janet teased.

"Then you don't get shit," Animal laughed and put the box back in the bag.

Janet poked her forefinger into one of the dimples of Animal's smile. "You have the deepest dimples. You know what they say about people who got dimples?"

"We're good in bed?"

"Nope. But you're close. Dimples are where your father porked your mother when she was pregnant with you!"

Animal guffawed, "You are so fucking sick!"

"But you love me!"

Animal pulled the box out of the bag again and slapped it on the table. "Who's a retard now?"

"More ink? You bastard!"

Chapter 25

Cole was cornered against the brick wall. Puke stood behind Vanessa with a scowl aimed at Cole. Toad lingered behind his little brother and stared at the back of his sister's head without blinking. Cole tried to get him to look at her, but he either didn't want to or had been told he couldn't. She willed something else to happen, like a car crash or all of the crumbling walls of the old factory behind them to finally fall into its complete ruin at once. She waited.

Vanessa opened the tin of cookies Cole had carried to the Pit. She smashed a soft butter cookie into Cole's chest. "What's the big idea scaring a little kid, huh? What do you have to say for yourself? He was the only one who actually liked your lame crap talk about P.T. Bunghole." She stuffed one of the circular treats in her mouth. Spitting cookie bits into Cole's face, she went on, "Then you fucking petrified my baby brother and you're just gonna stand here and pretend you all of a sudden got nothing to say?"

"We were just hanging out." Cole's voice came out much softer than she intended.

"I know you were. He told me everything. You waited 'til we were gone and then you made him listen to all your dead father bullshit!" The force of the bullshit's "t" sprayed more wet crumbs into Cole's flinching face.

"I didn't want to go out. He came and got *me*," Cole tried to reason.

Vanessa mocked her, "He came and got me." She jabbed Cole again. "What the fuck does this little retard know?" She turned around and pushed Puke.

"Hey!" he whined.

"Shut up!" Vanessa pointed into Puke's face.

Cole and Toad's eyes met for a moment. He looked away and shook his head, a signal Cole couldn't decipher. She looked past the trio at the brick and garbage rubble that used to be buildings. Sometimes the older kids smoked and broke bottles against the lingering half-walls at the far side of the once-factory. Cole listened for voices but no one was there that early. They usually waited until after sundown to jump the fence.

Vanessa turned around, saying, "I was up all night with him crying about the dead bird. He was afraid to go to sleep. You're lucky I didn't come over and leave him at your house. Your mom woulda been really pissed then, wouldn't she?"

Cole folded her arms and shifted her weight to one foot. The corner of her mouth twitched so she bit her lip.

"I said, 'Wouldn't she?' Answer me!"

"Yeah," Cole said. She kept her eyes on the ground in front of Vanessa's feet. "I didn't mean it though. We just were playing...."

"Playing? Playing? You were just playing. Well, how would you like to play now? You wanna play a game now? Some fucking game where *you* cry all night? Would you like that? Huh?"

Cole was afraid of Vanessa all the time, but this made her insides tremor. She kept her arms folded and tucked her fingers into her armpits, to push hard into where she felt her fear twinge. Cole answered, "No."

"Well, good. Because we aren't gonna do what you want today. We are gonna do what Puke wants." Vanessa turned around to Puke, "What you want? You want to help me?"

Cole raised her head and used her eyes to plead with Puke. He scratched the top of his head with both hands. "I don't know," he muttered.

"You see that? She's trying to get to your dumbass brain. Don't fall for it, you stupid turd."

"I guess so," Puke quickly changed his answer.

Cole felt tears coming so she tilted her head all the way back. She escaped for a few peaceful seconds watching the fast-moving clouds and blinking, fantasizing that when she lowered her head she would be alone.

Vanessa rushed toward her and pushed Cole hard. Her head smacked the wall. She attempted to gasp. In a terrorized flash she worried that the part of her brain that allowed her to breathe had been knocked out of order. Her back arched and a piercing pain on the left side of her shoulder made her gasp again and a tiny amount of air got in. She folded to the ground as she took air in short huffs and let it out pursed lips.

When she almost got back to normal, she looked up to the three faces above her.

Vanessa kicked her left knee hard. "You done being a baby? Get up!"

She stumbled up to her feet but dizziness kept her from standing up all the way. Hands on her knees, Cole tried breathing deeper.

"Toad, take her over to the cove!"

He pulled Cole's elbow but she didn't move.

"Come on! Move it!" Vanessa demanded.

Cole shuffled her feet in the direction Toad pulled.

"Put her over there," Vanessa directed.

The "cove" was a small room of the building that still had three tall walls. A pickup truck cap was propped at the top of it. The cap's louver windows were all busted off and the rubber seals were dry and cracked, but it was still the place the younger kids could wait out the rain or hide from the noonday sun. The older kids didn't like that side since it was partly visible from the street.

Cole stood in the cove facing the wall. Vanessa told her, "Turn around. This isn't math class! You need to face what's coming to you, little girl!"

She turned around and kept her head down. Just a few weeks before this, Vanessa and Cole had played catch in exactly the same positions they were in at that moment. They tossed a beanbag that Vanessa bragged she had stolen from the health clinic's play area.

Vanessa held a chunk of brick in her hand and lifted it repeatedly like a dumbbell. Cole looked past Vanessa at the wire fence they had climbed many times. It was the hurdle they looked forward to jumping to get to where they were free to play, kick, run and yell with no adults around. The four of them even pissed together on the other side of the cove's outer wall for Toad's birthday. He joked that this is what he wished for when he blew out the make-believe candles on the four real Hostess cupcakes Cole bought at the corner store.

That fence, once a comfort, now felt like a trap, a pen for wild, vicious animals and their prey. Her instincts told her to run but her knees couldn't. She imagined trying to get away and the three of them pulling her to the ground. Standing there seemed safer than any other option.

"I'm sorry," Cole said. It sounded more like an exoneration plea than a statement. "Please. Don't. Really sorry." Cole kept her eyes on Vanessa's feet. Acknowledging the brick could call Vanessa's bluff and make her feel like she had to throw it. Vanessa beat up her brothers all the time, so Cole had no faith that she wouldn't hurt her even worse than her flesh and blood.

"You got me wrong. I'm not gonna throw it at you," Vanessa said as she paced the front of the cove. She grabbed Puke's arm and pulled him closer to Cole. "He's gonna."

Puke looked up at his sister and shook his head and whimpered, "Vee. No. I don't want to do that."

"Yes you do. You told me how she made you cry and said all that shit and scared you. Throw this as hard as you can," she handed Puke the brick piece. It seemed to grow twice its size during the transition from her hand into his small palm and fingers.

Puke dropped the brick and cried. "I can't throw it at her. Make Toad do it."

"Listen. You're the reason we are doing this so you gotta do it," Vanessa said. She stomped off to the other side of the wall. Cole, Puke and Toad noiselessly took this time to rebuke and plead with each other all at once. Hands and arms flapped while eyes squinted and widened, and heads shook until Vanessa appeared again.

She carried an open Styrofoam Big Mac container filled with dirt in both halves. Placing it next to the brick Puke dropped, she said to Cole, "Start whistling!"

"Whistle?" Cole asked.

"So, you heard me. Good job, fucking genius. Yeah, whistle!"

"What should I whistle?"

"You're always listening to your stupid tapes and radio. Just pick something."

Cole was too nervous to think of a song. Her right eye twitched a few times as she thought about the last time she listened to the radio.

"I don't hear anything coming out of your jerky face. Stop looking like such a mental case!"

Cole started to whistle but none of it sounded like what was in her head.

"What the fuck is that supposed to be?"

"Like, like, like it virgin," Cole stuttered out the title wrong.

"Keep whistling…even though you suck at it." Vanessa pointed at the Big Mac container. "Hey, Puke. Throw that dirt in her face."

Cole nodded her head at Puke and stood rigidly, readied. She kept trying to push the tune through her pursed lips. But it all sounded like someone making up a tune from the same four notes.

Puke grabbed a fistful of the dirt and took a few steps closer to Cole. He held the hand near his right ear and threw the sandy dirt overhand into Cole's face. She winced. It sprayed into her eyes and hair, as well as her mouth that still squeezed out a whistle. Her eyes closed and she went to touch her face.

"Don't move!" Vanessa told Cole. She pointed at Puke, "Keep throwing it until she can't whistle no more."

Again, Puke threw the dirt in Cole's face. This time she didn't flinch because she couldn't see it coming. She figured he must have aimed for her mouth this time since a lot of it landed there and stopped her from being able to whistle.

"Now lick your lips and keep whistling!" Vanessa yelled.

Cole stuck her tongue out the least amount that allowed her to keep making noise. Even though the grit in her mouth was disgusting she couldn't help mashing it between her teeth as she tried to swallow it away.

"You know what that is you're tasting there?" Vanessa asked.

Cole stopped whistling and shook her head.

"That's what we all pissed in! You just licked piss dirt off your lips! What do you two think of that?"

Toad and Puke laughed uneasily.

"Keep your eyes closed," Vanessa said.

She walked up to Cole and shoved her into the wall. Cole flailed her arms and moved her feet in any direction that would keep her from falling. She managed to stay on her feet.

"Fuck…," Vanessa placed her foot and leg behind Cole's calves and pushed her over them with her forearm, "you."

Cole landed on her back again. She opened her mouth wide and gulped air to make sure she didn't stop breathing again. Vanessa kicked her in the arm and then the chest. "You ever gonna make a poor stupid asshole kid cry again?" Cole breathed in fine bits of the dirt that tickled her throat.

"No," Cole choked out as she dusted the dirt out of her eyes. She opened them enough to see the outline of Vanessa's legs.

"Get over here and help me!" Vanessa barked at the boys.

The boys shuffled over and kicked at Cole gently. "Harder!" Vanessa shoved Puke away, "Like this." She kicked Cole's knee again.

Puke cried, "I'm not gonna do any more stuff to her."

"You two are both pussies!" Grabbing Puke, she dragged him over to Toad. "If you two are going to be such faggots, why don't you kiss?"

"No," Toad said.

Vanessa folded her arms. "Then kick her."

"No. I don't wanna," Toad said.

"Well, turdface, remember this morning? What was it you said? 'Her ass is grass'?" Vanessa stepped closer to Toad to put her face close to his.

Cole sat up and crossed her legs and kept her head down. Vanessa picked up a brick.

"You two are pissing me off! Now, go over there and kiss him or I'm going to smash her head in," she raised the brick over her head.

Toad walked over to Puke, bent over and kissed the top of his head.

"Here!" Vanessa held up one of the little white paper cups from the tin of cookies. She lowered it onto Toad's head, "Kiss him on the lips now, pilgrim girl!" She snapped her fingers at Cole, "Hey! You! Watch these two pussies make out."

Cole raised her head, but everything was blurred by tears and the dirt in her eyes.

Toad knelt in front of Puke, grabbed him by the arms and kissed him on the lips hard for a few seconds. Puke squirmed but Toad's grip was strong. "That's better!" Vanessa clapped slowly. Puke pulled away fast. His small fists were tightly clenched as he scowled at Toad.

"Now Puke, kick him in the nuts."

The little cookie cup slid off Toad's head as he tried to scamper away on his knees. Puke swung his leg and landed his foot squarely in Toad's crotch. Toad cried out as he rolled to his side.

As Vanessa cackled, Cole took the opportunity to scoot back a few inches away from her. Cole wished that her evil laughter would change into a naughty giggle and that she would say she was just joking and just wanted to scare the shit out of them.

Puke sat on the ground. Vanessa stepped out from the cove and craned her neck to see up the street. A few cars passed but none slowed down. Still holding the brick, Vanessa paced in front of Cole, saying, "You want to make us feel like shit because our father's locked up? You think you're better than us 'cause you got your own room and your mom works. You think I care your father died? I don't feel bad for you. Your father's just feeding worms. Then you get this dildo to cry about your damn dead bird? You piss me off!"

Vanessa swung around and threw the brick fast and hard at Cole. Puke's mouth dropped open and Toad stopped moaning. She picked up two more chunks and hurled them.

Puke started to cry loudly as he sobbed out, "Vee, stop…hurting…her." The first one took Cole by surprise for its timing but the next two rage-fueled ones shocked her.

As Vanessa kicked her, Cole heard Puke's crying fade away. She was afraid that she had passed out but then realized Vanessa's voice was still nearby. Was he running away to go get help? Toad screamed at Vanessa, "Stop it! You're getting us in trouble!" Cole hoped that meant someone was coming toward them or watching and Vanessa would stop.

Curled into a ball with her forearms over her face, Cole rolled around trying to diffuse the blows. Gritting her teeth made the dirt crack against them. She felt like throwing up. Vanessa's voice started sounding far away but this time it happened while she was still being kicked. A final rubbery thud on her left ear sent Cole under.

When she woke up, she didn't know how much time passed since everything faded away. Lying on her side she looked at the fence again. The same part she looked at earlier. How was she going to make it over it? She stayed still but tested different body parts for pain. Everything hurt. She tried moving but the only comfort was when she gave in to gravity completely. When she felt that she had pissed herself she wondered if she was dying. She had heard that dead people go to the bathroom all over themselves.

Chapter 26

Vladimir packed a large brown paper grocery bag with three repurposed jelly jars filled with water carefully wrapped in toilet paper, a sleeve of Saltines, a jar of peanut butter, a metal butter knife, a blanket and his toaster.

The Sunday dawn bounced off the hills behind his apartment, appearing much later than 5:45 a.m. He put the phone on the couch cushion next to him and dialed the number written large in black marker on the back of an old phone bill.

"Hello?" Tony answered the phone on the fifth ring.

"I'm ready," Vlad said.

"My brother was picked up last night."

"We're going to Coney Island, remember?"

"I can't, Vlad. I got to get him out. It's big. Big time."

Vlad's voice quivered, "We have to go today."

"Listen to me. I can't go. I didn't know he was running up in and out of Massachusetts. He's in big trouble. I can't do shit until we can get him out," Tony sighed. "I am really sorry, Vlad. Maybe we can go in a few weeks?" he offered.

"Is this because of the ferry?" Vlad wondered if Tony changed his mind because he had insisted they take the ferry and drive across Long Island. "I told you I'd pay you."

"Vlad! I just told you," Tony yelled.

"The hell with you, then." Vlad slammed the phone onto its cradle so hard the bell inside jangled.

Vlad was ready to go with or without Tony. Now, what was he going to do about the note to Cole? He was going to get Tony to write it and leave it on the coffee table.

In the kitchen, Vlad brushed everything magnetically attached to the front of his white QE refrigerator to the floor. In Magic marker he wrote in letters about four inches tall, "I love you Cole." He thought about what to write next. He wanted to tell her about how everyone dies. He started with "We all" and then scribbled over it. She knew that. He wanted to tell her the truth about her birth. She didn't know that.

He didn't think that was something that should be revealed on a refrigerator. She would have too many questions and he was the only one left with answers. He sighed deeply and wrote, "Be a good girl," but it ended up looking like "Bla goof give." He threw the marker without its cap onto the counter and used the kitchen phone to dial the number he had memorized from the 1979 calendar still hanging next to the phone. He told the dispatcher to have the driver pick him up at the street entrance of Fireside Apartments at the end of Palisade. He didn't want a car honk to wake anyone.

In another paper bag he placed one of the scrapbooks he had wrapped in a blue towel. The day was already sticky hot. He moved even slower than usual since he was going to need his energy for the lengthy train ride into the city and out to Coney Island. Clutching the paper bags with one hand and his cane in the other, Vlad stepped out of the apartment. He leaned his cane against the wall to close the door, but he didn't bother to lock it.

Chapter 27

Vladimir walked into the Coney Island surf in the middle of the night. No one was there to notice the old man navigate the craggy boardwalk slats to the yielding sand. Using a cane for stability on his left side and holding his toaster by its slots with his right hand, he walked like Frankenstein into the water until he felt the seawater percolate up his thighs. He bit his bottom lip, scrunched his brow and grunted as he pitched the toaster underhand a few feet away where it sounded its last metal jiggles before gurgling under.

Seeking the aid of buoyancy he lugged his stiff knees to get him out to deeper water. His loose-fitting linen shirt took a few moments to relax into sogginess. Vlad stood facing the invisible horizon. Each swirling current sucked his slippered feet and wooden cane further into the sandy muck.

A dull glow flickered beyond where the toaster landed. It was almost his height and size but it didn't move when he did. The new moon made Vladimir's night no darker than the glaucoma that had pilfered his vision of the past fifteen years.

The Atlantic's cold heart never held any warmth for long. Vlad shivered and whispered, "What am I doing here?" No one answered.

Maybe in order to justify taking such a long journey he imagined P.T. Barnum's ghost told him the answer was in these waters. Or perhaps he just craved something extraordinary after the last sparkless twenty years.

Letting his bladder empty brought Vlad some comfort. The piss created a warm pocket around his crotch and thighs, and he had a sense that Red was there with him or maybe could see him. His calves trembled as he pulled each foot from the sand that had swallowed his slippers. As the gentle waves followed him, Vlad used his cane to struggle back to the shore.

On the beach, Vlad scuffled around until he found his paper bag. Plopping down in the sand he wrapped himself in his blanket and let his memory dredge up whatever its tides carried. He remembered when his five-year-old Oleg held his privates next to the Christmas tree while little baby Vera cooed, cradled in her mother's arms. The eager boy had hopped from one foot to the other in his new red pajamas as Vlad performed the Vanishing Handkerchief trick from the A.C. Gilbert Mysto Magic Set left by Santa.

When Vladimir handed his son the fake rubber thumb for him to try, Oleg hesitated and then shook his head. The boy whined, "I don't like to pretend things."

Vlad turned to baby Vera and put the thumb in her tiny outstretched hand. His wife Wilda plucked it away, threw it at Vlad and said, "What's the matter with you? You want her to choke on that?" That was the first time Wilda scolded him for putting Vera in harm's way.

Over the years, the fourth generation of shifty criminals fizzled. In the late 1960s Vlad canceled his magic act's Yellow Pages ad. The phone company had always suggested he list under the "Entertainment" heading but Vlad insisted he be the only business under Magicians. The deserted-looking entry advertised, "Magic for events and occasions," falling perfectly flat. He was a successful marketer for magic that never was and would never be. There were a couple of years that he didn't get even one phone call. Then when he gave up his unlawful ways, he needed no masquerade to hide his illicit income.

The memories of the old days were difficult enough when Oleg and Vlad were alive together. Ever since his son was born, Vladimir never went to the beach without him. Every time. At home it was easy for Vladimir to pretend Red had just left or was at work. And there were walls that served as borders between where Red wasn't and where he could be. He looked to his left and then to his right. Even though he couldn't see it clearly, his eyes fixed on the horizon. He was alone. The sand and ocean's vastness wouldn't let Vlad lie to himself any longer. For the first time he wept for Red, for his Oleg, his dead son, Oleg.

He called him Red sometimes but when he did, Vlad felt like a traitor to his Russian-born grandfather, Boris. The Slavic name "Oleg" had been converted into the communist color by his grade school pals.

The day after Red's death, Vlad explained to Helen how he hadn't left his apartment since December. He told her that the wintery day was just too cold and he couldn't risk falling. The truth was that he didn't go to his son's funeral because he didn't want to face his ex-wife after their decades-long estrangement. He had wanted to face her one more time before he died, but not at their only remaining child's funeral. This excuse now seemed as defenseless as he felt sitting on the sand; wet, cold and shoeless, wiping his tears with a corner of the blanket.

Chapter 28

Cole gulped in short breaths as she slumped against the refrigerator and slid down onto the floor. A stinging pain pulsed in the rough gash across her upper arm. Her face had hurt like this once before, when she was eight years old. She had tied the leash of her neighbor's German Shepherd to her bike handles and madly pedaled down their street. Inspired by her galloping companion and the open road, she decided to ride beyond the neighbor's house on the way back. But the loyal dog stopped in front of his house and sent Cole airborne several feet beyond. Now, her gentle tap on her puffy cheekbone dough made her eyes tear, just like after that accident.

A dog. That's what Vanessa had called Cole as she pushed her into the wall. If Cole hadn't worn pants her legs would have been as battered as her top half. The last time Cole hung out with them she had to come up with an excuse for her mother about her scratched up legs. That day she had worn shorts and knelt down in the decaying building's rubble to play catcher in their illogical four-player baseball game. The rules were simply that everyone was to try to hit or throw the ball as hard as possible at someone else. When someone had the stick, someone else threw the tennis ball at the batter's body while he or she tried to dodge the ball and hit it hard in the direction of any of the other players. When the catcher had the ball, he or she could throw it at anyone but the batter, who usually shouted to the catcher the name of the person to be pelted.

Cole should have known Vanessa was up to something. On her way to Vlad's the day before, Vanessa asked her, "When's your mom working again? We're going to play the pit tomorrow."

"Tomorrow night. She's going to work late," Cole answered. Cole's availability seemed to intensify Vanessa's nervous energy; she chewed at the inside of her bottom lip, cracked her knuckles one-by-one instead of all at once and her right heel pistoned up and down. She told Cole, "Let's pit at seven o'clock then. Bring those tennis balls and get me some of those metal box cookies."

The last time they played Cole brought one of the five dented metal tins of butter cookies from Caldors that her mother stashed in their pantry. Her mother noticed and told her to not eat so much sugar. She warned, "You're getting chubby and besides, we don't got money for any of your cavities." This time, Cole wrapped a few cookies in a tissue and gave them to Vladimir, and told Helen she gave him the whole canister. When Vladimir thanked Helen for the cookies, Cole's scheme was complete. Now, all that deception made it feel as though she stood guilty as a cruel accomplice to her own demise.

Using the refrigerator door handle to get up, Cole's head hurt inside and out. Her ears rang, and time and plans blurred. This isn't what she thought would happen at the pit. After shuffling to the bathroom she sat on top of the toilet lid. The landlord's cigar smoke wafted up from his bathroom below. He often smoked a cigar while taking a crap. She thought of how her father had taken the newspaper into the bathroom and would not come out for a long time.

He would not have liked Allan. He didn't like smoking and he would have thought play-acting about the Civil War was a waste of time. When Vladimir tried to teach Cole card tricks, Red told her, "All that is pretending." Cole thought about what he would say if he could see her now. Could he see her now? Wouldn't that mean he saw Vanessa throwing the bricks at her and kicking her?

Her father would have poured hydrogen peroxide on all her cuts. He used it on her cuts and scratches, and he gargled with it after brushing and flossing. For many nights after he died, she sniffed from the bottle after she brushed her teeth. The mixed aromas of the peroxide and toothpaste made it seem like he just went to bed or off to work. Not just gone. She hadn't opened the bottle since the day she unpacked it during their first weekend at Sheridan. Now, the new aromas of musty Civil War uniforms and cigar smoke blurred older memories and shoved them further into the past. She poured peroxide over the cuts as the red-streaked runoff soaked into her pants and pooled on the toilet lid.

Breathing deeply, she started thinking about what she should do if the cut didn't stop bleeding. She once read a story about a soldier who had made a tourniquet. When she asked her grandfather about it, he tore off a long strip from his bed's top sheet to make her one, saying, "It's not like I'll need it much longer anyways. What the hell, right?" He wrapped the sheet around her bicep and used a wooden ruler to twist it tight. "Your arm here is turning colors down here and it looks fine up here. That means it's working. The blood's not getting there because we stopped it here," he told her while pointing at the fabric knot pushing into her arm. After he released the tourniquet it took a while for Cole's fingers to not feel icy numb.

Where would she put a tourniquet to stop the bleeding on her face and on her bicep? She wished she could call Vladimir but he would ask too many questions. What happened? Why don't you call your mother? Why don't you just come over?

After she wet and wrung out a facecloth she put it in the freezer. Every movement seemed to hurt her somewhere. When they moved in, they had put a shoebox of odds and ends under her mother's bed. That's where Cole had tossed the Ace bandage after she rolled it up. The two metal-fanged tabs kept it tightly wound in a way her father told her not to store it, telling her "It's going to lose its elastic powers." She hoped it would still work even though it had been stretched out for two months.

Kneeling beside her mother's bed she lifted the chenille bedspread leaving blood on a few of the twisted white thread tassels. She bent from her hips just enough to see the shadows of two boxes under the bed. Were there two or was she hallucinating like the people in movies stuck in a desert? She pinched her nose between her eyes and bent over again. She dragged the closest box toward her as the other one stayed put. There were two after all.

Her fingertips felt the relief of cool metal. This was a Saltine tin not the cardboard Thom McAn box she expected. She leaned down to one side and eased herself to the floor so she could reach the shoebox. Once she flipped the top off the shoebox and could see the bandage, it reminded her of the stuffed cabbage rolls her grandfather used to get from a neighbor lady. He would say, "Golubsti for my golubtsi-poopsy" and share them with Cole. The fasteners' teeth still bit the bandage as hard as the day she pulled them onto it. She took the clips off and put them on the floor with the teeth facing up. They looked like silver bugs that died on their backs.

Sitting up cross-legged she unraveled the bandage all the way to its tight little crumpled core. Each orbit around her arm and shoulder proved that moving around was making her feel better not worse. By the time the bandage ended just under her armpit her breaths were deeper. The oozing blood had slowed. The quarter-sized bloodstain on the bandage's top layer looked as if it were coming from a small bullet hole now rather than the wide deep gash.

Cole put the lid back on the shoebox. A tie clip and a Bicentennial pin that her father wore to a Father/Daughter Dinner at her school were in the box because Cole didn't want to see them but didn't want to get rid of them either. She picked up the Saltines tin as she pushed the shoebox back under the bed. As soon as her fingernail split through the masking tape holding it shut she wondered where she last saw that roll of tape. She was going to have to put things back the way they were.

A look down into the tall rectangular metal canister was like checking a full mailbox. Envelopes of different sizes were folded and bent to fit in. Cole tipped it over but only two fell out. Were these cards from after her father's funeral? But those were all in a wicker basket in their new pantry. Pulling them all out, she let them fill the space in the middle of her crossed legs. Some of the envelopes hadn't been opened. Some had yellow post office stickers with numbers at the top and reading:

FORWARD TO: Sevic
P.O. Box 1137
Bridgeport, CT 06610

The letters from QE and their lawyers had these stickers on them but she hadn't thought about why they were sent to a post office box.

"Nikolaevna" was handwritten on many of the envelopes but someone added "Kim" as if it was her middle name. A few were stickerless. The postmarks were from a few places in New York. She opened one. It was as if someone had delivered a bag full of her mail from the past, but from a time before she ever lived.

> Dear Kim, I really, really hope you don't mind me calling you Kim. It's not like I am calling you a name you never had. I named you. I'm still trying to make enough money to take you back with me again. My friend here is helping me with that. I know it's hard for you to not have more to go on but I can't risk anyone finding me here. You know I love you. I know you know. Sweet baby Kimberly. I probably won't stop calling you that ever. Even after you are grown. Love from your real mother. Never stopped loving you. Your True Mother Forever.

Cole's face flamed hot from her cheeks down to her neck. What was this? *Who* was this?

Exhausted, she slumped down, closed her eyes and let her chin drop. Just above her head she heard a bug use the screen as a horizontal trampoline.

She took a few breaths and tried to sort it all out. But this was all like when she saw *Star Wars* with her father. The scenes blurred together as spaceships chased each other down and then shot at them. Both Cole and her father were confused and leaned in at the same time to ask the other what was happening. She tilted her head to the left while thinking about how their heads bumped, and he took her hand and squeezed it and let go.

Vanessa's rage was impossible to shake. Cole couldn't stop the flashes of raw memories. Vanessa biting her lower lip while lobbing the bricks and rocks at her. Toad and Puke's windmill arms beating her when she tried to get away like a car speeding out from under the berating car wash brushes' slaps. Then the blood. Maybe there was blood on the bathroom floor.

A breeze picked up and carried faraway voices. Kids playing, yelling, laughing. It sounded so normal from far away but she knew it could be Puke crying out for help and Vanessa laughing cruelly. Or it could be some other neighborhood kids. Miguel's ball could have flown over a fence or Shara's shirt could have been lifted, revealing her new padded bra. The voices continued but stayed distant.

An envelope's edge poked into her thigh. She crumpled it and threw it over the bed and across the room. One loose card did an aerial cartwheel as her arm flung out. She squinted at the cartoon on the card's front. It wasn't any character she knew from television. Was this something she should recognize too? Did she have a concussion? She wondered what amnesia was like and how people know they have it. When she opened the card, it had writing all the way to edges. Then the woman drew an arrow and cramped in the message, "Open it up. More in here." Cole unfolded the card vertically. The woman wrote across the opened card as one large sheet of paper. In almost every paragraph the woman repeated that she was Cole's mother.

Was this woman crazy? It sounded like she was hiding somewhere so that no one would find her until she came to get Cole. How could all this be true? She must be lying. If it were true, how could she have not felt that she was not her parent's kid? Wasn't it part of being a human to know who your family is?

Something sounded like water swooshing. Was it her blood? She put her fingertips against the side of her neck. Her grandfather showed her how to feel her pulse after she got woozy on the kiddie's Ferris wheel at the Bridgeport Fair. He told her, "Count the beats and breathe." Maybe she was having a heart attack. The hard thuds didn't slow or dull.

The words "I wish I were dead" floated through her mind. She had heard the phrase in movies. Her father loved to watch that old movie every Christmas. The one where the guy wished he had never been born. She couldn't stop her reeling thoughts. She wanted to know what it was like when she was born. And when she existed but no one knew who she was yet.

Trying to get up made gave her bowels urgency. She grabbed a picture frame from her mother's dresser mid-stumble from the bedroom to the bathroom. Gas and her upset belly raged into the toilet bowl. To break the wafting stench she pressed her thighs together. She placed the frame flat on her lap and studied it. Her father and mother looked more like each other than she resembled either of them. Their noses, eyes, hair.

Cole closed her eyes. Too tired to cry she shook her head as she remembered her last birthday. At Denny's her father snapped a photograph of her smiling with her arms around the plate, hoarding all her pancakes and bacon.

All the snapshots from that day were still in the pocket Instamatic camera that smelled like her father's waffles and Old Spice cologne.

How could they have celebrated her birthday every year as if they had anything to do with her being alive? The shock of it all was less rooted in the fact of the deception than the act of their dishonesty. Cole's eyes squeezed tighter as she tried to think of the opposite of keeping a secret. Was it telling the secret or could someone deny ever knowing it? Maybe her mother hid these letters because they weren't at all true. Cole settled on this explanation until she could talk to Vlad.

She wiped herself, flushed the chaos, and left her underwear and pants on the floor. Stepping into the bathtub, she slipped then steadied herself with a fistful of the plastic shower curtain as it ripped from the first three rungs. Cupping her hands under the faucet, she rinsed off the blood, dirt and brick bits. It stung like something other than water. It felt more like sharp wet snow whipping her skin during a storm.

When her hands felt soothed by the warm water, she pulled up the lever to divert the water to the showerhead. She braced for it to hurt or be cold but it was if the water knew to gently cascade over her skin. Using just her hands, she lathered white streaks of Ivory soap up and down her legs, arms, across the small mounds on her chest and under her arms. After she rinsed off the grit with the soap, she tried to plan what to do next. She stood under the water, eyes clenched. She would have to leave. It was just a matter of figuring out where to go.

Once she shut off the water, she heard Allan downstairs put away dishes and play his stereo. Cole knew it was Elvis because her father used to sing the now muffled song, "Blue Suede Shoes." He'd used his finger to dry his gums on one side of his mouth and hitch his lip on it. With that classic Elvis sneer he sang, "You can do anything, but stay off of my blue suede shoes," over and over until Cole would squeal because she couldn't take it anymore.

Songs, people, places, smells. Some made her miss her father less and others made it worse. To get out the door and over to Vlad she had to shut out everything. Without thinking about the blood on the floor, she wiped it up with her ruined pants and threw them in the kitchen garbage. Pulling on loose-fitting clean clothes over her cuts and bruises, she thought about the last time she got sunburned. As if they were just schoolbooks, she tossed the picture and the canister full of letters onto her bed. She wondered if pushing through pain is what it takes to be an adult.

Chapter 29

Wilda peeked through the curtains to her front porch and scowled. An anemic old man leaned on the cane that he had just rapped on her front door.

Since he faced the door squarely, she took the opportunity to pull aside her lacy shield and take a good look. A few paper bags were strewn at his feet. A large Nathan's bag made her wonder if Animal asked someone to deliver hot dogs. But this man was in no shape to be a delivery person, even in service to someone as lazy as Animal. As the man doddered in place, the joints of his neck, hips, knees and ankles wavered like Popsicle sticks held together with glue that couldn't dry. But with doglike resolve, his eyes were locked on Wilda's front door.

She looked down at what she was wearing and smoothed her thin white hair as if there were enough body in it to be out of place. Closing the snaps on her baby blue seersucker housecoat, Wilda went to the front door.

As soon as the door opened, the man's shoulders swayed back as his knobby knees moved with more conviction than appeared feasible. She opened the door wider to accommodate his walking cane. "I can't wait for you to invite me in, Wilda. I feel like I haven't pissed since the last time you saw me!"

"Vlad!" Wilda bellowed.

"Yeah. Yeah. There's more of that for us. I need a bathroom," Vlad said as he continued walking down the hallway into the kitchen.

Wilda used the words she had always said to direct people to the bathroom, but this time with a dazed tone, "It's down there and on the left. Off the kitchen?"

Still at the front door, she picked up the paper bags and carried them into her front room. Most people would call it a living room but Wilda called it "the front room." In turn, she called her bedroom "the back room." But the only people that knew this were Maddie, Animal, the few men she had dated, and the guys she hired to paint her walls and lay down new carpets.

Wilda set the bags down on the floor in front of the sofa. Unrolling the top of a large brown paper bag, she stole a glimpse inside. Then she hovered her hand outside of the Nathan's bag and it was as warm as it smelled. Hands on her hips, she rolled her eyes, thinking, "After all these years he barges in with peanut butter, crackers and a bag of hot dogs."

Back in her armchair, she pretended to watch the television. The sound had been on the entire time, but she didn't really hear it until she focused her eyes on the screen. Her efforts to pretend to be too distracted to care about Vlad made her jump slightly when he stepped into the room.

"You have a nice place here." Vlad almost said her name but just let out a sigh in the sound of the "Wil."

"Thanks. It's been good to me. Ginny's son rents the upstairs," she said. She didn't look away from the television.

Vlad sat on the sofa on the end closest to his bags. He rearranged them on the floor but placed the Nathan's bag on his lap. "You hungry?" he asked.

"Are you?" she asked back.

"Yep. I slept on the beach last night," Vlad opened the bag.

"What the hell did you do that for?" Wilda asked as she finally faced his direction. "Don't get that shit all over my couch. Go eat in the kitchen."

"I always eat on the couch. I'll be careful," he said as he reached in the bag and took out some catsup-streaked napkins.

"Fine."

"You want some?"

"If you got any fries."

"Got a couple of orders. I remembered," Vlad smiled.

Wilda gave him a cautionary side-glance but he couldn't make out that much detail.

He held the cardboard container of fries in one hand and grabbed his cane with the other. She shook her head as two long French fries flopped to the floor. The remaining fries survived the trip to her.

The NBC Sunday night movie played as they ate. Neither of them paid attention to the weak-plotted military flick that cut back and forth from military men barking orders in a submarine.

Wilda glanced from her fries to her surprise visitor every few moments. Vlad moved so slowly that she had to remember not to care if he was ever going to get the straw into his fountain soda, finish the hot dog, wipe his mouth, get the wrappers back into the bag.

After there was no more food in his hands and he was sipping his drink, Wilda said, "I don't know what you're up to, mister. But I sure as shit don't think you came here just to eat on my couch."

"No. I didn't know I was going to do that. I was just so ravishing," he said.

She said, "Ravished. You were ravished. It's been a very long time since either of us was ravishing."

"You know what I mean. I'm not the one who went and got an education. Remember?"

"Oh, shut up. I was a just a nurse. I cleaned a lot of shit. That's all. From the patients *and* doctors."

Vlad pointed at the television, "Can we shut that thing off? I can't hear you at the same time."

Wilda didn't have to look at the remote to press the power button and she knew she didn't have to aim it at the set either. The room went quiet except for the distant music coming from her tenants, two floors above.

"Good. I got to hear myself think to talk," Vlad said.

"Well, I figured some sort of speech must be coming. You came all the way here when you know how to dial a telephone?"

"I tried calling you. Back when …. When he died. But I got no answer. No phone machine. No nothing. But since I already lost you so long back. It was just more of your silent treatment, I guess," Vlad said. He had tilted his head back and closed his eyes. Wilda took in his face, coloring in the pale and wrinkles with the flush and texture of the younger skin she once knew, once caressed, slapped.

"Whatever you were going to say was for you. Not me. I made peace with him a long time ago. Did you?"

"Peace? With Red? Oleg?" Vlad often could not say his son's

nickname without his given name.

"Yeah. Did you apologize for killing his little sister?"

Vlad shook his head. "That's not what I would call it."

They sat in silence that fell when Wilda left him in 1953, two years after Vera died.

Through the closed door, they heard the music upstairs throb as heavy footsteps plodded down the stairs. The front door slammed shut and a car engine started. Vlad turned his head toward the front windows with eyes that begged for another passive distraction.

"Yes, apologize. That's what people do. I've seen it over and over. Good people do, anyway. Shitty people always find ways to not do it. But good people. They say sorry when they screw up, Vlad. And you ... you fucked up."

With his eyes still closed, Vlad smirked, "I think they should tell sailors that they swear like nurses."

"You never changed. Neither did I. The last time I saw Red he told me that you were too old to drive, and I really felt bad for you. I did. You loved your cars. I thought that would have killed you. Not being able to take your drives. But you're too stubborn to die, aren't you?"

Vlad's eyes opened. He turned his face in Wilda's direction and said, "Who's the stubborn one? You didn't even go to his funeral!"

"I wish I had."

"Is that an apology?" he asked.

"Why the hell would I apologize to you?" she asked.

Tears swamped Vlad's eyes. He said, "Because I would have gone if I'd known you weren't going to be there."

"Oh, save it. I didn't goddamnwell go because I thought you were going." Wilda shook her head. "But, listen. I am sorry, Vlad. Sorry my mere existence made you stay home. Somehow it didn't stop you from coming here to blubber on my couch, did it?"

"That's the way you always were. Blame everyone but yourself," he shot back.

"Look in the mirror when you say that, Buster Brown."

Vlad leaned forward and stretched out his neck toward Wilda, saying, "You still don't get it. I didn't do anything. You think I *wanted* the place to burn down? That I *wanted* Vera to play with the matches? That I *wanted*...."

Wilda interrupted, "You let it happen, Vlad. You and your bullshit. Your whole life. Lighting fires, stealing cars, anything to keep from getting a real job. At least your mother didn't want to kill anyone. She told me before she died. I'll never forget it. She said, 'Wilda, I ruined a lot of lives, but I never killed anyone. Vlad has. I feel like I'm to blame.'" Wilda got up and stomped over to sit on the other end of the sofa from Vlad. She shook her finger at him, "And you know what else she said? 'I am sorry. I will have to find out if those people are on the other side and tell them I'm sorry too.' That's what she said to me. See? She was a good person. She apologized."

"But I didn't kill Vera! I didn't light the fire that killed her. I didn't even know she was in the house!"

"You didn't know this. You didn't know that. What the hell *do* you know, Vlad?" Wilda's voice shook and the apples of her cheeks blazed red while her jowls stayed crêpe-white. Vlad crossed his arms and bowed his head.

She went on. "I know something! I know that you left the matches and the gasoline in the kitchen. I know that you dropped Vera off to her friend's house without checking if the people were even there. I know that you *did* manage to run into our house, while it was burning, mind you. But did you try to see if anyone was in there? Maybe be a hero? No!" Angry tears pushed from her eyes as she went on, "You ran into the flames to save the only thing you really ever cared about. All your Barnum crap!"

With his face in his hands, he moaned, "I didn't know. I didn't know. I didn't."

Talking over his remorseful mantra, Wilda asked, "To see you in the street with those cases! You saved all that bullshit about people you never knew! You never knew them! Vera was in there too. And you … just ….," Wilda pounded her fist on her knee. "And then you kept that ratty cursed mermaid. I fucking hate you for that too." She turned away and plucked a balled-up tissue from her housecoat pocket. After smoothing out half of it, she blew her nose and looked at the leaden television screen.

Vlad used his cane to get up from the sofa and shuffled to stand in front of Wilda. He reached out his free hand to touch her head. She pulled back.

He bent at his hips and let his cane fall to the floor. Placing his hands on her knees he struggled to kneel in front of Wilda. She faced him, put her hands on top of his and told him, "Whatever you're going to say. Don't."

"I'll tell you what I was never going to say," Vlad said with a vigor that seemed out of character for someone so frail.

But the temporary emotional façade disappeared as if a director yelled, "Cut." Vlad's mouth opened and closed as his throat let out sounds like a small animal was trapped inside. His tears didn't leave his eyes, which made them look like bluish watery marbles swimming in egg whites.

Wilda looked into them but they did not seem to see her.

His voice, like a bell pealing through fog, burst out, "I'm sorry."

His whining desire was fraught with fear of someone or something farther away and more powerful than Wilda. Sniffles and other noises from Vlad's nose and throat dissipated like a summer rainstorm. Every few moments it seemed to diminish, but it just wouldn't stop completely.

Wilda squeezed his hands just to hold onto something but not to console him.

Vlad turned his head and appeared to talk to his right shoulder, saying, "There ya go." He used her lap for leverage to stand.

Handing him his cane felt strange to Wilda since he moved like a toddler dressed in his father's oversized shirt. Wilda closed her eyes.

Vlad tottered over to his array of paper bags. He grabbed the large brown one and walked down the hallway to the back of the house.

After her bedroom door shut, Wilda gathered the rest of Vlad's paper bags and brought them into the kitchen. His acquitted snores sounding from her bedroom taunted her. She opened the freezer door to let the cold fog roll over her face. She grabbed something square that was wrapped in aluminum foil. On a large band-aid stuck on top, someone had written "Wilda Keep Out" next to a drawing of pot leaves. Shaking her head, she walked out the back door, sat on her back steps, unwrapped the brownie and bit off one of its corners.

Chapter 30

As Cole pulled a comforter out of her dark green duffel bag she leaned against the wall for strength. Two months before, she had punched it into the bag to get it to fit. Now, she had to use patience to pull it out a little at a time until the bag was free to fill with the cracker tin, the letters, some clothes, her tape recorder, batteries, cassette tapes, bandages, the half-full bottle of peroxide and a mason jar of water. When she grabbed the Pound Puppies top sheet from her bed, she pushed her arm down between the bed and the wall to find her special folder of pictures. The pain that seared up her arm into her neck forced her to give up the search. After she dragged the bag behind her as she swiped the framed picture of the three of them off of her mother's dresser. From the pantry she added crackers, peanut butter, a jar of maraschino cherries and a tin of kipper snacks.

An ant army snaked across the counter from behind a large coffee can to a drawer. She opened it. The insects swarmed a brown Necco wafer that had found its way to the top of the stack of the newspaper articles about Mexico's earthquake. She carried the papers to the sink and shook the insects off. One walked onto the back of her hand and inspected a deep scratch near her middle knuckle. The ant's shiny head was the same size as the cut's bloody bead that collected at the widest part of the wound. She lifted her hand to see it more closely and picked another ant out of the sink and put it next to the one on her hand. It walked away from the cut until she directed it back to it. The other ant greeted it and they both turned around and started to feed on her blood. She puckered her lips and sucked the ants into her mouth. Her tongue pushed the ants against the back of her front teeth. Then she nibbled on them, their sour, earthy tang mingled with her blood's briny metallic taste.

Back in the pantry, she tucked the now insect-free papers into the tin with the letters and put the tin in the duffel bag. She didn't know where she was going or for how long. What else would she need? She packed a fork, a spoon, a steak knife and the can opener. The bag was heavy; even dragging it on the floor was hard. How was she supposed to carry it between the apartment and the next part of her life? She never thought that this is why some of the downtown street people pushed around shopping carts. For a moment she wondered if she might become one of them.

She left her heavy bag outside the Civil War room and was careful not to make much noise. When pain shot up her thighs, she sat on a nearby wood and canvas folding camp chair.

Having looked through everything in there when they first moved in, Cole knew there were guns in one of the boxes. She remembered the large wooden box marked with a masking tape strip that read "Pepperboxes." When she opened it months ago, Cole thought she was going to find salt and pepper shakers. But now she knew what she would find: pistols that looked like the ones she saw in the Westerns on television on Sunday afternoons. Careful not to make any noise, she lifted the lid. She tiptoed with the pistol out to her bag and stuffed it into the middle of the clothing clump. After gently replacing the lid, Cole went back into the kitchen.

From a paper bag in the freezer she took half of a small pile of cash. She knew it was there to pay their rent but if Vlad couldn't help her, she needed to get away. Her head ached with fear. What if her mother called before leaving work? She went back to the bathroom for a roll of toilet paper.

Ready to leave, she sucked in air and let out a hiss to get her arms through the handles of the duffel bag. She could not look back and had to keep moving. One night when her mother was at work, Cole had watched a Tina Turner interview. She taped it on her recorder and played it back a few times. At the time she couldn't imagine how anyone could ever have had power over this larger-than-life celebrity. Explaining how she left Ike Turner, Tina said, "The way out is through the door. Nothing is more important than your own life."

Cole had never tested her own determination but with her bag packed, it ran so deep it felt as if she were being pushed out of the apartment. All the thoughts and feelings that brought her to that moment were now behind her. All she wanted was to leave and see her grandfather. Her head throbbed with the words, "The way out is through the door."

She tiptoed down the back stairs and found her way across several backyards until she reached Boston Avenue. Relieved that no one seemed to see her, especially Vanessa and the boys, she rested her bag against a tree to catch her breath, her t-shirt already sweaty. Usually she could run at least halfway to her grandfather's house before slowing down but every lungful of air pinched coming in and going out.

Before slipping through the hole in the metal fence behind Vlad's apartment, she checked his lightless window. He was either sleeping or just sitting in the dark. She didn't want to go to him until after her mother searched for her there. She had always wanted to go camping but this felt more like being homeless or a fugitive.

Ever since she was a little girl they had spotted foxes in this area. Her heart dropped when she realized she forgot to bring a flashlight. What else did she forget? She brought a notebook to write out a plan but she couldn't use it in the dark. Walking into the woods, she ventured deeper than she ever had dared. The trees were far enough apart to let some moonlight through. On a bald spot of dirt under a short tree she sat down with the pack on her back and then let her arms out of the handle loops. The lack of gravity dragging her shoulders increased the pain in her side. "Fuck!" her voice cracked as she started to cry.

She wrapped herself in the sheet decorated with frolicking Pound Puppies. Her head lowered onto the end of the bag stuffed with her clothes. A hot gust blew some leaves into her face but she was too tired to brush them away. Their innocent dirty scent helped her sleep as she imagined being buried there under the tree.

Throughout the night she woke up scared, yet each time her exhaustion overtook the fear. The Mason jar's water was warm, offering more relief when she splashed her face, rather than drinking it. Through all the new scratches on her digital watch, she read 9:53 a.m. Without the evidence of the previous day Cole carried in her bag and on her body, she wouldn't have believed what had happened. The day her father died had seemed to be the worst day of her life. But now she suspected that life was a catalog of worst days, organized by categories such as the death of someone you love, getting beat up and other awful moments she had yet experienced but were sure to come.

After she ate some of her rations her thoughts raced less, but confusion was constant. She had never just sat in the woods before and it felt like someone was going to find her at any moment. Her only connection to staying outside this long was made a few months earlier when her class read *The Adventures of Tom Sawyer*. Someone was always snooping or finding things out while hiding. The most important parts of the story had to do with people seeing things they shouldn't have. In the book it made sense, but she wasn't sure yet that any of the books they read in school made any sense of the bad things that happened in real life. There wasn't a word she could ever read that would come close to making sense of the past twenty-four hours.

Under the sunlight she made a list: "See Grampa, ask about letters. Knows? Leave. Surprised? Ask—help you run away. Either way—take socks." Now that she had written the list it seemed a much simpler plan. She had thought it would be much more complicated and that writing it out would give her a chance to doubt herself. Instead, it made her certain that if she had to, she would run away.

This was the first time she used the words "run away." She had previously thought about it as "going away" or "leaving." Now, having slept her first night alone away from home, she saw herself as a runaway. Whenever she heard the words "runaways," "dropouts" and "druggies" before, she had never thought she'd be any of them. Each word seemed like a title for an army whose soldiers remained anonymous until they defected to being normal civilians. But being a runaway sounded less scary than any of her other options. At least she had control over this, for now.

She got up and leaned against the tree and moved her body as if it were made of three wooden planks: her legs, her torso and her neck up to her head. In a wide circle, she walked around her simple camp. A few empty beer cans and a shredded plaid flannel shirt were the only signs anyone else had spent time there. She wrote a note to put on top of her bag: "Do not steal this. Thank you."

She stopped herself from writing her name underneath. Was she going to have to make up a new name if she was a runaway? As if someone asked her name, she said aloud confidently, "Kim." If she used the name the woman called her in the letters maybe they would find each other and figure out the truth. She hadn't looked at every letter but, so far, the woman had not revealed her name or whereabouts. She was ready to wonder what would happen if this woman was her mother. If they ever met, was Cole going to have to call this woman her mother? What should she call a woman whom she never met but who was the person who gave birth to her? If she ever found out this woman's first name, she would call her that. Having one mother, even a fake one, was enough.

She pulled up her shirt and tugged the bandage on her arm but the dried blood stuck it to her skin. Her hands shook a little when a pain shot into her chest from the gash. Tugging her shirt away from her body she pulled the bandage off of the wound. The absence of the bandage made it feel as though she had sensitive newborn skin, not her bruised and slashed lived-in shell.

Watching the ground for protruding tree roots, she walked down the hill to slip through the fence. To appear confident, she drew her shoulders back as she walked up to Vladimir's front door. To avoid using her scratched knuckles, she tapped a small bit of loose patio cement on the door. Looking in the window, she tried to think of a time that her grandfather hadn't been there when she stopped by. He had always been there, even if it took a long time for him to get to the door. When she turned the wobbly brass doorknob it wasn't locked. She called out, "Grampa? You here?" She stood still as if her voice was searching the rooms and she didn't want to interrupt.

A visual sweep of the apartment verified that all the large things were where they always were: the couch, the refrigerator, the lamps, table, chairs. But the small things were pieces waiting for a determined puzzler. The first place Cole inspected was the table near the window. On it was a Caldor receipt, a dime and four pennies. Someone must have picked up something for him. But seeing that Caldor logo made Cole feel as though her mother could come by at any moment.

She didn't want to see her mother. Urgency took over. As if she were on a game show, she rushed to each strangely placed object and unraveled its meaning. The magic marker on the floor in the kitchen: her grandfather wrote something on the refrigerator. A vacant spot surrounded by crumbs on the counter: the toaster was gone. An empty bank envelope open at one end on the floor: Vladimir always dropped things. A naked stack of Pringles lying on the coffee table: no explanation. Her first tape recorder, the brown Fisher Price one that she used to play with years ago: cassette tape slot ejected, empty. Four C-batteries scattered on the bedroom floor next to cellophane wrapping: new batteries in the recorder held in with fresh masking tape.

In the bathroom she opened the cabinet. A few generations of ointment tubes, Band Aids in yellowed wrappers, two Barbasol cans, a crumpled tube of Poli-Grip, some razor blades rusted into a pile, plastic bottles of rubbing alcohol and peroxide. The directions on a glass bottle marked "Empirin Compound with Codeine" said to "Keep out of children's reach." She shook three tablets from the bottle directly into her mouth.

Cole wondered if kids weren't considered runaways if they thought like adults and didn't do childish things any more. Maybe it wouldn't matter if her mother found her as long as Cole was able to take care of herself. The bottle looked old yet the pills bit her tongue with a medicinal tang. She let her jaw drop and looked in the mirror at the wet white mounds stuck to her tongue. Her t-shirt was loose around her neck, half-covering bruises on her collarbone. Every time she blinked it felt like there was dirt in her right eye. After she splashed some water onto her face, she cupped her hands under the faucet and drank.

The longer she stayed in the bathroom the less she worried about her mother showing up. She lay down in the empty bathtub to pour peroxide on her wounds. The bubbles gasped around the blood and her pale skin, sounding like Coke fizz. With a towel under her head Cole leaned back and closed her eyes. She didn't dream. Dreaming would offer visions from another time or another part of herself. Instead, the hazy doze was full of her real and very present problems. As if on a dubious merry-go-round, every several minutes a vivid concern shocked her eyes open. First, she thought she heard her mother's voice. Next, she thought her chapped lips were bleeding but it was only drool. When Cole heard Vlad's neighbors turn on their water, she thought she had unconsciously turned on the tub's faucet and was going to drown in her sleep. After a deeper sleep took over, her arms lifted up to cover her face, jerking her awake. She dreamed that Vanessa hurled a brick at her head. Two hours had passed and the struggle to rest had exhausted her.

Sucking in her breath to get out of the tub, she couldn't tell if it was her bruised ribs or the summer's humid air that was making it hard to breathe. The school nurse always put ice on twisted ankles and bumped heads, so Cole wanted to see if that would help her side not hurt when she breathed. In the freezer she found a Pringles can, three empty metal ice cube trays and a cassette tape with a label in her handwriting, "Grampa songs." The green-crayon printing and the red cassette were from a few years back when she got her first tape recorder. In his shaky scribble, Vlad had used a black magic marker to change the "o" in songs to a dotted "I," but it looked more like a jagged lightning bolt.

Cole grabbed the tape and the canister. The cassette's cold plastic felt good on her rasped fingertips. She held the tape against her temple and then slid it to her forehead. In cartoons people who were beat up sometimes put a raw steak on their faces and heads. Maybe the feeling of dead animal flesh on your face made everything else seem a little less horrible.

She sat on the couch to rewind the red cassette in her old recorder. Looking down at the machine in her lap, she listened to Vlad's voice say, "Testing…one…two…three…four…five…. How long do you have to count? This ought to be fine. I pressed the two buttons like you showed me and I see the wheels turning so…. Ah…so, kid. I can't write steady so I hope you find this tape here. You're pretty smart so I bet you're listening to this thing and it's not just sitting in the freezer forever. Ahhhh…let's see. There's all this stuff going on and Tony didn't get here and you didn't either. I don't know. Ahh…" Cole turned her head and bent over closer to the speaker. She could hear the tape fine but didn't understand what Vlad was trying to say.

"Tony?" she said aloud to try to grasp what the security guard had to do with anything.

Vlad went on, "Well, that ghost. He got something to say. Every damn day he told me, 'Coney Island.' It's not where I would ever think to go but I guess we don't know things until we know them. I think it's got something to do with your grandmother. I think I got to look in her face and take care of things. Barnum wants me to and I think he wants me to take him there too. I didn't know if it was real 'til all this with the toaster and the fridge. I think I can say for sure now that I'm his grandson. It would explain a whole hell of a lot. Well, I don't have all day. I just wanted to tell you all this in case I don't make it back here. Listen. I got a case with something special in my closet. It's yours now, kid."

Cole rolled her eyes. She needed answers, not more questions.

"Now, you're gonna find this tape. So, I put some stuff in the freezer for you in the thing. You'll see it. I plugged the fridge back in. If the anything in the kitchen thing talks to you or something, it's for me not you. That green stuff is for you and your mother. Maybe she can get another car or something. Your mother. She never liked me and I think you should know why." He paused. Cole felt her pulse in her armpits. He sighed and said, "I used to steal things and light fires. And so did your father."

Cole's shoulders fell as she let her hands fall palms-up onto the couch. What was he talking about? Fires? What about all the letters she found? Maybe her grandfather had no idea about anything in the letters. Maybe the letters are from some crazy lady who hallucinated all the things she wrote.

"We got rid of places that nobody wanted any more. People paid us. But your dad didn't like it. He just hated it. Especially after little Vera…," he sighed and then paused.

Cole cupped her hand behind her ear to help her concentrate. "So, anyhow, Helen didn't like our business side of things. I did something for a guy so that Red got the job at that QE. You should know that I haven't done much in a long, long time. So don't go thinking like I did. Things just got so bad in Bridgeport, New Haven, hell, everywhere. No one cared any more. Not even the insurance companies or fire departments. So people started their own fires or got some dummy cousin to do it." Cole let out a frustrated grunt at the machine. She had always wanted to hear more about her father's little sister and Vlad yet again successfully dodged the subject.

"My grandfather taught my mother and showed me too. He was a real cracker jack. Someday you might hear about all the fires he did for P.T. Barnum. You already know, but Barnum was my grandfather, your…your…your great, great grandfather. I guess that's what he would be to you," he stopped and clicked his tongue a few times, as though he was thinking about what to say next. Cole had hoped the tape would tell her things about her that she didn't already know. Helen often complained about Vladimir's selfishness, but Cole was yet to recognize it. "Well, I think you ought to know all that so you can make up your own damn mind about Oleg…uh…your dad, Red and me. You're young but after you live a lot longer you'll think about all this and know what I'm saying. Every day. Every day I wonder why I'm not dead yet," he said angrily. "When I sit on the crapper forever and can't go and my damn balls hit the water, I think, 'The hell for? What the *hell* for?'"

She stopped the machine, fearing that he was launching into of one of his old-man rants. To keep things moving she carried the tape player into the bedroom. After placing it on the bed, she pressed play as she searched for the case. Vlad went on about P.T. Barnum and something about a ghost but Cole couldn't hear everything as she opened the creaky closet door. On hangers were white shirts with stained collars and a couple of polyester dress pants, including a maroon pair that Cole remembered he wore on her birthday a few years ago. He wore a tie too. That was the most dressed up Cole ever saw him. When Helen asked him about it, he said, "I went to see a man about a horse." Cole thought that he meant that he brought her a horse and rushed out to the front yard to look for her four-legged birthday present. Why didn't he just give her this thing for her birthday? Why did everyone keep important things from her?

Bending down under all the clothes in the closet forced a groan out of her. She opened up a cigar box, but it was only full of rubber bands and a package of unused postage stamps that she held in her teeth as she searched behind a white plastic trash bag full of old pillows. His voice was still droning on, making it seem as though he were talking to himself while she looked for something he misplaced.

A square black case was attached to a luggage caddy with bungee cords. She gripped the caddy's handle and pulled the case out of the closet and next to Vlad's bed. There was a piss smell coming from the bed but when she patted the spot where she was about to sit down it was dry. Seated on the edge of the bed, she undid the case from the caddy and laid it flat. Just as she sprung the brass latches open, Vlad's voice stopped and the tape recorder clicked off.

Chapter 31

Finally home from work, Helen wasn't surprised that Cole was asleep. The longer her work shift, the more it seemed like Cole had worked a long day too. The boredom compounded during the ten hours in the apartment alone. Waking up late the next morning, it was as though she suffered from an overdose of tedium.

The apartment was dark and stone quiet. Helen turned on the kitchen light. There were no dishes in the dish drain or in the sink, yet the cupboard doors were all open at different angles. She thought it strange that Cole had cleaned up but left things undone.

Helen sat down at the kitchen table and bent over to untie her shoes. There were red spots on the floor; her steps had smeared some. She placed the tip of her middle finger into one of the dots expecting it to be hard, like a dot of paint. It smeared when she rubbed it between her finger and thumb. She looked around the kitchen to see where else this red liquid had splattered. A red streak across the white refrigerator ended with a handprint next to the door handle. Helen stopped taking off her shoes and stumbled toward Cole's bedroom.

Fearing something was wrong with Cole more than worrying about waking her, Helen switched on the light in her bedroom. "Cole?" Her voice probed the empty space for something her eyes already knew but her brain had not yet accepted. Cole's absence made the question tighten in her throat and repeat in a higher octave. "Cole?" A ballpoint pen and half a roll of cherry Life Savers sat in convincing permanence on the narrow, blond-colored dresser. Out of the open closet door dribbled random socks and an empty black plastic bag. The stained facecloth in the middle of the room brought everything together. Helen immediately recognized the red substance now as blood.

The kitchen's red stains then registered as blood in the playback of the memory that was only a minute or so old. She was afraid to say Cole's name again. What if she were calling out to Cole and she was dead? She thought about the night Red died and how many times she had called numbers where there were no answers.

Vague terror rang in Helen's ears as if a cherry bomb had blasted next to her face. She heard nothing but a high-pitched tone in her right ear. The other ear seemed useless, or the apartment had been silenced by whatever happened.

Helen rushed to her bedroom and flipped on the light switch. Usually she used the lamp in the room since the ceiling light was so bright. She gripped her fingers around the doorjamb when she saw the spot where a picture of Red, herself and Cole had been.

She got down on her hands and knees and searched under the bed. The tin can of letters was gone. The blood on the bedspread reminded Helen that Cole hadn't even had her first period yet. She knew there was a chance that she had but didn't come to Helen. There didn't seem to be an end to the ways Helen felt like a lousy mother.

The evidence of what happened to Cole added up to what Helen had feared. This woman, Cole's biological mother, was obviously very smart. There was no sign of her breaking in and so far, there was no weapon left behind. Helen went out to the kitchen and opened the drawer in a white metal stand-alone cabinet where they kept the silverware. There were four matching serrated knives, the large knife they used to cut up big things and a paring knife. The scissors, along with a few pens and pencils, were in a Mason jar on the counter. Of course, the woman's weapon could be anything at all; Helen just didn't want it to be something she got from the apartment. There was already a substantial list of things she'd messed up that she recorded on her internal mothering scoreboard.

The woman's letters had grown stranger but there didn't seem to be any urgency to them. Helen tried to remember what the last letter said but they all seemed the same. One refrain was that she was making money so that she could come get Cole. At first this worried Helen but after a few letters she wondered if maybe it would be better if Cole did go with real mother. After all, now that Red was gone, what was the difference between this woman and Helen?

Helen panicked that the woman could have taken Cole in order to bring her to the police and let them know how Red and Vlad took her from the hospital. But why wouldn't she have gone to the police already and had them come and arrest Helen and take Cole away? There were too many questions.

Chapter 32

Cole opened the case. It smelled like Allan's boxes of old Civil War boots and socks she had snooped through. It was full of crumpled newspapers that she tossed out onto the floor. Her fingers briefly touched something sharp. Her hand snapped back before she eased herself onto her knees to lift more paper wads out. A small hideous face looked back at her. It was a small, petrified body of some sort. The monkey-like face had perpetually bared fangs. It looked like it was trying to tell her something by holding its cheek with one creepy claw-hand while it tucked the other one under its ear.

Afraid to touch it again, Cole used one of the discarded newspaper pages to push the rest of the papers out of the way. The creature's fishlike tail curled up and part of its very end had broken off. After she pushed it to the other side of the case, visible at the case's bottom were a small envelope, three small teeth, fish scales and some fragments that had chunked off the freaky being. The stiff creature had small sagging breasts with dark nipples that looked like the rubbery necks of steamer clams.

Cole fixed her eyes on the envelope and snatched it out. Unsealed, the envelope contained a thin, brittle piece of paper folded in half. When Cole opened it, the paper snapped and cracked apart at the crease. She held the two pieces together to read the neatly printed letters written in pencil, "This is the real Fee-Jee Mermaid owned by P.T. Barnum. My grandfather gave it to me for my 8th birthday. He told me it could make me rich one day but I will never sell it. Promised by Vladimir Sevic. December 19, 1915."

Cole turned her face away from the Fiji Mermaid but couldn't stop staring at it. It was not only hideous; it smelled like a sour rag mop the school janitor used to clean the bathrooms. The face looked as if it screamed until its very last living moment and then froze in that screeching state. One of its hands was stiffly stuck next to its cheek, like it was killed mid-horror. The other hand was withered. It looked angry and scared and the thing's dead eyes made Cole almost as uneasy as she would be if it were alive. Cole twitched the edge of her mouth as she did whenever she was tense and first met someone. Imagining that it could come to life and bite her arm, she lifted it with the crumpled newspapers packed under it. The tail part didn't look at all like any image of a mermaid Cole had ever seen but it did have scales and fins. It was bigger than any fish she'd ever seen but only a portion of the size of a real woman.

Perhaps she never knew what a mermaid actually was or maybe there are pretty ones and ugly ones, like dogs. Maybe it was one of those words that she just learned wrong and didn't hear often enough to get it right. But what about the commercial with the blonde mermaid cartoon? The jingle was sung calmly, "Ask any mermaid you happen to see, 'What's the best tuna?' Chicken of the Sea." No one would dare ask this mermaid anything. And if they did and it could answer, Cole imagined it would let out a bizarre high-pitched screech.

If the mermaid had any powers, maybe she could be her good luck charm. Once, Cole had convinced herself that if she had the guts to steal Dave Johnson's milk money from his desk, she would get the Radio Shack remote-control car she wanted for Christmas. After she snatched the two quarters and put one in the bottom of each of her sneakers, she endured the nerve-racking one-hour shakedown their teacher led. Everyone was forced to empty out their pockets and turn them inside out. They had to take everything out of their desks and shake their books to see if the coins would drop out. No extra quarters were found, so that Christmas she got the Blue Shark car she had circled in the Radio Shack newspaper ad. When it didn't work unless she was right next to it, she thought maybe that defect had something to do with stealing Dave's milk money.

Taking a closer look at the gruesome face again, Cole told herself that if she touched three of the mermaid's teeth, she would get away and live somewhere else and her life would be fine without anybody but her new lucky mermaid. Cole's mouth twitched as she touched the tip of her forefinger onto one of the nastiest and longest teeth. It was hard and dry. The mermaid's lips were poised as if she were about to brush her gnarly teeth. Cole touched a long tooth coming from the bottom of the jaw. For extra luck her finger glided over the top row of teeth. She grunted a little as she pulled the papers over its face and closed the case.

Cole pulled the bungee cords back around the mermaid's case and the luggage caddy the way Vlad had them. She stepped back a few feet to look at it. It didn't look too bad. It was only as big as it needed to be, maybe about the size of two and a half rulers. If people didn't know that the case was filled with a bizarre pathetic creature, they might guess that Cole had been chosen to haul something like a vacuum cleaner or a few volumes of an encyclopedia set to a shut-in with dirty floors or a sick student writing a big report at home. Vlad's note said that it could be worth some money and she was going to need some cash after the Pringles can money ran out.

When she was a lot younger she saw a movie on television where a robber took the cases off some pillows in order to fill them with what he stole. He slung the full sacks over one shoulder like a reverse Santa Claus. Cole yanked the pillowcase off Vlad's pillow and filled it with the Pringles cash can, a few spoons and forks and his cassette tape recorder with the tape in it. She also grabbed a variety pack of hard plastic combs that she had given Vlad after she took a pink one with a long pointy handle and Helen chose the yellow one with the large round handle.

Only one of the two scrapbooks was left on the coffee table. It was the older one with newspaper clippings about P.T. Barnum and pictures of Vlad's mother and grandfather. Now that she was probably not even related to these people, Cole wondered if she even wanted to take it. And her overall load was already so heavy.

The scrapbook almost filled the rest of the pillowcase. As she tested its weight a knock on the door startled her. The door handle jiggled and then turned. She regretted not locking the door earlier.

"Hey! You're Vlad's grandkid," Tony said softly. The hush of the quiet space made him speak in hushed tones. He kept his hand on the doorknob to stop from entering the apartment any farther.

"Yeah," Cole said softly.

"Is he in there?" he asked, pointing at the bedroom.

Cole pointed at the bedroom too and said, "Yeah." She closed her eyes and tilted her head to mime sleeping.

Tony motioned for Cole to step outside to talk to him. She left the pillowcase on the floor and rushed out. He closed the door once they were both standing on the small patio.

"We were supposed to head out to Coney Island Sunday and I couldn't make it. He was mad as hell, but it was a family emergency," Tony explained.

Cole thought that she should probably say something about his family problem but by the time she did, Tony had already continued. She accidentally asked, "Sorry?" instead of giving condolences. Tony thought Cole meant she didn't understand. He repeated, "We were supposed to go to Coney Island. He said something about going to see his ex-wife and something about P.T. Barnum. I think he just wanted to go down that old memory lane and go to the park and stuff."

Cole agreed, "I think that's all. Nothing really to think about any harder than you already have thought about it." She was pleased with her attempt to get Tony to stop analyzing the situation.

"You know, I've been doing this for a while now. Over ten years. I think I know these old people better than their own families. The secret is that they are just little babies again. They want to eat and sleep a lot and do things that just make them happy. It's all like they are all living in rewind," Tony rubbed his chin and looked to Cole for her reaction.

"Rewind. I like that," Cole said.

"I just thought of that. Just now. Just like that," Tony said proudly.

"That's incredible," Cole said. She loved using the title of one of her favorite shows this way. It made her feel smart and sneaky. *That's Incredible* wasn't on television any more but when it was she never missed it. When they all watched together, Red and Helen seemed to enjoy the ghost stories best. But Cole loved when they showed kids who did things better than adults. Her favorites were a 4-year-old boy who walked a tightrope and another kid named Tiger who played golf since he was only three years old. Whenever she watched it, she wondered if someday she would ever do something that would impress anyone. The closest she ever got so far was that winning the Stevie Wonder tickets for Gwen and getting a medal for her P.T. Barnum science fair project.

"When your grandfather wakes up, will you tell him that I stopped by?" Tony asked.

"I will," Cole assured him. As soon as he turned the corner she rushed back into the empty apartment.

Riding the adrenaline from the surprise visitor, she felt little pain as she gathered up everything. She locked the door behind her. No one was out on their concrete patios or in their miniature yards as she hauled the case and the pillowcase toward the hole in the fence. She stopped at the neighbor lady's wooden yard ornament. It was a cutout of a cartoon bear with a bee about to sting its nose. It read, "Grin and bear it." The bear's face looked worried but happy at the same time.

No one's back door was open. No curtains moved and she didn't see any faces in the windows. When she pulled the bear out of the ground, it was attached to a garden stake with some wire and staples. She stuffed the decoration upside down into the pillowcase with the stake sticking out. This new item along with the scrapbook made the sack look less like a pillowcase and more like something really made to haul things.

Her bag was where she left it near the tree. A bird had dropped a grayish white splatter on the note. Her father told her that a bird crapping on her was a sign of good luck. She piled the mermaid case, her duffel bag and the pillowcase into a pyramid and pulled Vlad's bungee cords around the lumpy shapes. She folded the note carefully so that none of the feces was lost. As she slipped it into the pillowcase she thought, "Shitty luck is better than no luck."

Sweaty from pulling the case up the hill and afraid that someone had spotted her, she decided to get a bus going downtown. The load was easier to pull once she got to Boston Avenue's even pavement.

She felt around inside the pillow and pulled out the Pringles can. She shook it to listen for coins but it was the real Pringles can and she just heard the chips hop up and crunch down. As the bus pulled up, Cole held the other can up to her ear and shook it. Nothing jangled. As the bus pulled up, Cole tucked the canister under her armpit. This jacked her collarbone up, giving her relief from the ache she had there since Vanessa had knelt on her chest.

Being nervous that she didn't have the right bus fare gave her added strength to heave her load onto the bus. As the bus drove on, she opened the canister to see if there was a one-dollar bill. On other trips she saw people ask for change and now that she was on her own she would have to do these things. The bus driver's eyes shifted from the road to Cole as she struggled to steady herself. She saw his eyes change from curiosity to concern once she popped the lid off the canister.

"You forget about the paying. Just go sit down," the bus driver said as he winked at Cole. He leaned toward her, pointed at the can and whispered, "and put that away."

Her face flushed red just before she put the lid back on and said, "Thanks, sir."

After she sat in one of the front seats she looked back at the rest of the bus and at least five people watched her. She stuffed the cylinder down the pillowcase and lifted one of the bungee cords to hold it in place. Now that she had to protect herself, the money and the mermaid, she was going to have to be more careful.

Cole felt less adrift now that she knew that Vlad went to visit his wife. When she was younger, Cole used to laugh when Vlad told people that he and Red's mother were "estranged." It sounded like a joke about them both acting strangely by not speaking to each other. Back then she couldn't imagine why he would want to erase someone so important from his life. But that's what she was doing now. Laying down distance and time between her and her mother was all she could think to do.

As the bus made its way downtown she bit at her thumb nail. Her thoughts bounced from how she was half runaway and half something else, maybe a "run-to." Finding her way to Coney Island was going to be hard but at least she had somewhere to go. Even though she wasn't really Vlad's granddaughter she hoped that their time together would make her at least half his grandkid. But it probably wouldn't make her related to P.T. Barnum. But what if she never found out who her real great-great-grandfather was? Does that mean she just wasn't allowed to have any? Kind of like a mermaid was half lady and half fish, Cole didn't fit in to any of her worlds anymore. She gave the mermaid's case a light kick.

Chapter 33

Helen was back home from Vlad's with more questions, the foremost being where the old man was that late at night. She had banged on his door and peeked through his window. The apartment's forsaken, yet homey, ambiance turned into a whey-colored blah without him there.

After making herself pancakes, she sat up all night smoking at the kitchen table. She put all the lights on in the apartment so nothing could take her by surprise. In the bright kitchen she noticed the blood smear that arched across the white refrigerator door looked like the tail of a falling star. But there was nothing at the beginning or the end of it. Helen wondered when she was supposed to clean the blood. Who was the criminal and who was the victim in this kidnapping? Helen reasoned that Cole could both benefit from and be a victim of it all.

Back when Red brought her home, he believed that they would give Cole a life that no one else could. But after a few weeks of foul diapers and feeding her baby formula, Red and Helen laughed at how much they missed their simple life before dragging this tiny new person into it. Helen joked that she would sneak the baby back into the ward so that a nurse would think that someone had merely misplaced the infant. But for all of her joking, Helen tried to come to terms with being a mother.

After her miscarriage she wept for days and it took months for her to talk to Red about it. Although it appeared to him that Helen had finally opened up about her pain, she had kept her secret fears buried. Her mouth told him, "After everything we did to get ready and how happy you were when I told you. I just need time." But her heart knew that her post-miscarriage despondency dipped far down into her soul, even though she sometimes doubted she was born with a soul in the same way everyone else seemed to have been.

She couldn't tell Red that she was sure that their baby died because it sensed that she was not capable of loving it. Despite Helen trying to talk to the baby and rubbing her bump the way women did on television commercials, she hadn't felt a connection. Most nights were filled with long dreadful nightmares that picked up where they left off when she awoke to pee and then went back to sleep. After working long hours, Red slept through the nights and didn't know how many nights Helen spent sitting on their couch flipping through the Sears catalog. The depression Helen felt after the miscarriage was sadness for herself much more than it was for their lost baby.

Now she regretted lying to Red. If she had just told him the truth, he might not have gone to his father. Cole would have ended up with a different family. Helen knew that just about any mother could have done better. She would probably have both parents living and her biological mother certainly wouldn't have known where she was and kidnapped her.

Chain smoking, Helen watched the clock's minute hand go around a few times and the sun come up before she called Gwen.

Gwen rushed over and sat at the kitchen table where only Cole had ever sat since moving to Sheridan Street. She pretended she didn't notice the streaks of blood on the floor.

The gravity of what had possibly happened was clear but Helen wasn't ready to put it into words. They sat in expectant silence until Helen answered a question that wasn't asked, "I don't know."

Gwen waited.

"I don't know where to start. Shit. Oh my God. Sorry. I know you're religious."

"I kind of like that you think I am so innocent. But you know I grew up in this city and my mother was a psych ward nurse for thirty years. I can handle more than you think," Gwen said.

"Well, this is a loony bin for sure," Helen swept her arm out to gesture toward the crime-scene-esque room.

Gwen took a quick look around but couldn't make sense of it all.

Helen lit a cigarette and looked out the window as she told Gwen, "Okay. I came home last night after a long shift and Cole wasn't here. I thought she was asleep. Sometimes when I work a really long day she gets sad and sleeps a lot."

"Do you think she went to her grandfather's place?"

"No. I went there and he's missing too," she said.

"Maybe Cole's with him at a hospital or something?"

"I don't think so," Helen said. Looking Gwen in the eyes, she asked, "Can you keep something secret?"

"Sure. I think so."

"I think Cole was kidnapped."

"What? What do you mean? By Red's father?"

"No. By her real mother."

"Wait. Cole isn't yours?"

"I got home last night and there was that blood all over the place," Helen pointed at the floor. "It looks like they had a fight or something. Maybe Cole didn't want to go with her and the lady stabbed her. She took a picture of us out of my bedroom too. Maybe she's going to the police. I don't know. Oh God."

"You're making no sense."

Helen sat up and looked back out the window and took a drag from her shaking cigarette. "Lookit. It's hard to explain but here's the best I can do." She took a breath and made a fist with her other hand and used it to help get the words out by keeping time with it on the table as she talked. She told Gwen about Red and Vlad stealing Cole and how she never really knew the details until recently.

"Yep. A nurse there told Vlad about the baby. They just went in there and took her. That's it," she said. Then she continued the story up through when she came home the night before. "The tin was gone and so was Cole," she said as she shook her head. "Then I thought maybe I should go to the police."

"Please don't. It always ends bad. I've seen it too many times. No matter how right you are somehow they see it opposite," Gwen warned.

The phone rang.

Helen rushed to phone and then stopped. "What if it's the

police?"

"Don't ask questions. Don't answer questions. Just listen," Gwen advised.

"Hello?" Helen sounded like a scared child.

Listening was too stressful so Gwen bowed her head and prayed. She asked God to give her strength to help Helen and for Him to give Helen strength to pull herself through this mess. She pictured Cole's face framed by those blunt bangs and lots of light surrounding the girl. Her prayer turned to Red as she thought, "Helen can't do this alone. You have to protect them."

"Hey," Helen's voice pulled Gwen out of her thoughtful state.

She opened her eyes calmly and asked Helen, "Who was it?"

"It was Red's mother. She wanted me to know Vladimir was there."

"What? Helen. This is confusing. So, you know where Cole is now?" Gwen's tone was taut with frustration.

"I'm sorry. I don't tell things in the right order when I'm nervous. No, Red's mother has Vladimir. Not Cole. I don't know. I still don't get why he's there."

"Where is 'there'?"

"She moved to Coney Island after she left Red and his father here," Helen said as she lit another cigarette.

"Well, we know where Vladimir ended up. God is good. Did you tell her about all of this?" Gwen asked.

Helen shook her head. She took a long drag and let out the smoke over her shoulder, then said, "You've always been so good to us. Getting me this place and spending time with Cole. You're a nice lady. I'm sorry I put this mess in your life."

Gwen shook her head at Helen as she held the crucifix and ran it along the chain on her necklace. When she heard Helen's stomach growl as the scent of bacon frying wafted up from Allan's kitchen, she asked, "Can I get you something to eat?"

"No thanks. My gut feels like hell."

She thought that making Helen a piece of toast anyway would be the right thing to do, the most Christian thing to do. But Gwen stopped herself. At her bible study group a deacon talked about how Christ moved around a lot. This way the same people didn't rely on him all the time. He helped and then moved on. The elder told Gwen that this was something she needed to work on. She made a plan to stay with Helen for only another half hour.

Helen said, "Last night I was wide awake in bed trying to figure out what to do. So, in the middle of the night I got up and made myself some pancakes. If she was here maybe your mother would have gotten out the straitjacket for me?" Helen's good-humored eyes made her downturned lips seem like a smile.

"When we played all wild, my mother always threatened to tie us up into what she called a cuckoo suit," Gwen said. They each glazed out a laugh and then breathed a deep sigh. "I think you just have to do what seems right for you," Gwen said.

"Yeah, you're probably right."

Gwen shrugged and said, "Maybe."

"Red always said that we could win the lottery and I would just go fix myself a grilled cheese sandwich, smoke a cigarette and then go to bed."

Gwen smiled and nodded her head, saying, "Red was one funny guy."

"He was," Helen shook her head.

"Don't you think you ought to go to Coney Island? It seems you could get them to figure this all out. You have to at least tell old Vlad. She adores him," Gwen checked her watch. She had five more minutes.

Helen tilted her head and squinted at Gwen, "You always know what to do. I just never think of things like that."

"I guess I got that from my mother," Gwen said.

Helen stubbed out her cigarette and swirled the filter around in the ashes and other butts.

"Well, maybe I don't always. Sorry. I forgot that Cole told me you didn't have a…."

Helen grabbed Gwen's hand, "I'll be ready in about thirty minutes. I'll pay for gas."

"But, I wasn't…," Gwen retorted.

"You better not argue with me. I got to get out of these clothes and pack," Helen rushed into her bedroom and shut the door.

Gwen checked her watch again and sighed. Then, standing outside Helen's bedroom door, she said, "Helen, I can't drive there. I can't…I can't do this." Alone in the kitchen with Cole's smeared blood, a shaky faintness came over her. "I think I have to go back home now. I don't feel so well."

Still in the bedroom, Helen said, "Don't go, Gwen. Maybe you can just stay here? You know, maybe sleep on the couch later? I don't want to be alone."

Gwen said, "God help me, Helen. I can't stay here. You need to call someone else. You have all day to find someone."

She startled back from the door when Helen opened it to say, "I just don't have anybody."

Gwen threw her arms up, "I don't know. Maybe someone from work?"

Helen shrugged, "I don't know what's so hard about it. Why can't you? Am I that...?"

"Don't you dare. Look around! Can you see?" Gwen motioned to the refrigerator and floor. "You're seriously out of your mind if you think anyone but you could stay here with this, this, this...Cole's blood all over the place! Jesus fucking Christ!"

Helen, stunned, held her hand over her mouth.

Gwen grabbed Helen's shoulders. They locked eyes as she leveled with her, "Listen to me. Clean this place up. Then you have to figure out how you want to be Cole's mother. Maybe even *if* you want to be. You read those letters and you didn't do anything about it. Think about it."

Helen nodded and then dropped her head. Gwen let go, opened the door, closed it behind her. Her footsteps thumped down the stairs like dwindling cranky goodbyes.

Chapter 34

Janet had rolled down all the car windows to smoke a joint as she drove. After parking in the Carvel Ice Cream parking lot, she flipped open a pizza box on the passenger's seat. Two slices sat in the car for a day and a half, but the summer's humid air had kept the dough from getting too hard to eat. She tilted her head back to hold a slice above her mouth. Her hand hit the car's roof so she slid down in her seat to lower her face. After half of the slice dipped past teeth, she chewed it into a ball inside one cheek. Squirrel-like, she did this again and filled her other cheek. She sat back up and sipped from an open Coke can until she gradually broke down the pizza wads to swallow them. She flipped the pizza box lid back down and let out a long, deep burp.

An automated beep went off to let the business know someone had entered. Janet stepped back to make it go off again. The girl behind the counter didn't stop reading a *People* magazine. Janet resisted doing it a third time and made her way over to the cake freezer. She selected a Cookie Puss ice cream cake and brought it to the counter, the counter girl finally looked up and asked, "Do you want something written on that?"

"No," Janet said, annoyed. "There isn't even room there for a name. Even something like that," Janet pointed at the girl's nametag that read, 'K.' "What's the matter? They too cheap to put your whole name on there?" Janet asked.

"Name's Amy," she said with an enthusiasm she did not show earlier.

"Hmmm," Janet said as she nodded her head.

"Remember?" the girl asked.

"Remember what? Are you from the donut place next door, too?"

"No. I used to work at a place in Bayonne," Amy said. She nodded in a way that made Janet feel like she should remember her. "You came in there once a while back. Got a bunch of things out of the walk-in fridge."

"Oh yeah! Shit. I was so lost! Well, as you can see, I got to Coney Island just fine." Janet added, "But I just got here yesterday so I don't know if your directions were that great." They both let out three-beat compulsory laughs.

Amy chattered on about how her uncle hired her to work at the shop for the summer. She motioned to the back of the shop, "Yep. I'm his eyes and ears so no one…." Amy interrupted herself, "Did you say you wanted me to write something on this Cookie Puss?"

Janet rummaged around in her bag and pulled out a fistful of fifties. Half pissed off that so many were wadded together and half proud she had so many, Janet said, "I'm not asking for free shit this time."

Amy's eyes followed the money as Janet shoved it back into her bag.

Janet opened the ice cream cake box. "There's no room anywhere for his name. Look." The face's upside-down ice cream cone nose took up most of the cake's real estate.

"I fit stuff in there before," Amy pointed out a small area underneath Cookie Puss's chocolate smile.

Janet walked over to look at the other cakes in the freezer. "You know what? I'm not gonna be a pain in your ass but I think I might want this one instead." She took out another Cookie Puss cake.

"That's okay. People change their minds all the time. Last week we all got to eat a cake because we wrote on it, 'To a Whale of a Mom!' When they came to pick it up they realize that she's fat and this wasn't good, right? You know what I mean, right?" Amy's hand over her snicker showed Janet a temporary tattoo on the back of her hand of a cartoon dog on roller skates.

"It's my friend's birthday. So, I want it to say, 'Happy Birthday Animal.'"

"Animal? Like the word 'animal'?"

"Yep. That's his name."

"It's going to take a few minutes."

"Okay. I'll be back," Janet made a show of placing a fifty-dollar bill on the counter. She tried walking through the front door quickly in hopes it wouldn't beep, but it did.

Back at the car Janet choked down another few bites of pizza. She fished her flask out from her bag to swoosh around just enough Jack Daniels in her mouth to cover her pizza breath.

The Laundromat next to Carvel was full of people moving slowly in the heat. Since moving in with Animal she didn't have to leave the house to do laundry since there was a washer and dryer in Wilda's pantry. Her life was getting better. Maybe she would be able to get her baby back soon. She had a lot of money and some friends, even though all of it was counterfeit in one way or another.

From the car, Janet watched Amy come back out to the counter with her uncle. As she lowered the cake back in the box, he made change with the cash register and placed it on the counter. He tucked the fifty it into his shirt pocket, left the store and drove away in a baby blue Cadillac.

As she swung the shop's door open Janet talked over the door's beep, "He's going out to spend that right away, isn't he?"

"Yeah. Sometimes he does that. I guess that's what makes him the boss," Amy said. She put the cake on the counter.

"Speaking of that. I meant to tell you I almost have enough to get my little girl back. Remember? That's why I'm out here. Now I can move somewhere nice and get her in school and get a job."

Janet's breath and sweaty odor drifted toward Amy. She stepped to the side while she attempted an enthusiastic response, "Really? That's awesome."

Amy spun the cake around on the counter and tilted it just enough so that it wouldn't slip. "See? It came out okay, right?"

"That's better than okay. It's awesome." The last word she said surprised Janet since she seldom used "awesome" but was trying to seem as though she fit in. She smiled and leaned on the counter to make it seem like she was comfortable with the lingo.

"Oh! Here's your change." Amy picked up Janet's money that had been sitting on the counter.

Janet took it and then handed Amy back a dollar. She pointed at a cardboard fundraiser placard from the counter. "Can I get some change? I want to stick some money in this thing for these poor crippled kids."

She handed her ten dimes. Janet's ink-stained fingers

captivated Amy as they took their time tucking the coins into the March of Dimes fundraising placard. "My little girl is healthy but what if she wasn't? Right?"

"That would be really horrible, yeah," Amy agreed.

Wedging the last one in, Janet said, "Well, that should help get some crutches or something for little Jimmy there." Janet put the placard back on the other end of the counter and pulled out another fifty. She slapped it on the counter and told Amy, "That's for you! I can't believe we met up again. It was fate! Everything happens for a reason, right? What time you work until tonight? Maybe you can come over."

"Wow. That's too much. You got to save money for your daughter. I can't take that," Amy said.

"No. No. I'm doing a lot better and you helped me out that night. I remember." Janet tapped her temple. "You should really come on over tonight!"

"I work late." Amy rolled her eyes and leaned both elbows on the counter. She eked out another smile and said, "But have a fun party."

Janet grabbed a pen attached to the cash register by a long thin chain. She pulled Amy's arm toward her and wrote "Janet" and the Watchtower's address on the inside of Amy's forearm. "In case you change your mind," she said. As she left with Animal's birthday cake, she peeped, "Beep, beep," along with the electronic tone.

Chapter 35

Cole took the bus from the stop before the downtown bus terminal. If Helen were looking for her that would be a place she would search. She walked away from the busier streets and found shelter from the midday sun under an overpass. Not much of the graffiti made sense and some people painted over each other's messages. Cole chose to stay on the side of the road that said, "Don't stop" and "Shit Hole." The other side had a colorful and fun "Brenda" in letters that looked like balloons. Below it someone sprayed "is a slutbag!" There were some things left on the other side that looked like someone's bed sheets or clothes, so she stayed on the side that seemed to have unmistakably unwanted things.

When she made it to the top of the steep ramp with her stuff, along the ledge she spotted cigarette butts, empty pizza boxes and beer bottles, some with what looked like piss in them. Somehow there was a large stone that far up the incline. Cole kicked away a small Table Talk Pie box that someone used to get rid of a bloody tampon and steadied her load in place so it wouldn't slide down the cement slope.

Her new spot was equally out in the open and hidden. Cole could see who was coming from every direction but the people driving through were looking at the road. From the pillowcase she pulled out the money canister and a short stack of Hydrox. She nibbled a cookie and looked down at her black Converse sneakers.

She thought that maybe she should go home and tell her mother what she knew but tell her that she just wanted to forget it all and go on living as if she didn't know. The next thought was to find this woman who said she was her real mother. Maybe they wouldn't be at all alike. Even so, what if she felt that this woman was her mother? What if she also pulled her fingers to crack her knuckles? Did she love ketchup on grilled cheese sandwiches? Did her face spaz out when she was nervous? She imagined talking to a woman who looked like her but with everything longer: hair, arms, legs, nose and feet. If she recorded their first conversation would it sound like an older Cole talking to her younger self?

What if she had to be with her? Maybe there's a law that says once you're found by your real mother, you have to go live with her. Over time could they both forget that Cole had ever lived with someone else? How long would Cole have to live to forget the people she thought were her father, mother and grandfather? Would she forget their names first? What if she never said their names ever again and tried not to think about them? Would she forget the dead ones first?

Cole pulled out the cracker tin of letters. Some of the letters were postmarked Brooklyn, New York. A few were mailed from the zip code 10013. She didn't like these ones and didn't open them. Ever since the movie *Friday the 13th* had come out when she was in first grade, she hated the number thirteen. In the movie trailer a man counted to thirteen as people seemed to be killed or hunted by someone. Whenever it came on the television, Cole left the room but the blood curdling screams made her feel as if they were chasing her.

She opened a greeting card that was written by someone with pretty and uniform handwriting. It said, "Dear Helen, I hope this helps you until Red's company pays up. I hope you bring that your girl of yours to visit me again someday. Red always wanted me to get to know her better. Love, Wilda."

Cole was angry that her mother hid these letters. All of them were about her from people looking for her. She had listened while Helen called Wilda to tell her Red had died. Near the end of the conversation, Helen called out to Cole, "You don't want to talk to your grandmother do you Cole?" Before she could answer, Helen told Wilda, "She's too upset. Maybe another time."

Cole opened a few other letters. They were from the woman who said she was her mother. She searched for the woman's name. Many of the letters were signed off with, "Sent with love from your True Mother," but none mentioned her name. Cole skimmed the letters for clues but for as often as she wrote, her True Mother didn't reveal much. Most of the letters were about getting money in order to take Cole back.

What if Cole went to look for her and then the woman came to find her in Bridgeport and she wasn't there? Helen wouldn't know where to send her True Mother to find her. One letter said, "I mail these from places I don't live so you can't find me. I don't want your family to get mad and send the fuzz after me, you know. After I make all the money we need I'll come get you, baby Kim." Cole didn't like being called a baby, even if this lady could be her mother.

Cole winced when she smoothed out one of the letters on her thigh. Even though she chewed the acidic Empirin Compound tablets before leaving Vlad's, her scabs and bruises throbbed. It was as if the deepest pains pushed to the surface to prove that they were still inside her.

Maybe Cole needed to stay away from everyone she knew and who knew her. She closed her eyes. Her tongue dug between two of her molars to mine out a paste made up of the hard Hydrox cookie, its white stuffing and her saliva.

Her eyes startled open as a train rattled across the bridge above her. The train's booming racket made it seem as if the cement shook beneath her but when she put her hand down on it there was only a slight vibration. Dirt shook down as she leaned back on her elbows and then laid flat on her back. Maybe after hundreds of trains clattered above and enough people littered, the garbage and grime could bury her.

She tried to fall asleep. Maybe she could die there. Above her, the metal bridge had many sections about the size of her body. The images from the Mexican newspapers in the pantry came back to her. When their world shook, everything collapsed onto that moment, no matter where people were. Photos showed a woman found alive days later who was protected under a table and one man who positioned himself in a bathtub and pulled a giant mirror over him. She shifted over to the right to be directly under one of the bridge's underbelly sections and lay back. How perfect would it be if an earthquake hit at that moment? Motionless, she stared straight up into the underside of the overpass. Riveted steel beams crossed to make dark vaults above her. Encased in a metal bridge tomb, there would be no place to go and no way to run. The only decision she would need to make would be when, and if, to scream. But what would happen when she needed to pee or crap? After a deep breath she concentrated on the movie version of her fantasy, where no one needs to use the bathroom.

No cars or trains passed. It was quiet while she imagined her bridge coffin. Motionless, she felt as though she needed nothing at all. Her eyes fixed on her metal ceiling. If she were finally found there alive and everyone she knew had died in the earthquake, what would she do? Imagining this scenario, she felt bad about her mother's death even though she wasn't even her mother now.

Maybe something in her knew she wasn't her mother's child all along. Or maybe she never treated Cole the way people treat their real kids and neither of them knew what was missing so they lived like familiar strangers.

A thought of a crushed Vanessa crossed her mind. In the Mexican newspapers, there had been a photo of a stiff bloody leg sticking out from under a pile of earthquake rubble. She hoped that this would be Vanessa's fate, just like the Wicked Witch of the West. Instead of the witch's legs retracting, she hoped Vanessa would bloat up and stink like an animal run over on a busy road.

What if the schools shook until they crumbled? What if she had to go to New York City and just learn how to survive on her own? Her parents brought her there for her tenth birthday. They left early in the morning after eating powdered donuts for breakfast. Her father also treated her to a cup of coffee with lots of milk and sugar, even though Helen argued against it.

They got a spot on the train where all three of them could sit together. Cole sat by the window and they sat in silence with the quiet people who took the train to the city every day. She didn't understand why everyone looked so grim when they were going to such an incredible place. It seemed like everyone on television and in real life loved the city, and that the train people didn't realize what those actors knew, or they understood something no one else did.

Pushed along by the crowds, the three of them rushed through Grand Central Station to another train that lurched forward out of each station on their ride to the Natural History Museum. As they pulled away from the third stop, the motion forced Cole to barf up a puddle of that morning's caffeinated indulgence. A well-dressed man stepped over it while he deftly covered her vomit with a few pages of his *New York Times*. He performed the elegant action while he kept his eyes on the subway car doors that opened just as he reached them. Then he stepped off into the rest of his day. As new people entered the train and walked around the newspaper, it was as if Cole hadn't puked at all.

Red rubbed Cole's back on their walk from the train to the museum. But none of them talked until they walked through some animal dioramas and Cole asked, "Are these real?"

"I don't think so," Red shrugged.

"They are probably plastic. They look really good though," Helen added.

Cole later read a wall plaque that said that almost all of the dioramas were real animals. She didn't tell her parents because she liked knowing something they didn't.

Thinking back on that day she didn't know how to feel. What if they knew she wasn't really their daughter, but she knew the dioramas were real animals? She compared the two secrets to make a connection, but nothing made sense. She was sure that there was no way for the museum to get taxidermists to stuff humans and put them in the diorama. So, all the humans behind glass were fake, just like Cole, Red and Helen might have been, a fake family.

Thinking, and thinking about thinking, tired her out. Her body ached hard. She sat up to pull the Emperin Compound bottle and the Pringles canister from the pillowcase. The tablets tasted as bitter as the previous ones, but she was getting used to it and didn't make a face.

Looking down the Pringles tube, she saw that Vlad had rolled up money like cinnamon rolls before stuffing it down the can. She pulled out the first wad and counted it. There were mostly tens and fives, with a couple of twenties, but it was two hundred and fifteen dollars. The next roll had more twenties and added up to two hundred and ninety-five dollars. The final roll had a thick red rubber band around it and was much smaller than the others. It was one hundred and thirty dollars. Cole's head hurt too much to do the exact math, but she figured Vlad left her more than five hundred dollars.

She grunted and dragged everything down the cement slope

and all the way to the New York City train.

When the train conductor shouted, "Tickets!" Cole held her ticket up as her father did on their ride two years earlier. Eyeing the middle spot of the three-seater filled with her bags and the black case, the conductor said, "You got a lot of stuff there. Somebody with you?"

"It's my grandfather's." She shrank a little and bit her lower lip. "I'm going to see him and my grandmother in Coney Island. Do you know how to get there?" Cole cocked her head to the side and was about to explain further when he held his hand up to stop her.

"With all that? You better get a cab. I bet it would be about twenty-five, thirty bucks." His gruffness flung spit from his lips while he told Cole, "Get the old man to pay for it. Shouldn't be sending you out alone like this anyway." He shrugged as he stepped over to take another passenger's ticket.

Cole looked out the window across the tracks to Bridgeport Harbor. Three seagulls floated in place but Cole wondered if it only seemed that way because the train was moving with them. She gently twisted around backwards to keep watching the birds until a northbound train obscured them.

She turned back around and maneuvered around her stuff to the aisle seat to look for the conductor again. Through the windowed door at the end, she saw him in the next car. As the train went around a sharp bend he held onto the back of a seat to hold steady as that part of the train screeched and shook over the curved tracks. The people in the other train car twisted out of her sight for an instant and then came back into view. Cole thumped her shoulder blades against the seatback as she synched with the train's fits and jolts. It hurt, but she didn't mind the train's twists and turns. Knowing what was about to happen, even in this small way, was comforting.

Chapter 36

Wilda ignored the knock on the front door and pressed the TV remote volume button up. If the knocker was for Animal or any of his derelicts upstairs she didn't care. It was enough that she was dealing with Vladimir in her house. Seeing him felt like a hallucination. The feelings it dredged up had been submerged deep inside her. That pain was always there but now she would have to be buried with it closer to her skin again.

Voices outside her door made her curious. She turned the volume down a little and heard Animal say, "That's right. You got the right address. She's in there."

Wilda looked at the door as three soft thumps sounded from it. She waited.

"Throw your wrist into it. Like this," Animal said. Five confident knuckle blows rang out.

She went to the front room door and opened it. Heading up the stairs, Animal told her, "I let her in. She was looking for you."

There stood Red's daughter. They had last seen each other a couple of years prior for Thanksgiving. She was older now but still had the same haircut though not as neatly trimmed. And if she had changed radically, Wilda would have known her from what she held. A stack of the letters Wilda had sent to Helen after Red died.

Like a breadcrumb trail, envelopes and pieces of paper dotted a line from the front door to where they stood.

Cole quickly looked away after her eyes met Wilda's. Decades as a nurse made Wilda adept at giving one look that could either make people feel like they'd died and met an angel or were dealing with the gatekeeper of hell. In this case, Wilda used her best-guarded body language.

It gave her time to take in details. The girl was just old enough to find her way there alone. And the case she had dragged into the house looked exactly like Vlad's musty guilty heirloom. She wondered if Vladimir was behind this visit.

Cole broke the brittle silence by spouting the linear list of how she ended up there. "I found your letters. I went to see my Grampa and he wasn't there. He had all this stuff there. Tony told me…." Wilda made a face at Tony's name. "Oh, Tony's the security guard. He told me that he was on his way here to see you." Wilda nodded her head so that Cole wouldn't be as nervous and slow down. Only bits of the story made sense. "So then I left…."

"Left where?" Wilda asked.

"Grampa's place."

"With your grandfather?"

"No. He wasn't there. He was already here."

"How do you know that?"

"Tony told me."

"How did Tony know?"

Cole's right eye twitched a few times. "I don't know," Cole was frustrated by all the questions. She flipped her hand in the air and said, "Something. He had a family emergency."

"How did you get here, then?" Wilda asked.

"I took the train and then that taxicab," Cole said as she motioned toward the street side of the house. Wilda's interrogation drove Cole to blink fast and chew on the side of her tongue a little. Her gradual melt down worsened after each question. Wilda decided not to ask about the girl looking roughed up.

Thumping coming from the house's front door interrupted the blurry debriefing. Outside holding two large flat boxes, Janet shouted to Cole, "Hey! Kid! Come open up this door for me will ya?"

Cole hesitated when she realized that she had dropped so many things in the hall. She wanted to pick them up but instead just rushed to the door. After she opened the door, Janet said, "Thanks, kid. She nodded toward Cole's black case, chuckled and said, "What are you selling there? Encyclopedias?"

Bowing her head, Cole's face turned red. She walked down the hall toward her grandmother. Wilda nodded her approval.

On her way up the stairs, Janet shouted to Wilda, "Hey! My

hands are full. Could you give this kid a Popsicle or something? She did good!"

Wilda called out, "I'll take of her just fine. She's my granddaughter!"

Cole started to pick up all the envelopes and letters she had dropped, until Wilda said, "Leave it. Just get in here and sit down. I'll get us something to drink."

Even though the iced tea cooled her down, Wilda's face flushed as Cole told her everything that had happened since Red died. Decades as a nurse gave Wilda the superpower of knowing when to let a pained person talk and when to give them something no amount of talking could achieve. In lieu of a morphine shot, she hugged Cole. A nurse's hug is like the ocean, made up of everything it's ever touched. In Wilda's case: countless flawless fingers and toes, a limp dull blue doll, jittery dad vomit, five pleading pounds of addicted newborn, the slippery rose-red blood of an enslaved legacy, the rat's nest hair of a homeless mother, faces, hands, sheets, ass cheeks, time clocks, 3 a.m. Styrofoam coffee cups, necks, clipboards, and handed to her by a fellow nurse, the burned shoes emptied of her daughter Vera.

After Cole's quiet sobs ebbed, Wilda whispered, "You're right about one thing. Your grandfather is here."

Cole talked into the tear-soaked spot on Wilda's housecoat, "Where?"

Wilda pulled Cole from her to tell her, "The trip here would have been hard enough but the old fool and slept on the beach all night. He wore himself out. You go back and wake him up. Gentle. Tell him to come sleep on the couch." Having put sedatives in a glass of orange juice for Vlad, Wilda added, "And you help him walk, okay? He's very unsteady."

Wilda sat out on her front steps while Cole rushed back to the bedroom and talked to Vlad before helping him get out to the couch. On her way to her bedroom, Wilda walked through the kitchen as Cole took a piece of bread out of her breadbox. Nibbling on a piece of Wonder bread, Cole followed her into the bedroom. "Pigs don't even eat where they sleep! Go eat that out there," Wilda pointed out to the kitchen. "And wash up before getting in bed!" Wilda brushed off the bed with her hands even though there were no crumbs.

Once Cole slipped into bed, Wilda pulled the blinds down. In Wilda's bed, they alternately sighed until Cole's legs twitched as she fell asleep. Wilda's attempt to rub Cole's back was met by a visceral flinch. The poor girl was a bundle of nerves. Wilda felt partly responsible because she had only write letters and sent some money, all while Helen and Cole needed what can't be read or bought.

Chapter 37

Janet was the first one awake the morning after Animal's birthday party. Although there was plenty of cake left over, Janet wanted donuts. Emboldened by passing off the forbidden sheets of currency, she spent it on every whim. Propelled by her donut impulse, she ran down the stairs to hop in her car. Near the front door, papers littered the floor. She picked up an envelope with a yellow post office mail-forwarding sticker on it. But the writing above the sticker was her own.

She screwed her face toward the stairs as she wondered if Animal was messing around with her head. The card she tugged out of the envelope had a drawing of a butterfly with its curlicue flight trail reading, "I miss you" over and over. The postmark read March 12th. Her hand snapped up another envelope. It was a letter she had sent to her baby Kimberly a week after that. Why were her letters here? A hot panic ran down her arms. Someone was probably there to stop her from getting her baby girl back.

In the back of the house, off of the kitchen, Wilda's bedroom door creaked opened. Janet watched a young girl walk out into the kitchen. She wore a sleeveless nightgown so long it covered her feet. It looked as though she floated to the sink for a glass of water.

Janet's morning head was clear enough to flash to the day before when the girl opened the door for her. The girl looked out the window over the sink as she drank the water. With the envelopes in her hands, Janet tiptoed down the hallway and stopped in the kitchen's doorway.

Cole turned her head just far enough to see Janet out of the corner of her eye. She put the glass down in the sink and turned around.

Janet held her breath as she inventoried Cole's eyes, nose, lips, chin, hair, hands, arms, all in one rapid, lucid scan. She exhaled as she walked around the kitchen table. Cole backed against the counter. Janet's arms wrapped around her in a capture-like motion, not a mutual embrace. She swayed them both from side to side, sing-songing, "Kimberly, Kimberly, Kimberly," until her throat filled with her cries. She gurgled, "I found you."

Janet turned Cole around to sit her in one of the chairs. She knelt in front of her and said, "You don't know who I am do you?" Cole shook her head and her eyes lowered to the letters, now on the floor.

"I'm...I'm...," Janet glanced over at Wilda who watched from her bedroom. "I'm the one who wrote all those letters. I'm your mother, your real one."

Cole's eyes searched Janet's face for something, anything that would show if she were lying or if she was just a crazy lady. Every part of the woman; her eyes, her arms, her mouth, and especially her tears, seemed sure that Cole was her baby Kimberly.

The night before, Cole asked Wilda if the letters were true. Wilda told Cole the truth as she understood it. She seemed defeated by the facts when she told Cole, "But nothing your grampa touches can ever really be called the truth."

All night, Cole had barely slept as she wondered where this woman was and how she was going to find her. Now she was face-to-face with her and couldn't trust it could be her. She finally looked at Wilda. Her eyes asked her grandmother if this was real. Her grandmother's lips tightened into forfeiture as she nodded.

Cole stretched out her arms and pulled Janet by her neck toward her. She didn't know this woman's name and couldn't call her "mom," but she could hold her close. That's all that made any sense.

Chapter 38

After eating some of Animal's leftover ice cream cake at the house, Wilda, Cole and Janet went out to stroll the boardwalk. The two women flanked Cole, each holding a hand. Wilda held her hand gently on the side where Cole's injuries hurt the most. Janet pulled Cole's other arm and squeezed her hand in tempo with her chatter.

She talked about what she was like when she was Cole's age but the stories drifted from when she ate Swedish Fish while peeing in a swimming pool, to when she half-whispered to Cole, "I smoked my first cigarette at a *Heart* concert."

Cole's jumbled anger at Helen didn't in any way push her toward wanting this lady as her mother. Janet tried to make Cole laugh by sticking out her tongue and making faces, but Cole laughed *for* Janet, not with her.

As they stopped at the defunct Thunderbolt rollercoaster Wilda told them, "When I first moved here I rode that thing every pay day."

Even though many of the amusement rides were still running, people stopped a while to take in the rollercoaster's wooden frame corpse. An old building sat at one end of the ride. It looked like an oversized wood-slat soapbox with windows. Some of the roller coaster's legs went through the building. It was as if the ride rose up from the earth to grow through the house or that the building had been blown under the rollercoaster like Dorothy's house in the *Wizard of Oz* movie.

Cole always felt a kinship with deserted places. Bridgeport was so full of them, it simply was one. When Red drove her around the city he pointed out the abandoned factories like someone would name people in an old photograph. But this rollercoaster seemed much more vulnerable than a building, naked. The out-of-place building's windows were open, as curtains lapped out into the beach wind. A radio played loudly inside. Cole knew the Bananarama song well. It was played at least every hour on the radio and the video was on Friday Night Videos all the time.

"She's got it. Yeah, baby, she's got it. I'm your Venus. I'm your fire at your desire." The lyrics swam out on the breeze as Cole thought about the mermaid-like lady in the video. She was a pretty blond in a big pink clamshell. Then there was the red devil woman with a tail dancing around in fire. For a moment she thought about the mermaid in the case sitting in her grandmother's living room.

Cole's mind drifted to the confusion that took place in Wilda's living room just before Janet proposed they go to the park. The three of them ate from a melting ice cream cake that Janet had bought that supposedly welcomed "Kimberly" home. Janet insisted that she eat two large pieces. Cole doubted Janet knew she was in Coney Island since Cole didn't even know she was going there until that morning. So, either the woman lied about the cake's purpose or the mermaid did have magical powers like Cole had hoped.

She sensed that Wilda and Janet didn't like each other. When Janet had stopped talking, Cole babbled on about things that no one would really care about. She told them, "Allan's our landlord. He's into old stuff from the Civil War. When I told him I was related to P.T. Barnum he said that he owned slaves." Janet and Wilda both acted distracted by their desserts as Cole continued, "I mean, my great-great-great-great-grandfather. Not Allan. Allan's just a landlord. He didn't ever have slaves. It's illegal now."

When Wilda went to the kitchen with the dirty dishes, Janet asked Cole, "So what else? I can't get enough of you!" Cole didn't want to mention her parents because she thought it would hurt Janet's feelings. She got up to grope around in her bag and pulled out Allan's Civil War pistol.

Janet waved her hand up and down, and whispered, "Hey! What the hell?" She looked over her shoulder at the doorway. "Get over here. Give me that thing!"

"It doesn't have any bullets or anything," Cole assured her as she walked over to Janet.

Janet held out her large shapeless pocketbook like a Halloween trick-or-treat bag and said, "Put it in here."

Cole felt like she was supposed to trust this woman because she was apparently her mother, but Janet didn't seem like any mother she'd ever met. Even Vanessa, Puke and Toad's mother seemed more like a person who knew what to do around kids than Janet.

Now, out in the sun on the boardwalk, Cole took in Janet's stained hands, dark stringy hair and guarded rabbit eyes. She wondered what made them different and what made them alike. Maybe that's what God was supposed to do, fill in all those details.

They moved along to the livelier part of the boardwalk. Cole stopped at the Astroland Park rocket that sat on top of one of the food shacks. It looked like a pencil as long as two school buses with red and blue wings that flared out from the bottom. She pointed at the flames painted on the rocket from its bottom to the top and said, "On the Space Shuttle Challenger, one of its rockets was on fire. I think that's what they said caused it to explode like that."

It was as if the shuttle disaster and Red's death conflated and no one wanted to continue that conversation. They took turns not saying anything but seeming like they were about to. The awkward silence was broken when Janet asked, "Who wants to go on the Wonder Wheel?"

Cole's palms were sweaty from holding her grandmother's hand so when they sat in blue metal cage, the air on her hands was a relief. As the Wonder Wheel lifted them up, Cole watched her grandmother get smaller and smaller. She wiped her palm on her shirt and gripped the metal grate that kept them from falling out.

The cage's metal creaked. Cole's other hand gripped the back of the empty metal bench in front of them. Janet said, "Look at that! The beach is so full today. How much piss do you think is in that water?" Cole kept her smile going even though she was thinking how often Janet mentioned pee.

This was the second time they'd been alone now. She thought about what to say but was jarred forward. While they had waited in line, she heard riders' screams coming from the swinging cars. Janet assured her that it wasn't as scary as it sounded. Cole closed her eyes and clenched her jaw to stifle herself. When her muscles tensed, her wounds stretched and stung.

"Hey! Which way is north right now? Quick. Point," Janet asked.

Cole's eyebrows dipped down while her nose scrunched. It wasn't so much that she didn't know the answer as much as the question seemed like something a clown would ask someone before blowing a horn in their face. Janet's eyes pulled an answer from Cole, even though at first she shrugged. Silently, Cole pointed up.

As she snatched Cole's nervous, sweaty hand, Janet laughed. She thrust it in the direction away from the ocean and said, "It's that way."

Janet drew their intertwined hands to her chest and said, "Your palm is soaked!" She wrapped her arm around Cole's shoulder and pulled her close. "See? It's not so bad!" Janet didn't notice Cole wince.

For relief, Cole let go of the cage to lean into Janet's soft bicep. "There you go," Janet said.

When Cole opened her eyes, she focused on Janet's fingers as they stroked her frightened rigid arm. Blotched with gray ink, Janet's fingernails looked like ashen flat pebbles.

Janet's handbag rolled forward and back like a misshapen football along with the car's lunges. A Coke can, a tampon and a few coins rolled out.

The first time they went around, Cole looked for Wilda. Both forced smiles as their worried eyes met. Their deceitful hands also took part in the façade as they waved at each other.

"See that thing out there. That tall red thing? They used to throw people off of that in parachutes," Janet pointed out the Parachute Jump. Her elbow nudged Cole's side as she added, "What you think of that, huh?"

The tall empty tower looked a lot like the fire-ravaged buildings in the newspapers in Vlad's scrapbook. Places burning down and companies closing factories made sense, but it didn't make any sense to her why at least two big fun rides had been shut down. She wasn't enjoying herself on the Ferris wheel, but everyone else seemed to love it.

Each time the car thrust forward Cole felt like it was going to slam into the white car in front of them. She broke out in cold sweat that was met with a hot breeze. "You're going to be okay. I got you." Janet put her arm around Cole's shoulder, giggled and pulled her closer, "See?"

Cole closed her eyes and inhaled the tangled aroma of hot dogs, popcorn and the citrusy pong of Janet's underarm. She forced herself to look down and took comfort in the hundreds of people walking around as if the Ferris wheel wasn't going to kill her. If reality were as terrifying as it felt, those people wouldn't take their eyes off of her. If she were about to plummet to her death, they would be worried. They probably would not be able to blink or move, like the people on television who watched the Spaceship Challenger explode.

The fear of falling made everything spin out and then back into Cole's vision. She longed to be in the ocean out in the distance. She would plunge under. The cool seawater would soothe her cuts and bruises, heal her. If only she could transform into a real mermaid, she wouldn't want to run back home with her grandmother, who seemed trapped but in a cage no one could see. Under the ocean waves, she wouldn't hear the creaking Ferris wheel, squealing children, the crowds or Janet's amateur assurances that they were just fine.

Their cage waited at the top for other people to be let off. Janet picked up the escaped Coke can and tapped on the top, explaining, "Look it. This is a trick here. This makes it so it doesn't spray all over you when you crack it open." The can hissed open. Janet held the can far out in front of her, but the Coke didn't bubble out. "See? What'd I tell you?"

The cage jerked forward, making her drop the can right into her bag. "Oh, Shit!" Janet's foot kicked out to move her bag but the Coke already dove in, top first. As if it was Cole's fault, Janet snapped at her, "What the hell was that?"

Cole let out an "s" sound. She was going to say sorry but she couldn't get it out. She started to cry.

"Oh, man. Don't start crying now, kid. I didn't mean it," Janet rubbed Cole's back. "We'll be off soon."

They held their feet up on the back of the front bench to avoid the soda as it dribbled back and forth with the car's movements. Avoiding the spill reminded Cole of the time she vomited on the train in New York City when she was with her parents. The rest of the way down she thought about how she would have to see Helen again. Her head throbbed from not knowing how they would move on. In comparison with meeting Janet, Cole's Vanessa horror seemed somehow in an unreachable past now. Cole and Helen could move away from Sheridan Street but what were they supposed to do with a whole other mother?

When they approached the bottom, Janet barked at the attendant, "Hey, man! Get us out of this thing. My poor kid was terrified the whole time!"

Janet held out her dripping bag as she climbed from the car first. The chubby ride operator pulled Cole's arm and flung her out. Her arms wrapped around Wilda like a wet towel.

Janet rushed away from Cole and Wilda as she shouted over her shoulder, "I gotta get to a bathroom pronto." Sometimes when a person walks away, it's a free ticket for those left behind to choose a new direction. Wilda followed Cole, whose inner magnet was pulled by Janet's emotional compass.

Outside Ruby's Bar, Wilda yanked on Cole's arm. "We'll wait for her over on that bench." Cole craned her neck to follow Janet until she disappeared into the crowd.

The bar was three-people deep with sweaty drunks. Janet shouted over the din and perspiring scalps, "Just a Bud. I got my kid with me." She warily unzipped her bag to find a sticky wet tossed salad of her loose counterfeit cash, another Tampax, cigarettes, car keys, wallet, tissues, pills and the old gun she took from Cole.

She plucked out a fifty and left it on the bar. Holding the bag away from her, she grabbed the drink and headed to the bathroom.

"I gotta an emergency over here!" Janet shouted as she held her bag up to cut ahead in the line. As she passed a pregnant woman standing in the line, she leaned a little toward her and said, "You're about to know exactly what I'm talking about. I got a disaster right here."

Standing in front of the sink, she smiled at herself in the mirror. She had done it. She found her baby girl. It was feeling good so far, but she also felt an unnerving desire to tell Kimberly everything she ever wanted to say to her. There were places they needed to go together. Once they all got back to the house Janet would need to make a plan to pry her baby girl away from the old lady.

She took a gulp of the cold soda, tossed her open bag into the sink and turned on the faucet. The water ran over the outside of the bag while Janet stepped aside to pull more than a dozen paper towels out of the dispenser.

Most of the women using the toilets avoided Janet. But one woman braved it and went over to the faucet and cupped one hand under the stream. Janet watched to make sure the woman didn't take anything from the bag. As the woman pretended to check her teased bleach-blond hair in the mirror, she looked down at the soaked mess.

Janet followed the woman's eyes to a few fifty-dollar bills spilling out of the bag. The money's ink was washing off, turning the tissues gray. When Janet rushed over and lifted the bag, the old pistol fell out into the sink.

Swiftly, she tucked it back into the bag. A quick perusal of the bathroom assured Janet that the only person who saw the gun was the nosy woman.

Janet slipped three faded and limp fifties into the woman's hand. She gave Janet a nod and folded the money into the right rear pocket of her cut-offs. Janet shut off the water.

Despite the bag's soupy turmoil, two dry pills were saved from drowning by a fold of nylon near the zipper. Without other pills to compare them to, Janet couldn't identify them. Cutting back on the pills had been going well. Having been clean all day, she thought she deserved something to calm her nerves. She popped them in her mouth. The day had been unbelievable. Something about being in Ruby's bathroom and holding her bag over the sink to drain made her wonder if it had all been one of her fantasies.

Her mind ran through what happened from the moment Cole opened the front door to when she ran to the bar, yelling back to her baby girl as she ran to keep up with her, "I am going to clean this thing. Then it's my treat! I'll get us all some good boardwalk grub. Sit tight!" She had wanted to clean off her bag and get a drink.

One of these fifties had to be in good enough shape to buy dinner or she would have to walk back to the house to get more. Using a paper towel, she blotted one of the least washed-out bills.

Her jaw relaxed as she drawled out, "Yeah." It was both an affirmation that the one fifty seemed salvageable and that the pills were cooling her out. Licking her lips, her mouth felt pasty. Tucking the cash into her bra, she bent down to drink from the sink's spigot. She grabbed her beer and used her dripping bag to cut through the crowd.

Cole had stretched out on the bench and rested her head in Wilda's lap. On the boardwalk, they were sandwiched between the amusement park's cacophony and the sound cloud of boom boxes and screaming children on the beach. Wilda stroked Cole's hair. It soothed them both.

Wilda twisted her neck to spot Janet. She didn't trust that Janet wouldn't leave them waiting while she downed a few drinks. After a while, she asked Cole, "Do you want me to get you a coke or a ginger ale or something?"

Cole rubbed her belly and said, "I don't think so."

Janet appeared above Cole and poked her belly, "I knew it. You're hungry!" She stood behind the bench, pointed inland and said, "So, I'm thinking we should go get something to eat at a restaurant over that way. What you in the mood for, kiddo?"

Cole thought Janet was about to call her Kim and was relieved that she said "kiddo" instead. "I don't know. Maybe a hot dog?"

Janet clapped and rubbed her hands together, "It's my treat! We can get surf and turf to celebrate. Steak tonight!"

Cole sat up and Wilda stood up to face Janet, their eyes fixed behind her.

Four cops approached Janet from behind. The woman she paid off in the bathroom stood several feet away and hollered to them, "Yeah, that's her for sure."

Janet glanced back and then stomped her right foot as if she was going to run but didn't. She turned around and faced the policemen.

One of the cops placed a hand over his holstered gun as he told Janet, "Ma'am. Could you please put your bag on the ground?"

"Hey, buddy. I don't know what she's talking about," Janet pointed at the woman. "I'm just here with my daughter. You see her? Wave to the cop, Kimberly," she nodded to Cole.

Cole waved small and quickly and then crossed her arms. Wilda pulled Cole close.

"See? There she is. I don't have nothing bad in here. What she saw was a toy gun. A prop gun kind of thing."

Another police officer said, "Ma'am, put the bag down. Now!"

Janet pleaded with the cop closest to her, who had not spoken yet, "I'm telling you, they can't do this. I just found my kid and the gun isn't even real. Tell your buddies. Tell 'em I'm good, alright?"

Cole stood ice still. She was scared that if the police knew where Janet got the gun, they would arrest her.

The cop shook his head and pulled his gun from its holdster, "Ma'am, you've got to drop that bag."

Wilda shouted, "No!" as other people screamed "cops," "gun," "look out," and "run." "You don't get it, do ya? I'll show ya. It's just a fake," Janet said as she reached into her bag.

A gun popped. Screaming, feet thudding on the boardwalk, cups and cans thrown to the ground. Janet looked around to see where the cop's shot went as a large red circle grew on her thigh. One of the other cops rushed her and grabbed her bag. Another police office pushed her to the ground and yanked her arms behind her back . An ambulance, blaring its siren and honking, scattered the foolish, brave and drunk spectators lingering on the boardwalk.

Wilda led Cole to a cop motioning to her. "Say hello to Officer Dan, Cole," Wilda said.

Cole muttered, "Hi," and looked at Dan. But then she went right back to watching Janet get handcuffed.

As one of the cops opened the mushy bag and lifted out the gun, Janet shouted, "It's a fake! So is the money! It's all for a play! I'm in a play! Aw, man! Why you going to do this in front of my baby girl? That's my kid there."

The EMTs rolled the gurney up into the ambulance.

"These crazies will say anything. Sorry about that. We're picking her up for some serious stuff. She's been passing phony bills all over the place. And then today some lady called to tell us she had a gun. We've been getting tons of reports on this one," Dan said.

Wilda turned her back to the other officers and leaned in to tell

Dan, "Listen. It's complicated, but I need you to let my granddaughter talk to her before they take her away."

"You know her? Damn it, Wilda. Oh, sure. You gotta…." Dan didn't finish but walked away to say something to the EMTs and the officer in charge.

Dan returned and held his hand out to Cole to lead her into the ambulance. Dan said, "Okay. You can talk here for a second."

Two cops stood close. Cole hoped Janet wouldn't say anything about the gun. Janet sniffled throughout telling her, "All I wanted was to get you back." Janet took a deep breath and winced. "I wasn't going to be great or nothing. Just your mom. You know?" She tucked her lips, bit down and closed her eyes. She opened her mouth again but all that came out was a crack of her voice.

For a moment Cole and Janet both held their breath and their tears while they locked eyes. Cole said, "I know." Her voice barely breached the din of EMTs talking and walkie talkies blaring. While Officer Dan squeezed Cole's hand, her face went hot and she started to cry. She pulled her hand from Officer Dan's to wipe away the tears. Realizing she could, she threw herself over Janet to hug her. Janet kissed the top of Cole's head before Dan pulled her away.

As the EMTs slammed the ambulance doors shut, Dan walked Cole back to Wilda. Cole wrapped her arms around her and rested her head on the side of her right breast.

Dan whispered to Wilda, "I'm sorry to say it but she's going away for a long time. You better tell whoever she's in cahoots with to split town. They'll be all over them real fast."

Wilda nodded to Dan as she put a hand on the top of Cole's head. "Okay, we better get you home." Cole squeezed Wilda tighter.

"We have to go. But could you tell Maddie to come by the house tomorrow?" she asked Dan.

"Sure. I gotcha," Dan winked and joined the other cops as they talked to people who asked about what had happened.

Wilda and Cole held hands as they walked past nosey eyes.

"Is she going to jail?" Cole asked.

Wilda answered, "Let's not worry about where *she's* going. Just worry about what *we're* going to do."

Once they got into the house, Wilda rushed into the front room and piled all of Cole's bags onto the luggage cart and pulled it down the hall. "I'm running you a bath," she shouted halfway down the hall.

Alone in Wilda's front room Cole pulled up her shirt. Her wounds had scabbed over and stopped oozing and the bruises were less dark. She lied flat on the sofa with her eyes closed. Finally, alone, Cole thought about running away from Wilda, from Janet, from all of it.

That's probably who a real runaway would be anyhow. A kid who doesn't run to something but away from everything. This new mother, the one she just lost as fast as she got her, seemed like she could have been a runaway when she was a kid. Maybe that's what made her like that. She's what Vlad would have called, "a little off," while he tapped his finger to his temple.

Cole worried that she was destined to be like Janet. Is there an age when people stop being what their parents have made them be and they start just being themselves? Red didn't seem that much like Vlad except that they both hated chocolate cake and sneezed when they ate minty things. Helen didn't have people or things that she appeared to need or people who needed her, except for Red. The day he died, the small part of Helen's heart that he kept alive, went into a coma. That could be what happens when no one is your person, and you're nobody's someone. Who was Cole's someone? Vlad? Grandma? A tear crept from the corner of her eye into her ear. She twisted her neck to wipe it on the coach.

Wilda shouted from the kitchen, "Go wake up your grandfather and then get in the tub."

Cole sniffed hard and rushed down the hall. The curly spiral of the phone cord swung like a lazy jump rope from the wall to where Wilda sat at the kitchen table. Wilda said into the phone, "No, you stay there."

Turning away from Cole, Wilda cupped her hand around the phone's mouthpiece. Cole's cheeks burst into a self-conscious flush.

She tiptoed into the bedroom. Vlad was breathing deeply and looked too comfy to wake. In the bathroom, Cole softly closed the door and turned off the bathwater. After peeling off her clothes, she lowered into the full tub.

Wilda's footsteps headed toward the front room and then sluggishly thumped up the creaky stairs. Cole smoothed a brand-new bar of white Dial soap over her arms up to the gash from the brick Vanessa hurled. Then she used it to wash her hair and face. Sliding down, she sank her shoulders and lips just below the surface and hummed as she blew bubbles. She focused on thinking about how the sounds trapped inside the bubbles were released as they popped. It didn't matter that this wasn't the way it worked, she needed the distraction of something she made happen, no matter how stupid it seemed.

In the Watchtower, Animal and Keith smoked weed and played records as they waited for Janet to get back from the boardwalk.

"What a trip! Can you believe that my mother set all that up? I didn't have the heart to tell poor Jan," Animal confided in Keith.

"You sure that really is her little girl?" Keith asked.

"Makes sense to me," Animal shrugged and nodded. "After all that went down with her being pregnant and all that, my mother told me to not bother with Janet. But I always liked her. I mean, what are you going to do?"

"Yeah, man. You stick by your people," Keith said as he pumped a fist in the air and then toked. Exhaling smoke, he rasped out a laugh and shook his head. "She's what you call an original."

What wasn't said held in the air longer than what was. It mingled with the turntable playing a women's moany voice backed by indecisive drumming.

"What you say this is? Linda Lunch? Sounds like she ripped off the Beatles. This is *Come Together*, man. Listen. Hear it?"

Animal agreed, "Yeah, it kind of does. I like her though."

"Kiss the bride and make her cry? Roll over and die? You're lucky it's your birthday. I let you listen to this depressing junk," Keith said.

They startled when Wilda barged into the Watchtower speaking loud and fast. "You listen fast and you listen good, buddy boy!"

"I never seen this woman up here before. Is this a ghost, man?" Keith joked to Animal.

"I don't know. I didn't know she could make it up those stairs," Animal said.

"You kidding me? She in way better shape than you!" Keith flashed a kiss-ass smile at Wilda.

"Spare me your whole Mutt and Jeff act! You are in deep shit," Wilda sat at one of the baggy-covered tables but didn't seem to notice all the drugs. "I just got back from the boardwalk. The cops hauled away your fucked up friend." Wilda added, "Janet," sharply, as though it were a foreign-language. "She was screaming all over about having a gun and all that money she's been waving around!"

Animal panicked that Janet possibly stole his gun. He thought to check where he had hidden it in his bedroom but he was too stunned to move.

Wilda continued, "They had to take a shot at the dumb-dumb! You're damn lucky that Maddie's fiancé was there. He told me they got so many calls about her handing out fifty-dollar bills like they were candy. You two listen! You are going to get the hell out of here. Everything's gotta go. The damn cops will be here as soon as they get their warrants and whatever the hell else."

"What? Oh! Shit! Is Janet okay?" Animal pulled on his beard.

"Are you fucking kidding me? Andy! Listen to the words I am saying. She is arrested. Kaput. The bullet grazed her leg, just a lot of blood. Now, get moving," Wilda waved her arms as if she were shooing turkeys out of a yard.

Animal shrugged, "How the hell are we supposed to ….,"

"Think! Just get all this bad shit out first. Get it the hell out of here." She pointed at the stereo speaker. "And shut that crap off. She sounds like a cat being strung up," Wilda demanded.

Keith pressed the stereo's power button off and then waved a big black garbage bag up and down until the air snapped it open. Starting where Wilda sat, he swept his arm across the tables and pushed everything into the bag.

"See? Follow him," Wilda said to Animal as she pointed at Keith. "Get it together," she said as she slapped Animal's jelly-sack gut.

Animal lumbered into Janet's room. He threw everything he could grab into the middle of the bed. Mostly empty things: beer cans, baggies, envelopes, underwear, cigarette packs. The closet was full of crumpled clothes and Janet's Tampax box. As the taboo fake money fluttered out, Animal shouted, "Fuck!" He picked through it to figure out how much Janet had used.

Wilda walked into the room and said, "Listen, you make sure you clear the hell out of here. I'll tell them I don't know who the fuck you are. I'll play the stupid old lady. But you make sure this place gets cleared the hell out. For now, I'll only talk to Maddie. After this all blows over let's figure out what to do. You got enough money? Real money, not fake?"

"Yeah, I got enough to take off. I'm so sorry. Wilda, I…," Animal started to cry as he flopped down onto the mattress.

"Get a hold of yourself. I told your mother I would take care of you and I will. You just got to get the hell out. Pull it together, kid," Wilda said in her nurse's tough, consoling voice.

"It's not that. I'm just fucked, Wilda. Just totally fucked," he said as he held up the Tampax box half-full of counterfeit cash.

"I say you better go someplace where no one knows you. Nobody. You can't get away from things if you don't really damn-well leave them behind you. Shave that beard. Cut your hair. Lose some of that gut. You won't be free until you forget who you were all this time."

"Jesus, Wilda, it's not like I killed somebody!" Animal half-laughed some snot out of his nose and then wiped it on the back of his thick hand.

"Doesn't matter," Wilda said. She softened a little, "But when the coast is clear, you let me know where you are."

Animal's struggled up, hugged Wilda and then went back out to help Keith.

"Man, there's so much all over. Do we need to clear every speck out of this place?" Keith asked.

Wilda butted in, "Get what you can. Call people to help. Just get it the fuck out. And, listen you!" she pointed at Keith. "You're driving to Bridgeport in an hour. It's in Connecticut."

"I know where it is, Wilda lady. In fact, I have got some cousins there," Keith smiled.

Chapter 39

At her kitchen counter, Wilda packed a large paper bag with three smaller paper bags. She told Cole, "You each got an apple, a slice of my banana bread and some peanuts. It's only a couple of hours but there's always that stupid I-95 traffic."

Cole asked Wilda, "Why do you wear your watch backwards like that?"

Wilda handed Cole a few wrapped peppermint candies. "Here, keep these in your pocket for when you get motion sickness on the ride. Don't give any to the old man. It makes him sneeze."

"How do you know I have motion sickness?"

Wilda smirked. "Well, first off, you looked a little shaky on that damn Ferris wheel. Second, I'm your grandma, so I know these things. And third, I'm a nurse. That's also why I wear my watch this way. You done with all your questions?"

"Yeah, I guess." Cole liked when Wilda said she was her grandma. It made her feel special and connected to Red again. Cole stuffed the mints in her pocket, and asked, "If that lady is supposed to be my real mother, why didn't she know how to make me not scared on that ride? And what about my mom, too?"

"Let's get some air outside for a sec," Wilda pressed her palm into Cole's back to guide her to the back door. Wilda nipped out a quick grunt as they sat down on the back steps.

Wilda pulled on Cole's earlobe. "Okay, kiddo. Listen up and get this straight. You ended up with what I like to call a 'pigeon mother.' Actually, somehow, you got two of 'em. You see, pigeon mothers make the best nest they can. But it's just junk, things like nails, hard twigs, pieces of string. And that's all. Nothing holds it together. They are just sitting there. It doesn't look like a nest in any way! I wish I had a picture of one to show you, you wouldn't believe it," Wilda explained.

"If they're such bad moms, why are there still so many pigeons in the world? Wouldn't they die off?" Cole asked.

"Well, aren't you a smartass? Well, the trick is that they're good mothers if you're a pigeon. But some human mothers act just like pigeon mothers. Not so great for kids. If they get scared and think there's nothing they can do about it, they abandon the baby pigeon. My guess is that you can relate."

Cole nodded and asked, "What kind of mother are you?"

"Ah…that's the question of the hour! If I only knew. I stopped being a mother. I probably should have let your father know. I didn't really know I'd stopped until…it just kind of happened," Wilda said.

"I think I know what you're saying. I kinda think I'm not a kid anymore but I don't think it all happened when my dad died," Cole pursed her lips and scratched her ear.

"Makes sense. You'd already been through a lot with Helen. Helen is one of those pigeon mothers. She tries, but…well, you know, she never learned," Wilda stopped. In unison, they tilted their heads back and scanned the sky, as if to spot the questions to match Wilda's answers.

"That makes me her pigeon daughter, I guess?" Cole said.

Wilda put her arm around Cole and playfully shook her, "Be happy you were raised a pigeon girl! You'll always make a home out of any damn place and find something to eat no matter what. Every time you need something you'll fly away to find it. You already showed me you're a smart pigeon. You took off and traveled real far to find a safe place. As luck would have it, you somehow crashed right into that other pigeon mother of yours."

Cole winced at the mention of Janet and leaned forward. She squeezed Wilda's knee and said, "Hey! What about pigeon fathers?"

Wilda let out a deep cynical laugh. "I'll need a stiff drink for that conversation! For now, just deal with the fact that both of these mothers of yours are pigeon mothers trying to raise you, a human person."

Cole got up, faced Wilda and tucked her thumbs into her armpits. She flapped her arms like a bird and lifted her right knee and then kicked her foot behind her. "Doin' the pigeon," she sang. She then switched legs and repeated the movement. "Doin' the pigeon," she sang again.

Wilda laughed, "What the hell is that?"

"It's from an old Sesame Street. It's Bert's dance," Cole kept moving her legs.

"Okay, I think I better get my crazy little pigeon on the road back to her pigeon mother," Wilda held her hand out for help getting up. Cole grabbed her wrist and leaned back to get Wilda upright.

As soon as they were back in the house, Cole lugged the case and her bag from the bathroom out to the kitchen. A question crawled across Wilda's face. She pointed at the case and asked, "What's that?"

With a trembling voice Cole answered, "What's in it? I think in this one I put lots of things. I put some clothes and stuff in it." She worried that Wilda knew there should be a mermaid in that case.

"Where did you get it?" Wilda asked.

"I got it from my Grampa. He gave it to me to put my things in it and stuff," Cole said. She remembered that she also put her tape recorder in there at the last minute. "Oh! And my tape recorder is in there."

Cole regretted not recording Janet's voice when she had the chance. She had figured that Wilda didn't want to talk about what happened to Janet but she had so many questions. Was she going to the hospital and then to jail? Were they ever going to see each other again? Why did Cole have to go back to Helen? Was Wilda serious when she said she wanted Cole and Helen to move in with her in Coney Island?

Wilda asked, "Was there ever something else in there? Something of Vlad's?"

"Nope." Like most people, Cole lied faster than she told the truth.

Wilda said, "Good then. Why don't you just leave it here? You're coming back in a few days anyhow."

The letters from Janet and her grandmother were in there now. Even though the mermaid wasn't in it any longer, Cole didn't want to leave the case behind. It connected her to the mermaid, her tragic ancestor.

Instead of being half-fish, half-human, Cole was probably half-Janet and half-Sevic. She was made up of all of Vlad's fumbled legacies. She reasoned that through the mermaid connection she could, in good conscience, keep saying she was related to P.T. Barnum.

"Put it in the pantry. Don't worry. It'll be here when you get back," Wilda assured her.

"I got to get something out first," she said.

As Cole opened it, Wilda craned her neck to look in, but then squeezed her eyelids shut. Cole tossed clothes and the metal cracker tin onto the floor. As Cole pulled out her tape recorder, Wilda opened her eyes and eased down on her hands and knees and crawled over. She swirled her arm through the case as if it were filled with water and she wanted to catch a fish with her hand.

Wilda sobbed into Cole's vagabond jumble with eyes that seemed focused elsewhere, like an invisible well.

Cole knelt next to Wilda and rubbed her back.

Wilda choked out, "It's okay. Take it away with you now. Don't ever bring it back here."

Cole dragged the case out onto the porch. When she walked back into the kitchen, something in her grandmother seemed to have cooled off. It reminded Cole of how their television set made tinkly static pings after she'd turn it off after being on all day.

Keith jammed Janet's car trunk with as much from the Watchtower as would fit. On top of the black garbage bags and loose LPs, he placed Cole's case from the porch and the golf club he found in yard.

Vlad, Cole and Wilda walked out to the car. As Wilda helped Vlad lower into the front passenger's seat, she asked Keith, "Getting this piece of junk away from here while we're at it?"

"You got it right," Keith said. He jingled the keys in the air. "Found them on the windowsill. And it's a free ride to go stay with my Bridgeport cousins. Yeah, right. I'm laying low until all this blows over."

"You're one smart guy," Wilda said.

Cole cautiously eased into the back seat and placed a soggy paper grocery bag at her feet. Duct tape hung from a long gash in the fabric just above her head. The generations of garbage that peppered the floor ranged from a Table Talk cherry pie box and tin, to a few empty Big Mac Styrofoam boxes, to a sprinkling of empty beer cans. There were too many things going on with the car's interior to focus on any one thing.

No one was left in the house to overhear Wilda's brassy voice as she told Helen from her front room phone, "They're on their way."

"I don't feel good about not coming to get her," Helen said.

"You just get ready for her. She's in a hell of a lot of pain. You just got to take care of her." Wilda's nurse's training prepared her to tell people what they didn't want to hear. When Cole was a baby, Red confided in Wilda about Helen's deprived mothering. She assured him that something would soon kick Helen's nurturing skills into gear. But now, a sticky remorse clung to her realization that Helen's motherhood had never surfaced.

"There was blood on the floor. I don't know why she would hurt her. Maybe Cole wouldn't go with her? Did they say what happened here?" Helen asked.

Wilda needed to rest. "Listen, Helen. I've seen this kind of thing a million times. There's just too much that we don't know and the kid is just tired and scared as hell. Do everyone a favor, especially yourself. Just give her a big hug, give her some Tylenol and put her to bed. Don't ask questions. She just needs her mother. You get it?"

Helen hesitated. Did that mean her? Or was she supposed to comfort Cole because she needed her real mother? She wished Gwen hadn't gone home because she would have handed her the phone at that moment. Maybe that's exactly why Gwen left.

"Hello? You got to keep it together. You hear me? She needs you," Wilda said. She sighed.

"Hold on. I got to get something," Helen put down the phone. She needed to think through what to do.

Her cigarettes had run out but she had been afraid to miss a call if she left. Every few minutes she dug her forefinger into the empty pack in hopes she would find that one elusive smoke. She wished she knew what to say to Gwen to make it right between them again.

There was something about Gwen that made Helen want to spare her from everything that was going on while still asking for her help. Helen realized that her troubles weren't the only things in her way, she was her very own headache. She wanted to ask Gwen why she cared about her and Cole, and what made her do life in the right ways. Helen was afraid she already knew the answer. And Gwen was kind enough that she would never tell Helen outright that she had figured out how the world worked because she was smart and confident, and Gwen just did what was necessary to be a functioning person.

Helen felt like the world was set up to punish black people for not following all the rules, the rules that people said and those that they just thought. So Gwen couldn't afford to not be who she was. She regretted not telling Gwen that she saw all these things. The ideas always sounded right in her head but she was afraid that once laid out before them, Helen's ideas would come between them.

Helen resolved to beg for Gwen's help this one last time. After that, she would find ways to mend things with her only friend. She picked up the phone again to tell Wilda, "I'll call Red's friend Gwen right now."

"Why the hell would you do that?"

Helen stood up to defend herself even though they were on the phone. "I'm not a nurse and I'm not much of a mother. So I might need help with Cole. You don't understand, I don't…."

Wilda interrupted her. "Oh, I understand alright. You're afraid. But listen. You are this girl's mother and it's not easy but she needs you."

"But I don't know…."

They were still on the phone because each had fought all her urges to hang up. That's what they would have done if Red were still alive. He would pick up the pieces and carry on for them.

"Cut the shit. You just hug the kid. Listen to her. Pretend you know what you're doing. You think I knew how to raise kids? You think it was easy? You know what's going to be a hell of a lot harder than raising her? Losing her! That son of a bitch killed my little Vera and you act like you're climbing fucking Mount Everest every time Cole needs a goddamn Q-Tip!"

Wilda and Helen were in a race to the bottom. Cole was still alive so Wilda won this round of their suffering contest. But the old woman still held one thing that Helen never had. An undeniable place in the world, a belonging. Helen's fearful anger took flight on words she didn't know she had. "I got home from work and she was gone. I just...I had to ask...I can't lie...I wondered if maybe it was better for her. To not be here with me. There doesn't seem to be much sense in me helping her live when I don't know why or how to get through this, that and a third."

Helen stopped. The silence muffled like pillows over their ears. The moment froze and tightened around everything that was already said.

In a softer yet tight-gripped tone, Helen continued, "But then I couldn't feel anything but wanting her here. But not like this. Not like we always are. I wanted her back.... It might sound bad but I think I'm getting a second chance. Maybe it's a third chance. It might be too late but I'm going to try." Their telephone hush settled like ice cubes melting in a highball glass.

Helen looked out the window. Cole's koala bear caught her eye. She squeezed its back so that the arms and legs released the blind's cord. As she rubbed its soft fuzz and its miniature rubber claws against her lips she listened to Wilda. "You'll be fine. Just please...please...keep Red alive for her. I buried my Vera a little deeper every time I tucked her picture away in a drawer. That makes shit sense to me now."

Helen asked, "Did Cole say something about Red?"

"That's why I know. She didn't mention him at all. That girl is gloomier than a drunk old Judy Garland."

Helen's ear searched for clues that Wilda's comment was more of a joke than a warning. She toed across the silent tightrope and muttered, "Nothing's easy, is it?"

"For fuck's sake! You're going to have to do better than that. She doesn't need me, she doesn't need that old fool, she needs you, Helen. You! Wake up!" Wilda slammed the phone down.

Helen threw the receiver against the wall, gusted into Cole's bedroom and tore the blankets and bottom sheet off the bed. She wondered what Cole had done with the top sheet as she whirl winded, making the bed. The old Strawberry Shortcake sheets were clean but she hadn't seen them since they had moved. She couldn't remember the last time she spent any time in Cole's room, let alone made her bed.

When she pulled the bed out from the wall, she found a green Trapper Keeper folder on the floor. Tucked inside was the article about Red's accident with Cole's name circled many times in purple ink. Beside it, she had written her name five times in a list in all capital letters.

COLE
COLE
COLE
COLE
COLE

Helen sniffed the names. The ink smelled candy-sweet. The day before Cole went missing, she begged Helen to look for fruit-scented pens at Caldor. Every time Cole ran out of something that Red had bought for her she tried to replace it. Wilda was right.

When they had moved, Cole carefully packed the box of Lucky Charms that she had taped shut their first morning without Red. She wrapped masking tape around and around a large brown paper bag full of her father's toothbrush, shaver, shaving cream, Ban roll-on and eye drops. In Magic marker she wrote, "Dad's sink." Grief had turned her into a petty archivist.

Slipped into one of the green folder's pockets was a picture the size of a Hallmark card. Red and about fifty workers crowded around a machine at Q.E. A name was written above each head or on the blank slate of a tan uniform shirt. Above Gwen was the word, "Me." In the other pocket were childhood pictures of Red that Vlad must have given to Cole.

Gwen hadn't told Helen about the Q.E. photo. While Helen was tuned out, Cole gave birth to and concealed a world all her own. No doubt, it was a suitable betrayal.

An odd couple, Vlad and Keith sat in the front seat as they drove away. Keith zigged and zagged through one-way streets.

He asked, "Do you mind me asking why you're going to Bridgeport?"

"I mind. But I'll tell you anyway. We're going home. She's my granddaughter," Vlad slurred. Wilda had continued to sedate him to keep him from finding out what was happening.

"I didn't know Wilda had relations! No one ever around for her," Keith said.

"Well, they'll be around now. She said we'll go live with her." Vlad shouted back to Cole, "How does that sound, Cole?"

This caught Cole by surprise. "Good," Cole said with less enthusiasm than she felt. She dreaded going back to Sheridan Street and possibly seeing Vanessa again. Maybe she wouldn't have to leave the house until they returned to Coney Island. The idea of being with Wilda and living in her big house made Cole feel safer already.

At a stoplight Keith twisted around and asked Cole, "What is that evil smell from in the back?"

The car's musty smell didn't overpower the stink wafting up from the paper bag. She pushed it with her foot to get it under the driver's seat but it only made the smell disperse more.

"There's a lot of garbage back here," Cole said.

"It didn't smell like this before, girl," he said to Cole, eyeing her in the rear view mirror.

Vlad waved his hand in front of his nose. "Stop at this gas station and throw out that crap."

Keith lined up the right back door with the garbage can. He pitched all the garbage into it along with random things like leaky pen and a pair of pantyhose. Cole kept her foot next to her bag in order to keep him from grabbing it.

When he reached over to her side of the car, his face moved close to it. "Girl, what is that?"

"It's mine," she said.

"Aw, no. It smells like something died in there," he said.

Vlad asked, "What the hell is it?"

"It's my dirty clothes. I want to keep them."

Vlad told Keith, "Take it. Get it out of here."

Cole protested, "No! I don't want to lose these!"

"Uh, uh, girl. That is foul," Keith told her as he grabbed the bag and threw it in the trashcan.

"Let's get going," Vlad insisted. As Cole sulked, Vlad told her, "Don't worry about a few little things like that. You'll get other clothes. Wilda will buy you lots of new things when you go live with her."

But Cole wasn't worried about her clothing.

Earlier at the house, after she got out of her bath, she had tried to consolidate her things. She wanted to tuck the tin full of letters into the mermaid case.

To reorganize everything, she took the mermaid out and placed it on top of the closed toilet lid. She thought about what Vlad had said when she went in to wake him up. He asked her if she still had the mermaid. She did. He told her, "Throw her in the water. You have to get rid of her."

Cole was stunned. Ever since she could remember, Vlad told Cole that he was P.T. Barnum's great grandson. He implicated her in his complicated farce by joking with her that this made her the "greatest granddaughter" of the showman. She always told anyone who would listen that she was related to Barnum. Now, it felt like she would be throwing that all away if she got rid of the mermaid. And even worse, she wouldn't have the thing that linked her to someone so famous.

Vlad gave the mermaid to her but maybe he knew a reason why it could never really be hers. Maybe he figured Cole wasn't Barnum's anything anymore. Not being related to Barnum was different than not being related to Red and Helen, but she didn't feel like she belonged to Janet either. It all made her feel like she had floated away from her spaceship with no tether.

After her bath, she took her time studying the mermaid. She wondered if it had ever resembled the beautiful creatures in the Barnum Museum newspaper ads in Vlad's scrapbook. Since it was supposed to be a mermaid, she tried to see it as a girl. But its head seemed like a monkey's. She never saw a monkey that looked female. Even the one wearing lipstick on a talk show looked like a boy monkey someone had made up.

The mermaid's eyeteeth were menacing but she wasn't afraid to touch them now. Cole downgraded the dirty relic from having magical fangs to being just an old thing from back when things were much better. She looked down at her tape recorder on the floor and wondered if someday it would be an artifact, like the mermaid or the rollercoaster. What if way in the future, like the year 2086, someone found her tape recorder and thought about how much better things were in Cole's life than they'd be at their cruddier future time?

Compared to the tape recorder and everything else in Wilda's spotless bathroom the mermaid seemed ancient and dull. Cole carried it over to the bathtub and did what her grandfather told her to do. She submerged it into her undrained bathwater.

At first it seemed buoyant but it took water quickly, shooting little bubbles out. It reminded her of the time her father filled the kitchen sink with water to squeeze her bike tire under water until he saw bubbles. She gently squeezed the mermaid under the water. Bubbles escaped where the mermaid had been sewn together.

As Cole's thumbs bore into the middle seam, the mermaid started to crumble. Parts of it seemed brittle while others were soft like the inside of a pillow. A chunk of its tail broke off and landed on the tub's bottom. As it came apart in her hands Cole succumbed to her curiosity about what was inside. Some of the mermaid bits floated while the bigger chunks sank.

She spread out her fingers and pulled her hands out of the water. Gray bits of the mermaid's skin were stuck to her forearms. What looked like wet pieces of dingy cotton balls clung to her fingers.

Wilda's voice rang out a second before a loud knock at the bathroom door, "You okay in there? We got a ride in about fifteen!"

"Yeah, I'm okay?" Cole called out as slightly more of a question than an answer.

Plunging her hand into the tub, she pulled the ring on the top of the rubber drain plug. She spread out her dirty clothes on the floor. The mermaid's silt clung to the water's surface, making it hard to make out the where the larger hunks were. As the water drained she scooped out mermaid bits and collected them on the clothing. When the last of the water sucked down the drain with a burpish gurgle, Cole used one of Wilda's facecloths to retrieve the last of the vague guts.

Cole rolled up the clothes around the soggy mess and then rolled that into a large towel. She stuffed it all into a brown paper grocery bag that she didn't want to put back into the case. It smelled bad so she thought giving it air would help.

After she hurriedly dressed, Cole opened a squat yellow canister of Jean Naté powder. She dabbed the soft white puff under her chin and then shook it all around the bathtub and a little over the damp paper bag.

When she walked out of the bathroom, Wilda said, "You look a hell of a lot better. Smell good too!"

Now, only an hour later, the car sped toward Bridgeport. All the windows were open making it too loud for any talk. The discarded bag's stink had already faded. Cole worried that maybe she ruined something that was worth a lot of money. To calm herself down she rubbed under her chin and then smelled her fingers. The powder's sweetness smelled like Wilda, who she had already started to miss.

Chapter 40

From the back seat Cole listened to Vlad snort air in through his nose and then rasp his breath out of his throat. He snored just like Red used to. She thought about how her grampa wasn't at her father's funeral so maybe he never went to his grave. Cole hoped that Helen would let them go to his grave before they moved in with Wilda.

Would they take trips back to Bridgeport to visit Red's grave? She was sad that the mermaid ended up in a garbage can and worried if she was supposed to have a funeral for the mermaid. What do people do when they don't have the dead bodies for a grave? What did they do for all the astronauts on the Space Shuttle Challenger? Now that she thought about it she felt lucky that she knew where Red was, even if she would end up living far away from him.

After they had made it onto I-95 Vlad fell asleep. Cole was disappointed that they didn't drive through Times Square and all its tall buildings. Although it already seemed crowded, she didn't understand why everyone in the world didn't want to live there. Now that they were probably moving to Coney Island, she wondered if she someday they could live in a nice apartment right in the middle of everything, like on *The Jeffersons*. But George and Louise had to have a lot of money to live there. Cole allowed herself the guilty fantasy of what it would be like if QE were to come through with a lot of money. In the parking lot in front of where her father died, there would be balloons and ribbons like they had at the new CVS grand opening. At a podium, a tall man in a suit would hand her a giant poster board check, like the ones Jerry Lewis gets on his Muscular Dystrophy telethon. It would be enough money for Vlad, Helen, Wilda, Janet and Cole to live in a giant apartment next door to the Jeffersons. She would have a television in her bedroom and a stereo system with speakers taller than her. Wilda and Vlad could make up and be together again. Since Helen wouldn't have to work, she could go and finish high school. They would get the police to make Janet be their maid as punishment for whatever she did.

Finding a place for Janet brought the curtain down on Cole's made-up world. Their short-lived reunion was still settling in. Cole was uneasy during most of her time with Janet. As they ate ice cream cake in Wilda's front room, Janet had sat right up next to her on the couch. The corner of Cole's mouth twitched while Janet pressed her chest into her arm and caressed her hair.

Janet seemed to be under a spell that she herself had cast. She told Cole, "I knew we're connected. This is a miracle that we just found each other, right? I mean, think about it. I think about you every damn day and now we're here. Right? You see? It's kismet. You know what that is right? It's when shit's supposed to happen and then it does. Like this." She kissed Cole on her hair just over her ear. While she thought of that moment, the squeaky kiss resounded in her head. Cole tried to sort out why she didn't feel the same way about Janet. Was she supposed to? She had a hard time believing they were once all in one body. Maybe this proved that her grandmother was right, Cole was a pigeon. She felt as though she had cracked her way out of an egg next to some scraps of metal, and not caught by a nurse and swaddled in a blanket.

Keith's voice interrupted Cole's thoughts as though he turned the dial on her mind's radio. He shouted, "You quiet back there, girl. Don't worry, we almost there."

"I'm okay. Just thinking," Cole answered. Vlad was still asleep with his mouth open as his head bobbled against the window. She became aware of knocking sounds coming from the back wheels and wondered if they had been making the sounds the entire ride.

Wilda was also right about the traffic. It seemed to Cole like it had taken a few hours until they finally passed signs for Bridgeport. At the first one, she sat up on the edge of the seat. She looked out the open window over to the southbound highway lanes. As they sped past the area where Barnum wintered his circus animals, a few floodlights silhouetted the one-story brick factories on that property.

She thought about when Vladimir walked with her all over that area, their shoes getting sucked into the muck around of the factory buildings. He told her the stories his grandfather had passed on to him. After a giant fire forced Barnum to winter his circus in Florida, they dug deep into the ground to bury the burnt animals and the building debris. As they tilled into the soil, they unearthed other animals that had been put to rest there prior to the fire. They mixed up all the remains and flattened the lot into a field and planted grass. Vlad's grandfather told him that this wasn't the only place in Bridgeport where Barnum's animals had been buried.

Cole settled back into the seat again, folded her hands in her lap and closed her eyes. She imagined her great-great grandfather, her father, P.T. Barnum and all of the buried elephants, tigers, monkeys, bears and horses at that very moment, running secret dead animal circuses under muddy lots all over Bridgeport. Now that Wilda taught her about pigeon mothers, Cole couldn't help but see how she was mostly made up of what had happened to her, more than what was running through her veins. Even though she wasn't blood related to P.T. Barnum, he was her great grandfather because that's what she had always felt was true. The blood she shared with Janet was supposed to be the real thing, but with her other pigeon mother, Cole was at home in the spaces between the bits and pieces of their nest.

Chapter 41

Keith parked Janet's car in front of the Sheridan apartment. Cole scanned the night streets for Vanessa, Toad and Puke. Whether it was three in the morning or three in the afternoon, they could be lurking.

Once outside the car, Keith stretched his arms out and twisted his torso. Joining him, she faced the same direction and copied his movements. Their arms and eyes swept across Sheridan Street's cracked windshields, chicken bones on the crumbling sidewalk, torn screen doors and tire-flattened beer cans. Almost midnight, the summer neighborhood air wrung out a couple of blaring radios and a couple's lazy shouting match farther up the block.

Cole was relieved that none of it seemed to bother Keith. He popped the trunk, pulled the case out from the sea of black plastic bags and lowered it down as if it held something delicate like an antique vase, or a treasured mermaid. She wondered if everyone else knew that an old bag like this one usually transported something so ancient and fragile that it had to be handled like her kindergarten teacher said to hold their class rabbit, "like a newborn baby."

Vlad yelled out the car window, "What the hell is going on here? Why am I just sitting here? I got to piss!" He honked the horn.

A glass bottle broke in the distance and several dogs barked out into their huffy chorus. Deciphering the crashing outbreak as a signal from Vanessa, Cole picked up the case and walked along the side of the house.

Keith shouted, "Hey! Wait til your mum come down! The old man beep for her." Vlad hit the horn again.

Cole ignored him and kept walking. She was sure that Helen

wouldn't hear the horn and think to look for her.

Keith called out, "Walk good, girl."

Cole's exhaustion and her fear of being exposed to Vanessa outweighed her regret for not bidding goodbyes to Keith and Vlad.

At the back of the house, Helen's voice jumped out from the dark before her body, "That was you!" Cole startled as arms wrapped around her torso and the soft pops of kisses synched up with her mother's lips on the top of her head.

They let go when the car horn blared again and Vlad hollered, "We're going. Call me later!" Cole listened for the telltale squeak that the car made all the way from Coney Island. As it faded out she felt a thin-stringed knot to Janet untie.

Helen said, "Good. Let's get you inside." She took the case and nudged Cole in front of her.

At the top of the stairs the door was open but Cole waited for Helen. She felt that she had messed up the apartment being both of theirs and needed to earn her way back in.

"Go," Helen whispered and motioned with her chin.

Helen plopped the bag down as Cole locked the door. She was finally safe from Vanessa but now she and Helen stood facing each other in the kitchen. Cole wondered if it was possible that someone else had greeted her downstairs. That embrace had made her feel like they were magnets but now in the light, they seemed mismatched again.

Helen flopped an arm toward Cole's room. "There are clean pajamas on your bed."

Cole edged into her room as if someone was going to jump out at her. One of their extra kitchen chairs sat next to her bed with the lamp from her dresser on it. Next to a stack of Hydrox, her little koala bear toy leaned against a glass of milk, holding one of the cookies. Her mother finally saw the bear, and used it to welcome her home. Cole felt a sense of victory. She wondered if any other runaway kids ever got to find out that their absence was much more important than their presence.

Helen called out, "Hey, it's late. You can just get in bed and wash up tomorrow."

"Okay," Cole said as she changed into her "Sweet Stuff!" candy nightie.

She slid under the Strawberry Shortcake sheets she hadn't seen since Red was alive. She couldn't remember if they were the ones she had slept on while he died. Perhaps some of the things she had frozen in time had thawed.

As her eyes adjusted, the lamp's weak glow reached farther out. Cole rose to her knees in the bed. Everything from her secret folder was taped on the wall. She ran her hands over the collaged shrine as if she could read it all in Braille. The newspaper crinkled under her fingers as she smoothed the creased obituary. In one of her baby pictures with Red she searched her infant face for anything that looked like Janet. Maybe her mouth? Janet held her hands in fists just like Cole's were in the photo, curled like miniature puff pastries. She searched Red's face for signs that he felt like he wasn't really her father. Even though she had wanted to ask Janet about a father, she didn't know how. It didn't seem right to call someone she never met "my father."

Cole had always just glossed over this photo. But now as she studied it, she was relieved that Red didn't appear puzzled or scared by Cole's foreign blood.

"So, I see your little bear friend shared his cookies with you," Helen said.

Cole jumped. Her hidden world was exposed. There was no way to cover it all up again.

As Helen sat at the edge of the bed, she said, "I like that nightie on you. That's the one from your dad." Her mother *had* remembered the Christmas gift.

Cole pulled it out from her belly to look at the candies on it, "Yeah. Me too."

Helen scooted more onto the bed and put her hand on Cole's knee. She sighed and said, "Um. I think you know that I'm not good with you like your Dad always was. I'm sorry I didn't try. I just didn't. But now I'm going to do my best. Anyway, it's not your fault though. You know that?"

Cole never thought about it that way. Nothing ever seemed like it was anyone's fault because nothing seemed to happen just because anyone tried or wanted for it to happen. She rested her hand on top of Helen's because it was easier than knowing what to say.

Helen looked at the pictures. "I miss your Dad too. He'd love to see you right now, I bet. Whenever you went up from one grade to another he was so excited. And I think this was all like that, you know? Now that you know everything, well…. This seems really horrible but it's like you learned something new. And now you got to do stuff with it in order to keep going. You kind of know everything now. I do too. We both do."

It was strange to hear her mother speaking about something other than what to make for supper, her job or other humdrum matters. Unsure what to say, Cole reached for the glass of milk.

Helen grabbed and hugged Cole. Cole embraced Helen as she realized that Helen thought that this is why she had leaned over. Each of their heads landed onto the other's shoulder.

"We can get through all this. Don't worry. You can talk about your dad all the time if you want to. I just…I just….," Helen wept.

Cole nudged her head into the crook of her mother's neck where her tears rolled down the valley between her jaw and Helen's collarbone. Cole's fingertips rubbed over the bumps of Helen's bra clasp. It brought back memories of when she was younger and Helen held her only when she was sick.

Now, Helen hugged her as if she were afraid that they would fly off into outer space if she let go. Cole squeezed her tighter to prove that she wasn't going anywhere.

Helen let out a pacified murmur. They sniffled and coughed until Helen laughed a little. She patted Cole's back and said, "My damn back is tired. I'm getting old. But I wish I could hug you all night though."

Cole leaned back. A sticky breeze blew through her window and kissed her where a continent-shaped spot on her pajamas was soaked with tears.

Helen handed her the milk. "Here, have something. You're hungry, right?" Cole picked up the koala and ate the cookie out of his paws. "You can keep all the pictures up here until we move to Grandma's okay? Then we can get you some frames and put them up in your room there if you want."

Cole nodded before she stuffed an entire cookie into her mouth. She had an urge to blurt out that she knew that she needed to keep them nice and not ruin them like she had the mermaid. On the drive from Coney Island, she promised herself to not tell anyone about the mermaid. She would even lie to her grampa. He had hid things from her and told fake stories about her very existence. She wanted one honest lie all her own.

Helen kissed Cole's head and stood up. "Well, it's been a long day. I'm going to bed. Are you okay? You can come sleep with me, you know."

Cole looked over at the pictures. "I'll stay here."

Helen said, "Good night. Don't let the bed bugs bite." Red sometimes said that when he sent Cole off to bed while he watched TV. Cole wondered if she were to record Helen, if she could better understand the difference between the Helen before she ran away, to the Helen who turned around in the doorway and smiled. The gesture wasn't forced and appeared to be a comfort her mother took, like resting her feet on an ottoman. In a blink, Helen vanished until Cole heard the bathroom faucet squeak on.

Cole shut off the lamp and plopped her head down onto her pillow. The darkness was dusked by the soft yellow glow from the bathroom light. She tried to make out the shapes of the exhumed pictures. Cole squeezed her eyes shut. Her father used to sit on her bed as he waited for Helen's evening toothbrushing. He sometimes teased that he had worked hard enough to make his hands so calloused he couldn't feel them. Cole gripped his hands as hard as she could while he pretended he couldn't feel it. She squeezed tighter and tighter until he finally winced and begged, "Uncle, uncle, uncle," until she let go.

Now, alone in her bedroom, she stretched her arms down by her sides under the covers with her palms down. She was afraid that the pictures being out in the open would make her father come back to play the game with her. It would mean everything to see him again but she didn't know what dead people did when they took someone's hand. Would he take her with him? What if he was there with her and she didn't know? She had never before felt like this. She remained stone still and pushed her palms hard into the bed.

Transfixed by questions about her father, she wondered if she would forget him faster when they moved out of Bridgeport. There would be fewer places that had been theirs. She was moving to a place where he'd never lived. Would there be new sounds that would remind her of him? Does he know that her old but new mother found her? Could he see Janet in the hospital or the jail?

Cole wondered if she would ever find out who her other father was and if he was a pigeon father like Janet and Helen were her pigeon mothers. For now, her dad was the only father she needed. Being with her grandmother made her feel a little like she was with her dad. What about his grave after they moved? Do people take pictures at the cemetery so they won't forget? Will they have to get other people to go to the grave so he doesn't think no one remembers him?

Gwen seemed to know a lot about God and just about everything else. Cole had wanted to ask her how to pray but was ashamed to admit she didn't already know how. Now that she had a list of things, Cole decided to go see Gwen in the morning. She would bring her tape recorder so she could bring her answers to Coney Island. A smirk lifted the left side of her lips while she thought about how to slip the prayer question in with the others.

Helen tapped her toothbrush against the sink. This had always been her father's cue that the bathroom was free.

Cole called out, "Goodnight." She paused, then said, "Mom." Her mouth remembered the word but her ears didn't. As it repeated in her head, the *m* sounds felt like they had looped out of and back into her mouth like a cassette tape reel.

"Goodnight," Helen called out.

Cole took a deep gulp of breath. As unease gusted out of her nose, it also rolled out of her muscles as they softened from the tip of her fingers, up her arms, to her shoulders and up through her neck. When she unclenched her eyelids, a glowing blur floated above her bed. She held her breath until it disappeared the moment her mother flicked the bathroom light off.

The room darkened. While Cole was in Coney Island, Helen had stuck glow-in-the-dark stars to the ceiling above her bed.

Enchanted beneath her very own outer space, Cole squinted to see all the way up to where she imagined her father had just skyrocketed.

She whispered, "Goodnight, Dad."

Acknowledgements

Kate Conroy is my love. A good spouse supports a writer while she writes a book, my amazing spouse was there for the idea, the obsessive focus, the lulls, the switchbacks, the hits, the misses, the MetroNorth rides to crumbling factories and everything in between. Kate, thank you for holding me up, respecting my vision and rolling with all of our *Pigeon Mothers* undertakings. You make me laugh every morning and exemplify how much a creative lesbeing can get done in a day. I adore you every day, Kate.

I couldn't have done this without Carolyn Dinshaw. Her English Professor eyes saved my manuscript from embarrassing mistakes and her queer heart always looks out for me.

Thanks to Marget Long, my Mr. M, my fellow Masshole artist. Thanks for the space to write and for taking this joker seriously when it matters.

How many times can a friend selflessly edit new versions of your manuscript without murdering you? Ask my mountain muse, Judy Rosen. She also lent me her place to research what it was like to live in a wood-stove heated home with no internet in the middle of a Catskills blizzard. Those scenes were edited out of this book. You're welcome.

My best friend Kim Perry never bullshits me. If you ever meet her, thank Kim for saving this book from some disruptive 19th-century chapters.

Jennifer Morgan, the outright opposite of a pigeon mother, knows when and how to be there for me and when to just let me be. She is the best kind of human there is.

Liz Margolies is the Jewish patron saint of *Pigeon Mothers*. Without Liz gifting me unlimited access to supreme writing space, I'd still be whining to her about how I can't finish this book. Hey, wait a minute. Maybe she just did that to shut me up! Either way, *Saint Liz* it is.

All the goddesses worked their magic to plop me in the paths of Peggy Shaw and Lois Weaver. As a butch lesbian East Village artist, I have the most generous King and Queen of Performance Art to thank. Through their work, they taught me to breathe desire, politics and feminist values into my creativity.

Caz Springer was my human Goodreads before there was an internet. He can melt away a crappy day with his laugh. Caz is also a patient educator, my favorite mensch and in him I've met my match for delighting in the oddest news stories.

Even when I insert myself into their family, Joann Schellenbach, Alida Rojas, Lauren Schellenbach and Kate Schellenbach do a great job of making me feel like I belong. They are the people whose pictures I keep in my proverbial wallet to show off that I have a family that loves and believes in me.

Thanks to Ellen Geiger and Nina Cochran at the Frances Goldin Literary Agency for believing in this book and going the extra mile and a half.

Bloodroot Restaurant in Bridgeport, CT was an oasis after long days of hitting the pavement while researching this book's environs. Meeting Selma Miriam and Noel Furie, and experiencing their feminist restaurant and bookstore influenced me to focus this story on its female characters. Please go treat yourself to exceptional vegetarian cuisine and savor their feminist space. It's a MetroNorth ride from NYC. Or if you're on I-95, GPS yourself there on your way to/from wherever. www.bloodroot.com

Don't worry. I won't quit my day job. Thanks to NYU and the Department of Social & Cultural Analysis and the people there who've supported me on the road to this book's release:
Julie Livingston, Phil Harper, Marlene Brito, Arlene Dávila, Mary Louise Pratt, Renato Rosaldo, Joseph Pisano, Ruby Gómez, Robert Campbell, Heijin Lee, Dean Saranillio, Sukhdev Sandhu, Thuy Linh Tu, Nikhil Singh, Awam Amkpa, Andrew Ross, Cristina Beltrán, Gayatri Gopinath, Ann Pellegrini, Deb Willis,

Anne Rademacher, Miriam Jiménez-Román (RIP), Juan Flores (RIP) and Jack Tchen.

My always-there-for-me friends:
Lisa Duggan, Kathleen Furin, Cyd Fulton, Amy & Dorothy Harbeck, Annise Weaver, Anastasiya Panas, Ché Valencia, Lola Flash, and my Shady Ladies Joan Carey and Ann Kirchoffer.

The Inner Arts Coven of Encouragement and Laughter:
Kay Turner, Mary Sanger, Pat Power, Madala Hilaire, Alexis Clements, Amy Jaime, Kelly Bedwell, Jackie Rudin, Nadia Conroy, Nejma Nefertiti, Nina Kennedy, April Gibson and Afua Kafi-Akua.

My Creative Writing Cronies:
Ellie Covan, Diane Fortier, Sarah Sala, CQ Quintana, Amy Finley, Jerome Murphy, Sultana Banulescu, Chuck Wachtel, Deanna Masselli, David Lipsky, Stephanie Schroeder, Lisa Haas, Andy Braunstein, Rick Moody, Jonathan Ned Katz, Kathleen Laziza, Sherry Mason and Heather MacDonald.

There at the perfect moment:
Amy Gissen, Judith Katz, Michael Teitler, Bonnie Marcus, Katharine McKenna, Mark Braunstein, Yoko Ono, Ellen Hegarty, Kelly Bigelow Becerra, Steven Amsterdam, Mary Witkowski, and Pamela & Chris McLain.

Dedicated readers:
Mimi McGurl, Ann Schroeder, Petuh Sam, Kali Lightfoot, Mary Summerall, Mary Hall, Dorothy Nuess, Leopold Krist, Deborah Hauser, Melissa Hoffman, Kelly Friedman, Michael Davis, Sharon Her, Katherine Gleason, Noeva Wong, Colleen Wagner, Marya Leonard, Maureen Singer, Bernadette Conover, Amanda Greenman, Nou Moua, Leslie Kang, Janet Doerge, Sharmaine Griffin, Caleb Savage, Elizabeth Heard, Emma Morgan-Bennett, Herman Bennett, Hannah Feeney, Sean Pagaduan, Elizabeth Mesok, Gina Rodriguez, Elaine Freedgood, Christopher Arp, Ben Beckett, Shannon Gosch.

Thanks to Ancestry.com for my new Aunt Kay, Aunt Shirley, Aunt Peggy, Lyn Fouts Rainey, Sharon Howe Brault, Camry Rose Brault, Kathy Rondeau, Debbie Mott, Danielle Martinelli Beauregard, Michael LaTour, Dianna Allen and all the other newfound LaTours.

Since 1996, I've been charmed by the unconditional love of the Conroy family.

Love and admiration for my birthday twins and the best niece and nephew this Aquarian could have asked for, Ben Dube and Abbie Dube. You are both always in my heart.

If I forgot to add you, forgive me. Please send me an email so that I can thank you in the next edition.

This project was possible thanks to:

Arts Center of Yates County
Millay Colony for the Arts
Dixon Place
Worcester Art Museum
Artists Anonymous
Lower Manhattan Cultural Council
Poets & Writers
Bridgeport Public Library
Bridgeport History Center
The Barnum Museum
Holiday Inn, Bridgeport
Greater Bridgeport Transit
Coney Island USA
Children's Friend of Worcester
New York University's Creative Writing MFA Program

In Memoriam

Johanna Lee
Allan Bérubé
Abel Correia
J. Michael LaTour
Edward J. Conroy
Paul Violi
E.L. Doctorow

 A triple-decker is a three-story apartment building where each floor typically consists of a single apartment. They were built in the Northeast, USA and usually housed working class people. We are a press dedicated to the work and ideas of people who value community. Even when there are floorboards between us, sharing our stories unites us under one roof.

www.tripledeckerpress.com